Black Sunflowers *is a riveting novel of one close-knit family's survival, resilience, and perseverance under two invading totalitarian regimes. Historically accurate, it takes place during the Soviet occupation of Ukraine from the early 1920s into Nazi Germany's invasion in 1941. It is vividly described through the experiences of a young girl and her father exposed to the injustices of two dictatorships determined to subjugate the population. At the core of the story is the Holodomor genocide. Veronika's father guides her, teaching her life skills to survive the Holodomor with humanity. This moving and engaging page-turner is suitable for students in middle years through to adulthood.*

—**Valentina Kuryliw, Director of Education of the Holodomor Research and Education Consortium, University of Alberta.**

Cynthia LeBrun

Fitzhenry & Whiteside

Text © 2024 Cynthia LeBrun

All rights reserved. No part of this book may be reproduced in any manner without the express written consent of Fitzhenry & Whiteside, except in the case of brief excerpts in critical reviews and articles. All inquiries should be addressed to Fitzhenry & Whiteside Limited.

Published in Canada by Fitzhenry & Whiteside Limited
209 Wicksteed Avenue, Unit 51, Toronto, ON M4G 0B1

Published in the United States by Fitzhenry & Whiteside Limited
60 Leo M Birmingham Pkwy, Ste 107, Brighton, MA 02135

Fitzhenry & Whiteside acknowledges with thanks the Canada Council for the Arts and the Ontario Arts Council for their support of our publishing program. We acknowledge the financial support of the Government of Canada through the Canada Book Fund (CBF) for our publishing activities.

Library and Archives Canada Cataloguing in Publication
Title: Black sunflowers / Cynthia LeBrun.
Names: LeBrun, Cynthia, author.
Identifiers: Canadiana 20230585566 | ISBN 9781554556434 (softcover)
Subjects: LCGFT: Historical fiction. | LCGFT: Novels.
Classification: LCC PS8623.E396 B53 2024 | DDC C813/.6—dc23

Publisher Cataloging-in-Publication Data (U.S.)
Names: LeBrun, Cynthia, author.
Title: Black sunflowers / Cynthia LeBrun.
Description: Toronto, Ontario : Fitzhenry & Whiteside Limited, 2024. | Summary: "A vivid account of the brutal realities of life in Ukraine under Stalin follows Veronika and her family on their farm in the close-knit village of Kuzmin in 1928. Life is good, despite the Soviet occupation, but soon everything they have known and loved is not just altered, but demolished. Inspired by real life, Veronika's story illuminates one of the darkest times in Ukrainian history: the Holodomor" -- Provided by publisher.
Identifiers: ISBN 978-1-55455-643-4 (paperback)
Subjects: LCSH: Ukraine--History--Famine, 1932-1933--Fiction. | Farmers--Ukraine--History--20th century--Fiction. | Families--Ukraine--History--20th century--Fiction. | BISAC: FICTION / Historical / 20th Century / General. | LCGFT: Historical fiction. | Novels.
Classification: LCC PR9199.3.L4 B53 2024 | DDC 813/.54 | dc23

This publication was supported by the Peterson Library Fund at BCU Foundation.

Design by Tanya Montini | Edited by Sarah Harvey | Copyedited by Penny Hozy

Printed in Canada by Copywell

fitzhenry.ca

To Veronika, because this is her story,

and to the millions of people who lived in Ukraine, who suffered and died under the oppression of Stalin and Hitler, and whose identities and life stories are unknown.

EUROPE

1929

SOVIET OCCUPIED UKRAINE

1921–1939

VERONIKA'S PROVINCE OF KHMELNYTSKYI

(PRESENT DAY MAP)

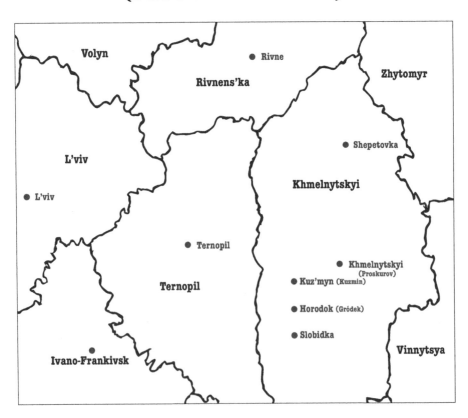

VERONIKA'S EXTENDED FAMILY

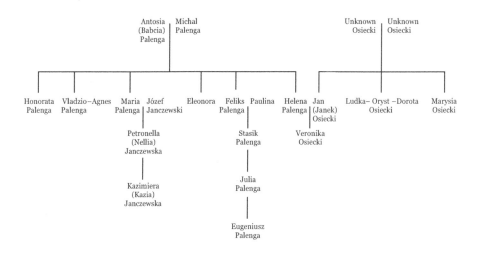

JANCZEWSKI BROTHER'S TRIPLEX

Dr. Julian Janczewski
wife, Truda

Józef Janczewski
wife, Maria
Nellia
Kazia

Ludwik Janczewski
wife, (name?)
Marek
Alina

PELENGA BROTHER'S DUPLEX

Vladzio Palenga
wife, Agnes

Antosia Palenga (Babcia)
Feliks Palenga
wife, Paulina
Stasik
Julia

I will die, I will die.
They will bury me,
And nobody will know where my grave is.
And nobody will come and remember,
Only in the early spring,
The nightingale will sing.

1
VERONIKA

Village of Kuzmin, Soviet Occupied Ukraine
November 1929

In the flickering half-light cast by the kerosene lantern, Veronika and her mother sat at the kitchen table, knitting. The kitchen was quiet except for the steady click of the wooden needles. Veronika felt proud that, at six years old, she knew how to knit her own scarf.

Veronika looked up as the front door opened. Her father came in with a bundle of horse harnesses in his arms. As he closed the door, a rush of crisp air from the autumn evening swept into the room.

"It's getting dark early," he said.

"It is," Mama replied. "I've been thinking, Janek. It's time for the women's sewing club to start meeting again, with these evenings getting so long."

A feeling of joy bubbled up from Veronika's heart.

"I'd like to hold the first one here," Mama continued. "Is that all right with you, Janek?"

"I guess so. Might as well take your turn now as later."

At that, Veronika jumped up, flapped her arms, and swooped over to her father. As she leaned into his lap full of harnesses, she could smell the musky sweet scent of horse sweat rising off the leather as she planted a kiss on his beard.

"Thank you, Tata. Are you going to come?"

"Me?" Janek laughed. "I'm not going to be here when forty or more women and children take over my home."

— ✳ —

The next day, anxious to share her excitement with her Aunt Agnes, Veronika hastily plowed through a breakfast of hot buckwheat pancakes smothered with honey, before pulling on her wool-lined boots, quilted coat, and scarf.

Even though it was sunny, a crisp wind gusted about. Most of the frozen puddles were in pristine condition, a bounty of ice crystal windowpanes, all waiting for her to break. Some she approached with care, stepping gently around the edges to create a series of shattering sounds. Others she leapt onto, and bounced on the thick ice as it swayed up and down under her weight until, with a slow groan, it gave way, and she plunked down into its muddy depths.

As she made her way down the road, sucking on a cleaner chunk of ice, she hoped she wouldn't see her grandmother, Babcia. A gloom settled within Veronika's spirit as she visualized Babcia sitting in front of the duplex, praying the rosary. Tata said the only reason Babcia sat out there was to keep an eye on everyone else's business. Mama got annoyed at him for saying that about her mother.

Babcia's sons, Feliks and Vladzio, had built the stone-walled duplex. Babcia lived in one side with Uncle Feliks and his family. Uncle Vladzio and Aunt Agnes lived on the other side.

Veronika pulled her coat closer around her neck. It only took ten minutes to get to the duplex, but even so, she couldn't wait to be at the door and out of the wind. She imagined herself already inside, sitting between her aunt and uncle, her fingers and toes warming by their woodstove.

Veronika sent a clod of frozen dirt scuttling across the road and felt guilty. She wished she liked Babcia. The neighbours all seemed to like her. They always marvelled at her keen eyesight and hearing.

"And she can work like a woman half her age, from dawn to sunset," they said.

They even found her hair remarkable. *"You still have a full head of brown hair? What is your secret, Antosia?"*

With a shrug of her shoulders, Babcia would just give a little half-smile.

As she plodded along the road, head down, Veronika resolved to say something nice to Babcia if she saw her.

Aunt Agnes's house was like most other homes in Kuzmin, with stone walls, a thatched roof, and a dirt floor. Inside it was clean and cozy, with a built-in clay oven as well as a wood stove to the side of a large wooden table. Aunt Agnes and Uncle Vladzio didn't have any children of their own. Mama said it was because they couldn't. Maybe that's why, when Veronika came for a visit, they treated her like their own special little girl.

As Veronika approached the duplex, her heart sank. Babcia sat on the front porch, a quilt wrapped around her legs, rosary in her hands.

Upon seeing her, Babcia said, "Aren't there enough children here already?"

The words stung, but Veronika did what she had seen her mother do—she ignored the remark and continued as if the words had not been spoken.

"I'm visiting Aunt Agnes, Babcia. Would you like to see the scarf I knitted?"

"Scarf? Maybe later, Veronika. I'm going in now. I'm cold."

Without a backward glance, Babcia went into her side of the duplex and closed the door. Just as happy with not having to talk to her, Veronika continued to the end of the building and knocked on the door. Uncle Vladzio greeted her as he always did with a hearty, "Hello, hello, hello," before tousling the top of her head with his hand. She hated having her hair messed up like that, but she knew it would hurt his feelings if she asked him not to.

Aunt Agnes sat peeling potatoes, a knife in one hand and a chipped enamel bucket of peeled potatoes between her feet.

"Veronika, you're here," she said, her face beaming with delight. She was short and stout with a plain face. A broken hip that hadn't healed right caused her to limp as she got up and walked toward Veronika. As Aunt Agnes hugged her, she felt herself disappear into her soft and squishy bosom.

"Look what I made," Veronika said, extracting herself and proudly holding up her scarf.

Aunt Agnes peered closely at the scarf, turning it over in her hands.

"You made this, Veronika, and you're only six years old?"

Veronika nodded her head, delighted with her aunt's reaction.

"Very beautiful. How about you go help yourself to some candy, such a good little worker."

Veronika dashed over to where her aunt kept the candy on a low shelf, where children could easily get to it. She pulled out the candy tin and pried off the lid to reveal her favourite candy—hard on the outside with soft fruit filling. After a moment's hesitation, she popped a red one into her mouth. Aunt Agnes sat in her chair and smiled at her.

"Mama's having the sewing club at our house," Veronika said, the candy making a lump in her cheek as she spoke.

"Yes, that's good. Such happy news you bring me, Veronika. I guess I'll run the *loteryjka*, the bingo game. They always like me to do that." Veronika felt her heart drop. She loved playing loteryjka with the women, but it cost a kopek a game, and she had already spent her few kopeks on candy at the village store. Now she couldn't play. Her face must have told Aunt Agnes what she was thinking.

"Do you have money for loteryjka?"

Veronika shook her head.

"Come with me."

Veronika followed her into the bedroom. She liked going in there. It was cool and dark and smelled faintly like soap. Best of all, it was where her aunt kept her treasures from Germany. Aunt Agnes pulled open her dresser drawer and took out a change purse.

"Here," she said, "hold out your hand." She poked through her purse, seeking kopeks to drop into Veronika's upturned palm. "Now you can play loteryjka."

— ✳ —

As Veronika skipped down the road and her home came into view, she felt a deep happiness. So strong and beautiful her home was, with its whitewashed stone walls and tile roof. Wisteria vines covered the front wall of the house; when it was in bloom, the wall was a mass of purple flowers. Against the wall of wisteria, was a stone bench. Beside the house was an enormous vegetable garden, and directly behind was an orchard of cherry, plum, pear, apple, and walnut trees. Beyond that were their grain fields, where Tata grew mostly buckwheat.

    Walking down the stone pathway to the door, Veronika jingled the kopeks in her pocket, liking the sound. She decided to ask her mother if she could sleep over at Aunt Agnes's house someday. Aunt Agnes could tell her stories about when she was a little girl in Germany.

> *... it had been ruled that a peasant could be penalized for not delivering grain even if it could not be shown that he was 'hoarding' any: he could be fined, and if the fine was not paid, expropriated ... and on the second offense a year's imprisonment ... Many 'kulaks' (land-owners the Soviets categorized as being prosperous) now sold up and moved into the towns to avoid this.*
>
> —Robert Conquest, *Harvest of Sorrow: Soviet Collectivization and the Terror Famine*

2
JANEK

Janek always found brushing out his horse, Dobroc, comforting. Time slowed down, allowing Janek's inner thoughts to form and develop. Finished with the brushing, but not quite ready to go into the house, Janek pressed his face against Dobroc.

"Life is good, isn't it, boy? A warm barn, a bucket of oats, someone to give you lots of pats."

Like a silent friend, Dobroc turned to look at him, wisdom in his deep brown eyes.

"For me, too, good fields, and a full root cellar, thanks to you, Dobroc. Isn't that right, friend? We're both fine, thanks to you."

Feeling Dobroc's nudge, Janek said, "All right, I get the hint. I'll get your oats."

As he filled a bucket with oats, Janek looked forward to the evening, when Helena would host the first session of the sewing circle. After dinner, he'd go over to his brother-in-law Feliks's house and have a few drinks with him and Vladzio while the women sewed.

At Feliks's they would likely talk about Yuri, the head of the newly formed collective, the pompous ass that he was. At last week's meeting, Yuri had encouraged his neighbours to join him on the collective.

"*Give up farming your own land, then all your troubles will be over. All fields will be joined together to make one grain factory. Machinery will come and do the work of a hundred men,*" he had proclaimed.

When someone from the back yelled, "*It works out great for those with worthless farms, eh, Yuri?*" Janek saw Yuri flinch. What were his neighbours thinking? You don't mock those in power and get away with it.

It's good that Veronika has her happiness now, he thought. Who knows what the future will bring with collaborators like Yuri extolling the wonders of communism?

— ✽ —

Janek helped Helena clear the dinner table, then put on his coat and cap.

"Leaving already, Tata?" asked Veronika.

"One little girl is fine," he said, tapping her on the nose. "Dozens? I'm gone."

"Tata," she giggled. "You're being silly. You should stay."

Helena walked up to him and gave him a hug, her cheeks bright with excitement. "You have a good time, all right?"

"Thanks. I always do."

He closed the door and walked up the dimly lit path toward the road, then glanced back. Veronika's little face peered out the window. Looking for children already, he thought with a smile. Well, she wouldn't have long to wait. Polish or Ukrainian, every woman and child within a fifteen-minute radius of their home had been invited, and dozens of children would be coming.

He pulled his collar closer around his neck, glad he'd be at Feliks and Vladzio's duplex in a matter of minutes.

Janek's mother-in-law, Antosia, and her husband used to own all the land around there. Fifty acres of it, following the road and the Smotrych River that lead to Kuzmin. After his father-in-law died, the land was divided into sections, one for each of their four children. Helena's parcel of ten acres connected to Feliks and Vladzio's, and their property connected to their sister Maria's parcel.

Janek wished he had met his father-in-law. He had been a fine man, from what people told him. Even though he had died a good ten years ago, he was still around, checking on his fields. Janek would see his ghostly outline from time to time and would stand in awe until the image faded away.

Antosia was another matter. Veronika called her Babcia, but she wasn't much of a grandmother or even a mother. Maybe because she'd been too old when she'd had Helena, the last of many births and miscarriages. People said she loved her children when they were babies but, once they grew up a little and developed minds of their own, she was done with them. Helena had had Veronika late in life, too, but luckily wasn't in any way like her mother.

A horse and buggy pulled out of the duplex's driveway ahead. Must be Paulina, Feliks's wife, Antosia, and Agnes on their way to his house. He smiled and waved his cap in greeting. Paulina, at the reins, brought the buggy to a halt.

"Janek, where are you going?" Paulina teased. "We want to play loteryjka with you."

Agnes laughed but Antosia ignored him. What a nasty woman that one is, he thought, and once again was glad that Antosia lived with Feliks and not with him.

When he arrived at the duplex, Feliks opened the door at his knock. "Come in, Janek! Sit down, sit down. I'll get you some *spiritus*. Vladzio is already here, eating cake the women left for us."

Janek settled back in a chair and accepted a glass of fruit vodka from Feliks. He felt great already, being with his friends. "I passed the women on their way."

"Yes, they took the buggy because of Agnes's hip," Vladzio said. "Still giving her a lot of pain."

"Your mother wouldn't even look at me."

Feliks shook his head. "She's getting harder to live with all the time. Every day she's onto Paulina about something or other, making her cry."

"Agnes has it easier," Vladzio said. "When she's had enough of Mother, she leaves. Paulina is stuck with her day in and day out."

"No woman is good enough for Antosia's sons, I guess," Janek said, with a wry smile.

Feliks snorted, took a drink, then looked into his glass. "Mother has been in particularly low spirits ever since they doubled our taxes. There's just no money in farming."

Vladzio pounded his fist on the table, his mood suddenly changing. "It's not right how much they take."

"It's the same with us," Janek said. "Sometimes I don't know how we're going to survive."

"The Soviets say they want more grain," Feliks said, "yet the heavy taxes force people to sell their farms and get jobs in the city. And they say Stalin is so clever. He's nothing but a *głupi dupek*, a stupid asshole."

The land (prior to Soviet collectivization policies) was fertile, and food always plentiful and the peasants were able to supplement their income by selling the products of the home industries which they carried on during the winter.

—Fedor Belov, former chairman of a Soviet farm collective
and author of *The History of a Soviet Collective Farm*

3
VERONIKA

Veronika was put in charge of opening the door when the guests arrived, while her mother bustled around the kitchen making a tray of sausage and pickles for the potluck supper.

Beside herself with expectation, Veronika stood on tiptoe, peering out their kitchen window as the daylight began to fade, looking for any sign of the guests. It was going to be so much fun. She could hardly wait for Kazia, her five-year-old cousin and very best friend, to arrive.

"Mama, when will they be here?"

"Soon."

"How soon? I'm bored of waiting. I want them to come now."

Veronika turned away from the window and watched her mother carry the tray to the side counter and set it down. She walked over to it. There they were, neat little circles of sausage, arranged in a mound of all their spicy goodness—Mama's special kiełbasa, "the-only-for-company sausage." Veronika took one.

"Listen, Veronika," Mama said with exasperation. "Why don't you just go and sit down? Look at the pictures in my prayer book."

That's boring, too, Veronika thought, but with Mama already annoyed, it was best to keep quiet and stay out of her way. With a sigh, Veronika plunked herself down on the bench and waited and waited.

Finally, she heard them, laughing and talking, sounding like a flock of chirping birds. She dashed to the window.

"They're coming!" she yelled and opened the door. A swirling blur of women in long coats brushed past her.

Veronika stood at her post, unable to move. The flow of guests had backed up as women struggled to take off their coats, greet each other, and set down their packages of sewing and party food. Veronika listened to the hum of a dozen conversations and the occasional peal of laughter as the women admired each other's knitting, embroidery, or crocheting. She felt her heart fill with pride to have her home like this, the centre of attention, with her mother the one in charge. The room grew quieter as the women took out their needles and began to work on their individual projects, and Veronika heard the sound of Kazia's laughter. She squeezed past the seated women and ran out into the yard for a game of tag. Other children joined in and they ran and ran, shrieking for joy.

With only the light from the window to guide them, Veronika played with the swarm of children until the stars gradually pinpricked the late autumn sky, and the air took on a bitter edge.

Veronika heard first one mother and then another urge them in. The children ignored them. Eventually Veronika could sense the mothers were getting annoyed, so she and the others trooped in, sweaty and red-faced.

Veronika could see women laughing and chatting in small groups as they sipped spiritus from Tata's still. Their sewing was nowhere to be seen. The savoury aroma of fresh bread, mingled with the pungent smell of kiełbasa and sweet pickles, drew Veronika over to the counter. She inspected the offerings: sour pickles, sweet pickles, red pickled beets, piernik, spice cake, honey cake, jellied headcheese—and candy.

Veronika sauntered over to Kazia as casually as she could and whispered, "Kazia, there's candy."

No point in alerting the other children. The two of them walked over to the bowl and stared at it. They knew the rules. No taking food until it was time. But a quick scan of the grownups showed no one looking, so they grabbed a few candies and scampered away to play with the other children in the bedroom.

After a while, Veronika's mother poked her head into the bedroom and asked, "Any of you want to play loteryjka?" Veronika ran to the kitchen table with her kopeks and joined the crowd of jovial women.

"I'm playing," she announced, and plunked one kopek into the pot, which already had thirty or more kopeks in it. As she looked around the table, waiting for the game to start, she felt a tingling surge of excitement. Maybe tonight she would win.

"All right," Aunt Agnes said. "No one touches that pot until I check to see if you really won it."

"We wouldn't cheat," said Kazia's mother Maria in a voice of feigned innocence.

"Like hell you wouldn't. You're all a pack of cheaters," retorted Aunt Agnes. At that the table erupted into laughter.

Aunt Agnes had grown up in Germany. They must play differently there, thought Veronika. Sure, we cheat, but that's part of the challenge, to see how much you can get away with.

Veronika waited in quiet expectation as the game sheets were pulled off the pad and passed around. She stared at the glistening pot of coins. She could visualize herself going to the general store in

Kuzmin and trading all that money for hard candies wrapped in a paper cone.

Each person took a sheet and then passed the rest along. When the sheets came to Veronika, she held them in her hand and had a good long look at the top sheet.

"What are you doing, Veronika?"

"Looking for good numbers."

"Just take one! You're holding up the game," someone said.

She took one.

Aunt Agnes picked up a cloth bag filled with numbered wooden balls. She reached into the bag and called out a number. Veronika had it! She covered the number with a little cardboard square. The first person to get a straight line going down got to yell, *Ja mam*, I have! Each time Aunt Agnes pulled out a ball, Veronika willed it to be a number that she needed. On and on they played. Tension grew, as any second someone would yell, Ja mam. Veronika only needed one more number.

Suddenly Kazia yelled, "Ja mam!"

"Let's see your card, Aunt Agnes said. Seconds later, "No, you don't have a win. You're missing a number."

"Oh, I'm sorry. I must have made a mistake."

Then the teasing began. Kazia tried to keep a straight face, but finally had to break out into a crooked smile. Veronika knew that smile. Kazia had a hard time keeping a straight face when she cheated.

Veronika didn't win that night, nor did Kazia, but she knew eventually their turn would come.

The evening went from loteryjka to eating, and it was past ten o'clock when her last friend left. Veronika crawled into bed exhausted, full of fresh pressed apple juice, sweet cakes, and candy.

She could hardly wait for tomorrow, when the sewing club would meet again at her house, and every night for the whole week. And the best day of all would be the last one, when the women wouldn't even bring their sewing, and the men would come for a night of dancing and partying.

— ✶ —

On the morning of the seventh party, Veronika and her father helped her mother prepare for the wind-up celebration. All their furniture had to be moved out of the living room and stacked into the bedrooms to make room for a proper dance floor. Specialty foods would be prepared. Her father said he would go into the cold cellar and bring in a bottle of plum jam needed for baking.

"I'm coming, too," Veronika said. She never missed a chance to go into the cellar. She was forbidden to go there alone—and she wouldn't want to. It was too scary. The entrance was concealed, not by intention, but because that was just the way a rectangle of weathered wood lying flat on the ground looked. But if you knew, and lifted the wood up, a gush of icy cold, dank, earthy-smelling air would be released, and you would see stairs leading down into the blackness of its stone-lined walls. Climbing down those stairs into the darkness deep under the earth filled her with fear and excitement. Once down there, feelings of comfort overcame her fear as she surveyed the stored-up food: sacks of potatoes, cabbages, beets, carrots, and onions, and deep sand-lined shelves of apples. Barrels of sauerkraut, pickles, and apple cider stood beside barrels of pork, preserved by layering the pieces of raw salted pork in lard.

After bringing up the jam, her father brought in a ham from the smokehouse and cut it into thin slices, while her mother swept and cleaned and fried *drożdżówki*, the special plum-filled buns. Veronika helped her father by eating the little bits of ham that were too small to go on the plate and her mother by cleaning off the extra jam that oozed out of the buns with her finger, until they both said that they didn't need her help anymore and shooed her out of the kitchen.

As the families started to arrive, Uncle Vladzio pulled up a chair, cupped his hands around a harmonica, and played folk songs. Drawn to the music, Veronika, Kazia, and other children gathered around his knee before darting off, only to be drawn back to the music moments later, sometimes bumping into Mama and the other women as they bustled back and forth from the kitchen to the table with platters of food. Veronika knew better than to bump into Tata and the other men. They sometimes scared her when they stood around looking angry and raising their voices about boring stuff like grain prices.

When Uncle Vladzio began to play polka music, the adults drifted into the living room, drinks in hand, and soon everyone was dancing, including Babcia. Veronika felt proud when people nodded and smiled and watched Babcia as she danced, whirling nimbly around them. She was quite the show at parties, even at the age of ninety-one.

Suddenly someone called out, *"Hopak! Hopak!"* Others took up the chant, until Uncle Vladzio struck up the familiar tune. Clapping and cheering, the crowd kept time to the music. First one and then another of the young men danced, backs straight in deep knee bends, flinging their legs out one at a time to the rhythm of the music. A roar of approval went up as older men dared to take a turn at the challenging dance. Even though the Hopak was a man's dance, someone shouted Babcia's name.

"Antosia! Antosia! Antosia!"

Others took up the chant, beckoning her to come out to perform, until Babcia could hold back no longer and walked to the centre of the floor. The clapping grew stronger, louder, and ever more insistent as she crossed her arms over her chest, dropped into a squatting position, and kicked her legs out in time with the music. Up and down, she bounced, a smile on her face, legs kicking out, faster and faster. The crowd went wild, with whoops and cheers, chanting "Antosia" over and over again, until she collapsed, energy spent, into a chair.

After an hour or two of dancing, Vladzio called for a break and people helped themselves to the meal. Veronika took a full plate of sweets with a token amount of ham and pickles on the side.

"Who would like to host the next round of women's sewing club?" her mother asked during the break.

"I can have it at my house," said Aunt Maria.

— ※ —

When Mama tucked her in that night, Veronika asked, "When is the next sewing club meeting?"

Her mother laughed and kissed her forehead. "You talk about the next already?"

Veronika nodded. "Parties are my best."

"Probably there will be a break of a week or two, then Aunt Maria will have her week. After that another break and then someone else will have a week."

"Can it be all year long?"

"Oh no, Veronika. In winter there is not so much to do, but the rest of the year we are busy! Besides, having it in the winter helps us to forget the early darkness and the winds that howl. We are inside, making our own fun."

4
VERONIKA

December 1929

Veronika's mother hummed *kolęda*, a Christmas carol, as she passed the shuttle back and forth on her loom. Veronika sat close to Kazia beside the warmth of the earthen oven. She felt a surge of happiness, being there so close to her cousin, playing with sticks they had shaped to resemble a human family.

"Let's sew rags on them for clothes," Kazia said.

Veronika's eyes widened. "I'll ask Mama if we can use her needles."

She walked over to her mother, taking in the work-worn face and deep-set eyes that always seemed to be concerned about something.

"May we borrow two needles and some thread?"

"If you're careful, I'll let you use one needle."

"Please, Mama, two. We won't lose them."

"I only have six needles. I can't get anymore."

Veronika remembered how her mother had dropped everything and rushed to the village when she heard that a limited supply of needles had arrived at the general store. Word had spread quickly throughout the village, and her mother had almost missed out on acquiring her last two needles.

As Veronika waited for her turn with the needle, she noticed her cousin's look of intense concentration as she lashed a bit of black rag to a stick by poking the needle in and out a few times. Kazia looked up, meeting Veronika's gaze. She flashed a smile that revealed missing front teeth.

"Do you like it?" she said, holding up the black-robed stick. "I made a priest."

"Oh, Kazia. We can pretend the boy and girl want to get married. I'll go see what else we can use."

Veronika went to her bedroom and pulled open the top drawer of her dresser, where she kept her candy and all her other treasures. She took out a few sparkly rocks, some dried red leaves, and two child-sized teacups and a teapot, the only gift that anyone had ever given her. Last Easter, a lady had been selling children's tea sets on the steps of the church as people came out of Mass. Veronika had looked with longing at the cups. They were glazed and painted with little flowers, much prettier than her mama's plain brown cups. Even though they didn't cost much, she knew better than to ask for them. The next thing she knew, the cups and teapot were in her hands.

"I will buy them for Veronika," was all her mother said.

Tata nodded.

All morning, Veronika and Kazia worked on their wedding plans. As they chatted, Veronika became aware of the smell of sauerkraut. Alarmed, she ran to the stove and watched as her mother plopped mounds of sauerkraut on top of pieces of frying pork.

"Don't worry, Veronika. I'm making this for Tata. I made you noodles and cream, but you should be like Kazia, not so fussy."

Relieved, Veronika went back to her play. Mama knows I can't eat sauerkraut or lumps she thought. Those were her two worst things. Whenever Mama made lumpy things like mushroom soup, she always strained the lumps out and gave her just the creamy broth.

When it was time to eat, Veronika's father stood outside the door and brushed off bits of straw from his coat so he wouldn't track any inside and make more work for Mama. He pulled off his knee-high boots and left them outside. Veronika liked to look at his boots. They were so worn and scuffed; they were almost colourless and had molded themselves to the exact shape of her father's feet, protruding bunions and all.

The sound of Tata preparing to wash his face drew Veronica and Kazia to watch expectantly, smiles already on their faces as he filled the washbasin with hot water from the stove and mixed in little homemade soap shavings. Nudging each other, they watched as he scooped water to his face with both hands and made spectacular sounds as he puffed out his cheeks and blew into the water. As always, he seemed confused by their giggles as he patted the moisture off his face and slicked back his hair with the family comb.

While Mama went back and forth from the stove to the table, they sat at the table and waited.

"Watch this," Tata said under his breath. "Let's see how long it takes." He picked up his knife and tapped his cup, over and over, ever so softly. In Mama came with a bowl of potatoes boiled in pork and sauerkraut. Tata tapped. She ignored him as she went back to the stove. In she came with Veronika's noodles and cream. Back she went, Tata tapped on. In she came with the round loaf of rye bread. Suddenly she snapped, "Janek, will you stop that!"

"What? Oh, sorry," he said. He put down his knife, looked at Veronika, and winked.

After helping clean up after the meal, Veronika wanted to play in the loft above the kitchen. Since she seldom went up there, it was a place of mystery. Her old baby clothes and cradle, as well as strings of dried fruit and Tata's trunk from the war were up there.

"Want to play in the loft, Kazia?"

"Is it scary?"

"Not too bad.

When they came down an hour later, dusty and thirsty, Mama didn't look right. Tata didn't either. Something about their mouth and eyes.

"What's wrong?"

"A man from the village hall came by. There is a meeting later this afternoon. Babcia has agreed to look after both of you and make your supper."

"Please, Mama, no. Can't Sofiya take care of us? She tells such good stories."

"All of our neighbours are going to the meeting."

"Aunt Agnes, then, please, Mama," Veronika said, grasping at alternatives, "They don't make her go because of her hip."

"Please, Aunt Helena, not Babcia." Kazia started to cry.

"Veronika, Kazia. The arrangements have already been made with Babcia."

Kazia howled. Veronika crumpled to the floor.

"Babcia is too strict, and her food is horrible," Veronika said.

Veronika thought back to the last time Babcia had to take care of them. Babcia had made carp stew, which, just by the smell, Veronika knew she wouldn't like. When Babcia had set a bowl of it down in front of her, her stomach did a flip-flop. It looked like cream of carp soup with bits of grey fish skin floating in it. Kazia's looked the same. When Veronika saw Babcia's bowl of carp stew, she felt like fainting in horror. Babcia's bowl had a huge fish head in it. Its mouth was open, in its last gasp, and a little row of teeth in its lower jaw lay exposed. Its enormous glassy eyes were clouded over and staring straight up at the ceiling. Babcia tucked into her fish head, grasping it in both hands and gnawing on it. Veronika had to look away. Pain radiated from her stomach up to her throat as she dipped her wooden spoon into the broth. It came up with long strings of something hanging off it. Next to her, Kazia was gingerly eating her stew. Next thing she remembered was vomiting on Babcia's dirt floor.

"Veronika," Mama said now. "Stop crying. I won't have it. Look, you're making Kazia cry, too."

More gently, she said, "It's only for a few hours, Veronika. Your cousins, Julia and Stasik, will be there, too."

Veronika thought about that. It would help having Aunt Paulina's and Uncle Feliks's children to play with. They were older and thought of interesting games.

"So, come on. Stop crying," Mama said, as Veronika's crying eased off. Picking Veronika up off the floor, she said, "Tell me, what is so bad about Babcia's food?"

"It's scary. I hate everything she makes."

Her mother was thoughtful for a moment. "It's terribly rude to refuse the food that has been offered. And Babcia is such a stickler about manners, too."

"She is, Mama. I have to sit up straight at the table and not talk while we're eating. If I forget, she reaches over and cracks my hand with a spoon."

"I tell you what. I'll sew pockets onto your apron and, when Babcia isn't looking, slip the lumps or things you don't like into a hankie in your pocket."

Sniffling and wiping her tears, Veronika reluctantly agreed to go.

When it was time to leave, Tata tried to cheer them up by offering a ride on his back.

"No, Janek, don't. It's too hard on you."

"Just for a little way, Helena, and one at a time. It'll be all right."

Gleefully, Veronika clung to his neck as she bounced up and down, teeth chattering, braids flying.

"My turn, Uncle, my turn," Kazia begged.

"No, no, I have to rest. Once we get closer to Babcia's I'll give you a turn."

They arrived at Uncle Feliks's duplex with Kazia still clinging to Tata's neck. Veronika's smile froze as Babcia opened the door and looked at them with disapproval. She wore a long dark skirt, a black sweater, and boots.

"Look at you, carting her like that. You'll spoil those children, more than they already are."

Tata quickly put Kazia down. Aunt Paulina and Uncle Feliks stood behind Babcia, putting on their coats. Aunt Paulina rolled her eyes at Babcia's remark. Uncle Feliks touched Babcia's elbow and said, "Mama, the way you were raised was not necessarily right, either. Sometimes showing children a bit of love makes them stronger, not weaker."

Veronika looked at Aunt Paulina and asked, "Where are Julia and Stasik?"

"At Aunt Agnes's. Four children are too many for Babcia."

Veronika looked at her mother balefully. Her mother looked back at her, giving her the look, which meant "not one word." Then Mama said, "Remember to have good manners for Babcia."

Veronika put her arms up and gave her a long hug. When Tata bent down to say goodbye, he grabbed both her and Kazia into a bear hug and growled into their necks until they couldn't help but laugh.

"We'll be back as soon as we can," he said.

"Thank you for taking them, Mama," Veronika's mother said.

Veronika watched as they got into the sleigh and covered themselves with heavy blankets. Suddenly her parents were gone and they were alone ... with Babcia.

"What are you making, Babcia?" Kazia asked.

"Pork cooked in sauerkraut. You like sauerkraut?"

"Yes, Babcia," Kazia said. She knew her manners.

Veronika was silent. Fear gripped her stomach, and she shoved her hands deep into her pockets, subconsciously measuring their capacity.

When it came time to deciding who was a kulak ... envy, personal grudges, and very often opposition to collectivization played a role. Consequently, many middle and even poor peasants were designated as kulaks or their helpers.

—Orest Subtelny, *Ukraine: A History*

5

JANEK

Fear consumed Janek's gut. He snapped the whip in the air, making a sharp cracking sound. Dobroc picked up his pace from a plod to a smart trot along the frost-covered road that followed the Smotrych River on one side and grain fields and farms on the other. Janek could not be late for this special meeting, and it would take twenty minutes to get to the village.

Why had this extra meeting been called just days before Christmas? What was so important that it couldn't wait until the regular monthly meeting? Was it to harangue them for selling their grain on the open market instead of handing it over to the state agent? But what were people to do? The state agent offered only one-eighth of what the open market offered. If they sold to the state, how would anyone pay their taxes? Whatever they called this meeting about, it couldn't be good.

"Janek, you better get that horse moving," Helena said, her face grim.

Janek cracked the whip again, and the horse resumed its pace.

As the road curved, the Polish Catholic church came into view. Janek exhaled heavily as he gazed at it. Just to look at it comforted him. It was like looking at the face of an old friend. God knows, he thought, making the sign of the cross.

When Janek pulled into the community hall, it was already so crowded, he had to search for a place to tie up the horse. At the back of the room, they found a place on a bench beside Feliks. Janek took off his hat and coat and felt glad for the woodstove's heat.

At the front of the room, Janek was startled to see Yuri, the head of the collective, talking to a man who wasn't local. The stranger's face was clean shaven, and his clothes were crisp looking, not handmade. His shoes were made to the shape of the left and right foot, definitely not village-made like theirs.

Janek nudged Helena and pointed the shoes out to her.

"Maybe a city man," she said, her face tense.

Feliks leaned toward Janek and whispered, "No one is going to make fun of Yuri's ideas, at least not today, not with that fellow sitting there."

"Just looking at Yuri makes me angry. The most lazy, good-for-nothing man in the village, and they make him collective leader."

Feliks nodded. "We can handle Yuri, but that city man, who knows?

Janek watched as Yuri walked across the room, gaunt as ever, with scruffy hair that curled over his ears and an untrimmed beard. He picked up a small table and carried it to the front.

As Yuri carried two chairs over to the table, Tomasz, an older grey-bearded man stood up and approached the front. Janek wondered why Tomasz would approach Yuri. There had been ill feelings between the two, ever since Yuri had wanted to marry his daughter and had been turned away.

Tomasz said something to Yuri then scuttled away when Yuri snapped, "Ask your questions later."

The city man sat down and opened up a case. He took out a set of papers and a pencil. Yuri stood in front of the crowd with an expectant look on his face. Holding up his hands, he waited for stillness as the talking died down and people readjusted their bodies to the benches.

"Soviet citizens of Kuzmin, Comrade Nicholai Zykov is the new director of our collective, sent to us from Moscow by our great Soviet leaders."

Throughout the room, groans and whispers could be heard that this city man, a Soviet outsider, would be living among them. Comrade Zykov stood up, cleared his throat, and said, "As collective leader, I will be working closely with Comrade Yuri to see that all Soviet directives are carried out. If I find any resistance, I will call in the military and the Soviet secret police to assist me."

Janek froze at the mention of the secret police. The people they took for questioning disappeared, often forever.

Comrade Zykov waited with an amused look on his face as he surveyed the anxious people. "To this end," he said when he had everyone's attention again, "here's my first directive. The shipment of grain from this year's harvest to the Soviet government is down from the year before, resulting in a two-million-ton deficit. Our government needed that grain. People in the cities have to stand in line for hours just to buy a loaf of bread. The army is no longer able to feed its men. Without grain to sell overseas, the purchase of new farm and factory equipment has become impossible.

"Why is the Soviet government short of grain? Because people have been hoarding. Burying it in the ground and waiting for better prices. Selling on the open market. They do not care about our country. They are only interested in making a profit and keeping their pig fat!"

Feliks whispered to Janek, "He probably doesn't know about our taxes. I'm going to tell him."

Janek gripped Feliks by the arm. "No! You say nothing."

At that moment, a woman to the side of the room rose to her feet. In a loud voice, trembling with passion, she addressed Comrade Zykov.

"We had to sell our grain on the open market to pay our taxes. The Soviet agent was paying less than it cost to grow."

"What is your name?"

"Alyona Pawlowska."

Zykov looked at Yuri. "Write it down."

"Alyona Pawlowska," Zykov said, looking up slowly from Yuri's notes, "you have many complaints about our government. Sit down. I would like your husband to stand up."

Her husband, shoulders bent, hat in hand, got hesitantly to his feet.

"Comrade Pawlowski, you share your wife's views?"

"No, I don't complain. For everyone, life is hard, but we will get by."

Eyebrows raised, Zykov turned to Yuri. "He complains, too. Life is hard for everyone, he says. Tell me, Comrade Yuri, did this man, Pawlowski, sell even one sack of grain to the Soviet agent?"

"No," Yuri said.

Comrade Zykov continued, "Not one sack, yet you and your wife complain. We will see what you can do for your country when we come to your farm."

Pawlowski slumped down onto the bench, then held his head between his hands.

Comrade Zykov continued. "To make sure that the government gets the grain that has been hoarded, a village troika has been formed to establish quotas."

He paused as moans and mutterings broke out throughout the

room. Janek felt his chest constrict. Not quotas again, he thought. Oh, God, not again. His two-year-old son, Vladimir, had died during the 1921 famine. The quota took everything. Then came the diseases—cholera, diphtheria, typhus, typhoid. He looked at Helena, quietly crying into her hands. She turned her face toward him at the touch of his arm around her shoulders.

"Janek, I can't bear to lose another child," Helena said, her face pinched.

"We'll be all right," he whispered. As he rubbed her back, he could see his son's face and a fresh wave of grief swept over his heart, constricting his throat. They just couldn't save him. He would have been eight this year.

After a moment's pause, Zykov continued. "The grain committee consists of me and Comrade Yuri, a representative of the secret police and the head of the village Soviet. Every man has been assigned a quota based on what class the committee decides you are in: poor, middle, or wealthy. Naturally, those with more money and land have higher quotas than those with less. You will be paid for your grain, but at government prices. Speculation and hoarding are criminal offences. Are there any questions?"

A man Janek had seen before but did not know, rose to his feet.

"I have not been hoarding. I only have three sacks of grain left. I must keep what I have for food."

Zykov turned to Yuri and said, "What class is this man in?"

Yuri opened a register and scanned down the list with his finger. Finally, his finger came to rest. "He is in the poor category."

"Ah, that is good," Zykov said. "Come up here."

Trembling, the man walked forward. Janek felt his breath catch in his throat. Zykov grabbed the man by his shoulder and turned him around to face the audience, then slapped him on the back and said, "You do not need to give any grain. Twenty-five percent of all the grain we gather, we will redistribute among the poor. That is the way it is with communism."

The astonished man walked back to his seat.

"Are there any other questions?" Zykov asked.

Tomasz, the man who wouldn't allow Yuri to marry his daughter, stood up. "What class am I in?"

Yuri looked at him. He did not look at the register. "You are in the wealthy class. You will give up twenty-five sacks of grain."

Tomasz sucked in his breath as if he had been punched. "I'm not wealthy. I don't even have that much grain."

Janek felt an explosion of fear in his chest. There must be a mistake. Tomasz had no more than he had, fifteen to twenty sacks, at the most. He struggled to provide for his family. Janek looked at Yuri and saw a slight smirk on his face.

Tomasz looked around the hall, bewildered at the blow that had befallen him. "Tell them," he beseeched those assembled, trying to make eye contact with them. People looked away, not meeting his gaze. "Tell them. I am not a rich man."

"Sit down," Zykov bellowed.

Hands reached up to grab him and pull him down onto the bench.

"Are there any other questions?"

No one said a word.

"No? All right, then, you can look at the posted list to see how much your quota is. You have three days to submit your grain in full or we will come and search for it. This meeting is over."

The few who were in the poor category, who were going to benefit from quotas, lingered to laugh and chat. Janek and his family walked past them, grim faced. They would not be able to make their quota.

6
JANEK

December 23, 1929

Janek stared out the kitchen window, his breathing laboured. In the back of his mind, he heard Veronika's happy chatter as she and Helena baked cookies to hang on the Christmas tree. How could he possibly make his quota of ten sacks? He counted again what he needed for food, for animal feed, for sowing. Always it was the same. He had fifteen sacks. The most he could give them was five. Maybe he could owe them the other five. Give it to them after next harvest.

"Tata, can you hardly wait?" asked Veronika.

"For what?"

"*Pierniczki,* gingerbread cookies, Tata. Can you hardly wait? We are going to cut them into the shape of little men."

"That's good," he said mildly.

He saw the joy in Veronika's face slowly fade.

"Mama, why is Tata sad?"

"He's just thinking. Let's leave him alone for a while. Later he's going to bring home a Christmas tree. Would you like that?"

Despite Veronika's happy exclamation, Janek continued to mull over his options. He had to protect the grain that he needed. Maybe he should hide a few sacks. And if they found them, then what? His eyes wandered over to Veronika. She caught his glance and ran over with a spoonful of cookie dough.

"Try some, Tata."

He forced a smile and made a show of pleasure. Veronika giggled and ran back to her mother, spoon held high in the air. Helena thanked him with her eyes.

Janek took a deep breath; he knew what he had to do. He walked over to the door and put on his hat and coat.

"Where are you going, Janek?"

"To Yuri's. Ask him if our quota could get reduced."

Helena gasped. "Do you think you should?"

"He owes us."

"Be careful, Janek."

As Janek's horse picked its way through the snow, he thought of Yuri, always taking the easy way out. Maybe if he had worked harder on his land and picked out more of the rocks and pulled stumps, he'd have something worth farming. Instead, he'd turned the farming over to his wife while he travelled the country peddling used clothes and rags. When that didn't work out, it was too late to plant, and Janek had given him grain so that at least they wouldn't starve. Now he had given his land to the Soviets and joined in with their *durne*, stupid plans.

Janek knocked on the door of Yuri's dishevelled-looking home. Yuri's wife Kateryna answered. She seemed surprised to see him and offered a weak smile. "I'd let you come in, Jan, but I don't know if Yuri wants any company."

"I won't be long."

A slurred voice called out from inside, "Who is it?"

"It's Jan."

"Well, let him in!"

Kateryna stood to one side, and Janek stepped into the kitchen. Yuri sat in a chair by the fire. Two children sat on the floor playing with rag dolls. Janek knew the older child. She was about Veronika's age.

"You know Alyona, but you haven't met our youngest," Kateryna said, scooping up the curly-haired toddler. "This is our Yulia."

The child stared at him in round-eyed wonder, thumb in her mouth. Kateryna put the child down and said, "Alyona, you two play in the loft. Father has company."

Yuri held up a jug. "Jan, come sit down. Have a drink. No one ever comes to our house anymore."

He poured Janek a drink with an unsteady hand, slopping a little onto the table as he poured. Janek looked around at the room and noticed no sign of Christmas preparations.

"Christmas blessings," Janek said, lifting up his glass.

"Christmas? No Christmas blessings for us. Not this year. Zykov says that we must be an example to others. Now my wife does not even talk to me."

Kateryna entered the room again, carrying a bowl of hard-boiled eggs and a dish of hot mustard. Setting it down on the table in front of Janek, she said, "First you turn our neighbours against us and now we cannot even go to church. How do I explain to Alyona that this year is no Christmas?"

Janek looked at Yuri in surprise. "Zykov can tell you what to do in your own home?"

"Zykov even tells me what to do," Kateryna said. "Says I have to make cloth for the collective. As if I don't have enough to do already. Everyone must do as the factory worker says."

"Factory worker?" Janek asked, raising his eyebrows.

Yuri smiled. "Oh, yes, that's our leader. He was the manager of a bicycle factory in Moscow. He hates it here. Says everything stinks like shit."

"Why did he come here, then?"

"Communists were sent to every village. *Find the blood-sucking lice*, they said. That's what they call us—lice. To them we are not even human. We're vermin."

Janek felt his gut clench.

"He called me a fool. That's what he did, in front of the village council. Said if I had been harder on people, he wouldn't have had to come here. Why did I ever join them?"

"Are you going to leave the collective?"

Yuri snorted. "Leave? They don't let you leave." He took a gulp of his drink. "Now I have to help make lists of people to ruin. Some I don't mind ruining, but others, people like you, it hurts. You've always been good to me."

"Is it possible, Yuri, to put in a word for me? To get my quota reduced a little."

Yuri looked at him through squinting eyes. "I cannot even help myself."

"When your family was starving, I helped you. Just put in a good word for me. Maybe my quota could be made just a little lower."

"All I can tell you is to cooperate. If he comes and finds you have been hoarding, then *zitt*." He made an explosive sound with his tongue.

"Then you'll do nothing to help me?"

"You'll be all right. I don't know about me. I just don't know."

"What don't you know?"

"This district has a grain quota. Can you believe it? Zykov is in charge of filling it. Until the end of the month, he has. But people don't have any extra grain. If the quota doesn't get filled, Zykov is holding me responsible. She doesn't know that," he said, flicking his head toward the back room, where they could hear Kateryna working on her loom.

Janek looked down at his hands. Yuri put his glassy-eyed face close to Janek's.

"Why?" he blubbered. "Why do I always have such bad luck? Can you tell me? I just wanted people to respect me. I wanted more than living day to day on this rocky farm. And now I'm trapped."

Janek stood and picked up his hat and coat. He didn't know what to say. Yuri had made choices; all along he had made choices. He was still making choices. "Zykov isn't here now. He can't see if you're praying for God's help." He called out to Kateryna, thanking her for the food, and walked out the door.

He sat hunched over his horse, as rain mixed with frozen ice particles whipped up by the wind hurled against his face. The pain was almost enough to distract him from the pain in his chest. *The web, we are all tangled in the web.*

7
VERONIKA

Veronika scraped the frost from the window, creating a peephole, then pressed her head against the window, trying to catch a glimpse of her Tata's return. Not seeing him, she left the window and wandered over to the kitchen table to watch as her mama make *kutya*, the special Christmas Eve dessert of honey, poppyseed and walnuts stirred into steamed whole kernels of wheat.

"May I lick out the bowl when you're done?"

"All right, but don't make a mess. Tomorrow Tata's brother and his wife come. We have to be ready."

"Where do they live?"

"In Proskurov. That's at least forty kilometres from here."

"That's a long way. Can I give Uncle Oryst his cookie as soon as he gets here?"

"Wait till he gets his coat off, but remember, Veronika, tomorrow is not about Uncle Oryst. It is about the vigil. We must keep watch and wait. And when the first star of the evening comes out, then we know that already the Baby has been born."

Veronika bent her head down to the cookies on the table and took a deep whiff, only half-listening. She wished she could ask her mother why Uncle Oryst's wife, Aunt Ludka, was so old, as old looking as Babcia, except Babcia had all her teeth. And what did it mean when people said he had married gold? Maybe she could ask Uncle Oryst when her mother wasn't around, but she wouldn't ask about Aunt Ludka's age. That would be rude.

She looked at the ribbon threaded through the pierniczki cookie. She picked one up. Yes, the little man still dangled there.

She wandered over to the dining room table where the other Christmas tree decorations sat in orderly rows. She felt a sense of awe that so many lovely things could be gathered all in one place: apples and walnuts tied up in ribbon, crocheted stars, paper ornaments and, best of all, candies that Mama had purchased from the general store to tie on the tree. The candies were counted, too, so Mama would notice if she took one.

"What are you doing in there, Veronika?"

"I'm just straightening the rows."

She heard Mama's snort of laughter. "Come away from those decorations. You need to practice the *kutya* blessing."

"Do I have to? I know it already."

"Yes, you have to."

"Why do I have to do it, Mama?"

"Because Babcia is the oldest and most important member of our family, and you are the youngest member of our household. That is the way it always goes, the youngest offers the kutya blessing to the oldest."

"Why is she the most important member of the family?"

"Because everything we have is due to my parents. After my

father died, Babcia divided up their land and gave each of their children a section."

Reluctantly, Veronika recited, "This bowl of sweet kutya your family gives to you, Babcia, to honour you and to thank you for all you have done for us and to wish you a very long life. There, is that good enough, Mama?"

"Yes, it's very good. We'll be proud of you."

Hearing a thumping in the front yard, Veronika shouted, "Maybe it's Tata." She ran to the kitchen window and licked a spot in the pane to clear away the frost, then rubbed it hard with her fist. "It is Tata. And he has a tree!"

Mama and Veronika rushed to the front door as Janek set the tree against the porch, then kicked his boots against the wall to knock off the snow.

"Tata, it's beautiful! Can we bring it in?"

"Not yet. It has to dry off." He bent down and rubbed his beard back and forth into the nape of Veronika's neck, making her laugh and wiggle.

"How did it go with Yuri?" Mama asked.

"Not good," he said, straightening up.

"What's not good, Tata?"

Continuing to talk to Mama, he said, "After Christmas, I'll go down, give them what I can, and tell them I have to owe the rest."

"How much are you going to give them?"

"Five sacks."

"*Matko Boska*, Mother of God, Janek."

"What's wrong, Tata? Why is Mama sad?"

"Don't you worry, my little one. Everything is very good. Tomorrow is Christmas Eve, is it not? Here, Veronika, put this hay under the table. I've blessed it."

Gleefully, Veronika took the sweet-smelling bundle that was pressed into her arms.

"We need another bundle for the corner of the room," Mama said.

"Don't know if there's any use, not this year."

"Janek, don't be like that."

"What is the use in hoping for a good crop of grain? The Soviets will only take it."

"You don't know. Things can change."

That night when Veronika went to bed, she kept thinking about their wonderful tree, the best tree ever, in the barn. She'd wanted to take it into the house right away, but Tata said they had to wait until tomorrow. The thought made her kick her feet up and down in bed. Why did everything have to wait? She forced herself to lie still. The sooner she could fall asleep, the sooner Christmas Eve would come.

8
VERONIKA

The sound of Uncle Oryst's and Aunt Ludka's voices in the kitchen woke Veronika up. She leapt out of bed and threw a shawl over her nightgown before running out to the kitchen.

"You're here," she said. "Now Christmas can start."

Uncle Oryst kissed her three times on the cheeks. "And look how big you've grown," he said, lifting her up and setting her down beside him.

How he and Tata resembled each other. The only difference being that Uncle Oryst was taller and his face clean shaven.

"Maybe she's too old for kopeks?" asked Aunt Ludka, smiling at her kindly.

"I'm not too old for that."

"Hold out your hand and close your eyes," Uncle Oryst said.

Veronika felt something dropped into her palm.

"Open your eyes."

Four shiny kopeks sat in her hand.

"Thank you," she said. "I'll put them in my dresser."

"Before you go, come here and give me a kiss," Aunt Ludka said.

Veronika glanced at her mother and, seeing the almost imperceptible nod, reluctantly slid across the sofa. Veronika felt her head squashed against Aunt Ludka's bony chest, then saw the almost toothless mouth gape open and come toward her. The soft, gummy kiss felt so odd, she couldn't wait to pull away from her but knew better than to move too fast.

She stayed pressed against Aunt Ludka's side until Tata said, "Go see the Christmas tree. It's on the side table."

Veronika jumped up and ran to the dining room where she stared at the beautiful little tree that filled the room with the spicy scent of Christmas.

After breakfast was over and the tree decorated, Veronika followed Tata and Uncle Oryst into the living room.

"I wish you still lived in Kuzmin," Veronika said, putting her hand in her uncle's.

"I do, too," Uncle Oryst said, giving her nose a playful tweak. "Then I could see you more often." Looking at Tata he said, "But it is better in the city. I work for myself. No one looks over my shoulder. I go to the city centre, set up my sharpening wheel, and wait for customers."

"Why do you work when you married gold?" Veronika asked.

From the look on Uncle Oryst's face, Veronika knew she'd said something wrong.

"Veronika," Tata said.

"No, let me tell her, Janek. There's no shame in what I've done. The only shame is when people hear gossip and don't know the truth."

"I'm sorry," Tata said. "I don't know what got into her."

Veronika felt her uncle lifting her chin.

"Look at me, child. Your Tata and I came from a very poor family. Every day was a struggle just to eat, and so I did not have an opportunity to learn a trade. I was desperate. That's when I met Ludka's son. He told me that his father had died, and he was worried about his mother. There was no one to take care of her. He couldn't because he travelled, sharpening knives. He offered to teach me the trade if I would marry her.

"There's no shame in what I did, Veronika. And yes, she does have gold. Her father left it to her, but we're saving it for our old age when I can no longer work. Do you understand?"

"Yes, Uncle Oryst," she said in a small voice. "I'm sorry."

"That's all right," he said, ruffling her hair. "People talk, and you were curious."

Veronika sat still, not daring to move. When the topic turned to the government and grain prices, they didn't notice her leave the room.

When the midday meal was over, it was time to sing kolędy. They sang until they could sing no more and it was time to go to Mass. Veronika helped Mama and Aunt Ludka clear away the dishes, while Tata and Uncle Oryst went outside to harness the horse to the sleigh.

After a sleigh ride, cuddled up in heavy wool blankets, Veronika welcomed the warmth as she entered the light-filled church. She sat between her Mama and Tata, gazing at the statues and smelling the incense that the priest swirled in a golden pot hanging from a chain. But not for so long. Today the Mass was double long, with two hours of singing. A long time to sit and look at statues.

Veronika looked at Kazia from across the bench. Their eyes met. Kazia smiled and then made her eyes bulge. Veronika snickered. Babcia knuckled Veronika on the top of her head. Mama pulled Veronika over, out of Babcia's reach.

Mass finally over, Veronika bundled up for the best part of Christmas, the feast of Christmas Eve, at Babcia's.

Upon entering Babcia's home, a round of hugs and kisses began—Aunt Agnes, Uncle Vladzio, Aunt Paulina and Uncle Feliks, as well as Julia and Stasik. Veronika endured it all, discreetly wiping off her damp cheeks. Veronika felt Mama's nudge as she passed her the bowl of kutya.

"Quiet, everyone," called out Mama. "Veronika is going to offer the blessing."

Veronika walked up to Babcia and stood in front of her, bowl held out. In a clear voice she said, "This bowl of sweet kutya your family gives to you, Babcia, to honour you and to thank you for all you have done for us and to wish you a very long life."

Babcia gave Veronika a half-smile and nodded her head. Her role of greeting Babcia over, Veronika set the bowl down and ran to play with Kazia. Every now and then, Veronika and her cousins ran outside to see if they could see the first star, the signal that the feast could begin.

At last Mama called everyone to dinner. To everyone's satisfaction, the traditional twelve dishes sat on the table. Veronika couldn't wait to eat the pierogi, made special for Christmas with white flour instead of buckwheat. After an hour or so of eating until no one could eat anymore, they sang kolęda after kolęda.

Exhausted from a long and glorious day, Veronika felt herself falling asleep and being carried to Babcia's pallet and covered with coats. She was not aware of the sleigh ride home or being carried into her own bed in the early hours of the morning.

The harvests of 1928-29 were poor ... Food once again became scarce, especially in the steppe region of southeastern Ukraine – but grain collection continued at the same pace.

—Anne Applebaum, *Red Famine: Stalin's War on Ukraine*

9

VERONIKA

On Christmas day, Veronika woke up and walked into the kitchen. Her mother sat by the earthen oven, mending a sock.

"Where is everyone?" she asked, rubbing her eyes.

"I'm sorry, but Uncle Oryst and Aunt Ludka are gone already."

"Gone? I didn't get to say goodbye."

"They didn't want to wake you. Uncle Oryst went in and kissed you while you slept. Said he put something under your pillow."

Veronika ran back into her room and lifted her pillow. Underneath were scattered candies and kopeks. "Mama, come see."

"Well, that's nice," her mother said, looking at the treasure. "Uncle Oryst certainly is good to you. Would you like to have breakfast now? Tata and I had to eat without you."

"Where is Tata?"

"Out in the barn. He took the hay from under the table."

Tears sprang to her eyes, "Oh, I wanted to see the animals eat it."

"Don't get so upset. He said he would wait for you."

"I'm going out right now." Veronika grabbed a coat, put it on over her long nightgown and thrust her bare feet into her boots.

"Wait, you'll need some kutya." Filling a small dish with the honey-and-walnut-soaked grain, Mama said, "There, that should be enough to do it."

Carrying the bowl to the barn, a sudden gust of freezing wind blew under her nightgown against her bare skin. She shrieked and bolted, throwing the barn door open so fast, she startled her father.

Laughing at how the wind swirled her nightgown and hair, he said, "Shut the door. Keep in what little warmth there is."

"Did you feed them the hay yet?"

"No, I was waiting for you." He put his rake down and picked up a bundle of hay sitting by the door, dividing it between the horse and the cow. "Put a spoonful of kutya on the hay."

Veronika watched as they chewed contentedly. They didn't look any different. It was disappointing. She gave some to the pig, and then scattered the rest of the kutya around the chickens and geese, watching as the falling kutya caused havoc as they tried to edge each other out of position. She dropped a clump down for the cats rubbing their bodies against her legs. They pounced on the kutya, smelled it, and nibbled a little, then walked away with disdain, tails swishing.

"I guess cats don't care if they eat blessed food or not," Tata said. "Let's go into the house."

"I want to watch the animals for a while. They still might do something."

"What do you think they might do?" Tata asked, a puzzled expression on his face.

"Well, Kazia told me that on Christmas the animals sometimes talk."

Tata snorted, "Oh, my little girl. Mama and I wondered why you were so anxious to see the animals eat the blessed food."

Trying to overcome her crushing disappointment, she asked, "May I play with Kazia today?"

He shook his head. "Christmas day is for resting after the late night."

"But I don't have anything to do."

"Mama is making a roast goose for dinner. You could help her. I'm going in now."

Veronika nodded. Not wanting to be put to work in the kitchen, she climbed into the loft.

Christmas day certainly isn't as special as Christmas Eve, she thought.

Veronika heard horses in the yard. Visitors! Tata was wrong. As she scampered down the loft ladder, the barn door opened and two soldiers walked in.

"You check the loft, I'll look down here," one of them said.

Veronika gasped and shrank against the wall at the foot of the ladder.

One of the men called out, "Over here, he's got grain."

She could hear Tata yelling in the yard, "I told you, I'm going to bring what I can to the collective tomorrow. I'll make arrangements to pay the rest in the fall."

Veronika bolted for the door. A hand reached out and grabbed her by the hair as she tried to run by.

"Tata," she screamed as she struggled to free herself from the soldier, who now had a firm grip on her arm. She could see Tata through the open doorway. A soldier held him back.

"Please, let my daughter go," he pleaded.

"She's fine where she is. Maybe she can help us find where you hid the rest of your grain."

The man dragged Veronika back into the barn and slid the door closed. She could hear Tata desperately calling to her.

"Where did your father hide the grain?"

"I don't know," she said staring at his thick fingers squeezing her arm.

His eyes bore into hers. "Sure you do."

She looked away, fear gripping her heart.

He shook her. "Children always know these things. Tell me, and I'll let you go."

"I don't know," she said through numb lips.

"Did he hide it in the cellar?"

He pulled her close to his face. The sour smell of tobacco assaulted her. "Tell me."

Veronika struggled to get away, away from that smell, from his eyes. "Yes, yes! In the cellar," she cried.

His fingers dug into her arm as he opened the door and released her.

Mama stood by Tata, crying. She ran to them.

"So, you hid no grain from the Soviet government. Your daughter says you did. How about we go see."

Mama held Veronika close while the soldiers rummaged around in their root cellar. They could hear barrels being moved and banged against each other. Moments later, they reappeared.

"You lied," a soldier said, glaring at Veronika, as he emerged from the cellar empty-handed.

Veronika's heart plummeted. She felt her mother trembling, clutching her, squeezing her breath away. Tata stepped in front of them, blocking her view.

"Of course, she lied," he said, his voice shaking with anger. "You frightened her." He turned to Helena, "Take her inside."

Veronika felt herself being led into the house. Together they sat on the bench. Veronika felt numb, mouthing the words of the rosary with her mother as they waited.

When Tata finally came in, his face was calm. "They're gone."

"Janek," Mama sobbed. The rosary fell from her hands as she walked hesitantly, disbelievingly, toward him. "Are you all right?"

"Don't worry. They didn't hurt me. I showed them where we hid the grain. I had to. They weren't going to leave until I did."

Veronika watched as Mama cried and Tata stroked her back.

"At least they only took ten sacks," he said soothingly. "We still have five."

Later, Mama cried again when she saw the tipped-over barrels in the root cellar.

10
VERONIKA

December 31, 1929

Veronika awoke with a start. She had been dreaming of the soldier who had grabbed her—the cold stare of his eyes, the feel of his fingers pressing into her arm. Bolting out of bed, she ran into the kitchen. Her parents sat at the table, holding hands. She wondered if Mama had been crying again.

"You look frightened," Tata said. "Did you have another bad dream?"

She nodded. "Will the soldiers come back?"

Tata looked down. Mama pressed her handkerchief to the corner of her eye then walked over to the woodstove.

"Will they?" Veronika asked again.

"Come here, my little Noosha," Tata said, using his pet name for her. "I don't know and that is the truth. But my way is to try to do as they say, then they have no reason to come." He took her in his arms and held her against his chest for a very long time.

— ✻ —

During the days that followed, a constant stream of relatives and neighbours came over to tell their stories of how their grain had been taken, or whose grain they thought would be taken next.

Why did they have to keep talking about it? Why couldn't everything be the same as before? At least she still had the New Year's dance at Aunt Agnes and Uncle Vladzio's to look forward to. Every year it was held at their home, and she would be given lucky kopeks to buy a paper cone of candies at the store.

"Mama, how many kopeks do you think I'll get? A whole bowl full, maybe?"

"I don't think we should go to the dance."

Veronika stared at her in disbelief. "Not go?"

"It just doesn't feel right with all that's been happening."

Tata slowly got to his feet. "I think we should go," he said softly. "It would be good for us. Why should we let them take even the dance away from us?"

Mama stared at him, her eyebrows furrowed.

"Come on," he said, putting his hand on her shoulder. "You know Veronika has been looking forward to this all year."

"Please, Mama?"

Helena shrugged and sighed, "All right, I guess we can go, but for now we must tidy the house. Tata's sister is coming over."

"Aunt Marysia?"

"Yes, and she has a gift for you," Tata said with a smile.

Veronika gasped. "What is it?"

"You have to wait until she gets here."

What could it be? Except for the tiny teacup and saucer Mama had bought her last Easter, no one had ever given her a gift.

When slender, dark-haired Aunt Marysia arrived an hour later,

Tata gave her a big hug. Veronika noticed how much alike they were, with their prominent foreheads and deep-set eyes.

"Come in, Marysia," Mama said. "Janek, take her coat. I'll put out something to eat!"

Veronika felt shy. She didn't see this aunt very often. She lived quite a distance away and only came to visit once or twice a year.

Aunt Marysia looked at her and smiled. "I have something for you!"

"We will have our tea first," Tata said firmly.

While Mama put out tea, cups, and sweet buns left over from Christmas, Tata told Marysia how the soldiers had come. Veronika stood at the kitchen window, looking out, trying not to listen. She didn't want to hear about it anymore.

"Come here, Veronika," Aunt Marysia said. "Let me see you."

Veronika walked over to her and stood looking down at the dirt floor. She felt Aunt Marysia's arm around her, pulling her close. "I'm sorry for what happened to you. It must have been terrible. Such times we're going through. But I have something for you that might cheer you up."

Veronika wanted to see it right now but knew it would be rude to ask. Veronika sat at the table and waited. One cup of tea, two cups of tea. Finally, as Aunt Marysia drained her third cup of tea, she looked at Veronika with a slight smile. Veronika felt her chest tingle with excitement.

"Is it time to see what I brought for you?" her aunt asked.

Veronika nodded, "Oh, yes, please," she whispered.

Aunt Marysia opened her sewing bag and held out a cloth doll. "I made this for you."

Veronika could not believe that such a wonderful thing could exist, much less be hers. She reached out for the doll. It was not at all like her stick dolls. This one had brown yarn for hair and an embroidered face with a pink smile. The doll wore a knitted blouse and skirt and even had socks sewn on. It was the prettiest thing she had ever seen.

"Are you not going to say thank you, Veronika?" her mother asked.

Veronika hugged the doll to her face. She ran to her aunt and crushed her tightly in heartfelt thanks.

"I have something more to show you," her aunt said, pulling out of her bag tiny knitted sweaters, skirts, and linen blouses with embroidered decorations. "So you can dress your doll for festive days and also for work. And there is something more."

She got up and went outside, then came in holding a wooden bed for the doll, complete with bedding.

As Veronika sat on the sofa, submerged in the glory of her presents, Aunt Marysia said, "Now, tell me who else got their grain taken."

When Veronika went with her parents on their rounds of visiting that afternoon, the doll never left her hands. Everyone marvelled at how beautiful it was, how well-crafted, then they seemed to forget that she was even there. They went right back to talking about grain and quotas and how they hoped it wouldn't be like last time when there was a famine. Once again, Veronika felt the weight of the stone slowly pushing down on her heart.

Stalin's orders were clear on one point: (collectivization) must be done rapidly and without regard to protest, difficulties or costs.
—Orest Subtelny, Ukraine: A History

11
JANEK

March 1930

Janek milked the cow, squirting some into the mouths of the cats sitting nearby. Usually, he took a quiet pleasure in his daily chores, but not so much anymore. His heart wasn't in it. Same as his neighbours. The women's sewing parties had ended abruptly with fear about the quotas and the new Russian man, Zykov. Each meeting seemed more menacing than the last.

"The vision from our great leaders was that agriculture production will rise by 150 percent. Instead, every year there are deficits. Why is this you may ask? Because of those who are deliberately sabotaging the plan. They don't want communism to succeed. I promise you one thing, soon they will be found out and expelled from the land."

He carried the pail of milk into the house and set it down on the counter for Helena. "There, all ready for your cheese making."

Janek froze and listened. There was a creaking rumble of a horse cart entering the yard.

"So early somebody comes?" Helena asked.

Janek went to the kitchen window and pulled the curtain back. Zykov and his new assistant from the collective were getting out of their cart.

"*Cholerny*, damn," Janek said, a tightness constricting his breathing. The assistant was wearing Yuri's black fleece coat.

Helena peered out. "What can they want with us?" she asked, her voice tense as the men entered the barn.

"Will they come in the house, Mama?" asked Veronika.

"I don't know, Veronika, maybe," Helena said, her voice brittle.

"Get her over to your sister's. Use the back door."

"Janek, I'm not going to leave you," Helena said, her eyes welling with tears.

He squeezed her shoulder. "I'll be all right. Go, before they come in," he said motioning with his head toward Veronika.

Helena grabbed their coats. "Come, Veronika."

"Why, Mama? We haven't had breakfast yet."

"Do as I say. We can eat at Aunt Maria's."

A wave of relief swept over Janek as they went out the door. Whatever happened, at least his little one would not be witness to it.

He put on his hat and coat, said a quick prayer, then walked toward the barn. He despised these men and how they could turn his life upside down, but especially he hated how powerless they made him feel.

Janek entered the barn. Zykov turned and approached him with a smile. "Hello, Comrade."

"Why are you here?"

Zykov's smile faded. "The Committee has asked that Comrade Kanygin and I make a report on the wealth of independent farmers."

"Wealth? I barely get by."

"That is for us to decide," Kanygin said. "Unless, of course, you join the collective."

Fear rippled through Janek. "Collectives are good, but I prefer to work alone."

"That kind of stubborn kulak thinking is what needs to be eliminated," Zykov said. He looked at Kanygin. "I'll finish checking the barn. You see how many hens he has."

"You don't have to count," Janek said. "I have eight."

Kanygin ignored Janek and continued walking. Janek followed Zykov, seething in anger that they could walk around like they owned his farm.

"She's a big one," Zykov said, looking at the pig. "Ready to butcher?"

Longing to call him a fool, Janek simply said, "She's about to have a litter."

"Oh, yes," Zykov said. "I can see that now."

Kanygin strode into the barn. Two hens dangled from his hand, their necks snapped. "I need a sack for these."

Through gritted teeth Janek said, "Those were Helena's best laying hens."

"You have more."

Janek turned away to get a sack from the stall where he kept them. He took his time, looking through the sacks as if to find a good one. He needed to maintain his calm. All their lives depended on it. He knew that, yet still, inside he raged.

Please God, be with me.

After making a note of the cow and horse, they asked him about his farm equipment, and took stock of his ten acres of land, writing down how many were in grain, and how many in orchard.

"Now we will see what you keep in your house," Zykov said.

Janek felt a tightness return to his chest as the two intruders silently took in the whitewashed stone walls, hard-packed floor, plank table and benches, the living room with the horsehair sofa and polished side tables. In the kitchen pantry, they looked at the food. Zykov made notes.

Kanygin wandered over to the kitchen table, ran his hand over the wood, then picked up Helena's prayer book and thumbed through its fragile pages.

Dangling it from his hand, he said, "You teach these lies to your daughter?"

"No, Comrade."

"Good," he said, throwing it in the woodstove. "We would not like to hear that you give religious instruction to a young Soviet citizen."

Helpless rage burned through Janek at its loss. The prayer book had been in Helena's family for generations, recording births, deaths, and marriages.

Kanygin walked over to the statue of Mary in the wall niche. He picked it up, turned it over, and looked into its hollow base. He scratched at the paint on her cheek with his fingernail, leaving a white streak.

Janek's heart jumped to his throat. "Please, Comrade, put it down. It was my mother's."

"Religion is the opiate of the people," he said, hefting it onto his shoulder and walking toward the door.

Stepping into Kanygin's path, Janek said, "Have you no feelings? I said it is from my mother."

"Out of my way," Kanygin said, shoving Janek aside and walking out to the porch. Swinging the statue by the base, he hit the head hard against a post.

The statue remained whole. Janek couldn't believe it. As Kanygin wound up for another swing, Janek tried to wrest it from him. Kanygin wrenched free and took another swing, and another, each time battering the head hard against the post until finally, the head fell to the ground.

Janek sank to his knees, gasping. How he longed to smash Kanygin's smug face in. How dare he destroy the only family keepsakes they had?

Kanygin nudged Janek with his foot. "Get your ladder."

Janek brushed himself off and got the rough-hewn ladder off its wall pegs and hooked it into the lip of the loft's floor. The two men scrambled up. He heard them move the storage trunks and baby cradle he had up there.

After they clambered down, Janek felt numb as they continued their room-to-room search, listing all the linens Helena had made by gathering flax from the field, then spinning and weaving it, the pillows she had made, and the plain and simple furniture he had hand crafted.

"That's about it," Zykov said, sitting down at the kitchen table. "Now it is time to talk. Sit down."

Kanygin pulled out a pouch of tobacco and rolled a cigarette in the palm of his hand.

Zykov drummed his fingers on the table. "Your name is Jan Osiecki, correct?"

"Yes."

"What kind of name is Osiecki? Polish?"

"Yes."

"That way of thinking is over," he said, his hand slamming the table. "No one is Polish or Ukrainian anymore. You should change the spelling of your last name to Russian."

Janek nodded, his lips dry. He tried to swallow but couldn't.

Zykov locked his hands behind his head and leaned back. "For now, your health is good, but things could change. Everything would be so much easier for you and your family if you signed over your land."

"And your health would remain good," added Kanygin, the cigarette dangling from his lip.

"You could keep your house and your orchard," Zykov said. "Just sign over your fields. You wouldn't have to worry about quotas anymore. You and your wife could work on the collective and your daughter, too, when she gets older."

He pulled out a paper from his pocket and slid it toward Janek. "All you have to do is sign here and all your troubles will be over."

"I cannot read."

"I've just told you what it says."

"I need to think it over."

"Maybe you need to think because you are a kulak."

A cold chill passed through Janek. "Kulak? What do you mean?" he gasped. Kanygin's heavy-lidden eyes seem to bore into him. "I'm not wealthy. I'm not. You've seen what I have, barely five acres of grain, a horse, and a cow."

"You have enough," Zykov said, leaning back and picking his teeth with a shard of wood.

They didn't believe him. But they had to. His life depended upon it.

"I don't hire anyone to do the work for me." Janek held out his calloused hands. "It's with these two hands I work the land."

"We are getting rid of useless people and replacing them with loyal Soviets, like Comrade Kanygin, here." Zykov went on, speaking quickly, forcefully, his eyes piercing Janek's. "Sign over your land, or you are also useless."

Kanygin took a drag on the butt of his cigarette then, stubbing his cigarette out on the table, said, "This is your last chance. Sign over your land."

"No, please," Janek said, getting up and backing away.

Kanygin pinned Janek's arms behind his back. Together both men dragged him to the doorway. Janek writhed and twisted, trying to get away. Zykov slammed him against the wall. Kanygin shoved Janek's fingers into the door jamb. Excruciating pain ripped across Janek's hand as Zykov pressed his weight against the door. Janek snapped his head back and let out a scream.

"Release," Zykov said, opening the door.

Janek yanked his mangled fingers out. Pain throbbed throughout his body as he cradled his hand against his chest.

"Ready to sign?" Zykov asked.

Janek shook his head. Once more he felt his fingers being forced into the door jamb. "No more, please," he gasped, before the pain once more descended on him.

Zykov eased off the door. Janek slumped to the floor. Through the haze of searing pain, he felt himself being pulled to his feet.

"Now we work on his other hand," Zykov said.

"I'll sign," Janek said, breathing heavily.

Zykov handed him the paper.

Janek took the pencil he offered and made an "X."

Zykov put the folded paper in his pocket. "We were careful not to destroy your hand. I'll give you two weeks to heal then report to the collective for work."

— ✻ —

Janek had his hand in a basin of cool water when Helena walked in.

"Janek!" she cried, rushing over. "What did they do to you?" She stared at his swollen purple fingers.

Stroking her cheek with his good hand, he said. "Don't cry. At least we are not registered as kulaks. We still have our house, our garden, and orchard."

12
VERONIKA

July 1930

Veronika felt chilled after paddling in the river, so she stretched out on the sand beside Kazia to warm up. As the mid-morning sun beat down on her, she saw a white stork glide downward, its black-tipped wings outstretched. She watched it land with barely a ripple at the water's edge.

"Look, Kazia, a stork. Tata says they bring good fortune if they nest by your home."

"Maybe the stork will make a nest here," Kazia said, her eyes bright, "and we get so much good fortune our parents quit the collective."

Veronika giggled. "I don't know if we could get that much luck. I just wish things could be the same as they used to be. Some days I hardly see Tata."

"Same as my Tata. All he does is sleep when he gets home."

Veronika closed her eyes against the bright sun. She felt hungry and thought of cherries. Yesterday they had picked the odd ripe cherry here and there in her parents' orchard, as well as all the ripe ones at Kazia's.

"Kazia, let's go to Babcia's orchard and steal her cherries."

Kazia's eyes flew open. "We'd get in trouble."

"Only if we get caught."

Kazia looked uncertain.

"Come on, Kazia. It'll be fun." Veronika pulled her dress on over her wet body, then tugged Kazia's arm. "Up you get."

"I'm scared," Kazia said, as she got to her feet.

"No one will be around. Everyone's at work on the collective."

"Babcia will be home," Kazia said. "And Aunt Agnes, too."

"Aunt Agnes hardly ever goes outside, and we'll just make sure Babcia is in the house."

Reluctantly, Kazia followed her. Creeping around to the back of Babcia's duplex, they walked as silently as they could through the brush, to the edge of her yard. As Veronica peered around a bush, she froze in fright. Babcia was on her porch, napping, not more than twenty feet away.

Kazia, in her nervousness, smothered a laugh with her hand, making an explosive snorting sound. Shocked, Veronika elbowed her. They looked at Babcia. She hadn't moved.

"Let's go," Veronika whispered.

They made a dash across her yard, hearts beating wildly, and into the cool depths of her orchard. Veronika's pleasure in the theft was infectious as they sat in a tree, dresses hitched up to their thighs, giggling and spitting pits at each other.

"I want to do some more," Kazia said, emboldened by her own success.

"You do?"

Grinning, Kazia nodded.

"Well, let's go pull out her onions, then."

Kazia gasped.

"She's sleeping. She'll never know."

Kazia shook her head, but Veronika could see that all Kazia needed was a little more coaxing.

"Come on, please, please, please? I'll let you play with my doll."

"All right," Kazia said.

They climbed down the tree and crept to the front of the house to check on Babcia. She was still sleeping.

"Let's go," Veronika whispered. Into the garden they scampered, up and down the onion rows, pulling up the odd onion here and there and flinging it into the air. Back into the brush they ran, hands over their mouths to muffle their laughter and snorts. They rested until their hearts calmed down and they could breathe normally again.

"Want to go again?" asked Veronika.

Kazia nodded. "Let's pull up her radishes this time."

They pulled as many as they dared, then headed back to the river through the brush, feet crashing, arms getting scratched in their panic to get as far away from their crime as possible. They collapsed on the sandy bank, panting and grinning.

"That was so much fun," gasped Kazia. "I wish I could see Babcia's face when she sees all those onions and radishes lying around."

"Yes," Veronika said. "I hope she gets upset."

> *Threatened by violence and afraid of hunger, hundreds of thousands of peasants finally relinquished their land, animals, and machines to the collective farms ... The fruits of their labour no longer belonged to them; the grain they sowed and harvested was now requestioned by the authorities.*
>
> —Anne Applebaum, *Red Famine: Stalin's War on Ukraine*

13

JANEK

Sadness overwhelmed Janek as he hoed the endless rows in the collective's sugar beet field. Already the summer sun beat down on his shoulders, and it was only mid-morning. All around him, he could hear the steady thumping and scraping of hoes as they struck the soil, and the occasional harsh clang of metal on rock. He took off his cap, pulled out a large grimy handkerchief that he had stuffed into his back pocket, and wiped the sweat from his face and neck.

He glanced up at the sky as a white stork silently winged its way overhead, long bony legs trailing behind its billowy, flapping wings. They were supposed to bring luck and harmony. *Harmony.* The word brought bitterness to his throat.

His thoughts went to Veronika. She had been asleep when he had left at first light for the collective. On a hot morning like today, she would be at the river, swimming with Kazia. Helena had the day off from the collective and would be working in their garden.

He glanced over at Vladzio and Feliks as their hoes slashed in steady tandem into the rich black soil. With a start he realized that he could be accused of slacking. He looked to see if anyone had noticed. As far as his eye could see, all were bent over their rows, slashing, slashing, hoes clicking and thumping. Once again, he bent over his row, as Zykov's latest tirade rattled around in his head.

"Those who shirk their duties on the collective are parasites. They are trying to make the plan fail. It is your duty to report them."

In only a few months, almost everyone he knew had given up their land and joined the collective. After the harvest was in, workers would get a share of it, according to the number of days each person worked.

Janek glanced at his fingers wrapped around the hoe, still bruised and mangled. Yet when the call went out for workers, he made sure to show up and work as hard as anyone else. It wasn't safe to stand out. Janek's thoughts went back to Alyona Pawlowska, how she had stood out at the meeting and admitted to selling grain on the open market. A couple of days later, shock workers paid her a visit, took her cow, and said she still had to provide milk for the collective. And to think that Feliks had been about to stand and complain as well. Would have been him, as well as Alyona, being ground into the dirt.

As the light faded from the sky, they were allowed to put their hoes in the tool shed and walk home. Standing at the water pump in his yard, Janek washed his hands and face in the cool water. It felt so good that he stuck his head under the pump and let the water stream through his hair. Squeezing the water out with his hands, he stood up. Helena stood in the doorway, watching him, towel in hand.

"They finally let you come home?" she asked.

He nodded, took the towel, and ran it across his face and hair.

"I have soup ready for you."

"Veronika?" he asked as he sat down.

"Asleep already. So much fresh air and playing with Kazia made her tired. All day she was at the river."

Janek smiled.

"I'm sorry I don't have more ready for your supper," Helena said, as she set a bowl of soup in front of him. "Mother just left. She seems to think Veronika and Kazia pulled up some of her radishes and onions."

Janek snorted. "Did she ever think it could be a dog?"

"That's what I told her."

"Soup's good. Thank you," Janek said, taking a spoonful of her borscht.

Helena reached out and put her hands on top of his. "I had a dream about you last night. All day it bothered me, because things like this are happening all the time now."

"Hmm?" he said. Helena was always having her dreams and telling him about them.

"I had a dream that they sent you away, and I was crying and running after you."

"You know my way is to cooperate. They have no reason to deport me."

"They don't need a reason to deport you! You know that. If you get word that they are going to deport you, I want you to promise me something."

Janek looked at her face; it was troubled but determined. Likely she had planned this conversation all day.

She continued. "I want you to go away from here. Find a job in the city or maybe in the mines. Other men do it."

"I'm not doing that."

Helena picked up his empty soup bowl and carried it over to the wash bucket. Janek went outside to sit on the front bench and be by himself. He knew she was probably crying. He fought the urge to go back in and hold her tight, to stroke her hair and say everything would be all right. He was just too tired and too sad to help her.

He looked up at the stars and took in a deep breath of the balmy summer night air. She was right, the Soviets didn't need a reason to deport him. All the time, men and women guilty of nothing were being deported, trainloads of them, from all over. Why? Maybe it was true, the rumours he was hearing, that Stalin needed labourers to develop Siberia, slave labourers to build railroads, work in the mines and forests. If that was the case, then even being compliant would not save him. Nothing would.

When he came back into the house, Helena was already in bed. He crawled in beside her and pulled her close. She put her head on his chest as he stroked her hair. He could tell that she had indeed been crying.

> Backed by soldiers and the secret police, these party functionaries (shock workers) simply ordered that grain be seized. Anyone who protested was declared a kulak ... and were exiled to Siberia and other remote parts of the Soviet Union. Others were imprisoned or killed or fled to cities to hide. The actions of the twenty-five-thousanders (shock workers) accounted for the removal of approximately one million men, women and children from the rural areas in 1931 and 1932.
>
> —Paul Magocsi, *A History of Ukraine*

14
JANEK

August 1930

Shock workers. The words made Janek's stomach churn. Everyone had been ordered to meet in the village square to welcome their arrival to Kuzmin.

"I'm not going," Helena said, her eyes troubled.

"You must," Janek said, rubbing his forehead. "We all must. How would it look if we didn't go?"

"What about Veronika?"

"We leave her with your mother. At ninety-two, they won't expect her to go."

That afternoon, Janek and Helena stood shoulder to shoulder with hundreds of others, staring at the red banners that decorated the storefronts and the raised platform where Zykov and Kanygin sat. Foreign looking in their city clothes, they chatted to each other, like princes of the nobility. Members of the Village Council and the Union of Tradespeople sat alongside them, while a choir of schoolchildren blithely sang Revolutionary songs. In front of the platform, the Communist youth groups of Kuzmin stood in military-like formation, feet slightly apart, hands behind their backs. Closest to the platform stood the Little Octobrists, fresh-faced children of about Veronika's age. Behind them stood the slightly older children, the Young Pioneers, and behind them stood the ones Janek feared—the fourteen to mid-twenties group called the *Komsomol*. Janek had seen some of them walking around in Kuzmin, almost with a swagger, like they owned the place. Janek glanced at his solemn, grim-faced neighbours who stood, like he did, waiting. He closed his eyes to try and calm his breathing.

Jezuz help me for what is to come.

Opening his eyes, he noticed a chestnut tree in bloom. How he loved chestnut trees. As a boy, he would gather whole piles of the shiny nuts, thinking them treasure. What a carefree time that was, the kind of childhood he wished for his little girl.

Janek's attention went to Zykov, who stood holding up his hand. "I have good news.

Twenty-five thousand shock workers have been sent into Ukraine by our Great Leader, Stalin himself. They will divide up in brigades and spread out into every village. Their mission will be to increase policing in the countryside. Their goals are to see that all fields are signed over to the collective, to find hidden grain caches, and to arrest kulaks."

Janek stomach tightened. *Who would they call kulaks?*

Helena gripped his hand. "*O mój Boże*, oh my God."

Smiling, Zykov continued, "Let us welcome these young shock workers, along with their leader, Comrade Kanygin."

Like everyone else, Janek waved his arms and cheered, while children in the Young Pioneers and the Komsomol youth marched across the square shouting slogans. Behind them came what he assumed must be the shock workers, a group of one hundred or so fresh-faced, flag-waving young men and women. Walking onto the platform, they stood behind the village council members.

All attention focused on Comrade Kanygin when he stepped forward. "As leader of the shock brigades, I will see that every field is signed over to the collectives. I will find and expose every grain-hoarding farmer for what he is, a blood-sucking speculator, waiting for higher grain prices. And when this happens, it will be the end of exploitation, the end of capitalism, and the end of food shortages. Are you for us or against us?"

Numb with despair, Janek stared at the chestnut tree as the crowd shouted, "For you!"

"Those who stand in our way shall be destroyed. What shall they be?" he asked.

"Destroyed!" erupted a chorus of voices.

From a building across the square, a stable door opened. A wagon came out, driven by soldiers. In the back, huddled together, was a group of men, women, and children. A gasp went through the crowd as leading families of the community were recognized. When one of them, a man, turned his blackened and swollen face toward him, Janek saw that it was Yuri. Beside Yuri sat his older daughter, Alyona, her face pressed into his side. Kateryna held their toddler, Yulia, in her arms.

"Matko Boska, Mother of God," moaned Helena.

Janek felt his chest constrict. Dizziness overcame him as the soldiers came closer, and he could see from the colour of their caps that they weren't regular army soldiers but soldiers of the Soviet secret police.

Zykov yelled into the assembled crowd. "These people tried to make the Revolution fail and cannot be allowed to live among us. They shall go live in Siberia."

Some in the crowd cheered. Many others, like Janek, did not.

Zykov pointed to Yuri. "This man had no stomach for tough measures and failed to report kulaks. He and his family must go."

Pointing to a teacher, he said, "This one dared to celebrate a religious holiday with students."

"These others," he said, pointing to Kuzmin's most prosperous farming families, "are an evil corruption among us! Greedy, grain-hoarding kulaks."

The crowd cheered again until Zykov held up his hand for silence.

"Those cattle cars are not heated. No water, no food. Many children don't survive the trip. The train stops on a bridge, and they throw their little bodies over. Let this be a lesson to you. Either sign over your land and give up your hidden grain, or you and your family will be deported."

Kateryna stood up. Wild-eyed, holding her toddler out to the crowd, she yelled, "Please, someone! Anyone! Take my baby."

Janek felt Helena clutch his arm.

"I'm going to take the children," she whispered.

"Helena, no," he said, holding her close. "You must remain still."

"How can I? This is murder."

Janek put his face close to hers. "You go up there, and you will mark yourself as a kulak sympathizer. Veronika, too."

He saw her eyes flicker then look away. Tears running down her face, she nodded.

Janek held Helena close to him, his heart aching as the wagon pulled away and Kateryna's shrieks faded.

Accused of collaborating with that secret organization, the church leadership was forced to call a sobar (church council) in January 1930 and to dissolve itself. Soon afterward ... dozens of bishops, and hundreds of priests were sent to labor camps.

—Orest Subtelny: Ukraine: A History

15
JANEK

Janek had just started a fire in the woodstove when there was a knock at the door. It was the priest, arriving unannounced. This alone frightened Janek. He never arrived unannounced. To them, he was their king. They took turns with other church members inviting him for dinner. Helena spent days cleaning, sweeping, and fretting over whether to fry or bake the fish. And always her china teacups came out and were placed beside her special coal-burning samovar. Now he sat in their living room, telling them that he was leaving, not just for a little while, but forever.

"I'm going into hiding. Already priests and bishops are being arrested."

"Where will you go?"

"It's best not to say."

"Who will give the Mass?"

"No one. All the churches are to be closed. Stalin has ordered it."

Helena stood up, hand over her heart. "I will bring you something to eat."

"No, I can't stay. I'm trying to say goodbye to as many as I can."

With tears streaming down his cheeks, Janek said, "Please, we have a few kopeks saved. Let us give them to you, for your journey."

Helena took her needle box from its hiding place behind her samovar and opened it. She dumped its contents on the table and swept most of the coins into her hand. She held them out to the priest.

He shook his head, no.

Janek took the coins and pressed them into the priest's palm. The priest looked down, blinking. Slipping the coins into his pocket, he said in a voice husky with emotion, "Thank you, my children. Please kneel and I will bless you."

They knelt down. He blessed them and was gone.

— ✳ —

When it was dinnertime, Helena told Veronika, "Let's have a quiet dinner. I don't think Tata wants to talk very much."

"Why? What is wrong with Tata?" Veronika asked.

"He's not feeling well."

After dinner, Helena put her arm around his shoulder and said, "You have to eat something, at least a little."

He took a long deep breath and looked at her.

"This world is not for me anymore," he said. "They take our land away, our freedom, and now they take away our church."

"Janek, they cannot stop us from praying."

He leaned into her and nodded.

16
VERONIKA

Veronika looked forward to spending the night at Aunt Agnes and Uncle Vladzio's home. She carried a cloth sack that contained her nightgown, hairbrush, and a picture she had drawn for them. As usual, she skirted around Babcia's side of the duplex to avoid being seen by her. Aunt Agnes beamed with delight when she saw her.

"Come in. Come in."

Veronika loved her uncle, but once he left for work and she had Aunt Agnes to herself, the real visit would begin. The moment the door closed on his back, Veronika asked, "Can I see your treasures?"

"All right," Aunt Agnes said with a half-smile. "We'll go see." She limped into her bedroom, pulled a varnished wooden box off her dresser, and carried it to her bed. Panting slightly, she set it down, then sat next to it. Veronika sat beside her.

A thrill of anticipation went through her as Aunt Agnes lifted off the lid and took out a small drawstring pouch. She pulled out the silver necklace with the red stones.

"They are garnets, real garnets. It was my mother's."

As always, she fastened the necklace around Veronika's neck.

Veronika lifted out the next treasure, German coins in a small coin purse made of a fine chain-link mesh. Next, she took out a tarnished locket that Aunt Agnes called a mourning locket, with a photograph of her mother on one side and her father on the other. At the bottom of the box, Veronika took out a comb, yellowed as an old dog's tooth.

"It's carved from an elephant's tusk," Aunt Agnes said.

"I know," Veronika said.

At the bottom of the box were her postcards from Germany. Veronika never grew tired of looking at them: a streetcar on a busy street, a castle on a hillside, and a picture of a hotel in Stuttgart where Aunt Agnes had worked as a maid.

"My next job was here in Kuzmin. It was your Tata who introduced me to Vladzio."

Veronika stared at the hotel, imagining herself in a building with hundreds of others.

"Tata told me that someday he's going to take me to Ternopil. It's a really big city."

"Ternopil? I've seen Ternopil. It's nothing. German cities are much better."

"Are you ever going to move back to Germany?"

"Me? Oh, no. I don't have family there anymore. They're all gone."

Veronika looked down.

"Oh, no, no, little one," she said, lifting Veronika's chin. "Don't feel sad for me. I have a new family now, lots of family. I have you and your parents. And I have Paulina and Feliks and their children. So much family," she said, laughing.

"When I grow up, I'm going to Germany to see churches like castles and ride in a streetcar."

"That's good! You'll like Germany."

After a cozy night all wrapped up in layers of quilts and sleeping on a straw mattress beside the earthen oven, Veronika ate breakfast with Aunt Agnes and Uncle Vladzio. Her egg was cooked just the way she liked it, so that it wasn't runny, and she was allowed to put as much jam on her bread as she wanted.

The only thing Veronika didn't like was watching Uncle Vladzio eat his eggs. His were all runny and slimy and he slurped them off his fork. She tried not to look. She got a little bit of a scare when he noticed that she had finished her egg and tried to give her some of his.

"Oh, no, thank you. I'm full."

"Are you sure? Because I could give you some. Here." He scooped up a slimy spoonful.

"No, no thank you, Uncle. I'm so full."

"All right, if you're sure."

"I'm very sure."

Before going to the collective, Uncle Vladzio ruffled the top of her neatly brushed head and pinched her cheeks. She tried to like it.

Aunt Agnes and Veronika had just started to clear the dishes when Aunt Paulina knocked on the door then burst in, her eyes flashing with anger.

"What is it, Paulina?"

"I try and try, Agnes. I really do. But I just can't take her anymore."

"Sit down. I'll make you a cup of tea and you can tell me what happened while I do up the dishes."

Veronika sat and stared at Aunt Paulina as she spoke. "I made a nice soup for supper, just how Feliks likes it, with soaked beans and salt pork, and as soon as Antosia sees it, she takes it off the stove and puts it aside."

Aunt Agnes turned and let out an angry breath.

"And do you know what Feliks did?"

When there was no answer, she continued. "He put the pot back on the stove and told his mother to leave it there. I'm proud that he stood up to her, but now she won't talk to either one of us."

She blew her nose and looked at Veronika as though she'd just noticed her. "I have interfered with your visit. I'm sorry. I know Agnes was looking forward to it."

"That's all right. Babcia makes my mama cry, too."

Aunt Agnes came over and sat down in her chair with a heavy sigh. She patted Aunt Paulina on the arm and said, "I don't know how you can live with that woman. It's bad enough for me with a wall separating us."

"I don't think Babcia likes me, either," added Veronika in a small voice.

Her aunts exchanged a quick glance.

"She likes you, Veronika," Aunt Paulina said. "It's just that she doesn't like children very much. They're all right when they're small, but once they grow up and get a mind of their own, she doesn't like them anymore."

Aunt Agnes pushed herself up. "Enough of this sad talk. Your mama will want you home. Go get your coat and mittens."

"Oh, someone's here," said Aunt Paulina. "Maybe it's your Tata to get you."

Veronika ran for the door and opened it. Her stomach contracted. "It's not Tata," she whispered. "It's … it's men." Veronika stood frozen as the men walked toward her. Pushing past Aunt Paulina, Veronika dove under the kitchen table for safety.

"Feliks and Vladzio are not home," Aunt Paulina said to the men, her voice unsteady.

"We are not here to see them. We've come for your horse. The collective has need of it," said a man wearing fancy shoes.

"Please, you can't do this to us," cried Aunt Paulina.

He slapped her. Aunt Paulina staggered, her head hitting the wall.

"You dare to tell me what I can and can't do?" Striding out of the house, he yelled, "Bring the horse around! Tie it to the wagon."

Veronika scrambled out from under the table into Aunt Agnes's waiting arms, nearly running into Babcia as she walked in.

"What are those men doing here?"

"They're here for our horse," Aunt Paulina said.

Babcia's face contorted in anger. She walked out of the house, shaking her fist. "You are not going to have our horse," she shrieked. "This land was my husband's. We will lose it if you take that horse."

Aunt Paulina gasped, her eyes large. "No, Antosia!" Aunt Paulina ran after her and struggled to hold her back.

"Let me go!" Babcia cried. "I'm getting our horse back."

Releasing her, Aunt Paulina ran to the wagon where the man sat, steely-eyed, holding the reins.

"Please, Comrade Zykov, she didn't mean anything," Aunt Paulina said, clinging to the side of his seat. "She's just an old woman."

"An old woman who talks like a kulak." He flicked the reins and pulled out of the yard.

— ✻ —

When Veronika got home, she burst into the kitchen and told Mama and Tata what had happened. Mama's face blanched.

Tata, his eyes serious, said, "Tell us again what happened, especially the part about being a kulak."

"I don't remember."

"It's very important. Think. Did he say they were kulaks or Babcia was a kulak?"

"I can't remember. What does kulak mean?"

"A rich person who is against the collectives." He looked at Mama and said, "I hope to God the district authorities haven't registered them as kulaks for that."

For Stalin, the peasants were scum.
—Nikita Khrushchev, Stalin's successor

17
JANEK

It seemed as if time were standing still as Janek waited, frightened that the secret police would arrest all who lived in Antosia's duplex. Janek had seen that happen. Except for the elderly and infirm, entire households were taken. Images of Feliks, Paulina, their children, and Vladzio being loaded into the back of a wagon kept running through his mind.

Walking home from the collective, hot, dusty, and tired, a peaceful scene greeted his eyes when he opened the gate to his yard. Helena and Veronika sat in the shade of the tree, shucking peas.

"Tata," Veronika said, getting up and throwing her arms around him. "I missed you."

"Don't hug so hard, you'll squish all the guts out of me," he said, tousling the top of her head.

"Tata!" she said with a giggle.

"Veronika, go get Tata a cup of water," Helena commanded. "Sit down, Janek. I have something to tell you."

"Oh? What?"

"Paulina came over today. Told me that Feliks had it out with mother."

"About her spouting off to Zykov?"

Helena nodded. "Seems he grabbed her by the shoulders and told her it was all her fault the family was in danger."

"What did she do? Go in her room and pout?"

"No, not at all," Helena said, her eyes round. "She started to cry and said she was sorry. I think she realizes what she has done."

"Why did Babcia cry, Tata? Veronika asked, coming back with his water.

"It wasn't a good thing to try and keep her horse. Those men are in charge of everything around here."

"Are soldiers going to take Babcia away?"

Janek paused and looked into Veronika's earnest face. Why did he have to talk to a child about such things? He glanced up at Helena. She lowered her head then gave a slight nod.

"No, they likely won't take her."

"It's been three days now," Helena said. "Maybe they won't take anyone."

"Anyhow," Janek said, "your Babcia is an old woman. Wouldn't look good for them to arrest her, and you could be sure she wouldn't go quietly."

Helena glared at him, fire in her eyes. "This is not the time to joke. She may be cranky and miserable, but she is still my mother."

As the days went by and there were no further visits by the shock workers or Zykov, Janek felt a sense of calm come over him. Likely the worst had passed.

— ✶ —

Janek glanced out the window. His heart sank. "Helena, Osip is coming to the door."

Helena clucked her tongue. "Maybe he won't stay long."

Veronika's eyes grew big. "I don't like him, Tata. He hurts Sofiya."

Osip was one neighbour Janek didn't like, either. A big man, he was often drunk and beat his wife. All the same, better to keep on his good side.

"Come in," Janek said, opening the door. "Join us for breakfast. We are just about to eat."

"Thanks, but no time. I'm on my way to the Pawlowski's. I heard that the shock workers and some of the Komsomol are at their place. The family is being thrown out."

Komsomol. The word struck fear in Janek's gut. Made up of local youth and young adults, they had turned against their own to become the right arm of the shock workers. Not wanting to expose his anti-communist feelings, Janek took a moment to clear his throat and spit outside the door. "Is it Alyona Pawlowska's home they're at? The woman who complained at the meeting?"

"That's the one," Osip said with a smile. "When the collective took her cow, they couldn't make their milk quota, so the collective is seizing their home. After the collective takes what they want, the rest will be left for whoever gets there first. Want to come with me?" he asked, his face eager.

Janek felt sickened. "Are they being deported?"

"Not deported. Moved into an empty shack at the north end of the village. The land is rocky and the soil dry."

"How will they survive?" Helena asked, her face rigid.

Osip shrugged. "To me, it serves them right. You have to work with these people, or at least appear to. Any fool knows that."

"I will come with you," Janek said.

"You are going to take from them?" Helena asked, her voice raised in disapproval.

Janek shot her a warning glance to say no more.

Osip put his arm around Janek's shoulder. "Don't worry about him, Helena. The secret police aren't there, and I'm on good terms with the shock workers. They won't bother us."

— ✻ —

When they got to the Pawlowski's, a crowd had already gathered. Alyona and her husband and children sat on a wagon in their undergarments. Alyona and the younger children huddled together on the bench. The two oldest sat stoically with their father, their faces drawn and pale.

Janek watched young Komsomol men, barely old enough to shave, load a second wagon with farm tools and a third wagon with furniture and barrels from their cold cellar.

Janek stared at a young man in a Komsomol uniform who was carrying a grain flail out of the barn. His face seemed familiar. With a jolt of disbelief, Janek recognized him as Helena's cousin's son, Aleksey. Anger burned deep within Janek. Aleksey had good parents. Why would he be here, a part of this abomination?

"I see someone I know," Janek said to Osip. "I'll go say hello."

Osip shrugged indifferently.

Aleksey's expression dulled when he saw Janek approach.

"How can you shame our family like this, and help these agents of Satan?" Janek hissed.

Aleksey's eyes welled up. "You think I want to do this?" he asked, throwing the flail into the wagon. "I had no choice. Stalin ordered that all Komsomol must participate."

"You could have refused."

"Refuse? I saw someone that refused."

Janek put his hand on Aleksey's shoulder. "I'm sorry, son. I didn't know."

Aleksey inclined his head toward the other Komsomol. "I need to get back to work."

— ✻ —

A few minutes later, Janek listened, cap in hand, with others in the crowd as a pimply-faced shock worker stood before the family and read the charges against them.

"Comrade Pawlowski and his wife, Alyona Pawlowska, will not be persuaded to try communism. Their taxes were tripled in an effort to get them to join us. Still, that did not persuade them. They are traitors to our cause, no longer fit to live among us. Even if they wanted to, they are no longer permitted to join the collective. Comrade Pawlowski must remain an independent farmer, as was his wish. They will have free land and a shack to live in."

As soon as the wagons pulled out, Janek and the rest of the people rushed to go inside the home. He went into the bedroom where it was less crowded and grabbed work pants, an armload of shirts, and a pair of boots before the room became too crowded to move. Squeezing his way out the door, he waited for Osip.

"Nice pair of boots you grabbed," Osip said, admiring Janek's load.

"Looks like you got quite a few things, too. I'll go home now, and Helena can wash them up."

Later that day, Janek went out to his barn and picked up a broken hoe he had put off mending. Veronika followed him around the barn as he searched for a new handle that he knew he had somewhere.

After the interest in the Pawlowski's had waned, he would find out where they lived and deliver the clothes, shoes, and hoe.

"Tata, what can I give?"

Janek smiled. "Do you have any socks you've outgrown, or dresses?"

"Would they like that?"

"I'm sure they would. I think a lot of other people are going to help them, too. But remember, you can't talk about this to your friends, or it could get us in trouble."

"I won't say anything, not even to Kazia. I just want to help."

"I know you do, my little Noosha. I know."

— ✱ —

The heat of late August was upon them. Janek stood with Helena admiring the collective's grain fields that promised abundance with July's lush green fields having turned golden brown.

"Look at those fields, Helena. Our share will be more than enough for our daily needs as well as to save for the future.

"Enough for bread every day?"

"Certainly, enough for that. It's been years since the growing conditions have been this good."

"That's good," Helena said. "Veronika needs a satchel for when she starts school next month. Maybe the store will sell us one in trade for grain."

"Perhaps at the meeting tomorrow, Zykov will give us a better breakdown of how the profits will be shared. Besides grain, there might even be some money shared out for us to buy a satchel."

— ❋ —

The collective hall was stifling when Janek and Helena settled onto the bench alongside other members of the community. For the first time the mood seemed light as those around them chatted about the good weather and crops.

As soon as Zykov, Kanygin, and members of the village council walked in, the hall became quiet and all attention focused on them.

Zykov strode forward. "This harvest promises to be the best one ever. In November, after all the collective's obligations have been met, all who have laboured will have a share of the harvest, depending on the number of days worked.

"As our leaders have said, holding all fields in common is the way of the future. Our forward-thinking leaders have now issued a new directive for the good of the community. Livestock will no longer be privately owned. All cows, horses, and pigs must be turned over to the collective to be held in common. Chickens may remain on individual farms, provided they can supply the collective with a weekly egg quota."

Murmurs of dismay spread through the room. Some began to shout, fists clenched in the air. Janek stared at Zykov in shock as Helena squeezed his hand. How could he bear to lose Dobroc? Their sow and piglets?

Zykov took a step forward, his eyes menacing. "You ignorant, backward people. Still, you question communism? Even after you see what working together has produced in our fields? Let me warn you, those who refuse to turn over their animals will be deported as kulaks, and traitors to the cause."

While those around him moaned and sobbed and some continued to shout in anger, Janek ran his fingers through his hair, and looked upward, tears welling in his eyes, *Jezuz, help me. What am I to do?*

"What shall we eat? Only bread and vegetables?" Helena asked, her voice trembling.

Janek looked at her, helpless, not knowing what to say.

For the last time, Janek hitched Dobroc to his wagon, already loaded with his sow and piglets. Anger and pain seethed within him as he brought his cow out of the barn and tied her up to the wagon. What right did the Soviets have to take everything that was his?

In the night, many of his neighbours killed their livestock rather than let the collective have it. They salted meat in barrels and hid it away. Janek couldn't do that to Dobroc.

Janek climbed into the wagon seat and snapped the reins. Helena waved goodbye from the entrance of the house. Veronika, too. Both were crying.

Driving Dobroc down the road to the collective, Janek let him take his time. No need to rush their final journey together. He wouldn't have much of a chance on the collective. No one took responsibility or cared for the horses they already had. Often, they were overworked and left without feed or water. It was the same with everything. Why take care of something that wasn't yours?

Nor did peasants give up their land without a fight. Their protests took different forms: the slaughter of livestock, the burning of fields, the driving out of the new collective farm officials (acts often led by women-the so-called babś ki bunty 'women's revolts'), and, finally, armed insurrection.

—Paul Magocsi, *A History of Ukraine*

18

VERONIKA

After a morning of playing with Kazia, Veronika walked home for lunch. When her house came into view, Veronika felt a deep happiness as she walked up its stone pathway. So strong and beautiful her home was. In all the world, this is where she belonged.

Walking by the barn, Veronika remembered what Tata had said about Kotka. *Any day now, she'll be having her kittens.*

With hope and excitement, Veronika opened the barn door to check. She found Kotka curled up on a pile of hay. The cat stretched her back and unrolled her tongue in a great big yawn, before lying on her side, a contented look on her face. Veronika stroked Kotka's swollen belly as she purred and bunted her head against Veronika's hand. The cat's belly was so taut and swollen that Veronika could see Kotka's pink skin and nipples through her fur.

Veronika loved sitting in the shade of the barn on warm summer days. She put her face down to Kotka's and they stared at each other, eye to eye.

A rustling in the loft above Veronika made her look up. The witch, Baba Yaga, looked down at her. Veronika ran screaming from the barn.

"Mama! Tata!" she cried, bursting into the house and running into Tata's arms.

"What's wrong?" he asked.

"Baba Yaga is in the barn! I saw her."

Tata grabbed a stick and went out. In a few moments he came back.

"It's not Baba Yaga. Her name is Anastasia, and she's just an old woman. She slept in our barn last night. I've invited her to come in and have something to eat. Is that all right, Helena?"

"Yes, of course it is. Where is she from?"

"I don't know, just that she's been walking for weeks. She was part of a rebellion of women trying to get their livestock back from the collective."

"Tell her to come right in. She's welcome to whatever we have."

"She's embarrassed about the way she looks. She wants to get washed up first. Could you pass me a bucket of warm water and some soap?"

When the door opened a few minutes later, Veronika saw a bent old woman in a headscarf. Not Baba Yaga after all. She wore a tattered man's coat and a dirty skirt.

Hands together, the old woman bowed to Tata and Mama again and again. "Please, some bread?" she asked in a gravelly voice. She cocked her head to one side in the watchful way of a stray dog.

"I have no bread, not even for ourselves," Mama said, "but I have potatoes."

The old woman gave a slight smile and shuffled in.

How could Mama let such a smelly beggar woman come into the house? She always fed them outside.

"Sit down," Tata said, pulling out a chair at the table for her.

Veronika stood at the far end of the room until her father motioned that she should sit at the table, too.

"Your daughter is so pretty," the old woman said as Mama set a cup of tea beside her. "I have a granddaughter about her age."

"Where is she?" asked Mama, resting her hand on the woman's shoulder.

"The secret police took her. Her mother, too," she said, her eyes filling with tears. "I got away."

"Rest, drink your tea," Tata said. "I'm going out to do my chores."

"Breakfast will be ready when you come back," Mama said, going to the counter and pulling out the potato bucket.

Alone with the woman, Veronika met her gaze briefly then looked away.

"Come here," she croaked. "You sit so far away."

Veronika stayed where she was.

"My granddaughter was very sweet, just like you."

"I think Tata needs me now," Veronika said.

The woman looked like she could see right through the lie.

Veronika got up and left. Standing beside Tata while he milked the cow, she asked, "Does she have to be inside our house?"

"Why do you ask?"

"She's a beggar."

Tata turned and looked her in the eye. "She's not a beggar. She had a home and a family just like you. She smells because she has nowhere to take a bath."

"But can't she eat outside?"

"Anastasia is someone's mother. What if Mama needed help and they made her eat outside?"

When Veronika came into the house with Tata, Mama said, "Wash up, then come eat." Boiled potatoes and fried onions were already on the table.

After the prayer, Veronika watched Anastasia pick up her fork and shovel food into her mouth. Long before anyone else finished, she had scraped up the last bit from her plate. When had she last eaten a real meal?

Tata poured her another cup of tea and passed the sugar jar.

She pulled out a large chunk of sugar. Veronika expected her to break it in half, like they did when getting too large a piece. Instead, she dropped it in her tea and reached for another piece. Veronika expected Tata to stop her.

"Take as much as you like," Tata said. "This area grows sugar beets, so of sugar we have lots. It's grain we don't have."

"You both are very good to me."

"Would you like to stay a day with us? Rest, maybe take a bath?"

Anastasia's eyes filled with tears.

"What is it?" Tata asked.

Her voice breaking, she said, "You treat me like family."

That afternoon, Tata set the washtub down in the middle of the kitchen floor and Mama filled it with hot water from the woodstove. After Tata went out to the barn, Anastasia stripped off her grimy clothing and stood naked.

Veronika gasped. She could see every rib; her arms and legs hung like sticks. She glanced over at Mama, gauging her reaction. Her lips were pressed together like when she was angry.

"Are you angry, Mama?"

"No, just sad and upset that this could happen to another human being."

Anastasia eased herself down into the hot water. "Oh, my, this feels good." She groaned with pleasure.

After her bath, she came out dressed in Mama's clothes. "Thank you, Helena," she said, touching Mama on her arm. "You don't know how wonderful it feels to be clean. It's like I'm whole again."

She spent the rest of the day washing her own clothes and helping them with their chores.

"Are you going to spend the night here?" Veronika asked her.

"Would it be all right with you if I did?"

Veronika nodded.

— ✳ —

The following morning, Tata came in from his chores with a smile on his face. "You better go out to the barn and see your cat."

Veronika found her curled up in some hay. "Kotka, you had your kittens."

"May I come see, too?" asked Anastasia, entering the barn.

"Yes, come see."

"Oh, look at them," Anastasia said. She picked one up and held it against her cheek. "Seeing these kittens reminds me of my granddaughter."

"Why?"

"She loved kittens, too. I miss her so very much."

"You will see her again, won't you?"

"I can only hope."

Veronika put her arms around Anastasia and hugged her.

The old woman spent another night. In the morning, Mama gave her one of her shawls, a few hardboiled eggs, and some dried fruit.

Veronika and her mother stood at the gate and watched as the early morning fog rising from the river gradually erased the outline of Anastasia's lonely figure walking down the road. She didn't look like a Baba Yaga anymore.

19

VERONIKA

"I can't go to school, Tata! Not without Kazia!

"You'll make new friends," Tata said. "I don't know what's wrong with you. Such a fuss."

"I thought Kazia would be going with me."

Mama put down her mending. "You are seven. Kazia is not. If she had been born a few months earlier, then she would be going with you. At least Alina starts with you."

Veronika paused and thought about that. Alina and Kazia were cousins and lived beside each other in a triplex. When Veronika went to play with Kazia, Alina often joined them.

"But she's not Kazia. Please let me start school next year."

"You should be happy you're going to school," Tata said, raising his voice. "Do you know what I had to do when I was nine years old? Quit school and get a job. For you, it will be different."

Gently, Tata pulled Veronika close and held her as she wept. "Veronika, Mama and I can't read or write. You will go to school and become a doctor. That is my dream for you."

Veronika sniffled. "Will Alina be able to sit with me?"

"I'll go to the teacher and make a special request for you. And I'll even go to Alina's house and see if she'll walk to school with you."

Veronika nodded. Tata gathered her deep against his chest and stroked her back while she adjusted to her fate.

— ✲ —

On the first day of school, Veronika knocked on Alina's door. Marek, her eight-year-old brother answered.

"Hi, Marek. Alina and I are walking to school together."

"I know. I'm supposed to watch out for the both of you."

Veronika felt a sense of relief. No one would dare pick on her or Alina with him there. He often got into scuffles and could hold his own.

"So, you have to listen to me and do what I tell you," he said in a firm voice.

"I'll listen," Alina said, coming out the door.

"Me, too," Veronika said.

As Marek and Alina got ready, Kazia came out from her section of the triplex and looked at them. It hurt Veronika to see the slump of Kazia's shoulders and the sadness on her face. Veronika ran over and hugged her.

"I want to come, too," she sobbed into Veronika's hair.

"I know," Veronika said, tears prickling her eyes.

"Veronika! Let's go," yelled Marek.

Veronika gave Kazia one last hug before she dashed off. "I'll see you later, all right?"

Kazia nodded and wiped away tears with the back of her hand.

Walking down the road, laughing and chatting with Alina and

Marek, Veronika turned every now and then to see if Kazia was still watching. She was.

Veronika enjoyed the walk, looking at the farmhouses that lined the road, the cats that ambled out, and watching Marek skip rocks into the slow-moving Smotrych River. Gradually, other Polish and Ukrainian children joined them along the rutted road.

"I wonder why there aren't any Jewish children living out here?" Veronika asked.

Alina shrugged. "The only Jews I've seen live in the village."

"Maybe because people don't like Jews."

"Tata says that's wrong," Veronika said. "He says there's good and bad in all people."

"Maybe," Marek said. "The man who runs the general store is good and he's Jewish."

"He always gives us a candy when Mama shops there," Alina said, smiling.

Arriving on the outskirts of the village, they came to the flour mill. Veronika lingered by the great wooden waterwheel as it turned and creaked, endlessly scooping up great mouthfuls of water on one side and spewing them out on the other.

"Veronika, you need to keep moving," scolded Marek. "You'll make us all late."

She resented his continuous urgings but said nothing. There was just so much to see, especially on the main street of the village—the bakery, the café, and the four Jewish-run stores, and the blacksmith shop built by her Uncle Feliks and Uncle Vladzio.

"Let's go in and see my uncles."

"No time, and anyhow, they're at the collective today," Marek said. "It's the start of the harvest."

— ✻ —

The first weeks of school terrified Veronika. Russian was the only language allowed, and she didn't know any Russian. Anyone who spoke Polish or Ukrainian, even on the playground, would be punished. In the classroom, she sat beside Alina in a double-seated wooden desk. They held hands and hoped the teacher wouldn't ask them anything.

At the break, Veronika played house with Alina under the trees, ever alert for Marek and his friends, who would try to swoop down and wreck what they had made. In the event of such an attack, Alina and Veronika had prepared long willowy sticks. With glee, they chased after the boys, whipping their sticks through the air, sending them fleeing. Alina and Veronika could hardly wait for their next attack, and the boys didn't disappoint them.

At first, Veronika thought of Marek as only a pest, as most boys were. Then one day, as they walked home, Marek offered to carry her books. For the first time, she noticed his blond hair and blue eyes.

During the next holiday from school, Veronika, Alina, and Kazia decided to play wedding by dressing-up in their parents' cast-off clothes.

"I'll pretend to marry Marek," Veronika announced.

Alina and Kazia giggled.

Veronika denied any deeper meaning to it, but she could tell Kazia and Alina knew.

Tata was wrong about new friends taking Kazia's place in Veronika's heart. No one ever could. But, after a few weeks, Veronika adjusted to playing with Kazia only on the weekends and bonded in friendship with Alina.

Although owned in theory by the peasants, the collective farms were obliged to deliver assigned amounts of produce to the state and were controlled by its officials. Only after a collective farm had fulfilled its obligations to the state were members allowed to divide what remained among themselves.
—Orest Subtelny, *Ukraine: A History*

20
JANEK

November 1930

Everyone in the community hall seemed happy, expectant. Janek moved closer to Helena and took her hand. Soon the meeting would start and they would know their payment for the year's labour. Janek smiled as Feliks and Paulina sat down beside them, and Vladzio squeezed his bulk onto the bench behind.

Helena leaned toward Paulina. "How about we get the women's sewing club started again?" she asked.

She nodded. "Maybe you start the round again?"

"What do you think, Janek?" Helena asked, nudging him.

He rolled his eyes.

"Look at you, acting like you mind," Helena said, giving him another poke in the ribs with her elbow. "As soon as the women leave, you should see him. He goes around and has another meal from all the cookies and cake they left behind."

Janek looked up when the hall grew silent. Zykov had entered, along with the Village Council and a dozen shock workers. The air in the hall seemed to close in around Janek's throat. He could barely swallow, his mouth was so dry.

Zykov approached the front of the platform and stood for a moment or two, surveying the hall. Everyone waited in expectant silence. Janek felt the hairs on the back of his neck rise. Three hundred days he had laboured in the heat and the cold, from early morning to sunset. Would these bastards keep their word and pay him?

Finally, Zykov broke the silence. "The harvest in this area has never been so good." He paused as clapping and cheers broke out through the room. He smiled indulgently.

"This is due to good management on the collective and everyone working together as one."

Feliks snorted, then leaned over to Janek and said, "It was due to exceptional weather, nothing that stupid ass did."

Zykov went on. "This year, we harvested several more tons of grain than last year."

Janek remained seated as thunderous cheers and thumping of feet broke out, reverberating within the wood of his bench.

"Now what everyone in this room wants to know is the payment for labour days. Likely you think the collective has many tons of grain to distribute. What you may not realize is the number of debts the collective must first pay off, to have made possible this bountiful harvest. Of course, you will get your due, but you must first understand the debts our collective has had to endure."

Janek felt a pit in his stomach. "What's he getting at?" he whispered to Feliks.

Feliks shook his head, his eyes fearful.

"Our primary debt, as you know, was to meet the grain quota set by the state. Next came paying the state for the use of their machinery, then the loan to purchase seed and, of course, the percentage of grain we are required to hold back for next year's seed. Just when we had all that accounted for, we were surprised last week with an announcement that each district would provide the state with a loan of money."

Murmurs of unrest rose from all parts of the room.

"What are you saying?" someone called out from the back of the room.

"Yeah, what's going on?" asked someone else.

Zykov held up his hands. "Silence. Listen to what I have to say. Again, due to our bountiful crop, I am pleased to announce that all debts to the state have been paid."

As if one, people rose to their feet in a volley of cheers. Janek felt himself able to breathe again.

"Before I discuss your labour-day payment, there is one more thing. A discrepancy has been discovered with our labour-day system. At first, it was thought that for each day worked, a person would receive one share of the harvest. Now it has been decided by our leaders in Moscow that management will receive three shares for each labour day worked, skilled workers, such as tractor operators will be paid two shares for each day worked, and unskilled field workers will be paid one-half share for each day worked."

Roars of outrage filled the room. Janek's breathing once again became constricted. He covered his face with his hands, not able to take in the immensity of half a year's work wiped out.

"Only half of what we should get?" Helena moaned. "Do they even care about us?"

"Quiet, and I'll announce the payment for a labour day."

The hall once again became quiet.

"It will be enough grain to make two loaves of bread."

The room erupted into chaos. Janek stared at Zykov in disbelief. That was only a fractional amount of what he expected. He worked one day for what? A loaf of bread? How could this be possible? It was lies. All lies.

When people began to storm the platform, Janek knew it was time to leave. "Come on, Helena. We can't be a part of this."

Together with Vladzio, Feliks, and Paulina, they pushed their way outside as shock workers formed a protective circle around Zykov and the council members and helped them exit by the back door.

Once outside, Feliks raised his fist to the fleeing collective members. "How could they cheat us like this? A loaf a day is about one hundred and fifty pounds. It should be eight hundred pounds, if not a thousand," he said, his face red, the vein on his neck bulging.

"That's because we're nothing to them," Paulina said, wiping away tears.

Janek took Helena's hand. "The secret police might be sent for. We need to get home."

"I was stupid to believe them," Helena said, her voice broken.

"Not just you, my sister, all of us were taken in," Vladzio said.

"With no grain to keep in reserve," Feliks said, "we will be living on the edge."

"We can't," Janek said. "Somehow, we must find a way to look after ourselves."

"Janek's right," Helena said. "If this is all they allot us in an exceptional harvest, what happens if the next harvest isn't as good? Will they give us nothing?"

"I can see it," Paulina said. "A famine is coming."

"Matko Boska! Not that," Helena cried.

"Stop it, you two. You're getting yourselves worked up," Feliks said. "We're a long way from a famine yet."

"Maybe expand our vegetable garden," Janek said. "Plant grain where it won't be so noticeable, thrash it in secret and bury it. That way we aren't completely reliant on those Soviet bastards."

"We should do that, too," Vladzio said to Feliks. "Maybe sell some of the grain on the black market for a Christmas goose."

— ❋ —

In the months ahead, an exodus of farmers headed for the Polish border or to the city to work in factories. Every time he or Helena went to work on the collective, there seemed to be another person or two missing.

As well as people leaving voluntarily, Janek saw the best and most skilled farmers in the region deported, their lands confiscated.

"It's good that they're gone," Zykov yelled. "We are better off without them."

Janek wasn't surprised that there was no women's sewing club that year or any Christmas to speak of. People were too depressed, with no Christmas Mass to go to, or roast goose for the meal.

"All the same, we should make something for Veronika," Helena said when they were talking about Christmas.

"I could bring in a tree."

"And Veronika and I can make pierniczki spice cookies and decorate the tree," Helena said.

"For this year, I guess it will have to do. Maybe next year life will be better."

21
VERONIKA

January 1931

Veronika walked on the snow-covered road with her mother, their boots making a crunching sound with each step they took. They were invited to Kazia's for lunch. After that, she and Kazia would go sledding while their mothers had a visit.

Veronika hoped Kazia's uncle, Doctor Janczewski, would be around. Everyone called him Doctor instead of his first name, Julian, out of respect.

Kazia's father, Alina and Marek's father, and the doctor were brothers; they lived beside one another in a triplex.

Veronika loved the doctor. It was like he was Veronika's uncle as well as Kazia's because he treated them the same, with lots of hugs and swings through the air by their arms until they were too dizzy to stand.

With the doctor's wife, Truda, it was different. Mama didn't like her. Kazia's mama didn't either. Veronika had heard about how the doctor would make house calls for free because he knew people didn't have money, then the next day, Truda would go around and collect.

— ⁂ —

Veronika sat with Kazia at the end of the kitchen table eating lunch, but she barely heard a word of her cousin's chatter. Instead, she eavesdropped on Mama's and Aunt Maria's conversation.

"She is a mean, kopek-clutching ... shrew," Aunt Maria said.

Veronika suppressed a snicker.

Mama picked up her spoon and dipped it into the steaming bowl of borscht in front of her. "I don't know how the doctor can take it."

"You should have heard the argument they had last night," Aunt Maria said, her face bright. "You can hear everything through these triplex walls. She said someone had to look out for their money, and then he yelled at her."

"She certainly does look out for money," Mama said. "I'll say that for her."

"But wait until you hear this. He went on to say their marriage was over and that he was going to paint a line down the middle of the floor. She has to stay on one side, and he stays on the other."

Veronika glanced at Kazia. She must have been listening, too, because she made big google-eyes at Veronika.

"It's terrible," continued Mama. "And such a good man he is. Any time of the day or night, you knock on his door and right away he comes."

"Mama, can I go see the line?" asked Veronika.

Her mother gasped. "No, you may not."

"Time for the both of you to go outside," Aunt Maria said. "Children do not listen to private conversations."

Veronika knew that when adults had that edge to their voice, it was best to agree. But how could she not listen when they were in the same room?

"All right," Veronika said, going with Kazia to get her coat and boots on.

Once outside, Veronika felt like a weight had been lifted off her. She had so many thoughts buzzing around her head that she could share with Kazia. "Are you happy that they aren't married anymore?"

Kazia hesitated. "Sort of. Everyone hates her."

"Do you talk to her?"

Kazia shook her head. "Not supposed to."

An idea for a game took shape in Veronika's mind. "Come on, Kazia. Follow me."

"Where to?"

"You'll see."

Veronika took Kazia's mittened hand and led her across the porch that ran the length of the triplex and down the two steps to the snow-covered path leading to the road. Pausing a few yards in front of the house, Veronika turned and surveyed its length. It was built like three identical white-washed cottages, with a continuous hump-backed sloping roof and multi-paned windows. Three doors were spaced equal distance apart. To the left and right of each door were white pillars, not thick enough to hide behind.

"What are we doing?" asked Kazia.

"Just looking."

"We can't let anyone see us."

Kazia raised her eyebrows.

"Good, no one's around. We can go back to the porch."

Veronika noticed a clump of dense bushes close to Aunt Truda's door. *Perfect.*

"Tip-toe," she whispered when they approached the door. She could feel her heart pounding.

Knock. Knock. Knock.

Kazia's eyes opened wide.

Veronika grabbed Kazia's hand and pulled her down the steps and into the bushes. "Down. Quiet."

Kazia's Aunt Truda opened her door. She was a tiny woman with thin lips and faded brown hair. Her eyes reminded Veronika of a bird's, sharp and always darting.

After peering around for a bit, she frowned and shut the door.

Veronika snorted with laughter.

"Let's do it again," Kazia said, her eyes sparkling.

"Not today. Tomorrow."

It was such fun that they did it almost every time Veronika visited. But one day when Veronika knocked, Aunt Truda's door burst open.

"Caught you, you little brats," she said, flying out the door with a wooden spoon held high over her head.

Veronika shrieked and ran for her life, abandoning Kazia to her fate, but it was Veronika that Aunt Truda took after. In and out and around the trees of the orchard she ran, Truda not far behind.

After a couple of minutes, Aunt Truda gave up. Hearing her stalk away, Veronika collapsed against the rough bark of a tree to catch her breath. Just before getting to the porch, Aunt Truda turned and looked back at Veronika.

"Be on the lookout for me," she shouted.

Fear like a thick blanket settled on Veronika's thumping chest. What had she done?

From a few rows down the orchard, she saw Kazia peeking out from behind a tree. "She's gone. Come back."

Kazia ran over, her eyes overflowing with tears. "She's going to tell on us, isn't she?"

"Yes," Veronika said, feeling sick to her stomach. "I wonder what my parents are going to do to me?"

"I want to go home," Kazia said.

Back at Kazia's, Veronika could see Aunt Maria peeling potatoes. She greeted them like nothing had happened.

"Let's go in your room," Veronika whispered. "She doesn't know."

As soon as Kazia's bedroom door was shut, Veronika felt weak with relief. "We are so lucky, Kazia. If your aunt was going to tell, she would have told by now."

A few days later Veronika asked, "Want to play the knock-knock game again?"

"What if she catches us?"

"We just have to be in the bushes before she gets the door open."

22
VERONIKA

January 1931

The January sky was a dazzling blue, a perfect day for sledding. Out in the sunshine, the snow sparkled as if a million diamonds had been cast upon its crusty surface. The wonder of it caused Veronika to stop in her tracks and marvel, until she saw the willows that lined the river.

So heavy was the weight of the melting snow on their slender limbs, the tops of the trees were bent half over. The branches seemed to call out and beg to be released of their burden. She ran to one and jerked on the tip of the branch. Up the branches sprang in a whipping flurry of flinging snow.

"Snowing, it's snowing," sang Kazia, flapping around under the cloud of descending snow particles.

In and out of the willows Veronika ran, helping them spring upright until the chill of snow melting down her neck ended the urge to continue.

"Let's take your sled onto the river," Veronika said. "I can pretend I'm a horse and pull you around."

Onto the river they went. Faster and faster Veronika pulled, swirling Kazia this way and that way across the frozen surface, her laughter spurring Veronika on to greater acts of daring.

Crack.

She felt a fleeting moment of dread before the ice gave way and she plunged down into the murky depths. Down, down she sank; the cold shock surrounded her body. In frozen deafness, she dimly heard Kazia calling to her.

"Get out. Please, Veronika."

Through the blur of water, she saw Kazia looming from above, her eyes wide with fear. Flailing, Veronika's feet scraped against the rocky river bottom. The panic subsided with solid ground under her, and she pushed upward and bobbed to the surface, gasping.

"Hang on," Kazia said, grabbing her arm and helping her place her sodden-mittened hands onto the icy edge.

Clinging to the edge, Veronika lifted her leg. It fell short of the icy shelf again and again. She felt herself growing tired. Would she die?

"You can do it," Kazia moaned, her face contorted in fear.

Finally, she pushed with all her strength, and Kazia pulled. Her body slid out and she collapsed on her back.

Breathe. In and out. Breathe. Her body on fire, she couldn't move. Her legs felt like blocks of wood.

"I'll go get your mama," Kazia said.

"No, take me to your home."

"But your house is just over there," Kazia said, pointing.

"Mama can't find out."

"All right." Kazia, pressed her lips together. "If you say so."

Veronika collapsed onto the sled, her legs barely able to move. Kazia pulled her along the road, a ten-minute walk.

"Mama, come quickly," Kazia called, when she got home. "Veronika fell in the river."

Aunt Maria's jaw dropped when she saw Veronika. "Why did you bring her here?"

"She didn't want to go home," Kazia said, dissolving into tears.

Veronika felt herself being lifted and carried into the kitchen. Aunt Maria hastily stripped off her clothes.

"Look at her. She's purple," Aunt Maria said, rubbing Veronika's arms.

"Please don't tell Mama," Veronika said, shivering uncontrollably.

"She's my sister. I can't keep this from her." Turning to Kazia she said, "Get me some blankets, then go to Veronika's. Tell them what happened."

Gradually, her shivering eased off as the warmth of the room radiated into her.

"Feeling better?" asked Aunt Maria, bringing her a cup of tea.

"Yes."

Within minutes, Tata arrived. "Are you all right?" he asked, stroking her cheek.

Veronika looked up into his troubled face. She nodded.

With his thumb, he wiped away a tear trickling down her cheek. "Thank God for that."

Swaddling her in a blanket, Tata placed her in Kazia's sled and dragged her home. Mama tucked her in bed with a hot stone wrapped in cloth.

Veronika waited to be scolded, but it never came.

After three days of not feeling well, Veronika began to cough and have feverish dreams of the witch Baba Yaga chasing her.

"I think we should get Doctor Janczewski to take a look at her," Mama said, after feeling Veronika's forehead.

When the doctor came, he listened to Veronika's chest.

"Make a warm mustard poultice and put it on her throat, then tie a wool sock around it. Twice a day give her a big spoonful of honey that has been steeped with garlic. Better than any medicine you can buy."

"Thank you, Doctor. Please, take some potatoes for seeing Veronika."

"That's not necessary, Helena. You keep them. Times are hard."

Mama insisted.

In the morning, the doctor's wife was at the door. She wanted money. Tata paid her. After the door was shut, Veronika heard her mother say, "Just wait until I tell Maria about this."

The value of goods confiscated from the 'Kulaks'....
about $90-$210 per household.
—Robert Conquest, *The Harvest of Sorrow: Soviet Collectivization and the Terror-Famine*

23
JANEK

May 1931

Janek and Helena sat on the long benches of the community hall, waiting for the meeting to begin. The smell of unwashed bodies and the rank, sweet smell of cow manure rising from the soles of work boots lingered in the air. People had been called away from their labour to attend the meeting. In the row ahead of them sat a young family. Their baby started to wail. The mother quickly lifted her shirt and put the child to her breast. Janek could hear the baby's noisy gulps.

Why did they always have to sit so long before the meeting began? Already they had been waiting a long time, and still no Zykov.

It was a good thing Veronika was at Babcia's. She would find it boring to wait for so long. Thinking of her, he looked up at the portrait of Stalin. Veronika had said she thought he looked nice, like a grandfather. Staring at Stalin's face, Janek could feel the evil pulsing from it.

At the front of the room sat a table and a row of empty chairs. A vase of yellow sunflowers sat on the table and, as he looked at the flowers, feelings of anger surged through him and he wondered why. The sunlight, too, annoyed him as it filtered in from the grime-covered windows. And suddenly he knew why he was angry. This was a place of despair, not sunshine. Yellow flowers had no business here. Black sunflowers, maybe, to symbolize death, for nothing good ever came from this room. Only orders of more hardship or long-winded speeches on how useless the people of Ukraine were. Pangs of sorrow washed over him. How he wished they could live like they did before, when they had plenty to eat and grain enough to trade at the general store for what they couldn't grow.

Finally, Zykov strode into the room, a sheaf of papers in hand, Kanygin following him. They sat down and still the meeting did not start. Janek stared at their hardened faces. They were both growing full bushy moustaches, Stalin moustaches. Dogs emulating their master. Helena whispered words of prayer.

Janek relaxed as Zykov stood up and began ranting about kulaks again, always the kulaks. There were no kulaks around here. Most of the ones they called kulaks were just hard-working farmers with good management practices. Now they were gone, even their women and children.

Janek looked at Zykov as his speech became more rabid. Spit flew from his mouth as he gestured with his arms.

"It is the kulaks in Soviet-occupied Ukraine who are holding back the progress of the Soviet Union. They are the ones who do not want the modernization of this great country. They riot. They burn the collectives' grain fields. They kill their animals rather than turn them over to the collective."

What was Zykov talking about? Riot? Burn grain fields? No one does that here. Kill their animals? Well, that might be true. Many horses and cows did sicken and die just before they were due to be confiscated.

Zykov suddenly slammed his fist on the table and said, "All kulaks must be rooted out. Exposed for what they are—tight-fisted, self-serving bloodsuckers. Once they are gone, the collectives will succeed. We can accomplish in ten years what has taken Western capitalists one hundred years to accomplish. We can do it and we will do it. Nothing can stop us.

"In addition to this year's district grain quota, we have been given a kulak quota. A list of kulaks must be submitted to the Soviet secret police on a regular basis.

"You may think that there are no more kulaks here. To assist you in your thinking, our leaders in Moscow have created criteria by which to judge who is a kulak and who is not. Comrade Kanygin, read the list."

"Anyone who has resisted in any way collectivization
Anyone who has a metal roof rather than a sod roof
Anyone who owns or has in the past owned a machine of any kind
Anyone who has hired people to help in the fields, including the hiring of relatives
Anyone who has more land than what can be considered normal
Anyone who has a kulak mentality"

Zykov cleared his throat and once again stood up. He surveyed the cowering, shuffling people and waited.

Helena pressed against Janek, crying softly. Janek felt his head reeling. He put his arm around her shoulder, as Zykov continued speaking.

"Does this list make you think of someone who might be a kulak? A neighbour, perhaps? Maybe even a relative? Don't be afraid to speak up. Remember, this is for the good of your country. Anyone who does not assist us in this purge of rot is also a part of the rot."

No one said anything.

"Maybe you wish to talk to us one at a time. You are welcome to come to me at any time to discuss those you think are kulaks. Don't worry that you are making a false report. Your word alone will not convict someone. We will read your report and from there make our own decision."

Walking home from the meeting, Janek felt like a pig swinging from a hook, waiting to be eviscerated. There was no mistaking what the Soviets had planned for the people of Ukraine.

*Give me four years to teach the children
and the seed I have sown will never be uprooted.*

—Vladimir Lenin, founder of the Russian Communist Party

24

VERONIKA

Veronika loved the Communist Party. Everything would be wonderful once the collectives really got going, then all the people could relax and let the machinery do the work for them. That's what their teacher said. When they sang songs about Stalin, Veronika liked to look up at his portrait high above the teacher's desk. She could hardly wait to sing the new song they had been practicing to her parents.

On the way home from school, Veronika, Alina, and Marek lingered in the village square, looking for lost coins where the farmer's market was held. Not finding any, they threw rocks at the mill's waterwheel then wandered over to the blacksmith's.

Uncle Feliks glanced up at Veronika as he nailed a horseshoe onto the hoof of a collective's horse.

"How was school today?"

"Good, Uncle Feliks. I like singing all the songs."

The sound of a hammer striking metal filled the room. Veronika ran over to where Alina and Marek stood watching Uncle Vladzio make a gate hinge. He held it in the fire until it glowed red and they covered their ears when he struck the metal with the hammer.

When done, he looked up and said with a smile, "Here, a few kopeks for candy for you and your friends."

Veronika felt proud that her uncle was so generous toward her in front of her friends. She savoured their looks of envy. When they were outside, Alina asked, "Does he always give you money?"

"Oh, yes. And at his house he keeps a whole tin of candy, just for me. And I can have as many as I want," she fibbed.

Their eyes widened.

They went into the general store that sold her favourite candy, the ones with the soft chewy fruit centres. The bells on the door tinkled as Veronika pushed it open. The Jewish store manager greeted them from behind his high wooden counter. She gave him her kopeks and he let her reach in the jar and pick out her cherry-flavoured favourite.

While Marek and Alina were deciding which one they wanted, Veronika wandered over to the bin of colourful bouncing balls. She wished she could have one. She remembered her surprise when they first came in. Never had she seen a plaything for children in any of the stores. When Kazia's parents bought her one, Veronika asked if she could have one. Tata shook his head and said that any money he had went to pay for the few things they had to purchase, like salt, spices, and sewing needles, and anyhow, it was the job of children to make their own playthings.

After saying goodbye to Alina and Marek, Veronika continued on alone.

Opening the front door, Veronika stepped over the threshold onto the hard-packed clay floor.

"I'm home, Mama," she called out.

Veronika's mother smiled. "Welcome home, Veronika! Why did

it take you so long to come back from school? I saw other children go by a long time ago."

"We were looking around the village. Uncle Vladzio gave us kopeks and we went and bought candy."

"You went into the store without me? What did the manager say?"

"Nothing. We always go into the store and look around, even when we don't have kopeks."

"What a bold girl you are. Change out of your school clothes and set the table. Tata's coming in now."

As Veronika set the table for supper, she cheerily sang: *"Stalin is our Father dear, the hero of our Motherland."*

Tata's eyes narrowed. "What is that you're singing?" he demanded.

"It's a song we learned in school today, Tata."

"Well, you don't sing it here."

Hurt and confused by his rebuke, she continued setting the table, blinking back tears. She glanced up at Mama. Their eyes met. Veronika could tell Mama felt sorry for her and was annoyed that Tata had spoken so roughly, because her mouth set in a hard line every time she looked at him. No one talked much during dinner, except to give the blessing and to ask for food to be passed.

After supper, Tata asked Veronika to come over to his chair. She approached him with her head down. He lifted her chin so she had to look into his eyes.

"Veronika, I'm sorry for telling you not to sing. You have a beautiful voice, and it makes me very happy when you sing, but not when it's songs about Stalin."

"But he's the hero of our motherland. Every day we sing about him."

"Stalin is not our hero. We don't want any part of him or the Soviet Union."

"Janek, stop! What if she says something to her teacher?"

"No, I'm going to tell her. They're trying to make a little Communist out of my daughter."

Veronika thought of Stalin's picture, hanging on the wall above the teacher's desk. He looked so nice.

"Teacher says he loves all his people."

"We are not his people. He doesn't care about us. All he cares about is taking our land and animals, so don't ever let me hear you singing that Stalin is a great man."

"Stalin did that?" Veronika asked. "I thought it was the men at the collective."

"Yes, the men at the collective took everything because he ordered them to."

"Janek, please, how can you be saying this to her? She's so young."

"The Soviets may have conquered us, Helena, but we will always be Polish. And I will teach my daughter that," he said, his fist slamming the table.

"Should I stop singing the songs at school, Tata?"

"At school, you do what your teacher says. Don't tell anyone what I said about Stalin, not the other children and not the teacher. They will report me, then they will come and take me away. You won't see me anymore."

Veronika's face crumpled. "Where, Tata? Where will they take you?"

"Here, Veronika," Mama said, grabbing her off her father's lap. "Don't think about that. Come, let's get your bath ready."

Tata went outside and lifted the washtub off its peg on the wall and set it in the middle of the kitchen. Mama filled the tub with warm water that had been heating on the woodstove.

Still upset, Veronika lowered herself down into the warmth and studied her reflection. Hypnotically, her image faded and rippled as she thought about Tata. Where would they take him?

Mama's voice filtered in, "How could you, Janek?"

Veronika looked up, startled. Mama never talked to Tata like that.

"I'm so sorry," Tata said. His voice was muffled, as if he were covering his face.

Was Tata crying? He never cried.

From that day on, fear followed Veronika to school. The teacher and the other children that she used to trust were now people who could make a bad report about her Tata. No longer did she want to sing the songs and shout slogans. If she could, she would always change them a little, under her breath, like: "Short live the Communist Party and Stalin is our country's stupid head!"

Open criticism, let alone resistance to, Stalin became impossible as a powerful and growing secret police methodically terrorized and later liquidated real, imagined, or potential opposition.
—Orest Subtelny, *Ukraine: A History*

25

VERONIKA

October 1931

"I'm glad Kazia and I are in the same classroom this year."

"Well, just make sure you concentrate on your studies," Mama said, as she wrapped a scarf around Veronika's head and knotted it under her upturned chin.

"Don't worry Mama. Kazia and I aren't sitting together. The teacher put me with Alina again."

"That's good. With Kazia, you would be talking too much."

"You'll study better, become a doctor," added Tata from across the room.

"I don't want to be around sick people. I want to become a teacher."

"Later we can decide. At least the Soviets give you children an education. That's one good thing they do."

Veronika had a sudden urge to run as she stepped out the door, schoolbooks in one hand and lunch pail in the other. Perhaps it was the freshness of the crisp fall air mingled with the scent of smoke and the aroma of overripe apples. Maybe it was the wind-blown, wizened clumps of leaves lining the road that caught her eye, that seemed to say, *kick into me*. It could even have been the white berries hanging in clusters that needed to be stomped on, just to hear them pop.

Out of breath from running, Veronika waved to Alina and Kazia, who were standing on the road waiting for her. Marek stood to the side, flinging rocks at tree trunks. Sharp cracks of stone against wood announced his accuracy.

She wished she lived in the same triplex as her friends. But that wasn't possible; there were only three units. Still, it would be fun just to open the door and be at Kazia's or Alina's.

They walked side by side, while Marek, as usual, walked a few paces ahead, scanning the ditch for frogs or dead birds. Suddenly he veered into someone's yard and disappeared.

"What is he doing?" asked Alina. "Mama said we're not allowed to go in other people's yards."

Daisy in hand, he reappeared.

"For you," he said, thrusting it toward Veronika.

She felt a flush of pleasure and then of embarrassment that Alina and Kazia could see his open display of affection.

Alina spoiled the moment. "You shouldn't pick flowers from other people's gardens," she said in a singsong voice. "I'm going to tell Mama on you."

He made a face and trotted ahead. Veronika slipped the flower into her satchel, as if it was something inconsequential, but when she got home, in the privacy of her bedroom, she knew that she would relive the joy that now suffused her heart. As conversation turned to other things, Veronika was glad, at least for now, that she would not be teased.

Hearing horses, she looked up and saw several men on horseback in the distance, followed by a horse pulling a cart.

"Just workers going to a field," Alina said, picking up Kazia's arm and swinging it wildly. Kazia laughed, her body jerking back and forth.

"No, I don't think it is workers," Veronika said. "Workers walk." A stab of fear curled around Veronika's stomach as they came closer into view. "Soldiers."

She ran with Kazia and Alina to catch up with Marek, who was staring at the approaching riders.

"I'm scared, Marek," whimpered Alina, clinging to her brother's arm.

"Let go of me," he said, shaking free of her. "They're not going to bother us. We're too young. Let's just keep walking and act normal."

Veronika took Kazia's hand and, keeping to the edge of the road, walked behind Marek and Alina.

"I don't like soldiers," Kazia said.

Veronika gave her hand a little squeeze, knowing she was close to crying. "Don't worry. We'll take care of you."

As the soldiers got closer, Veronika saw that they wore the uniform of the secret police. Her breathing tightened. She squeezed Kazia's hand a little tighter and kept walking, her eyes on the ground, only glancing up briefly as the horsemen and cart rattled by. An enormous sense of relief washed over her when the soldiers barely noticed them.

Marek turned and spat at the receding figures. "The secret police! Did you see them?"

Veronika nodded.

"I hope they're not going to arrest someone," Alina said with a shiver, making the sign of the cross like she had seen the grown-ups do.

Seeing her, Veronika and Kazia did the same.

"Can't be," Marek said, as the horses and cart rounded the corner and disappeared from view. "They always arrest people at night."

"Where do you think they're going?" Veronika asked.

"Maybe a grain search."

"I hope they're not going to my house," Veronika said. "The collective just gave us our grain."

"I want to go home," Kazia said, whimpering.

"We're not taking you back home," Marek said. "Anyhow, they're probably going to the next village."

"Are you sure?" Kazia asked.

"Pretty sure."

They continued walking, no one speaking much. When they were almost at the outskirts of the village, Veronika broke the silence.

"Mama told me the secret police will never come to our house because Tata always does everything right."

"It's not just your Tata that does everything right," Alina said. "My Tata does everything right, too."

"Mine, too," Kazia said. "But I'm still scared."

"I'm not scared," Marek said. "I've even talked to a secret police soldier."

"You have not, you liar," his sister said.

"I have, too. I've talked to lots of secret police. They don't scare me."

"I'm going to tell Tata that you're lying again."

Hearing yelling from behind them, they turned and looked. It was a boy, a friend of Marek's, running hard toward them, waving his arms.

"Marek," he shouted as he got closer. "Your house," he said, taking in deep sucking breaths. "The secret police are there."

Veronika felt dazed, as if the words he spoke had come out long and distorted.

"It's not true," Marek shouted.

"It is true. I saw the cart."

"Are they at my house, too?" asked Kazia.

Hand over his chest, he nodded.

Veronika shook, trying to make sense of what her mind denied. She looked at Marek. His books lay scattered at his feet. His face was pale. A dark stain gradually spread down the leg of his pants. Alina wailed, open-mouthed.

Marek bolted down the road toward home. Alina ran after him, yelling, "Wait!"

Veronika took Kazia's hand and ran after them.

"Don't go! They might take you, too," the boy yelled after them.

Veronika kept running, dodging the ruts in the road through tear-blinded eyes.

"Marek! Alina!" she yelled as their pace slowed. They turned and waited, gasping for air.

When they rounded the bend just before their home, Veronika heard the crying of children before she saw the cart and soldiers in the yard. Marek and Alina swept past the soldiers and through the door of their unit.

Veronika ran with Kazia into her triplex unit. Everything was flipped over—drawers, clothes, books. A young, sullen-faced soldier stood at the sideboard tossing what he didn't want on the floor and loading into a sack what he did. Kazia's father, Uncle Józef, sat in a chair in handcuffs.

Kazia put her arms around her father, "Don't let them take you."

"Don't worry. Maybe tomorrow they will let me go."

"Where is Mama?"

"Packing clothes for me."

Veronika and Kazia ran into her parents' bedroom. Kazia's mother took no notice of them while she frantically shoved pants and shirts into a sack.

"Mama," Kazia said, hugging her mother's waist.

She pushed Kazia away, her voice harsh. "Soon they will be taking him. Go help your sister pack food."

Veronika and Kazia ran for the kitchen. Kazia's older sister, Nellia, wept as she threw handfuls of walnuts into a sack. She pointed to the loft. "Go get dried fruit for Tata."

Another soldier entered the kitchen; this one was older, with cold, staring eyes. Veronika shrank against the wall.

He shoved Nellia aside and grabbed the sack. "You have enough for him already."

Nellia and Veronika fled to where Kazia's father stood, a rifle pointed at his back. "Time to go," the soldier said.

"Maria, come! They're taking me."

Kazia's mother ran into the room. "No! You said we had time to pack."

"You had time."

"Please, I beg you. Don't take him. He hasn't done anything."

Veronika watched as Uncle Józef was led out to the cart. Nellia and Kazia sobbed while their mother clutched their father's hands.

"I'll write, Maria. I'll write," he called out.

Frightened and alone, Veronika ran and clung to the wooden post beside the front gate.

Moments later, Alina and Marek came out of their home, clinging to their father and followed by their mother. She held a bundle to her chest and sobbed as he climbed into the back of the cart.

Another wave of anguish swept through Veronika when she saw her wonderful Doctor Janczewski being led to the wagon in handcuffs. Truda walked beside him, crying, clinging to him, telling him that she loved him.

Gasping, choking on tears, Veronika called out to him. He paused and looked at her, as if he were going to say something, but the soldier behind him prodded him in the back, and the moment was gone. He climbed onto the cart beside his two brothers. The secret police mounted their horses. Within seconds the cart rattled off down the road, women and children running after it. Veronika could hear Kazia's voice among the others, screaming.

A sudden spasm of pain hit Veronika in the stomach. She bent over and vomited, again and again until she couldn't vomit any more. Trembling and weak-kneed, she ran home as fast as she could, stopping every now and then to hold her side.

Opening the door and seeing Veronika, her mother rushed over, her eyes wide with alarm.

"What is it, Veronika?"

"They took them."

"Took who?" her eyes wide with terror.

"Uncle Józef, Alina and Marek's father, and the doctor."

Mama's screams brought Tata running from the barn.

When they got to Kazia's, all the neighbourhood men were standing outside, talking. Their wives sat in the living room crying with Kazia's mother and Alina and Marek's mother. Kazia had her head in her mother's lap. Veronika tried to put her arms around Kazia, but she shrugged Veronika away.

— ❋ —

Veronika had nightmares almost every night after that. She woke up shaking with deep gasping sobs. One night she had a dream that she was searching everywhere for the doctor. A large group of men sat in a field beside a forest, their hands tied behind their backs. A soldier came and took a few of the men into the forest. There were shots. The soldier came back and led a few more men away.

She looked into the faces of the waiting men. One turned toward her. It was Doctor Janczewski.

When she awoke, her pillow was wet with tears. She told her parents her dream.

"Don't tell Kazia your dream, or any of the other children."

Later, Veronika overheard her parents telling Uncle Feliks and Uncle Vladzio about the dream and that the secret police had arrested thousands of Ukraine's people—doctors, judges, lawyers, priests, musicians, and even storytellers. All were being shot and buried in mass graves.

"Veronika always sat right beside the doctor whenever he came over," Mama said with a catch in her voice. There was a pause as her mother blew her nose.

"Maybe his spirit came to her," Uncle Vladzio said.

"That means the men are dead. O mój Boże. My poor sister," Mama said.

"We don't know, Helena," Tata said. "Maybe someone said something and Veronika overheard, so then she has a dream about it."

"Why take my sister's husband?" Mama asked.

"He shared the same roof as the doctor. Maybe that was his crime."

Veronika felt sick to her stomach. She thought her dream was just a dream. She had believed her mother when she said that someday they would return.

"It must be hard for all three women, living in that triplex with their men gone," Tata said. "I'll go over from time to time and give them a hand in their garden."

"We can help, too," said Uncle Feliks.

Everyone was silent for a moment, then Mama said, "You can tell Truda is grieving. They must have loved each other in their own sort of way."

"You see," Tata said, wagging his finger at Mama's downcast face, "That's what I tried to tell you, when you and your sister gossiped about her. You can never judge what goes on between a man and a woman."

Mama looked at him and said, "Maybe I should drop in on her and see how she is doing."

Veronika felt a black wave of shame and panic come over her. She had always thought Aunt Truda was a bad woman who deserved to be teased. What if her parents found out that she and Kazia had been mean to her? In the morning, she would make Kazia promise once again to keep what they had done a secret; if they were lucky, their parents would never find out.

Although adept at coercion, Stalin and his cohorts were astonishingly inept when it came to farming. Frequently, the party activists who headed the collective farms would order the planting of inappropriate crops ... Because of poor transportation facilities, much of the stockpiled grain spoiled or was eaten by rats. Even more serious was the lack of draught animals, many of which had been slaughtered earlier ... tractors broke down almost immediately. As a result, in 1931, almost one-third of the grain harvest was lost in harvest.

—Orest Subtelny, *Ukraine: A History*

26
JANEK

November 1931

Janek slipped into the collective's barn and sprinkled a little bit of stolen grain into Dobroc's bucket. He didn't dare take much, only what he could hide in his pockets. Lingering close to the horse, Janek closed his eyes, and breathed in the sweet musky scent as he stroked its back.

It hurt to see how lean Dobroc was getting now that the collective owned him. Feeling the horse shuffle as he searched with its nose for more grain, Janek gave him a last pat then turned to go. Only then did he see Feliks walk toward him.

"I thought I'd find you here. Still thinking that horse is yours?"

"Makes me sick how no one takes care of the horses."

"Talk to Zykov about it," Feliks said.

"I did, weeks ago. He said, soon tractors will replace them anyway."

"Just shows how little he knows," Feliks said. "Tractors break down. Horses don't."

"We should go and see what they will give us this year for labour days."

"How much grain are you expecting to get paid?" Feliks asked.

"Who knows? But it better be more than last year."

"*Jezu Chryste*, I hope you are right. If the labour-day value is only enough for a loaf of bread, there's going to be a riot."

Janek motioned with his head toward the raised grain-weighing platform, where dozens of collective workers had already gathered. "Maybe that is why the meeting is outside this year—easier for the collective leaders to get away."

Janek and Feliks stood on the outskirts of the crowd, beside the dour faces of their friends and neighbours.

"With so many children to feed, we ran out of grain months ago," Stashu, a father of nine said. "When they give us our grain, I'm going to eat a whole loaf of bread myself."

"For me it will be a potful of buckwheat noodles," Pawel said.

Janek wondered about Pawel's youngest. The baby wasn't doing well. Now that Doctor Janczewski was gone, he and his wife were trying what they knew of natural remedies.

To the side, Janek noticed Nadzia, a woman in black. Her husband had died in the Great War, leaving her all alone in the world except for a sister and a niece. He wondered how she would make out with labour-day coupons. He hadn't seen her that often in the field.

Janek's eyes shifted to the platform when Zykov, Kanygin, members of the village police, and a few dozen shock workers walked up the steps.

"What are those bastards doing here?" Feliks said, jerking his thumb toward the police.

Janek knew quite a few of them. Grzegorz used to be a worker at the flour mill. Emil used to be a rag and bone man, and Danylo used to hire himself out as a farm labourer. Seeing an opportunity for advancement, they had put on a uniform and helped the shock workers torture people.

"Sell-outs, the lot of them," Janek said.

Zykov stepped forward. "Comrades," he said. "I know you have come to find out what your labour-day rate will be. As you know, we had a good harvest, but the harvest wasn't as bountiful as last year's. The state's grain target for Ukraine was twenty-two million tons, but only seventeen million came in."

"What does that mean?" said someone from the back.

"You will not get an allotment of grain. The state took the entire harvest, even that set aside for next year's sowing."

Janek felt numb. *Even the seed for sowing was gone? How would they survive?*

Nadzia, the widow, began to wail as others surged forward, anger contorting their faces. Kanygin and the other shock workers scrambled to move back. Several shots rang into the air as the police pushed their way forward, revolvers held aloft. Everyone froze.

Once again, Zykov came forward. "There is some good news in all this. Our collective managed to make their grain quota. Most collectives in Ukraine did not and were punished, some by having their potatoes confiscated. We did not get punished! And for your labour days, you will get a share of the collective's potatoes and sugar beets."

Anger pulsed through every fibre of Janek's body. He, too, surged forward with the crowd, yelling, his fist pumping the air.

"I have nine children," Stashu shouted. "What good are sugar beets?"

"Give us our due," Pawel said.

The police came forward once more. Janek felt Feliks's hand on his arm. "We need to get out of here."

The next few seconds were a blur of screams and shots being fired into the crowd. One moment Janek was looking at the platform, the next he was nearly knocked to the ground as people turned and fled in panic. Keeping low, he and Feliks ran for the side of a building.

— ✸ —

The next week, after everyone had brought home their share of potatoes and sugar beets, Feliks and Paulina came over to Janek's to visit.

"Lies! Once again it was all lies," Feliks said, banging the kitchen table. "They're taking so much grain out of Ukraine, there are no reserves left. What if there is a drought or the crops fail?

"Everywhere there's been riots," Helena said, staring into space. "My friend at the market told me even women are rioting."

Paulina raised her eyebrows. "Women riot?"

"In Proskurov, where Janek's brother lives, they attacked the collective leaders with sticks and hoes, and broke open grain storage bins."

"Maybe you and I should join up with some of the other women," Paulina said with a shaky laugh, "have Antosia as our leader."

"And you can be sure every one of them got deported," Janek said, shaking his head. "At least for our own family, we can stay away from that. All of us have a few sacks of buckwheat from our gardens hidden away."

Feliks raised his voice once again. "But what is going to happen to those trusting souls who gave up their homes to live in barracks on the collectives? What will they eat?" he asked, his face flushed.

"They'll be all right for as long as the collective's kitchens have potatoes to cook," Janek said. "After that, who knows? No vegetable gardens or fruit trees on the collective."

"I would think the worst off will be those who live in the village," Paulina said. "Their only food would come from their small garden plots, unless they have a bit of money to buy from the farmer's market."

"God in heaven, what will happen to them?" asked Helena, her gaze fixed.

Janek rubbed his neck, then said softly, "First the old and then the young will die."

On the Siberian taiga, if there was a village, they (those deported) were crammed in somehow, if there was not, 'they were simply set right there in the snow. The weakest died'; those who could, cut timber and built shacks; 'they worked almost without sleeping so that their families would not freeze to death.'

—Robert Conquest, *The Harvest of Sorrow: Soviet Collectivization and the Terror-Famine*

27

VERONIKA

November 1931

The next morning, Veronika was about to go to school, when Kazia burst in.

"Has something happened to your mother?" Mama asked, her face ashen.

Kazia shook her head. "Secret police," she gasped.

Mama covered her mouth and slowly backed away. "They took my sister?"

Kazia tried to speak but no words came out.

Tata grabbed Kazia by the shoulders. "Kazia! Did they take your mother?"

"Not Mama," she said, taking deep, ragged breaths. "The doctor's wife."

When they got to Kazia's triplex, the door to the unit belonging to the doctor and his wife was flung open. Furniture, clothing, and books spilled out onto the porch.

Tata joined her uncles and some of the neighbours in the front yard.

Veronika followed Mama into Kazia's unit. Aunt Paulina and Babcia were already there. Aunt Maria, pale and sombre, sat between them.

"I'm so glad they didn't take you," Mama said, as she hugged her sister.

"I just don't understand why I'm still here," Aunt Maria said. "Three women in this triplex and they take only one."

"Maybe because Truda didn't have children," Aunt Paulina said.

"Did they say where they were taking her?" asked Mama.

"Kazakhstan."

As the days went by, Veronika heard her mother and others in the family wish that they had not been so hard on Aunt Truda. With each day that passed, Veronika's shame grew for the mean tricks she and Kazia had played on her.

A few weeks later, a letter came addressed to Kazia's family. It was from Truda.

> *Greetings dear Maria and children,*
> *How often I think of you. I pray that your health and that of your children remain good. For me, my health is poor. My sentence is eight years of labour here in Kazakhstan. How much longer I live, I do not know. You are my sister through marriage, yet I did not act as a sister. I am sorry and ask if in your heart, you can forgive me.*
>
> *I came here by cattle car, stopping at villages, picking up more and more people until no one can even move. I thank God I am barren, the children with us suffered so.*

Bread was given sparingly. A loaf for every twelve people and half bucket of soup like water every other day. At stops, the dead are thrown out beside the tracks. Oh, unbelievable, what I saw. Yet I survived and now I am at a flat, snow-covered land at the end of the world. The camp was not ready for us, only numbered stakes in the ground where they planned to build huts. Kazakh families in the area were forced to take us in until spring comes. Then with our own hands we build mudbrick huts. Water is one tap in the centre of camp. People are desperate for clothes, for shoes. I wrap my feet in rags because there are no shoes. I work from sunrise to sunset clearing the land. Pull stumps, haul rocks. The food is not enough. There is no medicine. Always we are burying children and the weak who died from some disease that goes through camp.

Once again, I am sorry.
Truda

After hearing her letter, the secret burden of shame that Veronika felt intensified. In bed at night, she thought of Truda and wept. Finally, Veronika told her parents how she and Kazia had teased Aunt Truda, by knocking on her door then running away.

"It is not right, what you did," Mama said. "But it wasn't right what we did to her, either. We will ask Paulina to write a letter to her. We will say that we forgive her and hope that she will forgive us."

Sitting at the table together and writing that letter helped greatly to lift some of the shame from Veronika's heart. Truda did not write back, and Veronika wondered if she ever got their letter.

Some 100,000 kulaks were shot. The remainder were evicted from their homes and marched to the nearest railway. Huge lines of peasants converged on the trains which took two to three thousand people in cattlecars, on journeys lasting a week or longer, to the arctic.

—Robert Conquest, *The Terror-Famine in Perspective*

28
VERONIKA

January 1932

In the light from the kerosene lantern, Veronika's father knelt on the earthen floor as he worked on a tombstone with hammer and chisel. Veronika sat at the table, trying to memorize the words to a poem her teacher wanted the class to learn.

We live as light and burden free,

As birds that soar across the sky

Her mother sat across from her, eyes closed, murmuring the words of the rosary. Veronika found it difficult to concentrate with the steady clank of the hammer against the chisel. Ever since Tata had started work on the collective, he carved tombstones in the evening to trade for food or money. He hauled up stones from the river, cut them down to the right shape and size then sanded them smooth in the barn. Since he didn't know how to print, Kazia's older sister, Nellia, would come over and write what the family wanted on the tombstone with a charcoal stick. Tata would then trace over it with his chisel.

It made Veronika sad to see tombstones in the kitchen, especially those like this one, for yet another child on the collective who had weakened and died. The tombstone seemed to fill the whole kitchen with thoughts of death. She turned once again to her poem.

We live with joy that knows no bounds
Hearts and hands to Stalin pledged

She looked over to see if Tata had finished yet. He hadn't. The angel's face still needed eyes.

Veronika looked at her mother and watched how her lips moved as she held the beads between her fingers. Had her mother always looked so old, so worried? Ever since the secret police had taken Aunt Maria's husband and his two brothers away, Mama sat in the evening and prayed for some news about them, but weeks had passed and nothing had come.

At first, Kazia would say, "Tata is coming back."

"I know," Veronika always replied. Mama told her to say that. Mama also said to try and not hug Tata in front of Kazia.

At the end of her prayers, Mama got up to put her rosary away. Soon Mama would tell her it was time for bed. Veronika could feel that cold, sick feeling return once again to claw at her stomach. Night was the time that the secret police most often made their raids, taking a man here and a man there. No one could stop them. No one could question why they were being taken. Maybe tonight they would come and take Tata. She wrapped her arms around her waist and squeezed to make the pain lessen.

"Stomach ache again?" Mama asked.

Veronika nodded.

"Janek, I'm worried about Veronika. Every night she seems to get stomach pain, and in the morning, she doesn't want to go to school."

He put down his chisel and sat beside her. "My little Noosha, what's wrong?"

She shrugged her shoulders. She didn't want to tell Tata that she had nightmares of the secret police taking him away. If she said it out loud, it might make it come true.

"Why don't you want to go to school?"

She looked down.

He raised her chin. "You can't protect us by staying home."

Veronika nodded, unable to speak.

"I do everything they tell me. That is the best way I have to protect us."

"You should have told us you were worried," Mama said.

Veronika went deeper within herself. She didn't like it when she disappointed her mother.

Tata put his calloused hand over Veronika's. "Mama's right. It's not good to keep things in."

"How are Alina and Marek?" asked Mama.

Veronika shrugged. "Not so good, I guess." She thought of how quiet and pinched Alina had become. Marek seemed angry all the time, scowling and ready for a fight at school.

"I know my sister finds it hard to manage," Mama said. "She seems to have given up hope that Józef will come back."

"Is that why Kazia's hair isn't combed?"

Mama nodded, her lips pressed together. "It is hard for your Aunt Maria all on her own with the children."

— ✻ —

In bed that night, the door opened, and Tata came in. "Do you mind if I sit with you for a while?" he asked.

"I always like it when you do."

He sat at the edge of her bed and stroked her head. A slender shaft of light streaming in from the kitchen partially illuminated the love in his eyes.

"I made a vow to always take care of you, Veronika. First on the day you were born, and again not long ago. But I want you to remember one thing."

"Yes, Tata?"

"God is more loving and more powerful than I am. If someday I can't keep my vow, then ..."

"Don't say that, Tata."

Tata sat for a moment in silence, then she felt the soft brush of his beard on her face as he leaned down and kissed her.

"God is more loving than I," he continued. "And if I cannot keep my vow, He will take care of you. But I want you to promise me that you will always pray to God, even if I am not around to remind you."

"I promise," she whispered.

He kissed her one more time then walked out and closed the door.

After he left, she squeezed her pillow and prayed over and over, "Please, God, I'll do anything, just don't let them take my Tata."

The peasants ate dogs, horses, rotten potatoes, the bark of trees, grass - anything they could find ... And no matter what they did, they went on dying, dying, dying. They died singly and in families. They died everywhere –in the yards, on streetcars, and on trains. There was no one to bury these victims of the Stalinist famine.

—Fedor Belov, former chairman of a Soviet farm collective and author of *The History of a Soviet Collective Farm*

29
VERONIKA

February 1932

On the way home from school, Veronika saw a woman on her hands and knees, sifting through rotted leaves.

"I wonder what she's searching for," Veronika said.

Marek said, "Acorns."

"They're poisonous. Let's tell her."

Alina tugged on her arm. "Don't go near that woman; maybe she's not in her right mind."

"But she might die."

"Go if you want to," Marek said. "I'm taking Alina and Kazia home."

Veronika watched her friends leave, then moved toward the woman. Veronika wondered if it was a mistake to go near her, but the woman had already seen her approach and looked on with an expectant half-smile. She wore a long winter coat, and work boots to her knees. She was so thin, Veronika could see the outline of her jawbone. The gentle look in the woman's eyes reassured Veronika that it was safe to come closer.

"Hello, Auntie. You collect acorns?"

"Yes."

"My mama says they have poison in them."

The woman smiled. "Thank you, child. I soak them first, then boil them. It's all right then. What is your name?"

"Veronika."

"That is a beautiful name. I am Emiliya."

"Are you alone?"

"I'm with my husband. He's trying to see what he can find for us to eat."

"I live down the road on a farm," Veronika said.

"A farm is good. We used to live on a farm until we offered it to the collective."

Puzzled, Veronika asked, "You offered it? Why?"

Emiliya gave her a tired smile. "We thought we'd have a better life if we lived in barracks on the collective. My husband would no longer have to work by himself. I'd no longer have to cook or clean or even do laundry. We'd all live as one, having all our meals and needs taken care of. But we were wrong."

"Why wrong?"

"The collective has very little to make meals with. Everyone goes hungry."

Veronika's heart went out to her, and she thought of the leftover potato pancakes and dried apple rings in her lunch pail. She took off the lid and asked, "Would you like these?"

Emiliya put her hands to her face. "Yes, please. Anything."

In seconds, the pancakes were gone.

"Thank you, Veronika," Emiliya said, putting her hand on Veronika's shoulder. "The dried apple I will save for my husband."

Veronika felt good inside that she had helped her, and wished she could have done more.

"Mama," Veronika said when she got home. "I met a woman that lives on the collective. She was on her knees, looking for acorns to eat. I shared my leftover lunch with her."

Mama frowned. "Don't say anything at school about her. They will think it is a criticism of Stalin, but people who live on the collective have it very bad right now. Just not enough food."

"Will it happen to us?"

"No, my dear. Think of how many barrels of food we have in our root cellar and all the dried fruit in the loft. The collective doesn't have root cellars or dried fruit. That's the difference."

"Do you think Stalin knows people are starving?"

"Come here. Sit down beside me."

Veronika walked over to the bench. Her mother's face looked tired, her eyes troubled. Veronika's stomach tightened. Perhaps Mama was upset with her. Mama put her arm around Veronika's back and drew her close.

"You really need to understand how dangerous it is for us to talk about Stalin or people going hungry. Let's say you tell a friend, like Kazia, what you saw, and that friend tells someone else, and then they tell their parents. Maybe those parents will report you for talking against Stalin. All of us could be arrested."

Veronika's chest tightened. "But maybe Stalin doesn't know people are starving."

"He does know, Veronika. And he doesn't care."

— ❋ —

A month later, movement in the garden caught Veronika's eye. There in the garden stood a man in a grey coat. With a stick, he turned over clumps of soil in their potato patch. He picked out an old potato, left in the ground from winter, brushed it off and dropped it into his sack.

Veronika slowly walked up to him. "Why do you pick those up? They are rotten by now."

"Please? A little bread?" His toothless mouth puckered in and out as he spoke.

Veronika looked him over. His coat was creased and caked with dirt and was so worn that in some places it hung in shreds. A rope held up his pants.

"Bread?" he asked again, wiping away a stream of mucus that leaked from his nose with the back of his hand.

"I'll get my mother." She turned and fled to the house. Her mother looked startled when she burst in.

"Mama! A man is digging in our potato patch."

Mama's eyes opened wide. "From the collective?"

"No, an old man, all by himself. He asked for bread. He looks poor."

Moaning under her breath, Mama grabbed her shawl from the hook and went outside. Her face moved with pity when she saw him. "I cannot give you bread. I do not have enough even for us."

He looked downcast and turned to go.

"But I have soup. Please, sit down over there," she said, motioning to the stone bench outside their door.

Inside the house, Veronika stood in the safety of the doorway and observed him. Why was he out here all alone? Where was his family?

He fumbled around in his coat pocket for a while then pulled out a crumpled rag. He blew his nose. Veronika felt relived. She had been watching a blob of mucus dangle and bob back and forth, unnoticed.

"Thank you, daughter," he said when Mama brought him the bowl.

In some ways, Veronika felt frightened, because the way his lips got sucked right in and his cheeks puckered as he chewed on bits of potato and carrot in the soup looked grotesque.

"You come from around here?" Mama asked.

He shook his head. "South. Vinnytsia province." Bits of food flew from his mouth as he spoke.

"How is it over there?" asked Mama.

He shook his head. "There is no food. People are dying."

"Do you have any grandchildren?" asked Veronika.

"Veronika," scolded Mama. "You know better than to be a part of our conversation. Go inside and get him some dried plums."

Reluctantly, Veronika went in. She heard her mother tell him that he should soak the plums so they would be easier to eat. When Veronika came back out, she kept small and quiet so she wouldn't be sent away.

"I came here, thinking maybe things are better."

Veronika saw tears in her mother's eyes. The old man looked at her mother, then took out his rag and blew his nose once again and wiped the tears from his eyes.

After a few moments, he continued. "Mothers want to keep something for the children. But the soldiers don't care nothing for children. They took everything from our gardens."

Mama seemed to crumble into herself, weeping into her hands. "O mój Boże, I'm so afraid it might happen here."

Veronika's stomach clenched.

The old man took Mama's hand between his. "Don't cry, daughter.

Maybe it won't be so bad here. This region mostly grows sugar beets. It is the people in the wheat-growing regions to the south and east that are being punished."

"Here they take all our grain, too." Mama said, wiping her eyes. "Who knows what they will take next."

When he finished his soup, the old man stood up and took both of Mama's hands in his and blessed her.

"Thank you, Grandfather," Mama replied. "May the Lord go with you."

Later, Veronika overheard her parents say that he had died. He had shuffled around the village for days, knocking on doors, asking for bread. Sometimes he got something, sometimes he didn't. They found him in one of the collective shacks, the one that was used for storing tractor parts.

The decree required that the peasants of the Ukraine, the Don and the Kuban be put to death by starvation, put to death along with their little children.
—Vasily Grossman, Soviet writer and journalist

30
JANEK

August 1932

Janek stood at the side of his vegetable garden and surveyed the growth of his grain, hidden by the rows of corn. A feeling of pleasure went through him. Tall and thick, the heavy heads of grain nodded in the breeze. It would be a good crop—funny to think of these twelve rows as a crop, especially since the collective's grain fields were puny at best, and only about two-thirds of the land sown.

Any fool could predict that would happen with no seeds to sow, and those living on the collective too weak to work. At least Zykov had made an appeal to Moscow for a loan of seed, but by the time it arrived, the early weeks of the season were lost.

"Checking out your grain, Janek?"

Startled, he turned to see his brothers-in-law, Vladzio and Feliks, walking toward him. "You shouldn't sneak up on a man in times like this."

"We didn't sneak up," Vladzio said, putting his hand on Janek's shoulder. "You were dreaming of bread already."

Janek smiled, his heart warmed by his friend, the rock of the family, always ready to play a tune on his harmonica or lend a hand. Ever since Agnes's broken hip had left her unable to work, most of the chores had fallen to him, yet he never complained.

"It's been good weather for grain," Janek said. "Too bad the collective won't get a decent crop."

Feliks's eyes narrowed. "There will be no grain given out this year, and already it's desperate."

Vladzio nudged Feliks. "Tell Janek about your dog."

Feliks frowned. "Just before dawn this morning, I hear Paulina's dog barking. I go outside and see man with a knife. Sure as anything, he would have killed the dog if I hadn't got there in time. You know how Paulina loves that dog. She would have been heartbroken."

"Feliks recognized the man, too," Vladzio said.

"I recognized him all right. Won't do anything, though. He's from the village. Has six or seven children, all starving. I'd do the same if it were my family."

"I shudder to think of what will happen over the next few months," Vladzio said. "Right now, people can live on roots and wild leaves and fish from the river. What's going to happen in the winter, when everything is frozen over?"

"Just makes me sick to think of it," Feliks said under his breath. "But we better get to the meeting. Won't look good to walk in late."

"Is Helena coming?" Vladzio asked.

"No, she needs to stay and guard the garden. When the apples ripen, I'll really have to watch. That and potatoes is what kept us going most of the winter. I'll let Helena know I'm leaving, and we can be off."

— ✳ —

After the meeting, Janek sat on a rock by the edge of the river and watched the reflection of the sunset on the surface of its swirling water. He could hear Veronika laugh and shriek with her friends as they played in their front yard. The rhythmic motion and sounds of the river were calming, hypnotic almost, taking the edge off the raw, serrating pain that pushed up from deep inside with each breath he took, as the enormity of the meeting's announcements hit him again and again.

The collective's quota for this year's grain would be impossible to meet, unless they took the grain grown in family gardens. Harvesting of grain from family gardens was now forbidden under penalty of being shot. Watchtowers would be erected around the collective's grain fields. Guards would shoot to kill. Gleaning after harvest was also forbidden. Potatoes were under quota as well. Quotas must be paid, or the family's home and possessions would be auctioned off.

Janek rested his head in his hands. Already people were starving. With these new quotas, starvation would be beyond anything Janek could imagine, worse than when they lost Vladimir in the last famine. Through his exhaustion and grief, images that he normally suppressed fought their way to the surface: Vladimir's face, his wispy brown hair, his eyes, how he used to run into his arms, all smiles.

As the images faded, excruciating pain filled Janek's chest as he remembered the grief he had felt as they'd lowered Vladimir's body into the grave, unable to comprehend that he would never see his son again. And now there was another child, Veronika. Vladimir's face faded and he saw her mischievous face, full of life and quick thinking. He wouldn't be able to protect her any more than he could protect Vladimir. If he didn't hide grain and potatoes, Veronika could die. If he did, and they were caught, she might also die. Tears moistened the edges of his eyes. He wiped them away but could not keep up.

After a while, his grief spent, he opened his eyes and gazed at the hills across from the river. The setting sun seemed to be fighting the darkness that consumed its golden orb. Brilliant beams reached out from behind the darkened hills, clawing at the sky. Unbidden, words of comfort wove through Janek's heart, and loosened the bands of despair that compressed his chest.

I will lift up mine eyes unto the hills, from whence cometh my help. My help cometh from the Lord, which made heaven and earth.

Please God, help me, he prayed. *Help me find a place to hide my grain and potatoes where they will not look.*

He heard the crunch of footsteps on the gravel behind him. He turned and saw Helena and Veronika approach.

"Janek, what are you doing here? We worried for where you were."

"I was thinking about the meeting."

"What happened?"

"We will go in the house and talk."

When they got inside, Janek sat down at the table beside Helena and Veronika.

"Maybe we should talk after Veronika goes to bed," Helena said.

"Mama, I'm nine. I'm not too young to hear."

Janek looked at Veronika's innocent and trusting face as she searched Helena's eyes and then his. With a heavy heart, he said, "This time she needs to hear what I have to say. There is a new law. It says all fields, especially grain fields, belong to the state."

"They do now, Tata."

"That's right, but now they are saying no one is allowed to go in them, not even to pick the grain that's fallen after harvest. Anyone who goes in will be shot."

Veronika's eyes grew wide. "Even me?"

"Children will be whipped and let go, but their parents will either be shot or given ten years in Siberia."

"Matko Boska, Janek," Mama sobbed. "What has this world come to?"

"And there is something else I must tell you. We are going to hide our grain and potatoes, and Veronika needs to help by keeping it a secret."

Veronika's bottom lip began to tremble. "But they will come and search again. Just give them what they want."

"We can't. They want our grain, all of it, and our potatoes."

"What? We can't keep what we grow in our garden?" Helena asked.

"That's what Zykov said."

Veronika started to cry. "We can eat carrots, Tata, and beets."

"You need to listen to what I'm trying to tell you. People are so desperate for food, even dogs and cats are disappearing. Aunt Paulina keeps her dog tied up all the time now."

"Kotka? Is that what happened to Kotka?" she asked, tears running down her cheeks.

Janek felt miserable. He looked at Helena.

"Well, we don't know," Helena said soothingly. "Sometimes cats just go away for a while, then they come back, don't they?"

"She's been gone for a long time now."

"Here, Veronika." Helena handed her a handkerchief from her apron pocket.

Veronika blew her nose. "Do you think maybe she has gone away to have kittens?"

"Maybe," Helena said. "Maybe that's where she is."

Janek knew what Helena was thinking. He had found the cat's entrails and head behind the barn and had buried the remains deep in the garden.

"We will still have vegetables and fruit to eat, Tata."

Janek didn't answer.

"And walnuts and sunflower seeds. We can eat that, can't we?"

"We can live on the fruits and vegetables for a while, but we don't have enough nuts and seeds to keep us strong and healthy. We must keep back some grain and potatoes. And you must keep it a secret."

Janek took in Veronika's face, her little red nose and hollow, frightened eyes. How he wished he could give her a better life. As he gathered her in his arms and she put her head on his chest, he felt an outpouring of love for her. He closed his eyes and felt wetness form around his eyelashes.

"I'm scared, Tata," she said after a while. "What if I tell by accident?"

"Veronika, if they find what we hide or not, it's in God's hands, not yours."

Veronika lifted her head up from his neck. He saw a flicker of hope in her eyes.

"In God's hands?" she asked.

"In God's hands," he repeated. "Not yours."

"Will soldiers come and search?"

"I'm sorry, my little one, but probably they will."

Veronika leaned back against him and cried.

> ... teams (of Stalinist Shock brigades) operating in villages all across Ukraine began to search not just for grain but for anything and everything edible. They were specifically equipped to do so with special tools, long metal rods, sometimes topped by hooks, that could be used to prod any surface in search of grain.
>
> —Anne Applebaum, *Red Famine: Stalin's War on Ukraine*

31
VERONIKA

September 1932

They flailed the grain with a sense of urgency, between the house and the barn where no one could see. Veronika spread the grain-laden stalks of buckwheat on the ground for her father to flail while her mother separated the chaff from the grain. The hot and dusty work made Veronika's blouse stick to her body and the stalks cut her fingers in a dozen places. She longed to dip her head in the cool waters of the river but knew the importance of the work.

Watchful of the flail, she stood clear as Tata swung it again and again, the metal bar breaking the grain loose from the stalks. At the end of the staff dangled a short length of chain and attached to the chain, a metal bar.

After a couple of hours, Tata called for a break. Veronika sat on an upended bucket and blew on the tingling cuts on her fingers, while she waited for Mama to pass the jug of water.

"It looks like we will get four sacks," Tata said.

"Will it be enough?" Veronika asked.

"If we could keep it all, but I think we should leave out two sacks of buckwheat and maybe four of potatoes."

"Oh, Janek. So much you are letting them take?"

"If we don't give them enough, they'll search harder. Maybe they'll find it all."

"Such a life we have," Mama said. "It makes me sick."

Veronika's chest contracted. "Are we going to be all right?"

"Yes, we will. It's just that your father and I get angry sometimes. Let's talk about school. What do you like about it?"

Veronika smiled. "Walking to school with Marek."

"Marek?" Tata asked. "I thought it was Kazia and Alina that you liked to walk with."

"Well, them, too," she said, feeling warmth rise in her cheeks. "I'm going to go pick an apple."

"Looks like Veronika doesn't want to talk about it anymore," Mama said with a laugh.

When Veronika returned with the apple, Mama said, "Tomorrow is farmer's market. You'll need to get up early to help me."

Veronika knew better than to argue. "Yes, Mama," she said.

She didn't like going to the market anymore. She didn't want to see the tired, sad people, with sunken faces and swollen bellies. The ones that staggered, their hands out, were the ones that hurt Veronika the most when she and her mother walked by. Some older boys were wild looking, with filthy hair and dirty feet. They would try to snatch food from the vendors. Those ones scared her.

Veronika spread another bundle of buckwheat onto the ground and continued thinking about the market. All afternoon Mama would sit and hope for a few coins. Perhaps Mama would let her go play in the park for a while.

— ✹ —

The next morning, as Veronika walked beside her mother, pushing their wheelbarrow through the streets of Kuzmin, she saw a group of ragged little children—about four or five years old—move toward them.

"Don't look at them, Veronika. That only encourages them."

"Where are their parents?"

"Likely they don't have any. Maybe they were left here."

"Why?"

"So they have a chance to live. At their home, maybe there is nothing to eat. Maybe someone will come along and adopt them."

"Can we take one in?"

"Enough, Veronika."

Veronika tried to keep her eyes straight ahead. She didn't want to see their tattered clothes, their drawn faces, their swollen legs, but when they walked by a woman lying on the ground with a girl sitting beside her, Veronika couldn't help but look. The girl got up and approached Veronika with her grimy hands outstretched.

"Please, for my mother?" She grabbed the handle of the wheelbarrow and yanked on it.

"Let go," Mama said, as she wrenched her hand away. "I didn't come here just to have everything spill on the ground."

"Mama, couldn't we give her just an apple?"

"No, Veronika. Look how many there are around us. If I stop and give to one, everyone will want one."

"I feel so sorry for that girl."

"If she comes to us later, I can give her a few, but not here in the open."

When they got to the market, Veronika helped her mother spread the mat at her usual spot beside her friend who sold fried hemp seeds.

"Hello, Helena," said Mama's friend.

"Good afternoon, Lilka."

"That one beside you hoped you would not come today."

Veronika glanced over at the woman who had a stall next to Mama's. She also sold apples and plums. Mama would always mutter about her at home, how the woman would squawk if Mama's mat seemed too close to her stall or if more customers were buying from Mama than from her. She accused Mama of lowering prices or overfilling purchases just to steal customers away from her. That made Mama angry.

"How much has she sold?" asked Mama.

"Not so much. Mostly they are buying the pumpkins she brought in."

"Pumpkins?" Mama groaned. "I should have thought to bring some in."

Veronika watched as her mother laid the fruit out invitingly on the mat. Out of the corner of her eye, Veronika saw a boy of about seven, stealthily move toward the stand of the woman Mama didn't like, his eyes fixed on her pyramid of apples. Veronika was about to shout out a warning when he moved in, grabbed an apple and dashed past, dodging and ducking around people.

The woman shouted, "Stop! Thief!"

A man caught the boy by the shoulder. People gathered around as the woman punched and slapped him. He curled up in a ball, crying.

"Leave him alone!" Mama yelled. "He's just a little child."

The woman paused. The boy darted up and ran, leaving the apple behind.

The woman picked up the apple and glared at Mama. "Those boys are like vermin. They should all be rounded up."

Mama glared back at her and said, "That child was just trying to survive. May *Jezuz Chrystus* remember what you did."

When they got home from the market, Tata sat at the table, his face ashen.

"What is it, Janek?" Mama asked.

"You just missed them. They were here. Soldiers and some of those shock workers."

"What did they take?"

"They took the two sacks of grain and the potatoes we left out for them. They didn't find the potatoes I buried in the orchard."

"How about the grain?" Mama said, rising panic in her voice.

"No, but so close they came. When they were poking in the hay with their pole, I thought for sure they would find it."

Veronika knew the pole, the long wooden one with the metal spear on the tip.

"I don't know how they missed it," continued Tata, holding his head. He looked at Mama and then looked away.

"What is it, Janek? There's something you're not telling me."

"They took the flour out of the kitchen. And your wheat grinder. They said you had no need of it."

She walked heavily over to the table and sat beside Tata. Her lips pinched, Mama tried to hold back her tears.

Veronika walked through the house from room to room looking for more damage. In her parents' room the chest lay open. All of Mama's linens, pillowcases, and embroidered tablecloths were gone.

"Mama, your chest is near empty."

Mama groaned.

Tata looked sad. "They were angry that they didn't find more buckwheat, so they took from your chest."

"Maybe we should give up the farm, move to the city. You could get a job in a factory or the mines, maybe."

"It is illegal to move. A new law."

"If they're desperate enough for workers, maybe you can get on without being registered."

"And where would you and Veronika be if I were caught?"

Veronika felt tears well up in her eyes. She tried to be brave, but Tata must have seen her lip quiver. He motioned for her to come and sit on the bench beside him.

"You don't have to worry. Better we stay here." He patted Mama's hand and said, "Maybe in the spring I can go with my brother and sell knives for a couple of weeks. Make a bit of money and buy grain on the black market."

Mama nodded. "I guess you're right. At least here there will always be something to eat. In other places, who knows?"

Even those already swollen from malnutrition were not allowed to keep their grain. In fact, if a person did not appear starving, he was suspected of hoarding food.

—Orest Subtelny, *Ukraine: A History*

32
JANEK

November 1932

All day Janek worked in the collective's barn. He got home as the sun was setting, almost too tired to eat the plate of fried potatoes Helena put in front of him. After Veronika went to bed, he sat and massaged his temples, all the sadness of the day rushing through him as if he were a hollow reed.

"What is it, Janek?" Helena asked, her eyebrows drawing together.

"Dobroc finally died."

"What?" She dropped her mending and sat beside him. "Oh, that's a shame, Janek. You kept that horse so nice."

"They just weren't feeding him," he said, staring at his hands. "Probably half of the collective's horses have died."

"That many?" she said, blinking.

"Zykov is such a fool. Says we don't need horses, we have tractors now, but all the time they break down and we can't get parts."

"It's like everything else around here, Janek.

— ✻ —

Janek hunched his shoulders against the sting of the blowing rain against his face, as he closed the gate to his yard and turned toward Feliks's home. A woman walked toward him, a black shawl wrapped about her. Janek wondered why she didn't wear a coat on such a day. Could she be a neighbour in need of something? He waited by the gate.

"Jan, is that you?" she asked. She paused in front of him, her eyes haunted.

"Yes, I'm Jan," he answered, still uncertain who she was.

"I'm Alyona Pawlowska," she said. "You brought us a hoe and dresses for my girls after we were thrown from our home."

"Alyona!" Janek said, not believing the change in her appearance. Her face was elongated and skull-like, with sunken sags of skin where her cheeks used to be. "What are you doing out this way?"

"I was at my uncle's. Hoped he'd have something for me to eat, but he has barely enough for his own family."

"Now where do you go?"

"To the collective," she said, staring down the road.

"But you're not allowed there."

She nodded. "There's an old woman who works in the kitchen. Carrying wood hurts her back so I do it for her. Some days she puts a bowl of food scraps under the steps for me."

"Come into my house," he said, reaching out and touching her on the arm. "Helena and I can fix you up with some dried fruit."

She closed her eyes then opened them, her eyes glistening. "Thank you," she whispered. "Once again, I'm grateful to you."

As he opened the door to his home, Helena called out from the bedroom, "That you, Janek?"

"Yes, and I brought someone with me." Turning to Alyona he said, "Come in out of the rain. I'll take your shawl."

Helena came into the kitchen, a puzzled look on her face.

"You remember Alyona, don't you?"

"Yes, of course I do," she said, her voice halting. "Please, sit down, Alyona. I'll get some tea."

Janek took her shawl and felt an ache in his throat when he saw the round knobs of her spine protruding from her neck.

"I've never stopped thinking about you and your family," Helena said, bringing three mugs of tea to the table and sitting down.

"It's not been easy." Alyona said, staring into her mug of tea. "There are days of such pain," she said in a strangled voice, "I wish I had never been born."

Helena patted her on the hand. "Your husband, Petro, and the children? How are they?"

"They're gone. All gone."

A squeezing pain gripped Janek's chest. "Alyona," he said, his throat dry. "I'm so very sorry. Are you able to tell us what happened?"

She continued, her eyes a dull, empty stare. "We were hungry. That's when we had the children with us. Petro took our oldest son and went into the grain field and tore off a few heads of wheat. They were spotted by a guard. He struck them over and over with the butt of his rifle. Somehow, with broken ribs, my son managed to crawl home. Not Petro, though. He died in the field."

Alyona remained staring straight ahead, as if she were no longer with them. The only evidence of her emotions were the tears that ran unattended down her face. Helena moved beside Alyona and, pulling out her handkerchief, wiped Alyona's tears.

"And your children?" Helena asked gently,

"Oh, God, my children," she moaned, rocking back and forth with her eyes closed.

Helena grimaced. "It was wrong of me to ask," she soothed. "Please, forgive me."

After a few moments Alyona opened her eyes and said in a strained whisper, "I can talk. I want you to know." She took a moment to swallow, then after a deep, shuddering breath, went on. "With Petro, gone, I had no way to feed seven children. I took the four younger ones to a children's shelter. The three older ones, I don't know if they are alive or not. They went to Proskurov to beg. That was three months ago. Now all I can do is pray for my children."

How did this happen? An innocent family destroyed, and no one able to do anything. Maybe tomorrow it will be our turn to be thrown out with only the clothes on our backs. All the time, families were being thrown out, one from this road, two from another. All it took was for the search brigades to find grain hidden within a house or garden. How many times had they come to their house, slashing into walls and feather mattresses with their spiked poles. Seven, maybe eight times already?

Janek took out his handkerchief and wiped his tears, but still they kept coming, his body shaking as he wept.

Finally, when Alyona readied herself to leave, Helena filled a small cloth bag with dried apple rings, plums, and a few walnuts. The two women hugged.

"Do you have any plans?" Janek asked.

"When the weather gets warmer, I'll leave for Poland and someday, if God allows, I will return and try to find my children."

As the weeks went by, Janek wondered if she had made it through the winter or was buried in a mass grave along with others from the collective that had died of starvation.

*The whole atmosphere in the country from 1928 on was
one of increasing terror and hysteria ...*
—Robert Conquest, *Harvest of Sorrow: Soviet Collectivization and the Terror Famine*

33
VERONIKA

March 1933

Veronika sat at the table in Aunt Agnes's home, a bowl of cabbage and beet soup in front of her. Uncle Vladzio had to work late at the collective, along with Mama and Tata and almost everyone else who was still strong enough to work. She was glad she was only ten and not yet required to work at the collective, and that Aunt Agnes offered to take care of her until Mama and Tata came home.

She loved everything about her German aunt, from her soft hands to the love in her eyes when they were together.

She hoped Aunt Agnes would let her wear the very special garnet and silver necklace after dinner. It always made her feel like a princess when she wore it. When she had asked Aunt Agnes if it had once belonged to a real princess, she had smiled and said maybe it had.

Veronika was about to ask to wear the necklace when she heard Babcia yell, "*Cholera jasna*, damn it. It's lifting its leg on my onions."

Veronika ran to the door. "Babcia is chasing a dog through her garden!"

Aunt Agnes hobbled over and watched Babcia chase the dog through a newly planted row of peas.

"She's doing more damage to the garden than the dog is," Aunt Agnes said with a bemused smile.

"Get out of there, *ty głupi psie*, you stupid dog," Babcia hollered. "I'll kill you if I get my hands on you."

"If you stop chasing it, Antosia, it will go away," yelled Aunt Agnes.

"I'm going to make it pay."

The dog darted into a dense clump of cranberry bushes. Babcia dropped to her knees, crawled in, and yanked it out by its ear. The dog jerked free and lunged. Babcia stumbled backward. With a growl, he latched onto her hand, and shook it. Babcia's howls of pain sent chills down Veronika's back.

"Get," Aunt Agnes hollered, limping toward them, broom in her hand. Over and over, she hit the dog. It flinched but would not give up its grip.

A neighbour with a rifle ran toward them and smacked the dog with the butt of his rifle. The animal released its grip and loped off.

"*Mein Gott!*" Aunt Agnes yelled. A spurting stump was all that remained of Babcia's little finger.

Aunt Agnes took her apron off, then wrapped it around Babcia's gushing stump as she led her into the kitchen.

"*Ty durne wiedźma.* Why couldn't you have left that poor dog alone?"

The words shocked Veronika. She had just called Babcia *a stupid old witch.*

"How is she?" the neighbour asked, walking in.

Aunt Agnes looked at him wild-eyed. "Thank God you came, Jakiv. It took her finger right off."

"Keep it wrapped as tight as you can, but I don't know how much can be done. The dog has rabies."

"*Boże pomóż mi*, God help me," moaned Babcia, as blood flowed all over her hands and formed a pool on the hard-packed clay floor.

"Lots of men were out looking for it. That's why I came running when I heard all the yelling."

"Jakiv, please, go to the collective. Tell her sons they need to come. Have them bring a horse and cart."

"*Gott im Himmel*," Aunt Agnes muttered to herself, washing the blood off her hands.

"She always has to win, always has to be right, and now look where it got her."

She carried a bottle of spiritus to the counter and tipped a little into a glass, took a gulp and then another, before bringing it over to Babcia and holding it to her lips.

It seemed like forever before Uncle Vladzio and Uncle Feliks hurried in, their faces grave. Uncle Vladzio scooped his mother into his arms and placed her in the back of the cart. Uncle Feliks flicked the reins on the horse's back, and they took off at a smart trot down the road.

After they had left, Aunt Agnes sat down heavily, Veronika beside her. Aunt Agnes took out her handkerchief, blew her nose then wiped each eye.

"Such a day, we've had," she said, putting her arm around Veronika. "Are you all right? You look pale."

"I guess so," Veronika said, glancing at the blood-soaked soil by the counter. "It's scary, all the blood and that dog. Did Jakiv have to shoot it?"

"Oh, yes. That dog was out of his mind with rabies. Would have attacked another person, but let's not think of that. How about we go look through my jewellery box. Get our minds off everything."

"I think I just want to go home."

"You can't right now, my dear. No one will be home. Your Mama and Tata will be at the hospital with Babcia. Likely it won't be until after dinner that they come get you."

— ✳ —

A few hours later, when Veronika heard Mama and Tata at the door, she rushed to greet them.

"How is Antosia?" Aunt Agnes asked.

"They are sending her by train to the Proskurov regional hospital. She'll be there a few weeks getting rabies shots."

Veronika knew better than to say it out loud, but she pitied the nurses who had to take care of Babcia.

The most terrifying sights were the little children with skeleton limbs dangling from balloon-like abdomens. Starvation had wiped every trace of youth from their faces, turning them into tortured gargoyles, only in their eyes still lingered the reminder of childhood.

—Victor Kravchenko, Ukrainian-born Soviet defector, witness to the mass starvation

34
VERONIKA

Veronika watched as rain dripped against the kitchen window and gathered in wind-blown rivulets. She hoped that this time she wouldn't have to go with her mother when she went to visit Babcia in the hospital. Every Saturday, she and Mama walked the sixteen kilometres to the Gródek train station, then took a long train ride to Proskurov, a whole day of mingling with hordes of men, women, and children, all desperate for food. It was too sad to see.

As she traced the path of a rivulet with her finger against the cold glass of the window, she hoped this time they could go see Uncle Oryst and Aunt Ludka. At least she would have something to look forward to. Their home was close to the hospital. She came up to the counter and watched as her mother boiled cabbage, carrots, and beets for the evening meal.

"Do I have to go with you tomorrow to see Babcia? I could go over to Kazia's and play."

"You are with Kazia every day at school."

"Walking all the way to Gródek and back makes my feet hurt."

"A young girl like you shouldn't mind a three-hour walk to Gródek. Besides, it shows respect to Babcia."

"But she doesn't even say hello to me."

"She's in pain, Veronika," Mama said, sounding exasperated, "Which does nothing to improve her disposition. That is enough complaining from you."

"All right, I'll go, even though she won't even notice me."

Veronika lifted the lid of the steaming pot next to the vegetables and looked in. Two eggs rolled and bumped against each other as they boiled. They looked delicious. Ever since Mama had started to keep hens for the collective, they got to eat eggs sometimes. They only thing was, Mama had an egg quota. Sometimes the hens didn't lay regularly. If she came up short, she'd have to go from neighbour to neighbour, to try to buy or barter for eggs. She got a fine if she didn't. Veronika wondered if Mama would cut the eggs into three parts or if someone was not going to have one. She stared into the steamy pot. Her mouth watered just thinking of biting into one.

"Are we going to share those eggs?"

"They're for Babcia."

"Oh," she said. She swallowed her disappointment. Of course, they would be for Babcia. They didn't feed her well at the hospital. Mama always brought a basket of food to her.

After her father came in from outside, Veronika sat down at the table with her parents. When they had just about finished, they heard crying. Veronika froze and listened.

"Is that a cat?" asked Tata, going to the window.

Veronika bolted outside into the pelting rain. Maybe Kotka had come home.

"Veronika, your coat!" her mother yelled.

She kept going. The sound came from around the corner. Squinting through the wind and rain, she caught a movement. Getting closer, she saw a little boy of about seven crouched under the overhang of the back door, crying. He wore a ragged shirt and pants that came to his knees before they ended in shreds of fibre. Veronika stared at his bare feet and mud-splattered legs.

The boy got up and backed slowly out into the rain.

"What's the matter?" she asked. "Are you cold?"

The boy paused.

"Are you hungry?"

He looked at her. Veronika walked up to him and held out her hand. "Do you want to come in? My parents are nice." She reached for his hand. His fingers felt icy in her warm palm. He let her lead him into the house.

"Oh, my," Mama said. "He's soaked through and through. Janek, put him by the oven to warm up. I'll get him something to eat."

Veronika looked at the boy as he shivered, his chin pressed down to his chest, eyes averted. She couldn't see much of him except for the blond stubble of his hair, ears that seemed too big for his head, and thin, sloping shoulders. Mama came back with a bowl of the stewed vegetables. He ate it quickly, barely chewing before taking another bite.

Mama shook her head. "After we get those wet clothes off him, he can have a little more."

He lifted his head and looked at them. Veronika could see the outline of his skull and the sunken hollows where his cheeks should have been. He reminded her of Marek, with his blond hair and solemn eyes. Her heart went out to him. Now that he was in the light, he looked more like five years old than seven.

"How old are you?" Veronika asked.

He didn't answer.

"Let him be for now," Tata said.

"I wonder if he has a mother," Veronika said.

"Some woman took a lot of time and care making his shirt," Mama said. "Look at the fine stitching."

Veronika looked at his blue collarless shirt, fastened by buttons and loops off to the side.

"Janek, go get that old blanket from our room."

"Looks like someone else must have patched the shirt," Mama said as she unfastened the loops. A patch of grey fabric had been tacked to the front of his shirt in large, sloppy stitches, but the patch now hung in worn shreds as did the sleeves of his shirt.

When Veronika saw every bone of his rib cage and protruding hips, she felt sickened. How could he still be alive and look like that? From the look on Mama's face, she could see that she also felt very sorry for him.

When he had wrapped the blanket around his body, Tata carried him to the table and set him down in a chair. Mama brought over a bowl of soup. While he ate, Tata went out to the barn and got some straw and laid out a pallet in front of the oven. When the boy finished eating, Tata helped him to lie down. He fell asleep almost instantly.

"Can we keep him, Mama? I don't think he has a home."

"Well, I don't know, Veronika."

That night Veronika felt excited. Maybe she would have a little brother, but in the morning, when she dashed up to see him, he was gone.

"Where did he go, Mama?"

"I don't know. He was here when I got up in the night to check on him."

The eggs saved for Babcia were gone, too.

35

JANEK

April 1933

Janek walked between the rows of apple trees until he came to the place where he had buried potatoes in a straw-lined pit. Although the shock workers had searched his farm several times, they hadn't found the pit, perhaps because he had mounded tree limbs on top of it and set fire to the pile.

For months they had survived on potatoes from two other pits of buried potatoes, as well as grain slipped between the walls of their home. All of that was gone now. The last of their food lay here, beneath the charred limbs. Between that and what was left of the dried fruit, they'd get by.

As soon as Janek pulled back the straw layer, a musty odour of rot permeated the air. Fear constricted his chest. Frantically, he dug faster.

The potatoes were rotten. Some half-rotten, some entirely. He fell to his knees as the spectre of utter starvation hit him. Why had he been such a fool not to have checked the pit sooner? His family had counted on him and he had failed them. Unsteadily, he rose to his feet, then went into the house with a bucket of half-rotted potatoes. He set it down on the counter. "I thought we should use these up first."

Helena had a look. "Lots of rot on these ones. How are the rest?"

"They're all starting to rot. The dampness got to them."

"What will we do?"

"I'm going to the Torgsin store."

"Torgsin? What do we have that they would want?" she asked, raising her eyebrows in surprise.

"Ludka's gold," he answered thickly.

"Oh, Janek. How could we?"

"When they were here, Oryst said if things got bad, I should go see them."

"But that gold is for their old age."

"I don't know what else to do."

"We still have beets and some dried fruit."

"But is that enough to survive?"

Her troubled eyes searched his face.

"The only solution is to buy grain at Torgsin."

Janek closed his eyes and drew her to his chest. "We should let the family know I'm going."

— ✳ —

When they knocked on the door of the duplex, Vladzio and Agnes welcomed them in.

"Ask Feliks and Paulina to come over," Janek said. "What I have to say, they need to hear as well."

Vladzio's face darkened with concern. "I'll go get them."

Feliks and Paulina looked questioningly at Janek as they entered the room. Vladzio poured a round of drinks and after talk about the weather and crops, Janek asked, "How are you for food?"

"Not much left," Feliks said. "We get a few rubles from blacksmithing, but the stores are empty."

"We could always find something on the black market," Vladzio said, "if we dared."

"Or the Torgsin," Janek said quietly.

"Torgsin?" Agnes asked. "The state store? I thought only foreigners could shop there."

"It used to be that way," Janek said, "but now anyone can go. The only payment they accept is gold or silver."

"I guess they think it's better to have people turn over their wedding rings while they're alive, rather than dig up the ground looking for them after they're dead," Feliks said, his lip curling in contempt.

"No food for us," Vladzio said, "but they'll make an exception to fill the state's treasury. *Cholera jasna*, those Soviets. May they all ..."

"Vladzio," Agnes said.

He paused and then said, "What will you take to the Torgsin?"

"Gold."

"Gold?" Feliks said with a snort. "Have you been holding out on us, Janek?"

Janek took a deep breath. "Oryst and Ludka have put some gold coins aside for their old age." Choking a little on the words, he said, "Oryst gave me a few in case times got desperate."

He could feel his family's kindly eyes burn into him as he picked up his glass and took a sip.

"Well, there's no shame in taking help from relatives," Agnes said, patting him on the hand. "We all have to lean on each other sometime or other."

The shield Janek thought he had in place around his feelings crumpled with Agnes's sympathy. He felt grateful when Helena took over.

"With Oryst being Veronika's godfather and all, he'll want to see that she'll be all right when they go off to sell knives."

"Is it all right with Ludka that Oryst should give away her gold?" asked Paulina.

No one spoke for a moment, then Janek said quietly, "Ludka offered. She said her husband's family is her family."

"Well, I think she's a saint," Agnes said, with finality. "And Oryst is very lucky to have married such a kind woman."

After Agnes finished speaking, everyone grew quiet. Vladzio poured another round and then asked, "Would it be better to sell the gold on the black market? Maybe you'd get a better price."

"Maybe," Janek said. "But now that the Soviets have sealed the borders, I would have to sneak through the woods, but if I go to Torgsin, I'd get a permit to take the train."

"Still, it would be dangerous to go alone. You could get robbed," Paulina said. "Maybe Feliks will go with you."

Janek hoped Feliks would agree. He would be the perfect companion, quick with the tongue and the knife, if need be. Vladzio was too soft and mellow to fight anyone, even a thief.

"Sure, I'll go," Feliks said. "I wish I had something to trade."

"You have now." Paulina reached up to unclasp the gold crucifix around her neck.

"From our wedding day?" asked Feliks.

"It's better that we keep ourselves alive."

"And you can take my silver hairbrush, comb, and mirror set from Germany," Agnes said. "My parents gave it to me for my sixteenth birthday. It must be worth something."

> *But the state had foreseen ways to extract the peasant's family valuables in a more systematic fashion, and even in small neighbourhood towns or the larger villages he would find, and be able to use, the stores of Torgsin ('Trade with Foreigners'). These accepted in payment only foreign currency and precious metal or stones, and freely sold for them goods including food. Many peasants had the odd gold ornament or coins which would bring them a little bread ...*
>
> —Robert Conquest, *Harvest of Sorrow: Soviet Collectivization and the Terror Famine*

36
JANEK

The next day, Janek and Feliks stood in front of the Torgsin. It had no windows at all, just an opening on the side of a brick building with a soldier standing guard. Janek and Feliks joined the line of mostly older women in long coats and headscarves. While he waited, he saw emaciated men and women looking on longingly, among them a mother and three children sitting on the ground, their legs wrapped in rags. An empty pot and spoons sat on the ground in front of them. The mother's face, so contracted in starvation, sat as if death had already taken her. The older boy shared her gaunt feature. The younger ones still had some flesh to their cheeks, evidence that the mother and boy must have been sacrificing some of their portion to the younger ones.

"Don't even think of giving them something," Feliks said. "We'd be surrounded. Maybe lose everything."

Janek nodded, his heart saddened.

At the entrance, the guard asked to see what they had to sell. Satisfied, he let them in. For a few moments, Janek couldn't help but stop and stare at the curved glass counter before him filled with loaves of crusty bread and rolls. Clerks in white uniforms waited on customers, some obviously destitute, and others who were better off, likely factory workers.

Next to the bread aisle were multiple overflowing bins of potatoes, onions, garlic, beets, and carrots, and down the middle of the store, what looked like canned goods. At the far wall, rings of smoked sausage dangled from hooks.

A clerk glared at them. "Don't stand and gawk. What are you here for?"

"Grain."

"Over there," he said. "The assessing counter is past the smoked meats."

The savoury smell grew more pungent as they came to the counter of sausages and hams. Janek could not help salivating as he imagined snapping off a big piece of sausage and shoving it in his mouth.

"Let's get out of here before I jump over the counter and grab something," Feliks said.

After their coins and valuables were weighed and assessed, a steely-eyed clerk with thin lips said, "Here is your grain voucher. Take it to the warehouse."

Walking down an aisle of canned goods to get to the warehouse, Janek couldn't help but linger. Feliks picked up a can. The label had a picture of apples on it. "Apples? Why would someone can apples when they can be dried?"

Cans with a picture of a cow and a smiling baby made them wonder. Janek held a can to his ear and shook it. "Yes, it does sound like liquid. Do you think it's possible someone would actually can milk?"

"Not possible," Feliks said.

"Maybe foreign women don't know what their breasts are for."

Feliks guffawed. "Maybe that's what it is."

The next instant a clerk was upon them. "Come on, there is no reason for you two to be here. Get your grain and be on your way."

In the warehouse at the back of the store were sacks of grain, so many it took Janek's breath away, likely more than the entire harvest at Kuzmin. While they stood in line, Janek noticed a few of the sacks had grain spilling out of the bottom.

A burly-looking warehouse man took Janek's voucher.

"How much do I get?"

"Seven kilos of millet and two of white flour."

"Is that all? For seven gold coins?"

The man's face turned red. Poking a finger into Janek's chest, he said, "Then take back your coins. Chew on them until you die, you lousy kulak."

Helpless to do anything else, Feliks and Janek collected their flour and grain then left the store, only to be surrounded by men and women with pleading hands. The mother with the children also held out her hands.

"Please," she said, "For the love of Christ."

With a heavy heart, Janek shoved his way past them and strode toward home.

As starvation raged throughout Ukraine in the first weeks of 1933, Stalin sealed the borders of the republic so that peasants could not flee and closed the cities so that peasants could not beg ... Soviet citizens had to carry internal passports in order to reside in the cities legally. Peasants were not to receive them.
—Timothy Snyder, *Bloodlands: Europe Between Hitler and Stalin*

37
JANEK

April 1933

"You had plenty of notice to come and get me. I don't know why you didn't come sooner," Antosia said.

"Please, understand. It wasn't that we forgot about you. Janek had to go to Torgsin first, Mama," Helena said, a hint of exasperation in her voice.

Janek sat drinking chamomile tea with Helena and his in-laws. This was supposed to be a welcome home get-together for Antosia, but all she could do was complain. For Helena's sake, he tried to keep the irritation off his face.

"Here, Mama." Helena pushed a loaf of freshly baked "bread" toward her, the flour having been stretched with chaff. "You have the honour of cutting into it. It's the first we've had in weeks."

Janek hated the pleading tone in Helena's voice.

Antosia stood up and briskly made the sign of the cross over the loaf, before cutting into it with quick, rough thrusts, just to show everyone how angry she was. Janek glanced at Veronika and saw the fearful, bewildered look on her face. How dare this spiteful woman make everyone feel this way.

"Going to Proskurov isn't as easy as it used to be," Vladzio said. "Did you see any roadblocks, Janek?"

"Not roadblocks, but soldiers were at the train station, checking permits."

"Permits. Permits. What is all this talk about permits? I saw plenty of women leave my ward and nothing was said about needing a permit. Only I needed a permit," Antosia said.

"Probably those women were from the city. They are issued permits. People from the country have to apply each time they want to go somewhere," Feliks said.

"That's right, Mama," Vladzio said. "It's to stop people from the country going into the cities to beg."

"And do I look like a beggar?" Antosia asked. "Only thing I was begging for was someone to come and get me."

No one said anything. Janek chewed his bread slowly, trying to enjoy it. He wished he could be anywhere but here. He found himself smiling as a verse from the Bible came to his mind, something about it being better to eat in the corner of a rooftop than in a spacious house with a brawling woman.

"Seems like your husband doesn't have any thought about me," Antosia said. "He sits there and smiles."

"It's not that, Antosia. I'm thinking of another woman."

"Another woman? You're thinking of another woman? Your girlfriend, maybe?"

"Mother," Helena said. "How can you say such a thing with the children sitting right here?"

Janek watched as Feliks, who had just taken a swallow of his drink, exploded into a laughing-coughing fit. Vladzio, his eyes crinkling, and his shoulders shaking, pulled out a handkerchief to cover his laugher.

Antosia, catching the mirth going on around the table, grabbed a lock of her own hair and pulled. "Even my own sons don't care about me."

Helena leapt up and put her arm around her mother. "Calm down, Mother. Please. You're right. Maybe we should have come and got you sooner. Sit down," she said as she pushed her mother gently into her chair again. Antosia seemed mollified. Helena continued. "We just thought you would understand, with the children so hungry and all, that maybe it would be best to go to Torgsin first."

"Of course, I understand that the children were hungry. How could they not be when you didn't have the sense to hide more grain. If I were you, I would have found a dozen places to hide sacks of grain."

Everyone was quiet as Helena continued to rub her mother's back.

"Three extra days I had to wait for someone to come and get me. Do you know what that was like? I was hungry. They hardly even feed you there, and babies crying all the time."

No one spoke.

The silence was broken with Antosia saying bitterly, "Maybe no one even wanted me to come home."

"Of course, we wanted you home," Feliks said. "Even the children missed you."

The three children were silent.

Janek saw Helena give Veronika a nod.

"I missed you, Babcia," she piped up.

"Stasik? Julia?" Paulina asked. "You missed Babcia, didn't you?"

They nodded without much enthusiasm.

"Maybe I should just go and live with Helena and Janek." She pushed back her chair irritably and got up. "I'm going to my room."

Everyone sat in uncomfortable silence as she left the room and slammed her door. Stunned, Janek stared at Helena across the table, his eyes wide in silent supplication. Feliks, for some reason, seemed to find the situation amusing. His eyes gleamed in merriment. A faint smile pulled on the corners of his lips. He nudged Vladzio and said, "Maybe it's time for Janek and Helena to take a turn, don't you think? How long has she been here with us?"

"Oh, at least twenty years," Vladzio said, picking up on his brother's humour.

"You two stop it," Helena said, getting up. "Mama's feelings are hurt."

Calling through Antosia's closed door, Helena pleaded with her. "Mama, come back. We all love you. We missed you."

"When she gets like that, it's best to leave her be," Paulina called from the table.

Helena stood listening with her ear pressed against the door. "Mama? Are you all right? Mama?" Not getting an answer, she came back and sat down.

"She'll be fine in the morning," Paulina said. "And don't you worry. She'll never move away from her boys."

"Julia," Feliks said, "take Veronika to your room to play. I think our party with Babcia is over."

When the children left, Janek said, "All I can say is if I find that Antosia has moved into my home when I get back from selling knives, I'm moving into the barn."

Feliks and Vladzio erupted in laughter.

"Shh," Helena said. "Mother will hear."

Still holding his belly from laughter, Vladzio asked, "How did you get a travel permit?"

"I gave Zykov a few jugs of spiritus and a couple of my best knives and he put in a good word for me. He knows I'm not going to beg."

"Stay in this district," Feliks said. "Districts east of here have been hit hard by the famine."

Janek shrugged. "It can't be much worse than it is around here."

Starving villagers inundated train stations in the hope of traveling to areas with more food, but the trains were reserved for those with internal passports or to those who had documents identifying them as collective farmers on a work-related trip approved by the collective's board.

—Investigation of the Ukrainian Famine 1932–1933, Report to US Congress

38
JANEK

May 1933

As darkness overtook the sky, a feeling of pride went through Janek as he surveyed the thirty-five walnut-handled knives on the table before him. He held one in his hand, admiring the grain of the wood and the curve of the blade. When he got to Proskurov, Oryst would hone each blade to razor sharpness.

Janek wrapped a linen cloth around the knives, then tucked the bundle in his pack. As soon as Veronika finished her prayers with Helena, he would go in and say goodbye to her. He'd be long gone before she awoke in the morning.

"How is she?" he asked when Helena came out.

"She's worried, and I worry about you, too."

He looked up and saw the love that radiated from her troubled eyes. He put down the knife and took her in his arms, holding her close, breathing in the sweet scent of her body. He could feel her tremble beneath his arms. How was it that he sometimes forgot how much he loved her?

"I wish there was another way," she mumbled, her face pressed against him.

He pulled back and looked her in the eye. "I have to try, Helena."

"But it's so dangerous. All the time I have thoughts—what if you get killed or arrested? Or what if a brigade comes while you are away?"

"For everything, we have to trust God. I feel this is right that I go. I couldn't live with myself if I didn't at least try."

"I understand. Every evening I'll be by the window, praying."

Janek nodded. "And I'll come back. I promise you. Now I'll go see Veronika."

"Tata," Veronika said, when he opened the door.

As he bent over, she wrapped her slender arms around his neck.

"I don't want you to go."

"I have to. All those beautiful knives to sell." He felt her arms grip him harder. "You'll break my neck." He tickled her under the chin until she squirmed and lost her grip.

She looked at him reproachfully. "You made me let go."

He leaned over and kissed her forehead. "I'll be back before you know it. Sleep now, my little Noosha, and you be a good help to Mama while I'm gone. All right?"

His heart ached when he saw the forlorn look on her face and how the tip of her little nose had turned pink, a sure sign she was about to cry.

He walked out, not wanting to see her tears.

Early the next morning, Helena sat with him as he drank a cup of chamomile tea.

"You won't buy flour at the Proskurov black market, will you?" she asked, alarm in her voice.

"Too many roadblocks. I'll buy it closer to home, maybe Gródek, then cut through the fields."

Helena picked up a small sack and set it on the table. "It's not much, just a boiled potato and some dried plums.

"That will be enough. Oryst and I will work for our keep. Maybe sharpen knives for a bowl of soup and a place to sleep." He drained his cup and got up.

"So soon you go?"

"I want to be gone before Veronika wakes up and makes a fuss. Tell her Uncle Oryst will make me laugh all the way to Zhytomyr."

At the door, he put his arms around her waist and held her close, lingering in the feeling of her body pressed against his. He pulled back to kiss her and saw tears form once again in her eyes.

"Don't cry," he said, stroking a tear away with his thumb. "It's hard enough to leave you."

"Then stay."

"You know I can't," he whispered. He gave her one last kiss, picked up his pack and walked through the door. When he got to the gate, he turned and waved to where she stood in the doorway. He told himself he wasn't going to look back again, but could feel her eyes on his back, watching him walk away. After a while, he broke his resolve, but she had given up and gone inside. He was sad that he hadn't looked sooner.

Three hours later, he approached the Gródek train station to purchase his ticket. He felt his stomach clench. People were lined up to show their travel permits and have their bags searched. Off to the side, two secret police officers talked to a pale, trembling man. They had him pull everything out of his pack. Janek went to the end of the line and fingered his travel permit.

When he got to the front of the line, the officer had a cursory look at his permit then motioned him to the table to have his bundle inspected. They glanced through and, seeing that he carried no bread or grain, allowed him to board.

He walked down the aisle, wondering where he should sit. Very few seats were left. He saw an empty bench opposite a mother and her three children. In vain she tried to hush the toddler that squirmed and wailed in her arms. The mother looked apologetic when Janek sat opposite her.

"Sick?" Janek asked.

The mother shook her head. "Teething."

A man approached their bench, looked at the wailing child and moved on. Janek smirked. Maybe he would have the whole bench to himself. A woman wearing a tilt hat with a half-veil walked sideways down the aisle; even so, her protruding stomach rubbed against people's shoulders. By the look of the silky fabric of her dress and the almost regal way she held her head, Janek knew she had to be the wife of a Soviet official and sensed that she would be his seatmate. He groaned inwardly.

When she got to him, her eyes flicked from the children then to the empty spot next to Janek. With a sigh of resignation, she sat down heavily beside him, and set her packages down between her feet. The child stopped fussing to study her. To Janek's surprise, the woman smiled and reached out to touch his hand. "Are you a sad little one?" she asked in Russian.

The child continued to stare, then turned his head back into his mother's chest and, rubbing his face back and forth in frustration, resumed crying.

"Mustn't be feeling well," she said in Janek's general direction.

Janek leaned against the window and closed his eyes. With no one to talk to, the woman sat for a moment then pulled out her knitting. Janek watched her through the closed slits of his eyes as she counted stitches.

His thoughts turned to Veronika, and he could see her smiling face saying, *"Highest marks in math again, Tata."* Maybe she took after him. If he had been given a chance to go to school like Oryst, maybe he would have achieved his dream of becoming a doctor. Who knows?

Flashes of his boyhood flitted through his mind—his father's death, having to quit school and go to work. *You're the oldest. I need your help*, his mother had said. His mother had insisted that at least one of her children learn to read. He begged that it be him, but she selected Oryst, her youngest.

Nine years old when his mother got him a job as a scullery boy. Every spot of charred grease he had to get off the pots or it was a boot to his rear. When he got home, he had to help his mother with the only job she could get, stripping the shafts of feathers to make down. The feathers stuck to his hands and got up his nose, while outside, he could hear the neighbour's children playing.

Janek was stirred out of his reminiscing by the insistent whine of the older child.

He pulled at his mother's arm. "Bread, Mama, bread."

"Stop," she said in a hushed voice, "It's too soon to have more."

"You always say that."

With a sigh, the mother shifted the baby in her arms and reached for her bundle. Janek, seeing her struggle, reached down and got it for her.

"Thank you," she said. She pulled out something that resembled bread, likely made with powdered leaves or sawdust, and broke off a piece for each of the older two.

The Soviet woman groped in her bag and pulled out a loaf of ration-issued brown bread. She broke off a large crusty chunk and offered a piece to each of the children.

"Thank you," the mother said, her voice breaking.

The Soviet woman smiled. "Children must eat."

Janek closed his eyes, ashamed of how he had misjudged her.

An hour later, as they approached the city of Proskurov, he craned his head as they passed a hog feedlot. So many hogs, it took his breath away, their sides rippling in fat, snouts plunged into troughs. He felt his stomach churn in anger. What kind of vile government would have grain for its pigs, yet none for its people?

Pulling into the city, Janek gasped at the sight of the walking skeletons who lined the tracks. Arms outstretched, men and women pleaded for help, while some held children with wizened faces aloft. How he longed to gather the children into his arms and save them from death, but with what? A single potato and a few dried plums? The few kopeks in his pocket? A crushing pain pressed on his chest; he could do nothing. He would get off the train, turn his back on them, and walk away. And they would die.

Janek waited for a moment before walking down the crowded steps of the train. Below him on the platform, militiamen with strong bodies and crisp uniforms walked among the emaciated people along the tracks. A rage burned within him. Had they no feelings? How could they take part in the slaughter of villagers?

Shaken, Janek swung his pack over his shoulder and walked toward Oryst's home. A woman caught his attention, perhaps because she reminded him of Helena, with the same deep-set eyes and high cheekbones. She wore a black headscarf tied at the back, and sat on the ground, her legs swollen to the point where they looked like they were about to burst. A blonde girl sat close by; a dirty, sleeveless sack covered her torso. Janek longed to stop, to kneel down and help them. Instead, he walked by, his chest aching.

On the city sidewalk, a woman in a white headscarf and long coat lay sprawled half on the sidewalk and half on the street. She appeared young, maybe in her twenties. A few city people had gathered around her, to see if she was alive; others barely gave her a glance as they walked by. Janek stepped around her as well, despising himself for doing so.

What kind of human am I? Already like the militiamen?

Ahead he saw a girl of about eight years, wearing a brightly flowered headscarf that contradicted how gaunt her face was. Her dirty legs and feet were bare and covered in sores. She bent over to pick through the charred remains of a fire, putting morsels in her mouth to taste. Some she swallowed, others she spat out.

As Janek watched her, he thought of Veronika. This child was also someone's beloved daughter. Perhaps her parents were dead. He took the potato out of his sack and broke a piece off. "Here, child."

Ferret-like, she snatched it in her charcoal-covered fingers and shoved it in her mouth.

"*Zhdat!* Wait!" yelled a stern-faced militiaman from across the street. The girl pushed through a hole in the fence and ran.

Janek swayed in fear as the soldier approached, his young face both sullen and arrogant.

"You fed that kulak bastard?"

"Yes, but just a little."

"It's forbidden to feed them. Signs are posted everywhere."

"I didn't know." Janek took off his cap and bent his head.

"The dying need to die. If you give them something, it only prolongs the inevitable. Now get out of here before I charge you with anti-Soviet behaviour."

Janek hurried to Oryst and Ludka's home.

"Good to see you, my brother," Oryst said, slapping him on the back.

"And you, too."

"There you are," Ludka said, coming out of the kitchen. "I made dinner for you. Are you hungry?"

"Thank you, Ludka. I am," he said, giving her a hug.

Ludka gave him a toothless smile. "Come, wash your hands and then you can sit down and eat."

Janek followed her to the kitchen where she poured a basin of water and gave him a towel. After he sat down at the table beside Oryst, Ludka brought over a bowl of boiled potatoes and steamed greens.

"Smells wonderful, thank you. In the village there is so little to eat, with the Soviets taking the grain and then the potatoes."

"It's hard here, too," Ludka said. "Oryst paid a lot for these few potatoes at the market, and the greens are nettles I managed to find. With all the starving villagers here in the city, they seem to find them before I can."

"Why is it that Stalin lets the city people live, yet people from the villages must die?"

"People from the villages are against Stalin's plans to collectivize. He thinks they are planning a revolution against communism. Better that they die."

Janek's head swirled. "Better that they die?" he repeated.

Oryst nodded. "That's the sad truth. If the villagers die, they can be replaced with loyal Russian communists. The city workers in the factories, on the other hand, cooperate and are the jewels of Stalin's five-year plan to modernize the Soviet Union. For this, workers must be kept alive, and so they are issued food ration cards."

"Yet it's not so easy here in the city, either," said Ludka. "Not all who live in the city qualify for a ration card. You have to be a registered government or factory worker. And even if you do get a card, you still have to have money to buy anything."

"So, even here people starve?" Janek asked.

"Oh, yes," said Ludka. "Oryst being a knife sharpener doesn't qualify for a ration card, so we can't buy a loaf of good bread, or sugar, or oil, or anything, even though we have a little gold put away."

"You could go to the Torgsin," Janek said softly.

"Yes, the Torgsin, but then the gold is gone and what will we to do in our old age?" asked Ludka.

Oryst's lip curled in a sneer. "We are allowed to buy a bread of sorts. They call it Postyshev bread, but no one knows what shit they put in it."

Janek nodded. "A mother on the train had one of those loaves. Looked like sawdust bread."

"Probably it was," Ludka said. "All the same, you are only allowed to buy one loaf a day. All day people have to stand in line for it and, sometimes, just when they get close to the door, they run out. After a few days of bad luck, they become weak and can't stand in line any longer."

Janek rubbed his head. "Not what I thought living in the city was like. How long are we going to be here?"

"Just a few days, then if we haven't sold all the knives, head north."

"How far north?"

Oryst shrugged. "Don't worry about the train fare. We'll jump on a boxcar when no one is looking and hop off as the train is coming to a stop."

"They don't beat you for doing that?"

"Only the slow ones."

Physical elimination, straightforward killing, was indeed also a possibility. When the problem became too great for local officials bezprizornie (street children) are reported shot in large numbers.

—Robert Conquest, *Harvest of Sorrow: Soviet Collectivization and the Terror-Famine*

39

JANEK

The clatter of dishes in the kitchen woke Janek with a start. For a moment he was unsure of where he was and then realized that he was in his brother's home. He pulled on his shirt and trousers and ran his fingers through his hair. When he stepped into the kitchen, Oryst smiled.

"Good morning, sleepyhead."

Janek felt heat rise to his cheeks. On the farm, manhood and being an early riser were inexorably linked, and Oryst knew it.

"Pull up a chair. I'll get you some soup."

"Ludka not up yet?"

"She is in line for bread."

"When did she leave?"

"Around four this morning," he said, carrying over a steaming bowl. "After breakfast I'll set you up with the best place to sell knives, then I'll take her place in line."

Janek picked up his spoon and swirled it around the odd-looking soup. He tasted it and grimaced. "What the devil, is in here? Rocks?"

Oryst looked at him appraisingly. "Boiled potatoes with linden leaves and ground corncobs, but don't complain. Ludka and I had this every day for the past week in order to put aside a loaf of Postyshev bread for our trip. And hopefully today we can get another one."

Janek lowered his head. "Sorry. I had no idea."

After finishing the soup, Janek shouldered his pack and set out with Oryst for the bakery, located between the railway station and one of the city squares.

As they passed a vacant lot filled with weeds and scattered boulders, Janek saw thirty or more gaunt men and women. While some sat, others slept, sprawled out among the boulders.

"What are they waiting for?" Janek asked.

"The next train. They climb on the roof or hang on the side, hoping the next town will have work or something to eat."

After they crossed the street and walked the next block, Oryst said, "We're close to the city centre now. We'll begin to see where the *bezprizorniki*, the street children, sleep. They like to crawl in under stairways or by heating pipes, anywhere they can get some warmth. Lucky for us, most are still asleep."

"Why lucky?"

Oryst motioned to a stairway. "Go see for yourself."

Janek crouched down and looked into the gloomy space. In the far corner, where no one could reach them, a group of children slept huddled, arms and legs flung on top of each other.

"Like an infestation, they're everywhere."

Raising himself to an upright position, a pulse of raw anger flashed through Janek's head. "Since when did you start thinking of children as lice?"

"When they broke into my house and stole Ludka's laundry off the line. Everything has to dry in the house, or it's gone."

"That no one takes these children into their home and cares for them is tragic."

Oryst's eyes narrowed. "They are not like any children you know. They are street-hardened bastards. They'll do anything it takes to survive, even sticking a knife in someone for their coat."

Janek did not understand. Children knifing someone?

As he entered the city square, Janek gazed in shock. Everywhere he looked there were emaciated people with haggard faces. Some were lying down, others sat or staggered around.

On the corner of one of the ornately trimmed brick buildings, a mother slept sitting up, her back against the wall. Around her slept her children, not a blanket or anything between them and the sidewalk.

By a horse trough, a half-dozen boys, dressed in oversized, filthy rags, smoked cigarettes. Some looked to be no more than eight; others were in their late teens. Feathers blew in the breeze as one of the older boys plucked a magpie.

"Do you see those bezprizorniki?" Oryst asked.

Janek nodded, his stomach curling at the thought of eating magpie.

"Like I said, they're everywhere."

"Is that the bread line?" Janek asked, pointing to a queue that extended from the bakery down the length of the square before it disappeared around the corner.

"It is. The bakery hasn't opened yet."

"Do you see Ludka?"

"I'll have to go look. But this is where you set up, between the bakery and the administration building. That way you'll get businesspeople as well as those here for bread."

A woman in a black homespun dress approached them. Janek

tried to keep his eyes averted, yet he could not. She seemed so sad, all alone, shoulders hunched. She should be at home, with her garden and children. Her sunken eyes and gaunt face spoke of her hunger.

The woman pulled at his sleeve. "Please, two kopeks?" she asked, offering him a handful of old hairclips.

"Why do you sell those?"

She pointed to the bakery. "To buy bread."

"I don't have bread or kopeks to spare."

Eyes down, the woman walked unsteadily away.

"Janek, if you don't look at them, they will leave you alone."

"Something about her. Reminds me of our sister. Did you notice?"

"No, I didn't notice, because I don't look. You'll have to toughen up."

Janek slid his pack to the ground. He could feel his brother's irritation surround him as he fanned the knives on a black scarf from smallest to largest.

"Another thing. Keep a knife under your belt for protection against the bezprizorniki."

"Me? Stab a boy?"

"You don't have to use it, just show what you have. All right, I'm off to find Ludka. See you at home."

While Janek waited for a customer, the heady aroma of baking bread began to waft on the air. No matter that it was filled with sawdust, if only he could rip off a chunk, slather it in butter and plum jam and swallow it down in great mouthfuls.

Every now and then, a housewife leaving the bakery would come over and have a look at his knives. His hopes soared and then fell as they walked away without one.

Just as Oryst had predicted, a few of the older bezprizorniki began to gather around him.

Janek flashed his knife. "Get lost."

"Just looking, *staryi perdun*, old fart," said one of the teens who wore a Russian-style cap. He hocked a mass of phlegm from the back of his throat and lodged it on Janek's sleeve as he walked by.

Keeping an eye on the boys, Janek noticed two of them follow a woman with a loaf of bread tucked to her chest. A third boy and then a fourth joined in.

"*Złodziej, złodziej!* Thief, thief!" Janek yelled. At that moment, one of the boys rammed her in the back and another snatched the loaf.

Other people tried to block the gang's path while a militia policeman, baton in hand, sprinted after them. He reached an arm out and caught one of the smaller boys by the scruff of the neck. Again and again, he whacked the boy across the chest and shoulders.

Janek felt himself go numb as the beating went on and on.

The boy cried and held up his arms to protect his body, then dropped to his knees and begged for mercy. The militiaman picked him up by his hair and continued to beat him until he could no longer stand. The militiaman then dragged him out of the square.

Shaken by what had happened, Janek decided to gather up his knives and walk around for a bit. Midway down the queue, Janek spotted Oryst.

"Did you see that militiaman chase down that boy?"

"That happens a lot here. Sometimes the militia police will swoop in and capture a whole bunch of the bezprizorniki and take them away."

"Away where?"

"Officially, to a nice orphanage somewhere."

Janek looked away, as a flash of anger constricted his chest. "What kind of a man have you become?"

"Look, I don't like it, either. No one likes it. But it has to be done."

"What has to be done?" exploded Janek.

Oryst looked at him, his eyes wide in surprise. "I'm sorry, Janek. Maybe I shouldn't have said that."

"Just think of Veronika. She is from a village just like all of these children. If she were here, desperate for food, would you have such little compassion?"

Oryst looked down. "No, of course not, but all I know of these children is that they work in gangs and steal, kill if they have to."

"Not all are like that."

"I am only one person. What can I do?"

"You can help those that you can." Afraid he would say something he'd regret, Janek turned and walked away.

He walked back along the queue to the far corner of the square where a man, his legs wrapped in rags, tried to sell his own worn-out boots. Another man tried to sell just the soles. Janek squatted down and offered them each a dried plum. They nodded and clasped their hands to their heart to thank him.

Next to them sat a woman in filthy, tattered clothes. She held in her lap a burlap sack of weeds, mostly pigweed and sorrel. An emaciated child, her legs covered in sores, lay motionless beside her. Very little light was left in her eyes.

"You should eat those. Do you and the little one good," Janek said with a smile.

She shook her head. "I need medicine. Her legs are infected. I tried to give my little Inna away. No one would have her. It's this infection." she said, her eyes filling with tears.

"I'll take the sack," Janek said before he had a chance to think. "One ruble enough?"

She clenched his hand in hers. "God bless you. Perhaps tomorrow I'll have enough to buy ointment."

Janek walked back to his spot and once again set out his knives, a knot in his chest. Why had he so foolishly given that woman a whole ruble? Her child wasn't going to live, and he had his own child to think about.

A woman in a white coat with extra-large black buttons came out of the administrative building. Her leather shoes clip-clopped as she strode across the cobblestones toward him. Janek's heart beat a little faster. An office worker would have money.

She paused in front of him and scanned his knives. "You made these?" she asked. Her sullen half-lidded stare seemed more of a challenge than a question.

"Yes, the wood came from my own orchard. The blades from my family's blacksmith shop."

"Show me that one," she said, pointing a manicured finger.

As he bent to pick up the knife, a commotion in the bread queue grew louder. Forgetting about his customer, Janek watched the bedraggled line transform into a screaming, shoving mob, with fists pumping the air and rocks hurled. The bakery window shattered.

"They've run out of bread," the woman said, her eyes wide. "We need to get out of here."

Janek scooped up his knives and followed her into the doorway of the administrative building. He watched a group of men launch themselves again and again at the bakery door. Another crawled through the broken window. To the side of the bakery, a militiaman lay splayed on the ground, blood forming a pool around his head.

The woman clutched Janek's arm. "Those criminals will kill me if I'm seen."

"Get inside the building." He motioned to the door.

Her face white, she seemed frozen in fear.

"Go," Janek gave her a shove.

She bolted. "Let me in, please." She rattled the door and pounded on the glass.

"They won't let me in," she cried, her eyes wide in terror.

"Come back, woman, before you're seen. Put this on." He pulled the black scarf from his pack. "You won't be so noticeable."

A renewed uproar of shouts resounded as several men ran out of the bakery with sacks of flour over their shoulders, only to have them yanked off and pulled to the ground by dozens of hands. One sack exploded, sending flour pouring onto the cobblestones. A mass of hands scooped up the flour and people stuffed it down their shirts. Others jumped on their backs, fists flying.

Janek recoiled in horror as militia policemen on horseback charged around the corner and into the crowd. Wails filled the air. Mercilessly, whips slashed down. Hooves trampled the fallen. He looked for Oryst and prayed not to see him.

Within minutes, the crowd had fled, chased by the horsemen, leaving only the dead and mangled scattered in front of the bakery. The woman selling rusty hairclips lay crumpled, blood all around her.

Janek felt sick and wanted to get as far away as possible. "My brother was in line for bread. I need to go and see if he's all right."

"Here is your scarf," she said. "I can't imagine what my husband will say when I tell him that I was in the middle of a riot with those criminals."

"Criminals? All they wanted was food for their families."

The contemptuous look once again returned to her face. "Are they not criminals when they riot? When they kill an innocent militiaman, only there to keep the peace? The Party is doing the very best it can to provide bread. But what can they do when you people hoard grain and sabotage Stalin's plan?"

"No one hoards grain because there is no grain to hoard."

She glared at him and stood up. "You can keep your knife. I won't buy from someone who speaks against the Party."

Janek got up, his head in a daze. As he walked away, he wondered if he had lost his mind. Why did he speak to her like that?

Jezus Chrystus, from the stupidity of my own mouth, you saved me. So easily that woman could have had me arrested. And please, may the holy angels surround Oryst, wherever he is, and keep him safe.

Head down as he walked, Janek wondered if he would see his brother again. Those caught by the militia police would take the blame for the riot. Was he even now in a dark cell awaiting interrogation?

When Janek arrived at Oryst and Ludka's home, he steadied himself to face Ludka. He opened the door and grabbed at the doorframe in shock. Oryst sat on the sofa, a cloth held to his head.

"Matko Boska, I was so worried. You're all right?"

"I'm fine. Hit my head on the cobbles is all." He pulled the bloodied cloth away to reveal a deep cut on his forehead.

"But he got bread," Ludka said. "One of the last ones before they ran out."

Janek sat down beside his brother. "I know we planned to stay here for a couple more days, but I said something stupid and need to leave the city."

That night, Janek and Oryst said goodbye to Ludka and crept into an open boxcar headed north.

Ukrainian villages are in a state of visible demise, hollowness, abandonment and utter poverty, the cottages are in ruin, often with torn-down roofs, new dwellings are nowhere to be found, children and elders are mere skeletons, and there is no livestock. On a mere 1/5 of the worked fields has something grown ...
—J. Karszo-Siedlewski, Polish Consulate General in a report to Moscow, May 31, 1933

40
JANEK

"Now," Oryst said, throwing his pack from the moving train.

Janek dropped from the train and tumbled beside the tracks. He brushed himself off, while Oryst picked up his pack.

Janek looked at the meadow and woods that surrounded them. In the distance, he could barely see the thatched roofs of a village. He wished they could have ridden the train right into the village, but Oryst thought it too risky.

Neither one talked much as they walked along the tracks, chewing dried plums.

"How large is the village?" Janek asked.

"There used to be two or three hundred people, but who knows how many there are now. Some likely fled, others deported. Even so, it shouldn't be a problem to get a bowl of soup and a place to sleep in exchange for knife sharpening."

Janek tramped along beside Oryst, his thoughts on Helena and Veronika. What if shock workers had come and taken what little food they had? Maybe even roughed up Helena? A squeezing pressure filled his chest. Stop thinking these thoughts. Helena had a receipt that proved the grain came from Torgsin. But what if they didn't look at the receipt or worse yet, deported them? He was startled out of his brooding by the raucous cawing of a raven that looked down at them as they walked by, warning other birds of the danger of their passing. The bird's cawing suddenly struck Janek as odd. "Maybe it is I who should warn you," he said to it. "Have you not noticed that you sit alone? Fly away, out of this country, where even the birds are not allowed to live in peace." As if in answer, the bird arose and took flight in a great flapping of wings.

As they got closer to the village, the air took on a rank, pungent smell.

"Something's dead, maybe a horse," said Janek.

"Likely what attracted the raven here," said Oryst, covering his nose.

At the entrance to the village, Oryst pointed to a sign nailed to a road marker. A black flag fluttered from the sign.

"I don't like the looks of that. Let's go see what the sign says."

Getting closer, Oryst gasped, "O mój Boże!"

"What does it say?" Janek asked, frustrated that he couldn't read.

"It says there has been an epidemic. No one allowed in."

Janek's breath quickened. "Maybe even here, the air carries disease."

Oryst nodded, his eyes wide.

Janek and Oryst walked rapidly away from whatever disease lurked within the village.

"I wonder what it was?" Janek asked.

"Could be anything—typhus, cholera, smallpox, maybe."

Janek felt a chill go up his spine. "Good that the government had it marked like that."

From the corner of Janek's eye, he saw a group of children crawling in a patch of clover on the opposite side of the track. They grazed like sheep in a field, moving in a slow, deliberate manner, plucking and eating the flower heads.

A boy spotted their presence and froze. In a flurry of movement, the children fled into the bushes.

"Come back. We won't hurt you," Oryst called out.

After a moment, a young boy with solemn eyes and a gaunt face stepped out from behind a tree. Barefoot, he wore only a pair of ragged pants. Janek felt his heart go out to this desperately thin child, whose clavicle and ribcage protruded from his small body.

"Bread?" he asked, stretching out his hand.

"What is your name, boy?" Janek asked.

"Stepan."

"You have family?

He shook his head.

"Was it disease that killed your family?"

The boy's face twisted in anger. "There was no disease! My father said they blacklisted us for not having enough grain."

"Blacklisted?" Janek asked.

"Everything we can eat is taken away. No one is allowed in or out until the entire village is dead."

Janek felt numb. Could the Soviets be so cruel that even children and babies were sentenced to death?

"How is it that you and the other children are alive?" Oryst asked.

"We escaped." The child stretched out his hand again. "Please, bread?"

Janek opened his pack, broke off a chunk, and held it out.

The boy walked closer until he could reach out a bony arm for the bread. Janek put it into his grime-encrusted hand. The child thrust it in his mouth and chewed rapidly, as if afraid someone would take it from him.

Janek knelt and looked into the boy's face. "We have to go on," he said, putting his hand on Stepan's shoulder. "I haven't much bread, but I can give you another piece." Janek broke off another chunk and gave it to him.

For a moment, Stepan hesitated, like he was about to say something, then looked down.

"What is it?" Janek asked.

"My father," he said, tears trickling down his cheeks. "He was kind, too."

Then he turned and was gone.

"You gave him so much bread?" asked Oryst. "You have got to learn you can't help everybody."

Janek nodded. "You're right. I can't help everybody. I can only help those that God puts in my path."

... Soviet authorities introduced the "black list." According to this new regulation, collective farms that failed to meet grain targets were required, immediately, to surrender fifteen times the amount of grain that was normally due in a whole month ... this meant, again, the arrival of hordes of party activists and police with the mission and the legal right to take everything. No village could meet the multiplied quota, and so whole communities lost all the food they had. Communities on the black list also had no right to trade, or to receive deliveries of any kind for the rest of the country ... The black listed communities became zones of death.

—Timothy Snyder, *Bloodlands: Europe Between Hitler and Stalin*

41
JANEK

At the entrance to the next village, there was no sign or black flag but, all the same, a feeling of unease settled around Janek. "It's so quiet. Not a person or cart anywhere."

They stood in silence looking around.

"I've never seen it like this," Oryst said. "No people on the street, no sounds, no barking dogs, nothing."

"Maybe we should leave?" Janek asked.

"I think we should at least try to find a place to sleep."

The first half-dozen houses they walked past appeared abandoned, with doors opened wide, broken pails and other unwanted debris scattered in the yards.

Janek heard a faint sound.

Oryst stopped and listened. "I hear it, too. Let's go see."

Entering the house from where the sound came from, they found a woman with sunken cheeks lying curled up on the floor, groaning. A brown liquid oozed from her swollen legs. An emaciated child, his arms and legs like sticks, lay motionless beside her.

"Is the child alive?" Oryst asked.

Janek crouched down and touched the boy's cheek. "He's gone. Has been for a while."

Oryst sat beside the woman and gently lifted her head.

She moaned, her deep-set eyes clouded with pain. She tried to say something through parched lips.

"Janek, get her a cup of water. I'll see if I can get her to take a drink."

Janek dipped a mug into a bucket of water and placed it to her lips. After a few sips, she turned her head and reached for where her son lay. "My boy."

"I'm sorry. He no longer lives," Oryst said softly.

She looked at them, her eyes hollow with despair. "My daughter?"

"There is no girl here," Janek said.

"The loft."

Janek climbed the ladder to the loft. A girl of about nine or ten, rocked back and forth on her bed. A ripped pillow lay in her lap, feathers scattered about.

Janek walked over and touched her arm. She startled and grabbed the pillow.

"No, they are mine," she said, stuffing a handful of feathers into her mouth.

Janek gently pried the pillow from her grasp, carried her down the steps, into her mother's waiting arms.

"I thought you had died," sobbed the mother, holding her close.

"Mama, I'm hungry, so hungry."

"It will be all right," she whispered, kissing her daughter's head. "Just close your eyes and rest beside me."

Oryst's eyes filled with tears. Brushing them away, he said, "I'll get some of my bread, soak it in water for them."

"What's your name?" Janek asked, kneeling beside the woman.

"Daryna."

"Was your village blacklisted?"

She shook her head. "We made our quota. When we had no more to give, they took our food."

Oryst held a bit of soaked bread to her lips. She turned her head away.

"Let my daughter have it."

The girl threw her thin arm around her mother's neck. "Please, eat, Mama."

Oryst tried once again to bring the bread to her lips.

Janek held his hand up. "Don't force her. Maybe later she'll take some."

Janek and Oryst stayed the night, rising every now and then to offer them water and soaked bread. In the morning when Janek got up, the mother was dead.

Oryst held the girl and rocked her.

"What are we to do with this child?" Janek asked.

Oryst looked down at the girl in his arms. "I guess we take her with us."

"Do you think she can make it to the station?"

"We can walk slowly," Oryst said. "And if necessary, I will carry her."

Kneeling beside the girl, Janek gave her water and a bit more bread. "What is your name?"

"Tetyana," she whispered.

"Tetyana," Oryst said, stroking her head, "You're coming with us."

"I can't leave Mama."

"Your mama and brother have passed into heaven. They will be all right now."

When it was time to go, Janek and Oryst wrapped Daryna in a blanket and laid her on the road beside her son. Tetyana followed them, crying. Beside the bodies, Oryst took her hand and together they knelt while Janek recited the blessing of the dead.

"*Eternal rest, grant unto them, O Lord,*
and let perpetual light shine upon them.
May they rest forever in peace."

As they walked toward the railway station, it wasn't long before Tetyana became too weak and had to be carried. She had already fallen asleep on Oryst's back, when a horse and wagon from the collective slowly creaked by. In the back, piled high, were the bodies of the dead that had been hurled, one on top of another. Janek was glad Tetyana would not carry the memory of her mother and brother tossed on top of the pile.

> *Fathers and mothers sent their children to the cities to beg with very mixed results. Some children starved to death on the way, or at their destination. Others were taken by the city police, to die in the dark in a strange metropolis and be buried in a mass grave with other small bodies.*
> —Timothy Snyder, *Bloodlands: Europe Between Hitler and Stalin*

42
JANEK

They arrived at Zhytomyr late at night. Dread sat within Janek's heart as he searched the city park for a place to sleep. In the morning, they would have to find something to eat, especially for Tetyana. She had slept for most of the train ride but not the natural sleep of a child. It was a sleep that she could not be awoken from, and it frightened him.

Janek spread his coat on a park bench, and Oryst lay Tetyana down on top of it, then covered her with his. He and Janek lowered their weary bodies onto the dew-covered ground on either side of it. Eventually Janek drifted into an uneasy sleep broken both by hunger and the dampness of the earth.

At dawn, Janek was startled awake by the wails of children, kicking and screaming as the militia police dragged them away.

"Let me die out here in the air!" one screamed.

"I don't want to die," another cried. "Let me go."

Janek stood up, alarmed. What were they doing with those children? A militiaman approached Tetyana. "Is that girl with you?"

"Yes, she is," Oryst said, putting his hand on her.

He turned to leave.

"Where do you take those children?" Janek called after him.

"To the police station to be sorted. From there, some go to the children's shelter.

"Children's shelter?"

"You want to give her up?" the militiaman asked, coming back.

"I have to think about it. Where is it?

"Down from the train station, in an old factory building," he replied, voice trailing behind him as he walked away.

"I don't want to go to a children's shelter," Tetyana said. "I want to stay with you."

Janek knelt down on one knee. A lump formed in his throat, making it difficult for him to talk. "You can't. God knows I'd love to keep you, but you don't have the strength and we don't have any way to feed you."

Oryst stroked her cheek. "It's the only way."

"Both of us don't need to go," Janek said. "How about I take Tetyana, and you try to figure out if Zhytomyr is going to work for us. If not, I think we should head back home."

Oryst nodded, his eyes glassy as Janek led Tetyana away.

Tetyana held tight to Janek's hand during their walk to the railway station, asking questions he couldn't answer. Will there be bread? Will I have friends? Do I sleep there, too?

Janek felt the vibration then heard the long and short whistle of an incoming train. He paused, unsure. There would be a surge of people around the train, desperate for food or a train ticket out.

Perhaps he should wait until it left, but with each minute, Tetyana's agitation grew more intense. He decided to continue.

He kept a close hold of Tetyana's hand as groups of children, their eyes desperate for help, swarmed passengers that tried to disembark. Between the children, women with swollen legs held their babies, heads wobbling, up to the windows.

Janek's body stiffened in a surge of anger. *Why, God? Why do they do this to little children? Look down and see what is happening. May those that do this rot in everlasting Hell.*

"Ouch. You're hurting my hand," Tetyana said.

"Sorry, I never meant to hurt your little hand." He brought her hand to his lips and made a show of kissing it.

Tetyana giggled. "It didn't hurt that much."

A few buildings past the station they came to a derelict factory with several banks of windows facing the tracks and a decaying loading dock.

"This must be it, Tetyana," he said with false cheerfulness.

Tetyana gazed impassively up at the grime-covered brick wall.

"It's all right," he said, giving her hand a gentle pat. "If you're lucky, maybe soon you will eat."

Janek knocked on the door. When no one answered, he pounded.

A young woman, her hair short in the style of a university student, opened the door.

"I found this child. She has no family."

"Come with me, then," she answered in Russian. "I'll take you to the director."

She stepped aside and Janek walked in, Tetyana holding his hand.

"I'm Marta," she said, leading them past an empty office area, down a corridor lined with grimy windows, to a set of closed double doors.

While she took a key from around her neck, Janek asked, "How long have you been here?"

"A couple of months. I was studying medicine in Moscow and was told that I had to come care for abandoned children," she said, unlocking the door.

Walking into a large open room, Janek's breath quickened at the sight of a hundred or so skeletal children with spindly arms and legs and shaved heads. All were dressed in white gowns tied about the neck.

"It's hard to take it all in, isn't it?" Marta said. "First time I saw this, I just stood and stared, same as you are. Of course, I had no idea what I was walking into. It isn't talked about in Russia."

Unable to speak, Janek continued to stare at the children and the director, who stopped now and then to talk to a child or comfort another. If only he could reach out and feed every one of those children, hold them on his lap and tickle them with his beard like he did with Veronika.

"My God, so many beloved children ... beloved of dead parents," he said, his voice shaking with emotion. "How can you live with yourself, knowing you are a part of this?"

"I'm only trying to help. That the children are in this condition, falls on the heads of their parents. The government gave them every chance to cooperate, but they would not change. Something had to be done. Unfortunately, this is the result. Children paying for the sins of their parents."

"You know nothing of what you speak! The sin, my girl, is on the government, that they wanted the parents of these children dead."

Marta gasped. "Do you know what you're saying?"

"I say only the truth. Every law put upon the villagers has been complied with, yet still people are thrown out of their homes and left without food in order that they might die."

Her face darkened. "That can't be true. I've read dozens of articles in the *Pravda* about the hoarding going on and the resulting problems providing food to the cities and soldiers." Her mouth opened to say more when Tetyana tugged on Janek's sleeve and pointed.

"Oh, you've spotted Dmitri and Artem over there haven't you?" Marta said. "You should have seen them when they first came in," she said, walking toward two boys sitting on the floor, the older one spoon-feeding the younger, a metal pot between them. The younger leaned in, his eyes following every movement of the spoon. Janek could see his knobby vertebrae protruding chain-like from his exposed back. Marta crouched down and retied the strings of his gown.

"The stronger children help the weaker. Artem is feeding him gruel." Marta rested her hand on Artem's shoulder.

"Gruel?" Janek asked.

She nodded. "That's all we have to feed them, that and hot water."

"And children can live being fed only that?"

"Some have been here two years already," she answered with a shrug of her shoulders.

"Why is it that you work here? Do you even care for these children?"

"Of course, I care for them," she said, a flash of anger in her eyes. "It's important that they survive to become loyal Soviet citizens."

"How does a Ukrainian child become Soviet?"

"They will be given Russian names and raised in Soviet homes. In time, they will forget they even were Ukrainian.

"Forget or despise?"

She shrugged. "Does it matter? The girls will go on to be Soviet housewives or workers and the more promising boys admitted into the Soviet secret police training program."

Janek wondered what to do as he swallowed tears of grief and anger. Would it be better to leave Tetyana here where she had a chance to live, or abandon her in a city square to die or be picked up by the militia? He looked down at Tetyana standing forlornly in front of him, finger in her mouth. What choice did he have but leave her here?

"These children, will they all live?" he asked, his voice thin.

Marta's head tilted downward. "Every day some will die. But here comes the director. He will talk to you."

A slender man with round black wire glasses approached them.

"Comrade, this man has come with a child he found."

Janek bowed his head as the director greeted him.

"What is the child's name?"

"Tetyana. Her mother died and she has no other family. I am a peddler, passing through and cannot keep her." Janek looked into the director's face and saw a deep sadness in his eyes.

He rested his hand on Tetyana's shoulder. "She's not too swollen yet, so she may stay."

"Thank you, Comrade," Janek said, again bowing his head.

Turning to Tetyana, the director said, "Go with Marta. She'll give you some gruel."

Tetyana threw her arms around Janek. "I want to stay with you. Please don't leave me."

"You will be looked after here," Janek said, pulling off her arms. He gave her a little push. "Go on now. Go with her."

Tetyana looked at him, hollow-eyed, and took Marta's hand.

A sharp stab of pain shot through Janek's heart as he watched her walk down the corridor. He fought the urge to call her back.

"She will recover, do you think?" he asked, his voice tight.

"We'll do what we can. Sometimes we don't get our supplies and children die."

"Can't a doctor demand supplies?"

He smiled sadly. "Demand of the Soviet government? Doctors that cause problems don't live long. I do what I can to save lives while appearing to work within the rules."

"What rules?"

"It's against the law to treat someone whose main complaint is starvation. For these children, the government has made an exception, but there are other children's shelters that are designed to be more like prisons or death shelters."

Janek's head reeled as the director went on.

"I used to believe in the Soviet system, in all sharing for the common good. But now I do what I can to save children."

"You said that Tetyana wasn't too swollen and could stay here. What happens to the others?"

"I'm required to send them to the police station. That's where I have some leeway."

"What happens to those ones?"

"The hopeless cases?"

Janek nodded.

"They take them away, far from the city in freight cars, together with the swollen adults. That's all I know."

> *Special dining halls for officials of the Party and the administration were established in all the large Ukrainian cities ... Day and night it was guarded by militia keeping the starving peasants and their children away from the restaurant ... Around these oases famine and death were raging.*
> —Hryhory Kostiuk, *Stalinist Rule in the Ukraine: A Study of the Decade of Mass Terror*

43

JANEK

"So how was it?" Oryst asked, his eyes hopeful.

Janek joined him on the park bench. Unshed tears burned in his eyes for the little girl he had abandoned. "Not good. She didn't want to stay. I had to push her, tell her to go." He rested his face in his hands. "I'll never forget the way she stared at me—like I had betrayed her.

"Maybe you shouldn't have left her there."

"She needed to eat, today."

"Did she eat?"

Janek nodded. "Some gruel."

"That's good, then."

"They can't guarantee she'll live." His words were strangled.

What he wouldn't give for a glass of spiritus right now, anything to numb the guilt he carried. He kept seeing Tetyana's little face, the despair. Why hadn't he scooped her up and taken her out of there? Let her take her chances with them? And if she were to die, at least die among those who cared for her.

Janek looked up, his vision blurred. "And how did you do?"

"I've checked things out. I think we should stay for a few days."

"Find any food?" he asked, his voice flat.

"Yes."

"What?"

"Pig feed." He sounded pleased.

Janek winced, almost smelling the mass of rotting vegetables, intestines, blood, and bone. "Swill?"

"Not swill," Oryst said, giving Janek a playful punch on the shoulder. "I'm talking about potato mash left over from making vodka. It's dumped behind the factory, then collected for the pigs."

Potato mash ... Janek salivated at the thought.

— ✳ —

By mid-morning, Janek and Oryst arrived at the sprawling factory. Every breath held the bitter, musty smell of rotting potatoes.

Heaviness filled Janek's chest. "All we needed were a few potatoes, and we could have kept Tetyana with us."

"Not just Tetyana. The Soviets bastards could have kept the entire city alive."

Walking to the back of the factory, Janek's heart ached at the sight of men and women, faces lined with fatigue, crouched around a pit of grey slurry.

"O mój Boże," he said in a low voice. "It reminds me of the picture of hell in Helena's prayer book. People lying around a flaming pit, arms reaching out to be saved."

Not yet ready to try the foul-smelling mess, Janek squatted beside a woman who had a black shawl with gaping holes wrapped around her shoulders. She was a plain-looking woman, but in her plainness, there was a beauty that reminded him of Helena.

Helena … How he missed the comfort of having her by his side. Thank God she was home and not here as this poor woman was.

He watched how she dipped only the edge of her tin can into the grey slurry. He stuck his cup into the semi-liquid mass, tasted it and grimaced.

"Just take from the top," she said. "Underneath is rotten."

Janek swallowed a little of the sour, fermented mass, grateful that he had at least something in his stomach when so many were dying.

"See? Not so bad if you do it right," said the woman.

The next slimy glob refused to go down his throat. He spat it on the ground. He could see Oryst having problems eating as well. Janek tried again. He managed a few more swallows before his stomach began to heave. Wiping his mouth with the back of his hand, he choked out, "I need to get away from here."

Oryst stood up. "Let's set out your knives."

As they walked, Janek noticed cigarette butts scattered at the side door of the factory. "This might be good. Looks like they take their break here."

Oryst found a cement ledge to set out his whetstone and Janek his knives. After an hour or so, factory workers streamed from one building into another. Most walked by without giving them a glance. Others paused to smoke a hand-rolled cigarette.

A factory worker, his dirt-creased face shining with sweat, walked up to Janek's display. He had a moustache and, like Janek, a mop of uncombed hair. He paused to light a cigarette, then picked up a knife and tested the balance. He whistled.

"How much do you want for it?"

"Ten rubles."

"Seven rubles and tomorrow I will bring money to pay for it."

Janek nodded, trying not to appear too eager. "I'll be here." He set the knife aside.

The man scraped the glowing tip off his cigarette with a flick of a crooked nail. "I better get to the canteen." He opened his breast pocket and dropped in the blackened stub.

"Canteen?"

"Every day at noon we get some sort of slop to keep us going."

Oryst's face brightened. "Is there a chance of sharpening the canteen's knives in exchange for a meal?"

The man snorted. "I don't know if you would call watery cereal and a slice of sawdust bread a meal."

"We're not fussy."

The man shrugged. "When I go in, I'll ask."

Janek's hopes withered as the minutes went by. Finally, when the workers began to stream back into the factory, he bent down to pack his knives.

"Someone's coming." Oryst sounded tense.

Janek glanced up to see a man in white coveralls walk toward them. His face didn't seem friendly. Janek groaned. "Likely coming to order us off the property."

Janek took in the man's crisp coveralls and polished black shoes, before removing his cap and bowing his head. His gaze shifted to his own scuffed boots and greasy sheen of his rumpled trousers, then he forced himself to meet the man's piercing gaze.

"I'm the canteen manager. A worker told me that one of you sells knives and the other sharpens them. Is that so?"

"Yes," Oryst said. "Sir."

"Let's see the knives."

His hopes soaring, Janek set the knives back on the ledge.

"How much if I bought three?"

"Thirty rubles, sir," Janek said, astonished.

The man took out a wallet and counted the rubles. Janek's head swirled in disbelief.

"And I'll make you a deal. Give a large knife to the canteen, sharpen all their knives, and you can eat here for a week."

Janek almost gasped.

Thank you, sir," Oryst said.

"But you are not to come in until the factory workers are done eating."

"No, sir, we won't."

"I have family in the village, so I know how it is." As he turned to go, he said, "You might try selling your knives at the restaurant for Party members."

"Restaurant?" Oryst asked.

"Sure. Party members don't go hungry."

"Where is this restaurant?"

"Main street, to the right off the square."

As the manager walked away, Janek lowered himself to the ledge, his brain not yet functioning. Food for a week? And three more knives sold?

"Our luck has changed," Oryst said, with a gleeful smile.

"Luck? Nothing to do with luck. It's God looking out for us."

Entering the canteen filled Janek with awe. So many tables and chairs, enough to fill the length of the thirty-foot room, but best was the lingering smell of bread.

A woman in a white apron saw them come in. She put two bowls of what looked like buckwheat in some sort of broth and a couple of slices of bread on the counter. Janek trembled with anticipation as he carried them to a table and sat down.

After bowing their heads in prayer, Janek put a spoonful of grain in his mouth, wondering aloud at the explosion of flavour the bland food seemed to have.

"It's doing that to me too," Oryst said. "Probably because it's been so long since we've eaten."

After the first few mouthfuls, a sense of urgency filled Janek's being. He found himself bolting down the food, and as much as he tried to slow down, he could not until the bowl was empty and the bread gone. Gone. And it hadn't even taken the edge off his hunger.

After they returned their dishes to the counter, the women found more and more knives for Oryst to sharpen.

"This one has been in the back cupboard for years," said a woman with a laugh, brandishing a wooden-handled knife with a curved blade.

By late afternoon, Oryst had completed all the sharpening to the women's satisfaction. They left the factory and walked toward the restaurant. Eventually, they came across an area of vacant land where the poor had created places to sleep. Here and there, Janek saw people tending small fires. Beside one such fire sat a woman Janek recognized from the factory, wearing the same ragged black shawl around her shoulders.

At their approach, she looked up from her task of straining watery horse manure through a sieve from one bucket into another to capture the undigested kernels of grain.

"You're the one who tried to help me scoop up that potato slurry," Janek said.

She looked up, recognition in her eyes. "It does take some getting used to."

"I'm Jan. This is my brother, Oryst."

"My name is Natalia."

"What are you going to do with that grain?" Oryst asked.

"I don't know how it happened, but I seem to be taking care of a few bezprizorniki over there."

Janek looked to where she motioned and saw a lean-to of scrap wood and metal sheeting. Two street children sat at the entrance, one sucking his thumb, another, a little older, stood nearby.

"I'm making a pancake of sorts for them, by pounding the grain and mixing it with sorrel." She paused for a moment and cocked her head. "I shouldn't really call then bezprizorniki, though. Most are no more than four years old."

"Do they like your pancakes?"

"They like it better than the potato slurry. Just like you." She looked at Janek with a trace of a smile. "They couldn't swallow it."

A girl came out of the shack and stood quietly behind Natalia. Her light brown hair fell in messy tendrils over her face, partly obscuring her small mouth and perky nose. What captivated Janek's attention were her bright blue eyes. They had a stony coldness about them and yet, just below the surface, they told of the sorrow and betrayal carried within her. The girl squatted beside Natalia, resting her head on her boney knees.

Natalia gave her tousled head a pat. "This is Olena."

"Hello, Olena," Oryst said, bending down to her.

Olena turned her head away.

"Are you hungry, *kokhana*, sweetie?" Natalia asked.

Olena nodded. "The others, too." Her voice was low and soft, lower than Janek would have expected of a child about eight.

"Tell them soon it will be ready."

Janek watched Olena walk back to the shack and lift a child to her hip.

"Your daughter?" he asked.

"No, just another one of my strays, but she acts like a mother to the little ones. She even gets up in the night to see if their coats still cover them."

"Must have had little brothers and sisters herself."

Natalia pressed her lips together and looked away. "I don't ask."

Janek sighed. "Such a world. Reminds me of Tetyana."

"Tetyana?"

"A little girl we found. Had no one left in the world. We would have kept her, but we had no food to keep her alive. She was in a bad way already."

After a moment's pause, Oryst said, "Natalia, we are in need of a place to sleep."

Natalia sized up Oryst and then Janek. "What do you have to trade?"

"I could give you one ruble," Janek said. "It would only be for five days."

"A ruble?" Her mouth opened in disbelief.

Janek handed her the ruble.

She clutched it to her chest. "Thank you. It's so much."

A feeling of warmth went through Janek at her reaction. He knew it was too much but, in his heart, it was right. Exactly right. He glanced over at Oryst and saw him press his lips together and nod in approval.

"Maybe get something on the black market for the children." Janek rested his hand on her shoulder.

She reached up, eyes glistening with tears, and put her hand on top of his.

"We'd best go." He pulled his hand from under hers. "We need to find the Party member's restaurant."

Wiping her eyes with the back of her hand, she smiled. "Going there to eat?"

Oryst returned the smile. "I think not. We're not dressed for it."

"One of my friends used to work there until they replaced all the workers with Russian ones." She spat at the ground. "Guess they don't trust us to serve food to the Party bosses."

"What kind of food do they serve?"

"All kinds of roasts," she said with a sweeping motion. "Sometimes pork, chicken, goose. And always white bread and rolls. Even canned fruit and cakes, sweets of all kinds and, of course, wine and vodka. But they won't let you near the restaurant. It's guarded. Don't want the poor looking in and wrecking their appetite."

As they walked away, she called after them. "Maybe you'll see Olena there."

Janek looked at her quizzically.

"She goes to the market to beg."

In the late afternoon, they found the Party members' restaurant, its perimeter protected by an iron railing and militia soldiers. Janek set up his knife display and Oryst his whetstone as close to the restaurant's perimeter as they dared. Patrons could still see them, but not so close that the militia would chase them away.

While waiting for a customer, Janek stared at the restaurant and the steppingstone path leading to its doorway. If only he could go in and grab a bread roll and a thick slice of roast pork. He could almost taste the meat, still steaming hot, juicy. He turned away. It was no good to think this way, to torture himself so. A man in rags sat not far from him. Was he at one time a farmer like himself? That could so easily have been him sitting in the street had he lived more to the east. Perhaps the man had a family and they had weakened and died, maybe even in his arms.

Janek's thoughts turned to Veronika. What if he returned home too late? What if in his absence, she grew too weak to move? What if someone found her and put her in a children's shelter? Once again, he had to turn his thoughts away. He looked to the market square, where barefoot children wove in and out among the people, singing a sad, melodic song. Likely the song reflected their pain. Perhaps the hollowness of being left so totally alone in the world. He strained to hear the words but could not quite make them out. With a sharp intake of breath, he noticed Olena's little face among them.

"What is it?" asked Oryst.

"Olena. Over there," he said, pointing."

"So? Natalia told us she begged."

"But she's so young to be out here alone at night. I assumed it was in the day she begged."

"Desperation makes children willing to do anything," Oryst said with a shudder. "And what can we do?" After a moment's pause, Janek heard him say under his breath, "We can do nothing."

Janek's thoughts turned to Tetyana. Never would he forget when she slept in his arms on the train, nothing more than a slip of a child. He had gazed at her flushed cheeks, her innocence, and wondered how the world could have done this to her. How he longed to see her again, to make sure she was all right. *Stop it*, he thought, aggravated with himself. *She's fine.* She had gruel, and there are people there who are trying to do good by her. Better that she's there than on the street like Olena.

As the night darkened, he could clearly see into the window, and occasionally caught a glimpse of diners and servers in black uniforms carrying plates of food.

"They eat like noblemen, while out here people starve." Oryst sounded bitter.

"All we can do is ask God to see, and repay them with what they deserve."

— ✻ —

A few evenings later, Janek saw Olena and the group of children she was with venture too close to the restaurant. What were they thinking? Should he warn them? Before he could react, a militia soldier gruffly ordered them away. Taking a few steps back, hands outstretched, the children began their song. This time Janek heard the words.

"I will die, I will die.
They will bury me,
And nobody will know where my grave is.
And nobody will come and remember,
Only in the early spring,
The nightingale will sing."

Janek's throat squeezed shut. Children shouldn't know such things and yet these children did. The words echoed in his mind.

Nobody will know where my grave is. And nobody will come and remember.

He became distracted by a couple walking out of the restaurant, he in a suit and she in a fur-collared jacket. They didn't give the children a glance, although they were still singing. Did the words of their song not haunt them? How could those who had so much reject the little outstretched hands?

To Janek's surprise, the couple walked over to him. The man stared down at the knives, his breath reeking of wine and tobacco.

Janek pasted a humble smile on his face. "The handles are solid walnut, and the blades are the finest anywhere. Ten rubles for any one of them."

The man's thick fingers picked up Janek's knife and turned it over in his hand. "You need a knife?" he asked the tipsy woman with red lips beside him.

"Sure, I need a knife," she giggled, "but I need something more," giving him a slight bump on the hip.

The man smiled and reached around behind the woman.

She jumped and gave a little shriek.

The man smirked. "I'll take three for the lady."

She gave him a playful smack on the chest. "What do I need with three?"

"For you, I give everything."

Janek took the man's rubles, his joy at the sale all but smothered by the simmering rage that welled within him. How could a man have so much money that he would throw it away on knives he didn't need, and not even think about those little hands behind the rail?

— ✻ —

Janek's and Oryst's next few days were consumed by selling and sharpening knives. Between the market and the restaurant, he sold almost all his knives.

"I am blessed to have sold so many knives. More than I had hoped.

Thank you, my brother, for going on this trip with me."

Oryst smiled. "You'll have enough money to buy the grain you need?"

"I think so. Depends on how good I am at bartering."

"On the black market?"

Janek nodded. "In Gródek, close to home. But before we leave tomorrow, I need to make sure that Tetyana is all right."

"What if she's not?"

"Then we take her with us." Janek was surprised he had said that, but once said, it felt right.

"Home with us?" Oryst asked.

"Why not? Helena would welcome her. Veronika, too. Be a sister for her."

In the morning, they went to Natalia where she squatted by the fire, tending a steaming pot.

She smiled at their approach. "Potato peels this morning, thanks to your ruble."

"We go home today, you know," Oryst said.

Natalia stood. "I thought as much. I will never forget you or your kindness," she said, taking Oryst's hand.

Janek took her hand and pressed two rubles into it.

She stared at the rubles then looked skyward. "Truly, I have met the Lord's angels."

"You are an angel yourself, taking on so many," Janek said, shifting his pack. "I will tell my family, and you'll be remembered."

— ✳ —

It didn't take them long to walk to the children's shelter. At their knock, Marta once again opened the door. Her eyes flickered in recognition.

"I'm here for Tetyana," Janek said.

Marta looked down. "We ran out of food."

Janek felt his body become numb. The floor became a blur.

"What are you saying?" Oryst gasped.

"Tetyana died."

The famine was brought about in Ukraine in order to reduce the number of Ukrainians, resettle in their place people from other parts of the USSR, and in this way kill all thought of independence.

—Statement by Prokopenko, a party member government plenipotentiary, reported by the OGPU (Soviet secret police), 12 May 1934

44

JANEK

Janek settled against the side of the boxcar as it swayed on the rails. Spring's cold twilight made him shiver as it had done for eight days now, since he began his homeward journey with his brother. Home. He breathed a prayer that Helena and Veronika would still be there when he arrived—that the shock workers hadn't come. That they were alive. Oryst and some of the other men who shared their car stared out the open door at the countryside passing by.

Excited murmurs roused Janek from his stupor. He opened his eyes. They were passing mounds of steaming grain, partly covered by tarpaulins. Soldiers standing guard stared at the train as it swished by, and as quickly as the sight appeared, it was gone.

"Grain! Look at the grain," Janek heard them say. "Did you see how it was smoking? Burning up from the inside."

"They're letting the grain rot?" Janek asked.

"First time you've seen that?" scoffed one of the men. His stained clothes fit him loosely. "They're all over Ukraine. Piles of rotting potatoes, too. The fools took so much, they couldn't ship it all."

"Ship it out? I thought they took it to feed the army and city workers."

The man snorted. "I'm from Odessa. I've seen all the foreign ships coming into port to be filled with grain. There are so many, they have to wait in line at sea."

No one said anything for a while, each lost in his own thoughts. The man stretched out and went to sleep.

Janek lay back against the wall and closed his eyes. Unbidden, images of children singing in the market square, weaving in and out among the people, hands outstretched, blurred in his mind, along with villagers kneeling beside the tracks, and of ... Tetyana, so very frail, her trusting eyes. If only she were sitting beside him now. His chest ached with waves of pain that threatened to engulf him, then eased, only to rise again. Janek pulled his coat closer around himself and tried to sleep, not to think.

A ruthless struggle is going on between the peasantry and our regime. It's a struggle to the death. This year was a test of our strength and their endurance. It took a famine to show them who is master here. It has cost millions of lives, but the collective farm system is here to stay. We've won the war.

—Mendel Khatayevich, Soviet politician and main organizer of collectivization that caused the starvation of millions

45

VERONIKA

June 1933

The days seemed to go on forever as Veronika waited for Tata's return. "Do you think he'll come home today, Mama?"

"It's been two weeks, so he might."

On the sixteenth day, Mama asked the family if they could get together and pray the rosary for him. As they sat around the table at Uncle Feliks's home, Veronika secretly surveyed the faces of her family as they prayed—Aunt Paulina, Uncle Feliks, cousins Julia and Stasik, Babcia, and beside Mama, Uncle Vladzio and precious Aunt Agnes.

Veronika felt a wonderful warmth and power expanding out from the table and up, up into the universe where God would hear their prayers. With squinty half-closed eyes, she looked again around the table and saw Aunt Agnes wink at her. She winked back.

Two days later, when he still did not return, Mama spent the day by the kitchen window, looking out. Aunt Paulina came over to be with Mama. They had a cup of mint tea and sat for a while, not saying much. When she left, Mama stayed in her chair. Veronika warmed up a bowl of watery millet and shredded beet soup for her. Veronika hated it that way, but Mama said they had to stretch what little they had. Veronika put the bowl down in front of Mama, not daring to look into her eyes for fear of the sorrow she would see.

"Thank you," Mama said, pushing the bowl away, "but I can't eat."

Veronika slowly got ready for bed, her chest heavy. Maybe Tata was dead. Maybe that's why Mama wasn't eating or talking. She knew already. Veronika got into bed; missing him hurt so bad she could hardly breathe. *Tata! Come home, please come home.*

Mama's shouts of joy made her jump out of bed.

"Veronika! Tata's coming. I see him."

She ran into the kitchen in her nightgown, shoved her bare feet into a pair of boots, and ran into the yard as Tata swept Mama into his arms. Veronika wedged herself between them, hugging Tata tight. His coat felt cool against her cheek as she pressed her face against him, breathing in his familiar scent. Feelings of comfort and security flooded her being. He was home!

"Tata, I can feel your bones right through your coat."

He gave her a tired smile. She saw an edge of sadness behind his eyes. Maybe he just needed sleep. "What's in your pack, Tata?"

"Veronika," Mama said, in her tone of reproach.

"And here I thought it was me she was so happy to see," Tata said with a chuckle.

"I am happy to see you, Tata," she said, "I am."

"Look at us here in the cold and Veronika in her nightgown," Mama said. "We'll go inside. Tata needs to rest."

At the kitchen table, Tata pulled out a small sack and slit open the top. "In case I got stopped, I didn't buy much."

Veronika pulled the edges of the sack open and stared inside, not believing her eyes. "Wheat? You bought wheat, Tata?"

"Janek, why wheat? Millet is so much cheaper."

Tata shrugged. "I thought it was time for the taste of bread again."

Veronika dug her fingers deep into the sack, feeling the cool grain slip past her fingers, thinking of all the bread and noodles it could make. She looked at Tata and saw him smiling, watching her pleasure.

"So, you got a good price for your knives?" Mama asked.

"Not as much as I had hoped. There wasn't a market for them. Helena, you wouldn't believe how it is outside this area."

"How much did you get?"

Veronika pulled her hands out of the grain and glanced at her mother.

"After paying your brothers for the blades, maybe enough for three more sacks this size."

"Not enough to make bread every day, then."

"At least we have something. We have it good here."

"We have it good? With all the children and old people, thin like skeletons, coming to our door?"

"Whole villages have died, Helena, whole villages. And in others, they're eating earthworms, mice, and boiling shoes, anything, just to put in their stomachs."

"Oh, I cannot understand it, Janek. Why are they so cruel? What have we done?"

"In the cities, thousands have flooded in from the villages, causing such problems that the soldiers are putting them away."

"Where are they putting them, Tata?"

Mama shook her head at Tata. "We'll talk later. Come, Janek, sit down. You need to eat."

Later, Veronika heard how the militia hunted down homeless

children and packed them into boxcars, saying they had a special place to take them. But it wasn't a special place at all. They just unhitched the cars on a side rail and left them to die.

She heard her mother say, "Stop, stop. I cannot hear more, Janek."

All night Veronika had nightmares of the horrors Tata had seen. In the morning, she went to school and sang with the rest of the children, "Stalin is our Father dear, the hero of our Motherland, the joy of the nation far and wide."

46

VERONIKA

July 1933

The setting sun cast a pink glow as Veronika threw the weeds that she had pulled into the chicken coop. She smiled inwardly as they tried to outrun each other, wings fluttering, necks extended, and eyes wide in panic lest another get there first.

It was annoying that they belonged to the collective, because she and Mama did all the work of scraping out the chicken poop, pulling weeds, and digging earthworms for them. The only good thing about having them was if there were extra eggs, Mama would cook them up for dinner, except for Tata's. He ate his raw, sucking it right out of the shell.

Veronika went to the gate and looked up the road to see if her parents were coming. They always worked long hours. Tata said that soldiers had been called in to work the fields because there were no longer enough people alive to do the seeding or harvesting.

Not seeing her parents, Veronika went to the well to draw a bucket of water to wash the new potatoes and dandelion weeds she had picked for dinner. She wished she'd been able to find more of the small, tender leaves. These ones would be tough and bitter, not like the young leaves they ate in spring. Tata said they were very lucky to have so much to eat. She didn't feel lucky. It was boring eating the same things day after day, and she was particularly sick of eating stewed apples and plums.

Perhaps she should make a fire in the woodstove to cook the potatoes and greens. She decided against it. Tata didn't like her to do that when they weren't home. He said she had to wait until next year when she turned eleven. She wondered when they would get home. They were particularly late today. Lonely and hungry, thoughts of eggs frying until golden brown and crisp around the edges filled her mind. It would be so good along with the potatoes and greens.

She remembered how it was before Mama and Tata joined the collective. Mama would always be home. Tata used to joke around and play with Veronika.

In the fading light, Veronika pulled a chair close to the window and followed the silver clouds as they moved across the sky. September would arrive soon, and she would start the fourth grade. A tingle of excitement went through her at the thought of once again walking to school with Kazia and Marek and sitting beside Alina. She could hardly wait to have a math word problem to solve, the ones the teacher put on the corner of the board for those who finished early. The teacher never praised her for getting the right answer, but she didn't mind. Veronika could see his admiration in the flicker of his eyes and the slightest trace of a smile on his lips as he announced her name. The real pleasure came from reporting to Tata how smart she'd been in math that day. "That's good, Noosha," he would always say. "Doctors need to be smart."

When Veronika finally heard the gate open, she ran out to meet her parents.

"What took so long?"

Mama pushed a lock of hair from her grime-streaked face. Her hands were caked in dirt. "Comrade Zykov made our brigade stay until we finished weeding the north sugar beet field."

"Do you want me to get a bucket of water and a washcloth for you?"

Mama nodded.

As Veronika carried the bucket outside, she saw her father heading toward the chicken coop.

"Janek," her mother called, "you need to rest."

"I can't rest. The chickens need to be watered."

"I did that already, Tata, and I weeded the onion rows."

Tata smiled at her and walked over to the stone bench. He sighed and sat down heavily.

"I'm too tired to even wash."

Veronika took a satisfied breath. Because of her, Tata could rest.

Mama slowly dipped her hands in the water, and washed them with soap, then took the rag and wiped down her dusty legs and bare feet. She winced in pain. Veronika looked closer and saw a deep red scratch along the side of her foot.

"Do you want me to blow on it, Mama?"

She shook her head. "Just bring me the plantain salve."

After dabbing the golden salve on her cut, Mama sat on the bench beside Tata, watching the sunset. The sky had streaks of purple in a mass of vibrant red. Veronika waited. She had hoped her mother would go in and start supper as soon as she got home.

"I peeled the potatoes, Mama, and got dandelion greens ready."

Her mama didn't answer.

"Do you think we could have fried eggs with supper? I can go count how many there are."

"No. Even if we have extra, we have to save them until I make the quota. Then if there's extra, we can have eggs."

Veronika lowered her head. She went up to the loft to be by herself. All the work she did, all the waiting, and yet she couldn't even have one egg. If they at least had butter for the potatoes or sour cream to stir in. The sigh she gave deepened the longing in her belly. Why must everything go to the collective?

... by the Spring of 1933 most of the villagers were so exhausted and swollen that there were few people left who were able to till the soil at the collective farms. Under compulsion, the government organized the so-called brigades for work on the collective farms. Students, civil servants and laborers were required to go.
—Investigation of the Ukrainian Famine 1932–1933, Report to US Congress

47
JANEK

August 1933

The morning had already grown so hot and still even the bluebottle flies seemed lazy. Janek gazed absent-mindedly at them resting on the barn wall, moving only to flit over the back of another, jostling for what they perceived to be a choice position.

For almost an hour, Janek had languished in the heat along with Helena and his in-laws. A few dozen collective workers also waited for Zykov and Kanygin to assign them their jobs.

If they had to work, he wished they'd get started. He looked across the yard to where Zykov and Kanygin lived. Why were they taking so long to come out?

Likely he'd be assigned to join the endless rows of students and soldiers mobilized to help pull sugar beets by hand. Helena and the other women would follow along, cutting the green leafy tops with hooked knives, then throwing the beets into a horse-drawn wagon, that is, if the horses were strong enough to pull today. Otherwise, men and women would be hitched to the wagon.

He looked to where Helena stood with her sister, Maria, and sister-in-law, Paulina, chatting, waiting. The women looked rested in their clean work dresses and aprons. Soon they would be covered in dust and sweat, their bare legs and feet scratched from the thistles that had been allowed to infest the field.

Feliks cleared his throat, interrupting Janek's thoughts.

"They better not shorten the midday break because of this," he said, his jaw clenched.

"Probably will," Vladzio muttered. "They'll find some way to blame this on us."

"Could be they finally got the parts for the tractor," Janek said.

Feliks rolled his eyes. "Nah, those parts are never coming. Besides, Vladzio and I were told to sharpen the hooked knives. Have them ready for the morning."

"I wonder what's keeping them?" Vladzio asked, squatting in the shade of the barn beside Feliks and Janek.

Feliks half-smiled. "Maybe too much vodka."

Janek's gaze shifted to the dozen or so emaciated men and women sitting on straw pallets. Some ate boiled potatoes and greens, the weaker ones a thin porridge. Last week the Soviets didn't care whether people lived or died. Now those in various stages of starvation had been lured here by the promise of food to regain their strength.

Some were from the wheat-growing districts to the east, where the famine raged the hardest. Too weak to make their way to the Polish border, they had been brought here.

Others Janek recognized as former collective workers. He hadn't seen them for months and had assumed they'd left or died. But here they were, thin and hollow-eyed, with no more strength than to work for a few minutes before taking a rest.

Zykov and especially Kanygin had no tolerance for workers they considered malingering. Still, they now knew better than to push these people. A woman had collapsed after Kanygin threatened to order her off the collective for taking too many breaks. When they tried to revive the woman, her heart had stopped beating.

Not far from the adults, gaunt-faced children sat in the shade of a tree. Two older women from the collective were assigned to provide nursing care for them and regular feedings of milk and buckwheat porridge. Even with the feedings, Janek watched some of them aimlessly plucking at blades of grass, still intent on feeding themselves.

Janek's thoughts turned to the last time he saw Tetyana. If only he had cared enough for the child to have kept her alive. He could visualize her sitting on the grass with the other children, waiting for him to be done his shift. He saw himself scooping her up in his arms and carrying her home. As the vision faded, a hollow wrench of sadness went through him. Her eyes. Would he ever forget how her eyes had pleaded for him not to leave. He rubbed his head in his hands. Oh, God, would the pain ever let go?

"Comrade Kanygin is coming," someone said with urgency, stirring Janek out of his brooding.

Janek rose to his feet and took off his cap along with the others. He wondered where Zykov was.

Kanygin surveyed the workers, pausing for a moment before speaking. "Zykov will not be joining us today," he said, an arrogant edge to his voice.

Janek couldn't believe an underling would speak of a leader with such disrespect. Saying Zykov instead of Comrade Zykov?

"Is Comrade Zykov ill?" someone tentatively asked.

"Probably," sneered Kanygin. "They charged him with sabotage for failing to secure the grain quota. He refused to use the farm machinery sent to this district."

Janek looked at Feliks and Vladzio, their eyes speaking the words that Janek was thinking. Always the Soviets had to have someone to blame.

"Everything will go much better now that he and his kind are gone."

No one spoke. No one moved. Maybe this was some kind of trick to see who was loyal to Zykov and who was not. Maybe in a moment, Zykov would come strolling out of his house, walking like a czar over his collective kingdom. Janek looked toward the farmhouse. No one came out.

"Stalin has ordered all collective leaders who have caused such losses to be deported and replaced by loyal Soviets. Stalin has also announced that grain quotas everywhere are to be lowered. Everyone who works on the collective will have a share of this year's grain harvest."

"Yeah, right," said Feliks under his breath as all around, cries of joy and cheering rang out. Men slapped each other on the backs and couples hugged. Helena pushed her way over to him, her eyes glossy with tears.

"Did you hear what he said, Janek? The famine is over."

"Maybe it's over. Time will tell."

Helena looked at him and blinked, some of the shine leaving her eyes.

After a moment, Kanygin held up his hand. "The reason for this change of policy is that the converting of individual farms to collectives has been very successful." Kanygin looked pointedly at the workers, waiting for what pro-Soviet statements always required.

Janek and Helena clapped with vigour.

"Everything is in common now. All fields belong to the collectives."

They clapped again, some cheered.

Kanygin smiled benevolently at them. "Our Soviet leaders say they have made their point. Millions of kulaks, who have been at the heart of this great struggle, are now dead or deported."

Janek glanced at Maria. How would she take that statement when her husband, Józef, was one of the deported? But she, too, clapped. She had her children to protect.

After the day of work, Janek and Helena walked home, following the rutted road that ran along the banks of the Smotrych River. Watching the swallows flit in and out of their burrows in the clay banks, Janek's mind turned to Tetyana ... her little face, her tenderness, her innocence. Like the birds, she, too, had flitted in and out of his life. His chest ached with the pain of losing her as he tried to lend a perfunctory ear to Helena's prattle about chickens.

"Do you think we should raise the chickens more for meat or eggs?" she asked, a note of anticipation in her voice.

"You're giving too much thought to the famine being over."

"I don't know, with those feeding stations and all. Might be true. Oh, Janek, wouldn't it be nice to have a sow and a few piglets again?"

Janek forced a smile.

She gave an exasperated sigh and stopped in the middle of the road. "What is wrong with you?"

He shrugged. She didn't know about Tetyana. And his guilt.

"You don't seem to be the least bit happy that Zykov's gone and maybe the famine is over."

Janek took a breath then looked at Helena, her lips pressed together as she searched his face.

"I met a little girl when I was selling knives. She was nearly dead. Oryst and I took care of her for a while. Ended up loving that little thing but we had nothing to eat. Left her in a children's shelter hoping it would be better than with us."

He stared into the distance, taking a deep breath before he went on. "When we were ready to go home, I went to get her. Hoped you and I could take her in, be a little sister for Veronika." He stopped, his eyes misting over.

"Go on," Helena said, putting her hand on his arm.

"By the time I got there, she had died."

Tears brimmed in Helena's eyes. "Oh, Janek! It's not your fault. You did the best you could."

He shook his head. "It is my fault. I should have got her out of there sooner, but she would have been a hindrance selling knives."

"Janek, you have to forgive yourself. There were so many starving children. You couldn't help them all."

"I don't know if I can ever forgive myself."

Turning a bend in the road, he saw Veronika waiting for them by their gate. She raced out to meet them, grinning broadly, braids bouncing behind her. Tetyana had been so much like her, all tenderness and innocence. Veronika threw her arms around him, reminding him of how Tetyana had clung to him and the tenderness of his feelings.

Janek turned his head away, tears threatening to spill over.

"Mama, what's wrong with Tata?"

"Don't worry, Veronika. It's just that he loves you so much, he's reminded of another child."

"What child?"

"Tata doesn't want to talk about it anymore. Let's you and I walk ahead and let Tata be."

Janek sat by the river's edge, letting the sound of the swirling waters soothe his soul. Eventually he whispered across the waters:

Please Lord, forgive me for letting Tetyana die. I knew in my heart that I should check on her. Instead, my only concern was of selling knives and going home.

Let not her life or any of those who died without a grave be forgotten and lost through time. Help me explain to Veronika what I saw, so that she, too, can know and tell her children and her children's children.

As he slowly walked into the house, the words of the children echoed in his mind:

I will die, I will die.
And nobody will know my grave.
And nobody will come and remember,
Only the nightingale will sing.

> *(Although the exact death toll of the Holodomor famine will never be known) ... total number of missing Ukrainians 4.5 million. These figures include all victims, wherever they died—by the roadside, in prison, in orphanages ...*
> —Anne Applebaum, *Red Famine: Stalin's War on Ukraine.*

48
JANEK

August 1933

As the last light of the day faded from the sky, Janek sat on the stone bench and leaned his back against the wall of his house. Veronika was already in bed. He should be going in, too, yet he lingered, listening to the sounds of the river from across the way and the soothing drone of the crickets.

Janek scanned the sky, hoping to find the first star, but no, it was still too light. His eyes rested on the stubble left in the field beside his home and he felt content. There would be no starvation this winter. Stalin had created a new law in order to quickly rebuild food reserves. People were once more allowed to own livestock. They could grow food in their gardens, and this year, workers had to be paid their full grain allotment. Eight sacks of buckwheat he had taken home today. Not a lot, but enough so they could eat bread with every meal.

The front door opened and a shaft of light from the kitchen flooded the harmony of his retreat. Helena, in her long white nightgown, stood in the doorway. A shawl covered her shoulders. Her brown hair, loosened from the confines of its braided bun, flowed freely down her back, almost to her waist.

"Not coming in yet?" she asked.

"It's beautiful out here. Why don't you sit with me for a while?"

She closed the door, padded over in bare feet and sat beside him. As she threaded her arm around his back, he felt the flush of pleasure he always did when she was close.

"It's over, Janek," she said. With a sigh, she rested her head on his shoulder. "The famine is over."

He turned and kissed her lightly on the lips then pressed her against his chest, feeling the beat of her heart against his. Contentment rose from his soul. At last, he released her.

She settled her head back onto his shoulder and said, "Maybe tomorrow we can get our grain milled."

"I wouldn't mind having some ground, but I'm thinking of hiding some. What if they raise our district's quota again?"

Helena sat up. "I've been thinking about that, too."

"Maybe tomorrow night we should start burying sacks in pits. The east side of the garden would be good. The soil is already disturbed there."

Helena leaned forward. "Why don't we start tonight? It will only take me a minute to get changed."

"Really? Tonight?"

"Why not? At least bury a few sacks."

Janek let out a shaky laugh. "It would make me sleep better."

Two hours later, Janek paused from his steady shovelling. He put the shovel down and took a rag to wipe the sweat from his face. "That should be deep enough," he said as he sat down, his legs dangling inside the pit. Helena set the lantern down and passed him a dipperful of water from the enamelled pail beside her.

As Janek rested, he stared at all the stars shimmering in the night sky. As always, he marvelled at their beauty and at the infinite expanse of the universe overhead. He felt so inconsequential, one small man in the vast tapestry of time.

"You know, Helena, our lives are so short and then the next generation comes. And after we are gone and Veronika is gone, who is going to know about us or even care? Who will know we even lived?"

"Janek, I don't like to think like that. It is too depressing."

"Well, it's true. Every trace of us is going to disappear. Everyone we know will be gone. That's why for the short time we have on earth, we should be able to live freely, to be able to work our own land, go to church, and make a good life for our daughter. It's all we want."

"I know, Janek. But what can we do? We're slaves to the Soviets. We have to do what they say. They decide who lives, dies, or is deported."

"And we can do nothing about it," he said, resting his arms on his knees.

"I wonder," Helena said, "if the only reason they ended the famine was, if it continued, there would be no one left to work."

Janek rubbed his shoulder. "Yet still they deport people. Took Bilak, Evancho, and Panas yesterday."

"They did? For what?"

"Said they were malcontents."

"Matko Boska, Janek. What does that mean?"

Janek shrugged. Standing up, he said, "You know the Soviets. It means whatever they want it to mean. After this one, let's go in. I can't do anymore tonight."

"And I have to get up early. It's Veronika's first day back at school tomorrow."

49

JANEK

The next morning as Janek split pieces of kindling into fine slivers for the woodstove, he felt a flicker of happiness. At least now he didn't have to worry about starvation for the winter months. Tonight, if he had the strength, he would try to hide a few more sacks.

As the wood caught fire and orange flames leapt up above the round opening of the cast iron stovetop, Veronika came twirling out of her room into the kitchen, in her special-occasion black uniform and white apron.

"Don't I look beautiful, Tata?" she asked, her beribboned braids swinging.

"Is today a special day?" he asked with a trace of a smile.

"Tata, you know it is. I start the fifth grade today. Alina and I have it already planned. We're bringing the teacher flowers, and we get to join the Young Pioneers."

"The Communist youth party?"

"Don't scowl, Tata. I'm already in the Little Octobrists, and Young Pioneers is just like that.

"That's exactly how they start out, little by little. And what does it lead to? Becoming a communist."

Helena came down the loft steps carrying a string of dried apples.

"Helena. Did you hear? Today Veronika joins the Young Pioneers."

"Please Mama, don't be upset."

Helena looked from Veronika to him. "Janek," she said, touching him on the arm, "It has to be."

It felt as if Soviet fists were shattering his happiness.

He strode out the door and slammed it shut behind him. A moment later, Helena came out. He felt her hand slowly rubbing his back. She didn't speak, just rubbed in a slow circular motion. He felt the tension within him gradually loosen. Why did he always feel like this? He took a deep breath and let it out, his body involuntarily shuddering as he did so. As her eyes searched his, remorse weighed upon him. He could see the pain his outburst had caused her.

"Oh, Helena, I can't have them take her away from me. Already they have her memorizing so many communist poems and songs she can't help but absorb some of it."

"Janek, there's nothing we can do. Julia and Stasik go to Young Pioneers, and you know how Feliks feels about communism."

"She'll forget she's Polish," he said in a small voice.

"She will never forget," Helena said soothingly as she again rubbed his back. "We'll ask Paulina to teach Veronika how to read and write in Polish when she teaches Julia and Stasik. And when Veronika is old enough to understand and to keep what you say a secret, tell her what the Soviets have done to us. Tell her everything."

Janek gave her a tired smile. "You always know how to make me feel better." In broad daylight, in front of their house, where anyone travelling down the road could see them, he kissed her.

50

VERONIKA

Veronika took her usual place beside Alina in their double-seated desk and waited for the teacher to enter the room. The exhilaration she felt at being in school again faded as she looked around the classroom. Where were Aleksandra, with her bright blue eyes, and her little brother Symon, who used to sneak up and pull her braids? Where was dark-haired Milena? And Marko and Denys who used to play with her in the field with a homemade rag ball?

Veronika turned to Alina. "So many are missing."

Alina nodded, her face bleak. "Mama says I'm not to talk about it."

Veronika felt weighed down. Although everything in the classroom looked the same, with rows of double-seated iron desks and the familiar smell of pencil shavings and new notebooks, it had all changed. No longer did it seem like the safe place it used to be, where thoughts of deportation and the famine faded to the back of her mind. She took a deep breath and slowly exhaled as a sensation of sadness and loss rose and flowed through her.

To distract herself, she looked at the blackboard, where the teacher had already chalked math problems. Veronika took her time reading the questions over. Maybe she could be one of the first to solve them. It would be a good start to maintaining her status of top student.

As her classmates whispered, she turned to see what Kazia and her other friends were doing. Her eyes lingered on Marek. How handsome he looked with his blond hair slicked back, and a crisp white shirt under his blue uniform. She wished he would still walk to school with them, but he now chose to walk with a few of the other boys.

She thought of the flower he had given her years ago. She'd kept it pressed between the pages of an old notebook in her bedroom. Without warning, Marek turned and their eyes met. Veronika blinked and looked away as a rush of blood went to her head. Alina nudged her. Veronika ignored her. Refusing to be put off, Alina leaned into Veronika's shoulder and said under her breath, "My brother looks handsome today, does he not?"

Veronika shrugged.

"Well, just to let you know, I caught him staring at you, too."

"Really? For how long?"

"So, you are interested," Alina said, a smile in her words.

All talking stopped as the teacher walked in. Everyone rose to their feet and greeted him. They remained standing until he said, "You may sit."

Veronika liked her teacher. This was the third year she'd been in his room. He was an older man with grey hair. Deep creases between his brows gave him the appearance of having a perpetual frown. He wore round wire-frame glasses and had slightly protruding ears. Despite his stern appearance, Veronika could detect a certain gentleness behind his eyes; she knew that he liked and respected her as well.

After his welcoming greeting, Veronika heard a shuffling sound at the door, and the principal ushered a small group of students to the front of the room. They stood waiting shyly as the principal and the teacher conferred. Veronika recognized one of the girls, the one with wavy red hair, as the daughter of the Jewish general store manager in Kuzmin where her mother shopped. Alina and Veronika nudged each other with excitement as they stared curiously at the group.

When the principal left, their teacher said, "These children used to go to the Jewish school. Since their school only goes to the third grade, they have come here. I'm going to change the seating arrangements to help them make new friends. Would anyone like to change partners?"

A few children put up their hands—the ones who didn't get along with their seatmate. After there were no more volunteers, the teacher started moving children who didn't want to change. Veronika and Alina held hands, silently willing the teacher not to look at them. The teacher scanned up and down the rows of double desks. His gaze fell on Veronika and Alina's. Veronika held her breath and clenched Alina's hand.

"Yes," the teacher said, "I think that would be perfect. What is your name?" he asked the red-headed girl.

"Frania," she said, not raising her head.

"Frania, you will have Veronika as your partner. Alina, move to that desk by the window."

Veronika was stunned. Alina leave her side? Her seatmate for the past four years? She glanced to where he'd told Alina to move. Three whole rows away. She might as well be in another classroom, she was so far away.

As Alina got up to leave, they gazed mournfully at each other. Then she turned, notebooks and pencils clutched in her arms and walked away. Frania stood in the aisle, waiting to take Alina's spot. Instantly, Veronika's sorrow turned to anger. She would make the interloper pay. As Frania turned to sit down, Veronika scooted over, blocking most of the seat. Frania perched on the scant few inches left to her, sitting sideways with her feet in the aisle to keep from falling off the bench. Veronika glowed with self-satisfaction. It felt good to make Frania hurt, just like she was hurting.

The teacher strode down their aisle then paused by their desk. "Put your feet in," he said gruffly. "You'll trip me."

Pulling her feet in, Frania nudged Veronika over. Veronika nudged her back and pinched her. Frania pinched her back. Veronika scratched her arm. Frania punched her in the arm. On and on they fought, silently but with increasing fury. Veronika lost her mind. She lunged at Frania and bit her on the arm. Frania shrieked, tears gliding down her cheeks.

Veronika stared at her in shock and horror. What had she done? Shame engulfed her as all eyes turned to them. The next moment, the teacher towered over them. Veronika cast her eyes down to the black iron railing of their desk and awaited her exposure.

"Frania, what happened?" he asked.

Wiping tears and sniffling, she said, "My fingers got pinched in the desk."

When the teacher moved away, Veronika glanced at Frania.

"Thank you," Veronika said, a tremor to her voice.

— ✳ —

When it was time to go home, Veronika put on her coat with trepidation. Had either Kazia or Alina witnessed her fight with Frania? If so, it was bound to get back to her parents. As they walked, neither one mentioned it. Warmth returned to her body. She was going to survive.

Throwing open the door, she saw her mother washing potatoes.

"Hello, Veronika. How was school?"

A lump reasserted itself in Veronika's stomach. "Fine. A new girl sits with me now. Her father runs the general store."

"She's Jewish, then?"

Veronika nodded.

"That's good. Less talking and more studying."

Veronika picked up a knife. "Let me help you peel," she said, happy to put the subject of Frania behind her.

51

VERONIKA

March 1934

When Veronika came home from school, she knew something bad had happened. One look at Mama and she could tell she'd been crying. Tata sat staring out the window.

"Have a good day at school?" he asked, pasting a smile on his face.

"Yes, but what's wrong?"

He didn't answer.

Veronika dropped her school satchel. "Mama, what is it? I'm eleven now. You can tell me."

"The Soviets want to take our church away," she said, taking a ragged breath. "Convert it into something useful."

"Convert it? Into what?"

"We don't know yet."

Stunned, Veronika sat on the bench beside her mother. "Will they convert the Ukrainian Orthodox church, too?"

Mama nodded. "And the synagogue."

Veronika thought of Frania and the grief she must be going through.

"Why? Why do they have to do this?"

"They say there is no God, no more priests," Mama said, her mouth trembling, "So why have unused buildings?"

"We have to go vote on it," Tata said, his hands now clenched into fists. "So they can say it's the will of the people. Yet who would vote against it? A day, maybe two, then the secret police would be at their door." He dropped his head into his hands. Frightened, Veronika looked at her mother, but she seemed lost in her own world of pain. Veronika didn't know what to do.

After a few moments, Tata raised his head and wiped his eyes with the back of his hand.

"How can I vote that they should destroy our church?" Mama asked. "All the memories I have. I will never forget our baby's small casket being carried into the church. Do you remember, Janek?" she asked, her voice drifting off.

Tata nodded, lips pressed together.

"Yet once his body was in the church, I felt at peace. I had given him back to God," Mama said.

Veronika felt tears come to her eyes as she thought of Vladimir, the baby brother she had never met.

"And Veronika's baptism?" Tata asked in a strained voice. "As soon as that cold river water hit her, such a fuss she made. Do you remember?"

Mama smiled. "I remember."

"And when I think of the church, Helena, I think of our wedding day. I felt so lucky."

"I'm the lucky one. Good thing Honorata stole that lowlife I almost married."

"What? You were engaged to someone else, Mama?"

A shadow passed across Mama's face as her eyes hardened. "It's not for you to know. Come, help me get the soup ready. After we eat, we go to my brother's to pray the rosary."

That evening as they entered Uncle Feliks's and Aunt Paulina's home, it was full of their Polish Catholic relatives and neighbours. Except for Aunt Agnes, who sat because of her hip, they stood in small groups, talking in anxious voices.

Babcia's voice rang out above the rest. "If my husband were alive, he would never stand for this. Never. You are all a bunch of cowards."

"Mama, calm down," Uncle Vladzio said, stroking her back.

"I will not calm down," she said, her eyes bulging. "Every single person in this room is to blame. If they had stood up to them like I did, none of this would have happened."

Aunt Agnes smiled and motioned Veronika over. Warmth swept through Veronika's heart as she pressed a kiss to her cheek.

"I don't see you so much anymore," she said, taking Veronika's hand between hers.

"It's school. So much more homework now."

"How about after this meeting, you come to my house?

Veronika looked at her aunt's kindly eyes and nodded. Aunt Agnes flashed her a secret smile and a wink.

Uncle Feliks's booming voice cut through all conversation in the room. "Everyone is here. Now we will say the rosary. After that we can talk, with one person speaking at a time."

While Veronika prayed, the wooden beads slipping through her fingers, her mind drifted to what Mama had said about being engaged to someone else. Who was Honorata? Why would one not speak of her? Maybe if she pressed Aunt Agnes enough, she would tell her.

After the rosary ended, Uncle Feliks said, "Now we can talk. Stand, so we know who is speaking."

"What are we going to do?" a neighbour asked. "How can we live without at least being able to look at our beautiful church? Once it's converted, everything about it being our church will be destroyed."

"I know what you mean," Uncle Vladzio said, "To see it standing there, closed up the way it is, we could at least hope that someday they would relax the rules and let us reopen it."

"Isn't it just like everything else they have done to us? Keep taking more and more. Now they even take our hope," Tata said.

A neighbour who used to assist the priest stood. "In one village, they converted the church into a pigsty."

Veronika gasped. A shocked silence followed.

"The sacrilege," Babcia said, shaking her fist with emotion. "To think of having pigs live and urinate on that holy ground, where I had my children baptized and where my parents and my husband had their funerals ..." Her voice broke. She dropped into her chair, tears streaming down her cheeks.

Tata stood up. "I say we burn our church to the ground, rather than let them turn it into a pigsty."

"Sure, you do that and they'll come for you," Uncle Vladzio said. "Not only you but Helena and Veronika, too."

Uncle Feliks, his face flushed a deep red, violently shoved back his chair. Standing before everyone, he looked wildly around the room, then said in a thunderous voice, "I tell you what we can do." Again, he paused. "We can do nothing! We have to vote yes."

Silence lingered throughout the room until Babcia got up and croaked, "Cowards! All of you, cowards."

"Everyone needs time to think." Aunt Paulina said in her calm voice. "I'll go put out the tea. Come help me," she said to her daughter Julia. As the other women got up to help, Uncle Vladzio took out his harmonica and started playing a melodic folksong of longing and sorrow.

Aunt Agnes looked at Veronika and gestured with her head toward her half of the duplex. Veronika nodded.

"Not staying for tea, Agnes?" Aunt Paulina asked.

"We'll be back later. Veronika and I go to my house for a little visit."

— ❋ —

As Veronika walked into Aunt Agnes's side of the duplex, her spirits were lifted by their special relationship.

"Sit down, Veronika. I'll light the lantern."

In the glow of the hissing kerosene lamp, Veronika popped the big question. "Who is Honorata?"

Aunt Agnes's eyes widened slightly then became guarded. "Your mother never told you?"

Veronika shook her head. "No one ever talked to me about her."

"Because of her, my Vladzio went to prison for seven years."

"What? Oh, please, you have to tell me everything."

"I don't know," Aunt Agnes said, brushing invisible crumbs from the table with her hand. "I don't want any trouble from your mother."

"Please. I'm old enough to know." Seeing the flicker of indecision in her aunt's eyes, Veronika pressed a little harder. "I won't tell. I promise."

"All right." Aunt Agnes said, staring into space. "Maybe it's time you knew about this aunt of yours. You know that Babcia has four children."

"Yes, two sons, Feliks and Vladzio, and two daughters, Kazia's mother and my mother."

"That is right, but what you don't know is Babcia had two more daughters. One a twin of Feliks, the other a twin of Vladzio."

Veronika's jaw dropped. "Babcia had two more daughters?"

"No one speaks of Feliks's twin because she eloped and disappeared when Babcia tried to forbid her marriage. With Vladzio's twin, Honorata, it was something much worse."

"What?"

"She abandoned her husband and children and went off with another man. They took a freighter bound for New York to start a new life."

"That's terrible."

"But it gets worse. The man Honorata went off with was engaged."

"To my mother," Veronika said, feeling like a stone had lodged in her throat.

Aunt Agnes nodded. "The hurt must have been unimaginable, that Helena's sister was having an affair with her fiancé behind her back."

Veronika put her hand to her throat. "Poor Mama."

Aunt Agnes got up, opened the iron door of the woodstove, and stoked it. Veronika watched the sparks swirl and leap as she threw in another log. She sat down, her face solemn. "Maybe I shouldn't have told you."

"No, no. I needed to know. Please, go on. What did Mama do?"

"What could she do? She went into shock. Everyone went into shock. Then came the humiliation and gossip. To take away the family's shame, Babcia ordered Vladzio to go to New York and bring his twin sister home."

"How did you feel about Uncle Vladzio going?"

"I was worried sick. This was just before the start of the Great War." Aunt Agnes's eyes opened wide with meaning. "But Vladzio always had to do as his mother told him."

"Did he find her?"

"He found her, all right, in the immigrant slums of New York. She refused to leave and so, in the end, Vladzio gave up and started for home. The war was well underway by then. The French captured him and accused him of being a spy."

Veronika held her head. "How is it that no one told me this?"

Aunt Agnes went on. "For seven years they kept them in prison, and for all those years I waited for my Vladzio, not knowing if he was dead or alive."

"Oh, Aunt Agnes," Veronika said, her chest tightening with the sadness of it all.

"When he came home, he was in very bad shape, thin like a skeleton. They did something to him, what I don't know, but we couldn't have children. It was then that you were born to your mother and father, and you became like a daughter to us as well."

Veronika could barely speak. So much of what she had sensed about her family fell into place. Back at Uncle Feliks's and Aunt Paulina's, Veronika looked at her family in a new light, not just as a protective circle of adults, but people with their own weaknesses, hopes and dreams, and disappointments.

The Bolsheviks first liquidated the Ukrainian Autocephalous Orthodox Church, killing two metropolitans, 26 archbishops and bishops, 1,500 priests, 54 deacons and some 20,000 lay members of the parish councils. Not only was life destroyed, but 90% of Church buildings were either destroyed or convened into warehouses, museums, barns, dance halls, and so on.

—Andrew Wodoslawsky, *The Red Harvest*

52

VERONIKA

June 1934

Veronika sat at the kitchen table, studying for an exam, when Uncle Feliks walked in, his face tense. "I don't have good news. I found out the Ukrainian Orthodox church is being converted into a granary and the synagogue into an administrative building.

"What about our church?" Tata asked, his face rigid.

"A dancehall."

"Oh, my, no," Mama said, holding a hand to her mouth.

"Are you sure?" Tata asked.

"I'm sure."

Tata got to his feet. In a voice shaking with emotion, he raised his fist and said, "The idea of people dancing and drinking in the house of God, maybe even spitting … it's too much to even think of."

Mama said, "Janek and I will never set foot in that dancehall, and you won't either, Veronika."

"No, of course not," Veronika said, appalled at the idea.

Two months later, in the summer of 1934, the demolition work started. Everyone wanted to see what the Soviets were doing; they also wanted to mourn. Veronika and her parents walked to the hill outside the village where the three houses of God stood. At the base was the Synagogue and farther up were the Polish Catholic church and the Ukrainian Orthodox church.

A group of Jewish men stood at the edge of the road that overlooked their synagogue, its doors flung open wide, a smouldering fire of books and scrolls nearby.

Tata's jaw clenched. "How could they do that?"

"The same way they took our blessed statue of Mary and smashed it," Mama said, sorrow in her eyes.

"Come with me while I go have a word with Avraham. He was the one that always ground our grain at the mill," Tata said.

"Should we?" Mama asked, her eyes worried.

"Of course. I've known him for years."

Tata, Mama, and Veronika approached and stood silent watch over the synagogue for a minute for two. Tata walked up to Avraham and said, "We've come to see our church before they make it into a dancehall."

Pointing at the Soviet soldiers, Avraham said, "They can destroy the building but not our belief."

"So true," Tata said. "The Soviets haven't found a way to control our thoughts yet."

On their continued walk uphill to their church, Veronika had a new lightness in her step. Tata had brushed off Mama's fears about approaching the Jewish men. He did what he felt was right. Someday, she vowed to be like him and not let fear hold her back.

Ahead, throngs of people stood on the road in front of their church. Across the lane, others stood by the Ukrainian Orthodox church. Already, the crosses had been removed from both churches and thrown to the ground.

Everywhere there were soldiers working alongside the militia, some gutting the inside of the church, others carrying what they didn't want into the fire.

When a solider came out carrying a gold-edged book, Veronika gasped as others moaned and cried. That was the book the priest read from. The soldier tossed it in the fire with a flourish. Watching the flames lap the edges of the pages, Veronika wept, thinking of all the times the priest had read from that book as she sat in the soft illumination of the candlelight and smell of incense.

Another soldier came out of the church, a grin on his face, wearing their priest's vestments over his uniform. Veronika closed her eyes. When she opened them again, the vestments were in the fire, flames already lapping at the finely embroidered edges.

On the walk home, she asked her father, "I know the government says they are doing this to make use of empty buildings, but what is the real reason?"

"To destroy God in people's hearts. Remember this day, Veronika, as the day the Soviets were defeated in their goal. Never will God be destroyed within us."

They continued, walking in silence, each in their own thoughts, until Tata turned to Mama and said, "I feel I let God down by not doing anything to stop the soldiers. Daniel stood in the lion's den rather than deny God."

Taking his hand in hers, Mama said, "I don't think Daniel had a wife or a child standing beside him. Maybe he wouldn't have made the same choice if they were."

53
VERONIKA

October 1934

Eleven-year-old Veronika walked home from school, eager to share her excitement with her parents. As she turned into her yard, the smell of baking bread wafted from the outdoor oven. Good, they were home from the collective. With the harvest in, they were getting home earlier. Thinking of her good news, she ran the rest of the way in.

"You seem happy," Tata said. "You must have done well on that science test."

"Better than that."

Her mother smiled. "What is it?"

"Frania invited me to her house for lunch tomorrow. She's going to teach me how to write in Hebrew."

The smile faded from her parents' faces as they exchanged startled looks.

"Where does she live?" asked Tata.

"Her house is at the back of her father's general store on the main street of Kuzmin."

"Did she get permission to have you over?" asked Mama.

"Yes. Her mother said I'm welcome anytime." Veronika held her breath as Tata stroked his beard.

"I've had business dealings with her father. He's a good man, Helena."

Her mother frowned. "I don't know if it's such a good thing for her, Janek. They're Jewish. Things will be different."

"What harm can come of it? And if she doesn't like it, that will be the end of it." Tata put his hand on Veronika's shoulder. "We'll allow you to go. But tomorrow is Saturday, and farmer's market. You must help your mother before you go."

"Yes, Tata. Thank you." She ran to her room, and flopped on her bed, releasing the butterflies of excitement inside her. The only friends she had visited by herself were relatives. For the first time, she would be visiting a friend of her own choosing, just like a grown woman.

Early the next morning, Veronika and her mother packed their extra produce, filling their wheelbarrow with onions, pumpkins, and apples. Taking turns, they pushed it along the rutted road to the village centre. Already, vendors had spread out their mats and tables and set up displays of produce, home crafts, and used goods. Veronika usually liked to wander around, but not today.

Mama set her mat down beside her friend, Lilka, who sold hemp and sunflower seeds.

"Hello, Veronika. Helping your mother today?"

Veronika gave a curt nod then focused on unloading, not wanting to waste time talking.

"My daughters don't help me. Say they're too busy. But what's busy? They could bring their babies to the market. That's what I did when I was their age."

"Times have changed, Lilka." Mama turned and gave Veronika a cloth. "Give the apples a shine then set them out. You know how I like them, red side facing out."

Veronika sat on the far side of the mat with her back slightly away from Lilka. Best not to offend her, but Frania could be waiting already.

By the time she finished, her mother had set out inviting pyramids of pumpkins and onions.

"All right, Veronika, I guess you can go now."

"Where is she going?" asked Lilka. "Not staying to help you sell?"

"No, she's off to visit a friend."

Lilka shook her head. "So, your daughter, too, abandons you."

Mama said nothing; instead, she pinned back Veronika's hair where it had come loose, and helped her get her blouse all tucked in.

"Must be someone special you're going to see," Lilka called out.

Mama, her back to Lilka, rolled her eyes. In hushed tones, she said, "Now, make sure to use your best manners. And thank Frania's mother before you leave."

"I will, Mama."

"And take what they offer, even if you aren't used to that kind of food."

That was something she hadn't thought of. "What kind of food do they have?"

"They keep to themselves in the village, so I don't know much. I do know they are particular about how they slaughter animals, and they don't eat pork."

"I hope they don't have anything like carp soup," Veronika said, "Like that stringy grey soup Babcia makes with the fish head floating in it."

"They won't. That's Babcia's specialty. Go along now. Have a good time."

"Where's she going?" Lilka asked.

"To a schoolfriend. They're going to do some studying."

"Ah. Studying. That's good. She can work and support her parents in their old age. Not like my two. They say times are hard. Ha! They think they've had it hard?"

Once again Mama stepped in. "Bye, Veronika. Best go before you're late."

"Bye, Mama. Bye, Lilka. Good luck selling."

As she walked, she thought of how Frania was now an even closer friend than Alina had ever been. She especially liked how she could talk freely with Frania about anything, and it wouldn't get back to her parents.

When she got to Frania's house, she gave the door a tentative rap. After a quick patter of running feet, the door flew open. Frania's six-year-old brother, Izaak, stood there. He had the same red hair as Frania. Before she could say anything, Frania's mother approached. She was a long, lean woman with a smile that made Veronika feel at ease.

"Come in, my dear. We've been expecting you." Turning to Izaak, she said, "Tell Frania her friend is here."

While Veronika waited, an uncomfortable silence formed in which she alternated between glancing down and then up at Frania's mother. She appeared quite different from her own mama, more like a city woman. Her face wasn't brown from the sun, but silky and smooth. And her hair flowed freely in loose waves to her shoulders rather than rolled up in a bun.

At a loss for anything else to say, Veronika said, "Thank you for inviting me over."

"Of course. Frania often talks about you. It's like you're *mishpokhe* already."

Warmth flooded Veronika's cheeks. Did mishpokhe mean something bad? Maybe Frania had told her about their fight.

Frania bounded up to the door, her face aglow with happiness. "Veronika, you're here," she said, giving her a little hug. "Come on outside. I'll show you around."

Izaak ran out the door ahead of them.

Frania frowned. "No, you aren't tagging along."

The joyous exuberance faded from his face. Head down, he turned to go in.

"Oh, Frania, please let him stay. I've always wanted a little brother."

He turned, hope resurrecting in his eyes.

"All right, you can stay. But when Veronika and I go into my bedroom, you have to keep out. We want our privacy, don't we?" she said, looking to Veronika for affirmation.

Veronika gave a little shrug, not wanting to get between Frania and her brother.

"I promise," he said, with a grin.

"He's been so excited about your visit," Frania said.

"That explains why the door opened so fast," Veronika said with a laugh. "Nearly startled me off the steps."

Going by the garden, Izaak pointed to the clumps of freshly pulled garlic and onion drying on the ground. "I planted those myself."

"It's nice," Veronika said, amazed at what a tiny patch the garden was compared to her parents' field of vegetables. "Do you have a root cellar?"

"What's that?"

Veronika wondered what their mother did all day. She didn't work on the collective, and she had never seen her in the store. She didn't preserve food for the winter or fill a cold cellar. Probably she didn't even make candles or soap, and she surely didn't make Frania's clothes.

After walking around the yard, Veronika had an idea. "Izaak, would you like us to give you a swing?"

"How?" he asked, hopping up and down.

"Frania will take your feet and I'll take your hands and we'll swing you back and forth."

At first there was a little fear in his eyes, but moments later, he couldn't stop laughing. Tiring at last, they put him down.

"More, please?"

"I want to show Veronika inside now," Frania said.

Veronika touched Frania on the arm. Lowering her voice, she said, "Before we go in, I need to ask you about something your mother said to me."

"Oh? What?" Frania asked, her eyebrows furrowed with concern.

"She said I'm like mishpokhe already."

Frania laughed. "You silly goose. It means you're like family, probably because I talk about you so much."

Relief swept through Veronika. Her fight with Frania on that first day of school had not been exposed.

Walking into the living room, Veronika marvelled that they had wooden plank floors instead of hard-packed earth. Frania's mother sat in a chair by the window, sewing, but not the kind her mother did—mending socks or sewing on patches. Frania's mother worked on a picture, the kind you hung on the wall or decorated a pillow with.

Glancing up, she said, "I heard everyone laughing out there."

"We were swinging Izaak."

She gave a slight smile, then went back to her work while Frania showed Veronika around the room.

Veronika couldn't help but slide her hand over the heavily polished dark wood of the side tables, with their legs all curves and spindles. Veronika doubted their furniture had been made in the barn workshop like theirs. On the mantle, Veronika admired an oblong silver bowl with trailing clusters of grapes and leaves that stood in relief. "It's like you're rich to have such a bowl."

Frania smiled. "Maybe at one time in the past. It belonged to my mother's grandmother. Mama says it will be mine when I get married," Frania said, leading Veronika into the dining room. "This is where we have our everyday meals. For our evening Shabbos meal, we go downstairs."

"What's Shabbos?"

"It's like your Sunday, only ours starts on Friday at sunset and ends as soon as we see the first three stars on Saturday. Do you want to see our Shabbos room?"

"If it's all right."

Frania and Izaak led Veronika down a set of wooden stairs into a single room with a large table and chairs. In the centre of the table sat two heavy, twisted-silver candlesticks. Melted wax had run down the lengths of the candlesticks and sat in a solidified puddle at their base. She wondered why they didn't blow out the candles before it ran like that, but didn't say anything.

"My mother lights the candles in these special candlesticks and then says prayers. That starts the Shabbos," Frania said with pride. "These candlesticks have been in my family for generations. See the writing on the base? It's in Hebrew."

Veronika leaned over to have a closer look at it. "I've never seen letters like that. Can you read Hebrew?"

Frania nodded. "It's not so hard."

"I wish I could read Hebrew," Veronika said.

"It's not hard. I can teach you. Let's go upstairs now, and I can show you my room."

Veronika stepped into Frania's bedroom. Everything spoke of

the love Frania's parents had for her, from the clean, almost floral scent that seemed to waft about the room, to her feather bed with embroidered pillows.

"My mother embroiders," Veronika said, "but she doesn't have time with all the work she has on the collective." She paused to scan a picture tacked above the bed, drawn in a childish hand.

"I do it to please Izaak," Frania said half-apologetically. "He likes it when I hang his pictures. But let me show you one of my best treasures. My father made it for me."

Veronika waited, a shiver of excitement building within her. She loved seeing people's treasures.

Going to her dresser, Frania withdrew a small wooden box and held it out.

"Oh, it's beautiful," Veronika said, tracing her finger over the engraved rose with trailing ivy on the lid. "Your father made this?"

"He bought the pencil box in Germany, but the engraving is his. Open it up."

Veronika slid the lid back to reveal a top tray that rotated out from a bottom tray on a hinge.

"I'll bring it to school and share with you," Frania said. "You can keep your pencils in there, so you won't be losing them so much."

Veronika felt a lightness in her heart as they sat on Frania's bed, talking about school, which of the boys was the cutest, and the similarities and differences between their religions.

"We don't have a rabbi anymore. He disappeared."

"Our priest is gone, too."

"Is your family religious?" asked Frania.

Veronika nodded. "We're always praying. Why?"

"It's just that some of the other Jewish people in the village think

Father should keep his store closed on Saturday. But it's his busiest day of the week with the farmer's market and all." After pausing for a moment, Frania went on pensively, "It's like he kind of picks and chooses which of the religious laws to keep."

"My Babcia picks and chooses which Christian rules to keep. She thinks of herself as holy, but sometimes my family would just like to shake her, even though she's ninety-six years old."

Frania laughed. "Why would they want to shake her?"

"Babcia thinks everything her sons do is perfect, but she hates their wives. Aunt Paulina has it especially bad because Babcia lives with her and Uncle Feliks. Just last week we discovered that Babcia has not been letting Aunt Paulina have lunch."

Frania's eyes widened.

"When Uncle Feliks found out, there was a huge commotion between him and his mother, and now Babcia won't talk to anyone. But that's kind of a blessing, I guess," Veronika said with a snicker.

For the next little while, Frania showed Veronika how to print her name in Hebrew. As Veronika practiced, there was a knock on the door and Izaak poked his head in.

"Izaak. What did I say?"

"Mama said to get you. Lunch is ready."

On the table, Frania's mother had put out a bowl of pale, almost white meatballs. Veronika had never seen such oddly coloured meatballs before and hoped they would taste all right. When they passed the bowl to her, she took only two meatballs. She cut into one and took a small bite. It was amazingly savoury. She looked up and saw Frania and her mother watching her.

"Do you like it?" Frania asked. "My father says it's the best gefilte fish he's ever had."

"Oh, Frania," her mother said, appearing a little embarrassed, "I'm sure everyone makes it as good as mine."

"They're wonderful. How are they made?" asked Veronika.

"First Mother skins and takes the bones out of a carp, then she grinds the raw meat in our meat grinder. Then she puts in egg and onion and crushed breadcrumbs and rolls them into balls and boils them."

"You should taste them warm," Izaak added, "But the fire in the woodstove went out."

"We're not allowed to start a fire on Shabbos," Frania explained.

After they finished their lunch, the girls walked arm in arm down the main street to play on the swings in the park. Veronika felt Frania's arm stiffen and saw secret police soldiers on horseback approaching. A suffocating fear rippled through Veronika's body, even though she knew they wouldn't bother children.

"Just keep to the edge of the road," Frania said. "Don't draw any attention."

After they'd gone by, Veronika shivered. "I'm so afraid they're going to come and arrest my father."

Frania squeezed her hand. "My father is careful not to give them any cause to arrest him, either."

"At night," Veronika said, "when we hear horses go by, we just wait, praying they won't turn into our yard. And in the morning, we hear that another person in our neighbourhood has been arrested."

"Have you heard anything about Kazia's father or her uncles?"

"Nothing yet."

"I don't want to be out here with them around. Do you want to go in my father's store? He might give us candy."

"Sure." Maybe even the soft fruit-filled kind, Veronika thought.

The bells over the door jingled as they entered. Frania's father came out from behind the counter. He was a man of medium build with a long, full beard. He seemed delighted to see them.

"So, this is the friend we've been hearing about."

"Yes, Papa, this is my best friend, Veronika. She's the one who's been helping me in math and Russian."

"Thank you, Veronika," he said, his brown eyes twinkling. "You're a good person, just like your father." He paused to unscrew the lid of a big glass jar of fruit-filled candy. "Would you like some?"

"Yes, please," Veronika said, taking one.

He piled a few more into her hand and then Frania's.

— ✼ —

When she returned home, Veronika got out a piece of paper to show her parents how she could print her name in Hebrew. Her mother and father marvelled.

"Are you sure it says Veronika? Your name looks like a bunch of sideways numbers with a line over it.

"I'm sure, Tata. Her mother even checked it. May I go over to Frania's next week? Everyone was so nice to me."

"Of course," Tata said. He turned to Mama. "You see, Helena? All that worrying was for nothing. She had a good time."

Stalin gave rulings on the use of concentration camps not just for the social rehabilitation of prisoners but also for what they could contribute to the gross domestic product in regions where free labour could not easily be found.
—Robert Service, *Stalin: A Biography*

54

VERONIKA

March 1935

Frantic pounding on the front door startled Veronika out of her sleep. She sat upright in bed and stared into the inky blackness of the room, her muscles tense, a thick ache in her throat.

They had been waiting for this night and now the time had come. Her mind churned with visions of Tata handcuffed and loaded onto the wagon.

She heard the rustle of her parents' feet, the striking of a match. As the faint light flickered, Veronika felt around for her shawl and wrapped it around herself, stepping onto the chilly earthen floor. As she entered the kitchen, Tata was just lighting the kerosene lamp. Mama, hollow-eyed and wraithlike in her long nightgown and loose flowing hair, hovered beside him as he adjusted the flame. Tata's hands trembled as he set the lantern down in the middle of the kitchen table. Veronika stood, transfixed, staring at Tata. His eyes were wide with fear, his face pulled taunt, almost in a grimace.

Was it his death that stood behind the door, demanding to be let in? Tata walked to the door. They heard a voice, not a man, but a woman calling to them. Tata's fingers fumbled slightly as he tried to slide back the bolt.

"Quick, Janek!" Mama urged. "It's Paulina."

Weak with relief, Veronika grasped the table for support when she saw Aunt Paulina, Babcia, and her cousins huddled in the doorway, crying.

"Come in quickly," Tata said.

Mama grabbed Babcia and guided her to a chair by the table as she sobbed, "My sons are gone. They took them away."

Tata motioned Aunt Paulina and her children into the room then shut and bolted the door.

"Vladzio and Feliks are gone," Aunt Paulina said, her face twisted in agony. "The secret police took them."

"My brothers?" Mama gasped. "They took Vladzio? And Feliks?"

"Yes. Yes. They're gone," Babcia said. Burying her head in her arms, she wailed in the singsong way Veronika had only heard at funerals. "Feliks. Vladzio. You are gone. Why did they take you? Why are they always plucking at us? Why can't they leave us alone? Oh, my sons, I love you so much. Now I will never see you again."

That Babcia was already mourning their death struck Veronika so hard, she felt her knees give way. She stumbled over to a chair and sat, shivering and crying.

Aunt Paulina had an arm around Julia, who was sobbing. Stasik sat staring straight ahead, his eyes swollen from crying.

Mama said, "You children need something to eat." Looking at Veronika she said, "Bring some jam and bread out for them."

"She's too upset, Helena," Tata said. "I'll do it."

While Tata sliced bread, Veronika listened as Aunt Paulina struggled to speak. "The secret police banged on the door and when

Feliks opened it, they said, get dressed. You have to come with us. He hasn't done anything, I said. Tell me, what has he done? They laughed and wouldn't answer. While Feliks is getting his clothes on, they start poking through all our things and taking what they liked. When Feliks comes out of the bedroom, they put handcuffs on him and right away they take him out the door."

Crying, Mama reached out and held Aunt Paulina's hand.

Aunt Paulina continued speaking. "On my knees, I tried to hold onto Feliks. He needs clothes. He needs a blanket for Siberia, and some food, I yelled." At this, her face crumpled, and she couldn't go on.

Babcia, her face contorted in agony, said, "They let them take nothing. Nothing."

Mama gathered Babcia in her arms as Babcia seemed to lose all her strength. She looked old and vulnerable as Mama rocked her back and forth. Then Babcia started to cry in a way that Veronika had never heard an adult cry before, like a child.

Tata put the bread and jam on the table then sat beside Veronika, putting his arm around her and drawing her close. She rested her head against his shoulder while all around, her family cried.

After a time, Mama said, "How is Agnes?"

"I feel so bad leaving her there," Paulina said. "But she couldn't walk this far."

"Mama, I need to see how Aunt Agnes is," Veronika said.

"Someone should go with you."

"I'll go," said Tata.

"No, don't go, Janek," said Mama with a look of alarm.

"If they were coming for me, they would be here by now. And tomorrow, we'll go to Gródek and see if we can get a package to them."

"Oh, yes," Aunt Paulina said, her face brightening. "If we get up early, they should still be in Gródek. Did you hear that, Antosia?" she said, going over to where Babcia was slumped over, crying. Aunt Paulina rubbed Babcia's back briskly and shook her a little. "Did you hear? Tomorrow, we'll go see them."

Babcia lifted her head. She looked confused. "We'll go see them?"

"Yes. We'll bring them food and clothes and we'll see if we can speak to someone in charge. Maybe we can find out where they're sending them."

Veronika and her father got dressed then walked quickly to Aunt Agnes's duplex. When Tata opened the door, Aunt Agnes was rocking back and forth moaning, "Vladzio, Vladzio, oh, my husband, Vladzio, I need you. I love you." Locked in her own misery, she couldn't hear or see them.

Veronika rushed over and put her arms around her. Aunt Agnes looked up.

"Oh, Veronika. They took Vladzio."

Veronika nodded, tears streaming down her face as she looked into her aunt's pain-filled eyes.

"They wouldn't let me pack anything. They laughed when I asked if I could pack something for him. Please, I begged them. He'll die without food and a blanket, even before he gets to Siberia. They said he won't be needing anything."

Veronika felt a chill go through her.

Aunt Agnes continued, "They took my prayer books. I said, what are you taking those for? They sneered at me and said maybe I wanted to say my prayers."

They stayed with Aunt Agnes until she said she would lie down and rest.

When Veronika and Tata got home, Mama poured them each a mug of mint tea. As Veronika stared into the lantern and sipped on the fragrant tea, she felt a gradual loosening of the tension in her body, voices blurring together. She felt herself being led to her bed. She opened her eyes and saw Tata bending over, tucking the quilt around her, just like when she was a little girl.

"Tata, don't let them take you."

"Oh, my Veronika, they know where I live. There's no place to hide."

*Before any major project was begun, the NKVD (secret police)
received direct instructions about the number of arrests
it needed to make.*

—Evard Radzinsky, Stalin: The First In-Depth Biography
Based on Explosive New Documents from Russia's Secret Archives

55
VERONIKA

The rasping screech of the woodstove's iron door woke Veronika up. She pulled the quilt higher around her chilly shoulders and tried to sort the twisting nightmares she had had all night long. Her mind was so dull and heavy she was not certain what was true and what was a dream. She opened her eyes and wondered why they itched and burned. She sat up and was surprised to see Julia asleep beside her, and then she remembered. She felt tears well up and the sharp sting of her already sore eyes.

She lay back down and thought of Uncle Vladzio and how he used to muss up her hair. She remembered how he always wanted to give her the runny yolk of his egg, thinking it the best part. And Uncle Feliks, whose booming voice and the flash of his dark eyes sometimes scared her, but still, he was always good to her. She brushed away the tears and prayed that God would somehow find a way to bring them home.

Her breath formed a mist around her as she got dressed. In the kitchen, she could hear the low voices of Aunt Paulina and Babcia. They must have spent the night as well.

Julia groaned then opened her eyes.

"Come on, everyone is getting ready," Veronika said gently. She could see in Julia's face first confusion then fear as memories of the night flooded back. Wordlessly, Julia threw back the covers and started to dress as Veronika went into the kitchen.

Mama stood at the stove, stirring the buckwheat cereal she had made the night before. Aunt Paulina was setting the table. Babcia sat in the corner, mouthing the words of the rosary, beads clicking between her fingers, oblivious to the bustle of activity in the kitchen. Veronika could feel the tension that hung in the air. Who knew if the men would still be in Gródek by the time they got there?

"Veronica, go help set the table. Tata and Stasik will be in from feeding the chickens soon."

She went into the pantry and got bowls off the wooden shelf. She set them on the table just as Julia came into the kitchen. Veronika always thought Julia so pretty with her cute face, light brown hair, and blue eyes. Now she just looked so sad.

"I hope we can see your Tata soon," Veronika said.

Julia looked away, trying to hold back her tears. Veronika wished she hadn't said anything.

"Julia, pour the tea," directed Aunt Paulina when Tata and Stasik came in, stamping their feet and rubbing their hands. They washed their hands in a bucket by the kitchen sink while Mama brought the hot cereal to the table.

Tata stood at the end of the table while chairs and benches were pushed in and everyone sat down. Tata prayed over the food and for Feliks and Vladzio. As they ate, Mama said to Veronika, "When Paulina goes to get clothes for Feliks, you go along. You can help Agnes get clothes together for Vladzio."

"Yes, Mama."

"Tell Agnes I'll pack dried fruit and nuts for the men. Tell her we have some bread but need more."

Babcia said, "I'll go, too."

"Stay here," Aunt Paulina said. "We'll walk faster without you."

After grabbing their coats, Aunt Paulina and Veronika walked at a rapid pace toward the duplex, eager to get what they needed and be on their way to Gródek.

When they got to Aunt Paulina's door, she said, "Go help Agnes gather clothes and food for Vladzio. Tell her to hurry."

Veronika knocked on Aunt Agnes's door then walked in. She was sitting at the table, her hair uncombed, her face drawn. She looked surprised when Veronika came in.

"Aunt Agnes, get up. We need some bread and some clothes for Uncle Vladzio."

"You're going to see him?" she asked, her eyes brightening.

"Maybe. We're going to Kuzmin first. Tata says they might still be there."

"And I can't go with you," she said, the words coming out in a choking sob as she got up and limped to the bedroom. Veronika didn't know how to console her. There was no time. Veronika helped gather a few clothes and a loaf of bread in a burlap sack, kissed her aunt, and left.

Aunt Agnes stood and watched from the doorway as Veronika and Aunt Paulina walked rapidly down the road,

"Tell Vladzio I love him. Tell him I'll wait for him."

When they got back, Mama slipped the apples, dried fruit, and nuts into Uncle Vladzio's sack, as well as a few boiled eggs.

When Tata got on his coat to go with them, Mama's eyes grew big. "No, Janek. You stay here. Who knows if the secret police will grab you as well."

"You can't go either," Aunt Paulina said to Stasik. "You're thirteen, old enough to be taken."

"But I want to see Tata," he cried.

"No! I can't lose you, too. You must stay here with Babcia."

Their small group of Mama, Aunt Paulina, Julia, and Veronika walked down the dirt road as the sun rose, red and golden on the horizon. Mist rose from the river and gathered in a suspended layer just above the water.

When they arrived in Kuzmin, a small crowd of women and children had already gathered in front of the village Soviet hall.

"My God. How many did they take last night?" Aunt Paulina asked.

Three solders with rifles slung across their backs stood on the steps of the hall, casually leaning against the handrail, smoking cigarettes, chatting, and joking with each other. They seemed oblivious to the women and children below them.

Aunt Paulina and Mama worked their way to the front of the steps. Aunt Paulina waved her arm. When they noticed her, she said, "Please, we've come to see our men."

One soldier answered, "No one comes in," and looked back to his companions.

"Could you take this for them?" she persisted, as she and Mama held the burlap sacks aloft. When there was no answer, she said, "Could they at least have the food?"

The soldier replied curtly, "They have enough to eat."

"Where are they going?"

With growing irritation, he said, "Go home. You will know later."

Veronika and her family waited with the others, sometimes sitting, sometimes standing, hoping for a glimpse of the men, waiting to see if any of the other families would be allowed in. As the hours passed, children began to cry fretfully from hunger, cold, and fatigue. People began to drift away. They, too, left, cold and exhausted. Carrying the bundles of clothing and food, their tears would not stop.

When they went back the next morning, the men were gone. Grieving families who had gathered around the village Soviet hall told them that sometime in the night the men had been loaded into carts and taken to the Gródek train station.

From that day forward, Veronika and her family clung to the small hope of a letter, either from the men or from Stalin's officials, telling where they had been taken and for how long. They waited and waited. Weeks went by, and still no word from them.

"I'll write a letter to the vice president of the Soviet Union, Mikhail Kalinin. I'm sure he'll help me," Paulina said.

"The vice president will help you?" Mama asked.

"Others have written to him, asking him for help, and he writes back."

The next day, Aunt Paulina read the letter she had written:

Dear Soviet Secretary of State, Mikhail Ivanovich Kalinin,
How are you? I hope your health is fine and that of your wife and children. I humble myself before you and seek your help. My husband, Feliks Palenga, and his brother, Vladzio Palenga, have been arrested by some mistake. From the great power you hold, I petition you for their release. I do not even know what they were charged with or for how long their sentence is. Both men have always paid their taxes on time. They believe in Communism. They worked hard for the five-year plan to succeed. They love our great leader, Joseph Stalin, may he live forever.

Paulina Palenga

Two months later a letter came from Kalinin's office saying: *After ten years, then you can hear from him.*

56

VERONIKA

July 1935

Life went on for Aunt Paulina. It had to. With Uncle Vladzio and Feliks gone, all the outside work of her orchard—pruning the trees, preparing and planting the garden—now fell on her. Not only did she have to provide for Julia and Stasik, but for Babcia and Aunt Agnes, too. She also had to work on the collective when the call went out for more workers.

Four months after Aunt Paulina's husband had been taken, she came over to Veronika's house for a visit.

"Don't let me keep you from starting Janek's dinner," Aunt Paulina said, as Mama poured her a cup of tea.

"He won't be home for a while yet. We have time for a visit. In fact, you should stay for dinner."

"Oh, no, I can't. Babcia would have a fit. Wherever I go, she thinks she has to be invited. And there is Julia and Stasik I have to make dinner for."

"Veronika, would you like a cup?" asked her mother.

Veronika looked up from the sweater she was knitting for Tata. "Yes, please, Mama."

Veronika picked up her sturdy brown cup and the spicy, clean fragrance of chamomile caught her by surprise, as it always did. She closed her eyes and inhaled its calming scent. She wondered how Aunt Agnes was doing, all alone. Too bad she couldn't have walked over with Aunt Paulina. A thought began to form in her head and with it, a strand of joy. Tomorrow, she would go to Aunt Agnes's and then have supper with her. At least she'd have company for a little while. She opened her eyes and watched Aunt Paulina stir the sugar in her tea, slowly, methodically.

"Any word yet about Feliks or Vladzio?" asked her mother.

The question seemed to jolt Aunt Paulina. She took a sip of tea and shook her head. "I heard some talk. Don't know if it's true or a rumour, though."

Mama raised her eyebrows. "What was that?"

"Well, as I said, you can't know if any of it is true, but some people have been saying that all the men who were arrested around that time were sent to Siberia to build the railroad to Vladivostok. Those men have had it really bad there, such hard work, and the cold."

Mama took a deep sigh. She reached out and touched Paulina on her arm. "And my mother. How is she treating you? Without Feliks to stand up for you, I worry."

"If she picks on the children, I say something, but for me, I say nothing. With her being so old, it's better just to keep the peace, especially now, with what I've found out."

"Found out?"

"I'm with child."

"Oh, Paulina. Did Feliks know?"

Tears welled up in her eyes. "No," she said softly. "I was waiting. I wanted to be sure."

Mama got up and sat beside her on the bench. "Don't cry, Paulina. Don't cry. It's not good for the baby."

Aunt Paulina nodded, wiped her eyes, and blew her nose. Veronika could see that she was trying to stop crying.

"How far along are you?"

"I'm not exactly sure. I think about four months. But what am I going to do?" she said, pulling at the crumpled handkerchief in her hand. "I don't even know how I can provide for Stasik and Julia, much less a baby."

"I know it will be hard without Feliks, but we'll help you. Julia and Stasik should be able to help you quite a bit. They're certainly old enough now."

Aunt Paulina nodded.

Veronika tried to swallow her own tears as Mama tried to cheer up Aunt Paulina by talking about how much Julia and Stasik had grown.

As Aunt Paulina was leaving, Veronika said, "Please, could you ask Aunt Agnes if she would like me to come over and have dinner with her?"

"I'm sure she would love to have you. I'm at the collective most days or working in the garden, and she just sits alone."

"Babcia is all alone, too," Veronika said, trying to keep a straight face. "They should sit together and keep each other company."

"Those two? Not likely," Aunt Paulina said with a laugh. She reached out and kissed Veronika on both cheeks, then said, "Ahh, Veronika. How is it that you always find a way to cheer me up?"

— ✻ —

The next day, Veronika went for a morning swim in the river with Kazia and Alina. The sun's heat on her back followed by the cool water felt refreshing. When the sun rose to midday, Veronika said, "I have to go now. I want to give Mama a hand making pickles."

"We have to go, too. With both our fathers gone, there are always chores," Alina said.

"I'll never forget the day the secret police took both of your fathers and the doctor," Veronika said. "I cried for weeks."

"I don't remember much of that day," Kazia said softly.

Alina released a sigh. "I'm afraid when my tata comes back, I won't know who he is. I lie in bed at night, and try to remember what he looks like, but I only see parts of his face."

"It's been four years now, hasn't it?" asked Veronika.

"Four years," Kazia repeated her face glum. "I was in the first grade."

They were quiet for a while. Veronika's throat tightened with the pain of all the memories. Feeling close to tears, she changed the subject. "Did you hear Aunt Paulina is expecting a baby?"

"I probably heard minutes after you did," Kazia said, "with our mothers being sisters."

Veronika smiled. "That's always the way it is. Remember when we were little? If one mother caught you doing something wrong, the other was sure to find out."

Veronika said goodbye to Alina and Kazia at their triplex, then continued alone to her home. Coming into her yard, she was surprised to see neither Mama nor Tata working in the garden.

"Mama? Tata?" she called.

"I'm here," Tata called, his voice sounding muffled. He was sitting on his bed, his hands folded in prayer. He gave her a pained stare.

Veronika felt her breath catch. "Where's Mama?"

"She's all right but something terrible has happened. Sit down."

Fear raked its way down her body. "What?"

"It's the secret police. There was a raid."

"Where?"

"At Aunt Paulina's."

Veronika's mind spun in disbelief.

Tata went on, his eyes mournful. "Babcia is fine. They didn't take her, or Aunt Agnes, likely because neither of them can work. They took Aunt Paulina."

"Aunt Paulina?"

Tata nodded. "And Stasik."

"Julia?" Veronika asked.

Tata nodded. "Julia, too. Said they were sending them to Kazakhstan."

"But they can't! Aunt Paulina is pregnant."

"She told them. They said to take it up with the ministry of interior." Tata held her in his arms as she sobbed, "Why are they always plucking at us, Tata?"

When Mama got home, she looked pale and drained.

"How are they going to manage, Janek?" she asked. "My mother is ninety-seven and now she's all alone. And on the other side of the duplex is Agnes."

"Your mother should come and live with us."

"I told her that, but she won't. She says she wants to be there for when her sons come home."

Tata took a deep breath and let it go, his hands rubbing his face. "We'll have to go back and forth taking care of both her and Agnes."

— ✳ —

In the days and weeks that followed, the Soviet secret police continued to roam the neighbourhoods of Kuzmin. One evening, Veronika and Tata counted all the homes down their road where someone had been taken. In almost every home, at least one person had been taken.

She knew that it would be only a matter of time before the secret police raided their house. Tata would be taken first and then later they would come back for her and Mama. She waited and waited for the pounding on the door, week after week, month after month, not knowing when her family would be selected.

... about 850,000 were deported to the north where many, especially children, perished.

—Orest Subtelny, *Ukraine: A History*

57
JANEK

October 1935

A letter arrived from Paulina three months after she had been taken. Janek opened it carefully, wishing that Veronika was home to read it. Slitting the top of the envelope with a knife, he pulled out the folded sheet of blue tissue paper and looked at the writing, trying to glean meaning from the words.

"Can you make out anything of what she's saying?" asked Helena looking over his shoulder.

"Nothing that makes sense. Here, you have a look."

Helena held the paper close, her lips moving as she tried to sound out Paulina's words.

"Well? Do you get anything?" asked Janek.

She shook her head. "I don't know, Janek. I see the name Stasik and then after a bit she has Veronika's name and then she wrote Stasik again." Helena looked up at him, her eyes worried. "He's only thirteen. I hope everything is all right with him." She handed the letter back to Janek. He folded it and put it back in the envelope.

Setting it on the table he said, "We'll just have to wait until Veronika gets home."

"She's not going to be home for a couple of hours yet. Kazia and Alina came over. Said they were going over to Frania's but, by the way they were dressed and how long it took them to do their hair, boys are probably involved."

"Boys? Veronika doesn't have a boyfriend, does she?"

"Not that she'll admit to. But I think she's interested in Marek."

"He better come talk to me before he gets too serious with my daughter," Janek muttered under his breath.

About an hour later, Janek saw Veronika walk up the path to the house. "There she is," he announced.

Helena hurried to the door. "We've been waiting and waiting for you to come home," she said.

Janek saw Veronika's puzzled look as she came in. "You said I could go to the village."

"We got a letter from Paulina."

"Aunt Paulina?" Veronika gasped, as she threw her shawl down on a chair and snatched the letter from the table.

"Yes. Now sit, sit. Read it to us."

Veronika plunked down on the bench. Helena sat at her elbow. Janek remained where he was and listened from his chair by the window.

August 25, 1935
My dear Family,
I hope your health is good and the love of God blesses you always. Every day I long to be with you and hope that you will send me some word of Feliks or Vladzio.

Please remember us in your prayers.

We are living in a village on the steppes. So flat it is here. No trees, very windy. Never have I felt such heat before. The sun bakes our skin. So many mosquitoes you cannot even breathe without sucking some into your mouth and nose. Even into the corners of your eyes they get.

The head of the collective here ordered a Kazakh family to take us in. They do not want us. Already their mud house is crowded, such a big family they have with the grandparents and all the children. They have to share their food with us and they do not like that. We have to eat outside, after the family has eaten.

When the collective leader registered us for work, he asked how old Stasik was. I said ten, hoping to spare him work in the fields. Now it is my biggest regret. Stasik is the family's slave. I fear the family takes out their resentment on him. He has bruises on his back he won't talk about.

There is nothing I can do. To say anything, it will only make it worse. Do what you can to spare Veronika and Kazia such misery.

Pray the family will show mercy to my baby when it is born and allow Stasik to tend to it while I'm at work.

Paulina Palenga

After Veronika finished reading, Janek sat and stared out the window while Helena and Veronika cried.

After a time, Helena said, "We need to go read this letter to Agnes and Babcia, then if you are not too tired, maybe we can go to Kazia's and read it to my sister."

Veronika nodded. "I'm not too tired, Mama."

Helena walked over to Janek and rested her hand on his shoulder. "Are you coming?"

"You two go. I'll stay here." After they left, the knot that usually kept his feelings hidden deep inside him settled in his chest and each breath became shallow and painful. He knew where he had to go to ease his soul. Clamping his cap onto his head, he grabbed his coat and walked across the road to the Smotrych River. He clambered his way around the boulders until he found the flat granite rock that he was looking for. He sat, listening, breathing, taking deeper and deeper breaths as the rushing water swirled around rocks and into eddies. Paulina's letter had shown him the truth of what he faced. He was going to be arrested and deported, likely to Siberia. It was only a matter of time. Why should the secret police spare him? After he was taken, Helena and Veronika would be deported to Kazakhstan, and he would never see them again.

He wondered if it was fear that hurt him so? No, he decided, it wasn't fear. Mostly he was just sad. He was sad that he wouldn't be around to see Veronika get married, that he would never see her children, his grandchildren. He was sad that he wouldn't grow old with Helena, sad to think of Veronika and Helena, their backs bent, being worked like slaves. In his mind, he saw Veronika, the sun baking her body, the labour of hauling rocks and digging in the earth gnarling her hands, wearing her out, using her up long before her time.

"No, no, no." he shouted, slamming his fist into the palm of his other hand. Help me, God. That wasn't my plan for her. She was going to be happy. She was going to be a doctor. Please, please, don't let her get deported," he cried, his chest raked with sobs.

Eventually his crying stopped. He sat listening, thinking. *The only thing that could save us is if were liberated from the Soviets. But that won't happen. They are too strong, too powerful.*

He heard Helena and Veronika's voices carried on the air. They were coming home. Still not yet ready to go in the house, he lingered. And suddenly he knew the answer he was seeking. There was nothing he could do to change their fate. All he could do was decide how he was going to spend the remainder of the days he had left. Spending them in worry and sorrow would be a waste. Instead, he would cherish each day, use it wisely, find something good to talk about, to laugh about, to create good memories for Veronika, enough to last her a lifetime. Every day would be an opportunity to teach Veronika what he wanted to impart to her about life, about God and how to treat people. And with that thought, a feeling of peace settled over him. He got up and went into the house.

"Where were you?" Helena said. "I was worried where you had gone."

"I was outside, sitting by the river. Do you want to go outside and sit with me? It's beautiful. The moon is out."

"But already it's so late," she said. "We need to eat dinner."

"Later we can eat. Now I just want to hold you. I have something important to tell you."

Going outside, they sat side by side on the stone bench, Helena's hand in his, her head resting on his shoulder. So peaceful and beautiful my home is, Janek thought as he looked at the moon, a golden red in colour, rising above the willows. Janek leaned over and kissed her on the lips, the light shining through the kitchen window, illuminating her face.

Taking a deep sigh, he said, "You know, Helena, it's only a matter of time before the secret police come for me."

"For heaven's sake, Janek. Is that what you want to talk about? I don't even want to think of it."

"There are things I want to say. Once they come for me, there will be no time to talk."

A tear rolled down her cheek. Janek brushed it away with his thumb. Looking into her eyes, he said, "After they take me, maybe they will come back and take you and Veronika. I can't stand the thought of our last days or months together being spent in sadness, spoiling what is left of Veronika's childhood. Let's just try to be happy and not let this destroy what time we have left."

"That's all I ever wanted," she said, crying softly. "For us, but especially Veronika, to be happy."

Janek pulled her close and held her tightly.

"And I want to say something else, Helena." He pulled her back and looked again into her eyes. "I want you to know how much I love you. The only joy I have ever had in my life has come from you and Vladimir and Veronika."

"No, no. Stop, Janek," Helena said, sobbing.

Janek kissed her again, long and full on her lips.

58

VERONIKA

April 1936

Veronika vigorously brushed her thick brown hair, and then plaited it into one long braid. As she wrapped the braid up into a bun with her hair clips, she looked into the mirror and wondered if it was true what her friends said about her, that she was fortunate to have such perfectly shaped eyebrows, high cheekbones, and full lips. Instead of seeing these features, she saw only a pink blemish on her chin. She grimaced at herself in the mirror. Why today? Why, just before the dance, should this happen? She picked up her hand mirror and checked the back of her head. Well, at least when people looked at her from the back, she looked good.

"Come and eat," Mama called from the kitchen.

Satisfied she was as good as she could make herself, she took her place at the table.

"You look so grown up today, Veronika," Tata said. "And beautiful, just like your mother."

Veronika smiled. "Thank you, Tata."

"Where did you say the dance is going to be held?" Mama asked.

"Sonia and her older sister, Julianna, are having it at their house. They have arranged for some of the boys to play their harmonicas for us."

"Did you get permission from your teacher to go to this dance?" Mama asked.

"Yes, but he didn't even check my assignments. Everyone else who was going had to show him their work."

"That's good, Veronika. He knows you keep up," Tata said. "I wonder if he'll be there to check if everyone has his permission?"

"Probably."

"It seems like only yesterday you and Kazia climbed cherry trees and played in the river. Soon you will be growing up and leaving us," Tata said.

"Not for a while yet. I'm only in the seventh grade."

"It will go fast. Only three years until the tenth grade and then you'll be off to college."

"We've been saving for your college year," Mama said with a smile. "With every tombstone he carves, we get a little closer to having enough."

"Isn't college free?"

"It is, but the government is not going to pay for your train ticket or room and board."

"Oh. I never thought of that."

Veronika ate in silence, thinking about college. It was one hundred and sixty kilometres or so north of Kuzmin, in the city of Shepetovka. It would be exciting but scary to be so far from home. The farthest she'd ever been was Proskurov to see Uncle Oryst and Aunt Ludka. But after she earned enough money being a teacher, she would travel to Germany and see all those wonderful places Aunt Agnes saw growing up.

She wondered if Tata would be hurt or upset when he finally realized that she was serious about not becoming a doctor.

"You better quit daydreaming," Mama said. "Kazia and Alina are coming up the path already."

"They're early! Is it all right if I don't help with the dishes?"

"Sure, sure. You go," Mama said.

"I feel bad not helping."

"I'll help your mother," Tata said. "When you're older, you'll have work enough to do. Better you think back and remember this dance."

Veronika dashed over to the door to let her friends in.

"Hello, girls," Mama called to them. "Veronika, put on a headscarf. It gets cold in the evening."

"Mama, headscarves are old fashioned."

"Who cares what you look like? The main thing is that you keep warm."

"It will mess up my hair."

Veronika heard her father snicker.

"What are you laughing about?" her mother said crossly. "You should support me in this."

"I don't support you because she's thirteen now. You can't tell her every little thing to do."

Veronika went back into the kitchen and noticed her mother's petulant look.

"I'll take my shawl," Veronika said, leaning over and kissing her. "And if it gets cold, I'll put it over my head, I promise."

Tata walked them to the door. "Veronika, after the dance, wait at Kazia's and I'll meet you there to walk you home."

"It's all right. I'll ask Marek to walk me home."

"That's fine. As long as you're not walking by yourself."

As Veronika and her girlfriends got outside, Alina said, "You want my brother to walk you home?"

"It would be nice to spare my father having to come and get me."

"Mmm," Kazia said. "It's not because you have a crush on Marek, is it?"

"Maybe a little, but there are lots of other boys I like, too," she said, trying to hide the fact it was only Marek that she thought about. In the last year he had grown so much taller. When she lay awake at night, she often thought of what her first kiss would be like, imagining his lips on hers and the feel of his arms around her.

"If he wants to kiss you, are you going to let him?" Kazia continued.

"Maybe."

"Eww, who would want to kiss my brother?" Alina said, wrinkling up her nose. "What a disgusting thought. He always eats with his mouth open, and he farts."

Kazia giggled.

When they arrived at Julianna and Sonia's home, their schoolteacher greeted them at the door.

"Enjoy the dance," was all he said, with a twinkle in his eye.

"Come in!" Sonia said, taking Kazia and Alina's wraps. "The first dance is about to begin."

Veronika liked both sisters. Julianna, the older sister, was a fun-loving, blonde-haired beauty, who basked in the attention of boys. Sonia was more Veronika's type. With a broad face and grey eyes, she exuded a quiet strength and dependability.

Sonia took Veronika's wrap and gave her a little hug. "I'm so glad you're here."

Veronika glowed with excitement as she entered the room full of young people, laughing and talking in small groups, some of the older ones sipping spiritus that Julianna and Sonia's father poured from a jug in the kitchen.

"I'm going to ask for a glass of spiritus," Alina said, her eyes sparkling.

"I doubt he'll give me any," Kazia said, "but I'll try, too."

"How about you, Veronika?" Alina asked. "You look old enough with your hair all done up like that."

"What if our teacher walks in?"

"Just say you're holding the glass for someone."

Veronika shrugged and went with them, excited about her decision. Likely her parents wouldn't approve, but they were at home and she was here.

First to go up was Kazia.

"Not yet. Maybe in a year or two," the father said with a smile.

When Alina went up, he said the same thing. With Veronika, he poured some of the white liquid in the glass and handed it to her.

"See? What did I say," Alina said after they walked away. "Now you have to share that with us, then go up and get another one."

"I'm not going to go up again," Veronika retorted. "At least, not right away."

After each took a gulp or two of the fiery liquid, Kazia and Alina wandered off to chat with some of their friends and Veronika found herself standing alone. A strange kind of shyness enveloped her as she scanned the room for someone to talk to. Marek stood with a group of boys across from her. She wished he would come over and say hello when, without warning, their eyes met. Embarrassment flooded her being that he had caught her looking at him. Veronika gave what she hoped was a nonchalant nod, then looked away, her breathing constricted.

The tension melted away when the harmonica player started up the first dance.

"Women's round dance," came the announcement.

Veronika joined the rush of girls joining hands, as they hop-skipped around a circle to the lively tune. With leg kicks and whoops of joy, round and round they went to the rhythmic clapping from the boys.

"Men's dance," came the next call.

The girls disbanded and the boys formed a circle, arms on each other's shoulders, squat-kicking and whooping until it was time for the girls to take a turn again.

"Take a rest, have something to eat, to drink, and after that it will be polkas," announced the girls' father.

Flushed with the excitement of dancing, Veronika was walking to the edge of the floor when Kazia's cousin, Pavlo, walked up to her.

"Would you like to be my partner? It's all right if someone has already asked you."

Veronika smiled. "No one has spoken for me. I'd like to be your partner."

"You would? Thank you."

"I'll look for you when the next dance starts," she said.

Walking around the room, talking to friends here and there, Veronika made a conscious effort not to talk to Marek. She could tell Alina and Kazia were watching her.

When the music started up again, Veronika danced several rollicking polkas with Pavlo until the next dance, when Marek walked up to them.

"Do you mind if I have a turn with Veronika?" he asked.

Pavlo nodded and Marek took Veronika's hand. Dance after dance they remained partners, occasionally catching a glimpse of Kazia's or

Alina's knowing looks. She ignored them but wondered if Marek saw their smirks or even cared.

After the last dance, Marek said, "That was fun. Thanks, Veronika. I better get some water before the walk home."

"Me, too," she said, needing an excuse to be alone with him for a few minutes more. She stood beside him, sipping her water, then, mustering all her courage, said, "Marek, my father seemed tired tonight. I told him that you probably wouldn't mind walking me home."

Marek continued to drink, ignoring what she had said. Veronika felt heat rising in her cheeks as he drank. Why had she asked him? Obviously, he saw right through her ploy and thought her incredibly bold.

Putting his glass down, he flashed a charming boyish smile that always sent a zing to her heart. "Sure, I'll walk you home. Your house isn't far from mine."

After helping clean up a bit and thanking Julianna, Sonia, and their parents, Veronika walked with Kazia, Alina, and Marek to their triplex, laughing and joking about who seemed to have paired off with whom.

"You seemed to hit it off with my cousin, Pavlo," Kazia said.

"Oh, yes, he was a great dancer and a very nice person."

When they got to the triplex, Alina said to Marek, "I'll tell Mama you're walking Veronika home."

"Thanks, Alina."

Just before Kazia turned to go in, she said, "Have a good night, Veronika," and then gave that secret wry smile of hers, which Veronika pretended not to see.

After walking a while in silence, Marek stooped down to pick up a rock and pitch it with all his might against a tree.

Crack.

Then he pitched another. And another.

This wasn't the romantic walk Veronika had imagined. Maybe he didn't care about her at all. Maybe it was just her imagination that he looked at her in a special way.

"Thank you for walking me home," she ventured shyly, trying to lure him into some sort of conversation.

"That's all right. I don't mind walking you home. In fact, I kind of like it."

"You do?" she asked, her hopes soaring once again.

"Sure."

They walked again in silence.

Then it happened. He nonchalantly reached out and took her hand in his. Joy rippled through her, but she tucked it down as they continued to walk, as if both were unaware of their enjoined hands.

As they entered the path to her house, he said, "Anytime you want someone to walk you home, I'd be glad to."

"That would be nice if it's not too much of a bother." Not wanting their time to be over, she lingered, awkwardly, not knowing what to say, when he leaned over and kissed her on the cheek. Putting her hand on his shoulder, she pressed her cheek against his.

"Would it be alright if I kissed you again?" he asked.

Veronika nodded and closed her eyes. Their lips met, awkwardly.

Opening her eyes, she said, "I guess I better be getting in."

"I guess you better."

She turned and went into the house, elated.

59

VERONIKA

September 1936

Veronika picked up the white canvas shoes at the foot of her bed and admired them. A ripple of pleasure went through her. Canvas shoes! For the first time in her life, she would be starting the new school year in shoes. Normally she went barefoot until the ground froze and then she wore boots.

Mama had seen her admiring the shoes in the store and had her try them on.

"But Mama, can we afford it?"

"It's all right. You're thirteen and it's time you had shoes."

Veronika put her shoes down, then sat in front of the mirror and combed out her waist- length hair. As she braided her hair, she wondered what the eighth grade would be like. She'd be in a new room this year along with the ninth and tenth graders. Even the teacher would be new. He didn't raise his voice or slam his fist on top of the desks of those who annoyed him, like one of the other male teachers. She thanked God she didn't get that one.

Maybe Frania would be allowed to share a desk with her again. But what if she didn't? What if she had to sit next to Inna all year? Veronika used to be Inna's friend until she started gossiping about Veronika and Marek. Probably it had got around to Marek and he got teased, because now he acted indifferent around her.

When Veronika walked into her new classroom, everything seemed so strange, with double desks ranging from middle-sized to adult. Veronika began to feel comfortable as the morning progressed in a predictable manner, starting with the morning greeting by the teacher, and then a review of a seventh-grade mathematics assignment.

Veronika looked up from her work as a jovial-looking man of about thirty, wearing a brimmed worker's cap and clothing, entered the room. He was accompanied by a woman of nineteen or so, with a pleasant, open face and clear grey eyes. Veronika longed for a hairstyle like hers, short, loose, and tucked behind the ears. How much nicer it would be, rather than going around with dumpy old-fashioned braids.

After their teacher had greeted the guests, he said, "Students, your attention, please. This is Comrade Ivan Horenko, the local director of the Komsomol and his activities director, Symona. They are here to speak to the eighth-grade students, since they are now of age to join the Komsomol, along with the older students who may still be considering it."

Comrade Horenko stepped forward. "As your teacher said, I am here to extend an invitation to join the Komsomol, often referred to as the helper and the reserve of the Communist Party. Although we would like every one of you to join, not everyone can meet the strict requirements.

"First and foremost, you must have a commitment to Communist ideals of collectivism and atheism. You must be a disciplined person, dedicated to study and work. You must be healthy, and practice abstinence from drinking and smoking.

"If this sounds like you, and you'd like to join the Komsomol, you will need to fill out an application and have it recommended by a member of the Communist Party and two Komsomol. Not all applications will be accepted. Only twelve percent of all youth become a Komsomol. All the same, I hope you will fill out an application and see if you are successful in joining us, because I can assure you, the opportunity of going to university and having a choice career placement will be yours.

"Now here is Symona, to tell you some of the exciting activities we have planned for this year."

With a brilliant smile, the young woman came forward. "I am here to explain some of the clubs we have for members. There's a very active drama club, a sports club, as well as a photographic club. There are also weekly dances, but the big activity that all of our members are looking forward to is in August, when we form a construction brigade with other brigades and travel to Moscow."

Symona paused as excitement spread through the classroom.

Veronika gasped. Moscow! A place she had always dreamed of seeing. Images of the Kremlin and Red Square she had seen in books loomed in her mind.

Symona went on, "After some sightseeing around the city, our job will be to help paint the new line of the Moscow Metro subway."

Veronika had seen photos of the Moscow Metro. It looked like a palace with grand stairways, marble columns, and multi-arched ceilings through the passageways. But what excited her the most were the moving stairways called escalators. How she would love to go on one of those if she dared.

Symona held up her hand for the murmurs of excitement to die down.

"Our first event of the new school year will be held this Saturday. It will be a hike followed by a cook-out, then some singing and skits around a campfire. You don't have to be a member to come. Everyone is invited. Its main purpose is just to have a good time and get to know people. Before you go on break, there is a sign-up sheet for those interested in going on the hike, so we know how much food to prepare. Hope to see you all there."

— ✳ —

That afternoon during their lunch break, Veronika, Alina, and Frania sat under the trees where they used to play as children, and talked as they ate.

"I'd love to see Moscow, but not if it means joining the Komsomol," Veronika said.

Alina took an apple out of her lunch pail and said, "Same here, but I don't see why we can't enjoy the hike. It doesn't mean you want to join or anything."

Veronika nodded. "It does sound like fun. How about you, Frania?"

Frania gave her a sidelong glance, her eyes wide. "Are you joking? My parents aren't very religious, but going off with the Komsomol on Shabbos would be out of the question."

"Well then, Alina, let's you and I sign up before the list gets full," Veronika said.

— ✳ —

"How could you even think of it?" Tata said, his face dark with anger.

"It's not that I'm going to join the Komsomol. It's just this one hike," Veronika said, on the verge of tears.

"Veronika, that's enough discussion about it," Mama said. "Tata says no and that's it."

"You're both being so unfair. All the other girls are going. Besides, I signed up already."

"You what?" Tata asked, his voice incredulous.

"I signed up," she repeated, not so sure of herself. "Only so they know how much food to prepare."

"Matko Boska, Veronika," Mama exploded. "What were you thinking? And not even to ask us?"

"I'm not a baby anymore. I shouldn't have to ask just to go on a hike." With that she ran to her room and threw herself on her bed, weeping.

An hour or so later, Tata came into her room and handed her a mug of tea.

"Thank you, Tata," she said, her head down.

"It's time we talk about some things we've been keeping from you, because you're right, maybe we've been treating you like a baby."

Veronika looked up at her father's kindly face, the love in his eyes.

"Do you remember Alyona Pawlowska? How she and her children were thrown out of their home with nothing, and you gave up some of your dresses for the children?"

"Yes."

"The Komsomol did that. They are an evil group, disguised as something fun, to change you into one of them."

"But they don't do that kind of thing anymore. That was just to get people to join the collectives."

"Maybe not, but at any time, Stalin could once again order the Komsomol to do his dirty work. And you must do it, or they will torture you or maybe even shoot you."

"That can't be true," Veronika said. Surely Comrade Horenko and the lovely, sweet Symona wouldn't do anything like that.

"It is true. I saw your mother's cousin, Aleksey, at the Pawlowski's. He didn't want to be there, but Stalin himself had ordered the Komsomol to participate in destroying people's lives. Not long after that he disappeared."

"Disappeared?"

"His mother hopes he ran away to the city. She won't face the fact that his true feelings may have been found out and they killed him. You need to stay far, far away from those people."

Veronika blinked. "Sorry, Tata, I didn't know." She threw her arms around his neck. "I won't go."

"But you signed up already."

"I'll say I have too much studying to do."

Walking to school the next day, Veronika met up with Alina and Kazia. "I've decided I don't want to go on that hike."

"Why not?" Kazia asked. "You were excited about it."

"I've decided that I want to stay far, far away from those Komsomol. You just can't trust what Stalin will order them to do next."

"Well, I'm not going either," Alina said. "Mama and I had quite a row about it. She even threatened to get the wooden spoon out."

60

VERONIKA

April 1936

Veronika was jolted out of her sleep as her mother shook her roughly on the shoulder.

"Veronika, get up! You have to get up!" The hysterical tone of her mother's voice terrified her.

"What is it?" she asked, her chest heaving.

"The secret police wagon is parked across the road. Get dressed quickly."

Numb with the reality that the moment she most feared had finally arrived, Veronika got up, and with trembling fingers pulled on her clothes, praying silently with every short gasping breath she took.

She felt her way through the darkened house and paused for a moment by her mother who was praying on her knees in the kitchen. In the living room, her father stood by the window looking out, the curtain slightly ajar. Quickly going to her father's side, she whispered, "What's happening, Tata?"

He held the curtain open for her and stepped aside.

Hardly breathing, she peered out into the night. Across the road, a horse and wagon waited. A lantern on the driver's bench illuminated the darkness. Every now and then she could see a small red glow where a soldier stood, smoking. Hearing voices, Tata gently pushed Veronika away and looked out.

"Oh, no," he said.

"What?"

"They have Javik's sons and three of our other neighbours," he whispered, putting his arm around her.

"They'll be crossing the road and coming here next," Tata whispered.

Confusion and terror overwhelmed her. "Tata, you need to hide. Get into the fields, now!" Her words came out in sort of a strangled scream.

He just looked at her and said, "There is no use. They know where I live."

"No, Tata, no!" she shrieked, pounding him on the chest with her fists, trying to beat him into action, as a torrent of tears ran down her face.

Tata grabbed her wrists and held her. "Veronika, Veronika, don't," he said soothingly. Seeing the futility, she cried in his arms as he embraced her.

Once again they heard voices. He let go of her and looked out. The wagon and secret police were leaving. They looked at each other, speechless in astonishment.

"Helena! Come here!" Tata yelled, wonderment in his voice.

"Mama. They've left. The wagon is gone," Veronika said, scarcely able to talk.

"What?" Mama asked, joining them at the window. All three of them stood and stared at the empty place where the wagon and secret police had been.

"What happened? Why did they go?"

"I don't know," Tata said.

"Will they come back?" Mama asked.

"I would think so," he said, the elation gone from his voice. "Probably just unloading. I better gather up some clothes."

"Matko Boska, help me." Mama whimpered, "I don't know what to do."

"Why don't you stoke the fire and get the kettle going, Mama," Veronika said, taking charge. "Maybe Tata will have time for a mug of tea before he has to go. I'll pack food for him to take."

"Thank you, Veronika," Mama said, giving her arm a grateful squeeze.

An hour later, a burlap sack with Tata's warmest work clothes and a flour sack with bread, fruit, and walnuts sat on the bench beside Tata's winter coat. Veronika and her parents sat at the table, and stared into each other's white faces, sipping tea as they waited, the minutes ticking by. So much to say, a lifetime of things to say, yet all of it stifled deep in Veronika's heart for fear of upsetting Tata more than he already was. Better to say nothing, and to imprint upon her soul his hollow, pinched face, the touch of his cold hands on hers, the memory of these last moments together.

At dawn, when the secret police still hadn't come back, Veronika saw hope gradually grow in her parents' eyes. At last, her mother said, "Maybe they aren't coming back."

"They could still come yet," Tata said.

An hour later, Mama said, "Should I make breakfast?"

He nodded, went to the window, and looked out. After a moment, he turned and said, "I think they won't be coming today."

Mama put her arms around Tata and kissed his cheeks as she wept. Veronika hugged both of them.

"But why didn't they take you?" Mama asked after she released him.

Tata shrugged. "Who knows? Maybe they met their quota."

61
VERONIKA

August 1937

After a spring and summer filled with schoolwork, friends, and helping around the farm, eighth grade was just a blur, but Veronika's fears for Tata remained. She had finished the June exams once again at the top of her class in science and mathematics, much to Tata's delight.

"You're going to be a doctor yet, my girl," Tata said.

Veronika gave him her best pained look.

"Just stating what I see," he said with feigned innocence.

"Please stop bringing that up. I hate being around sick people, and you know that."

"Janek, don't tease her. You can see she doesn't like it," Mama said. "Her mind is made up to be a teacher."

"Thank you, Mama."

Veronika went into her room. How is it that her parents could get her upset so easily? It never used to be that way. Pushing open her bedroom window, she took in the balmy summer air. Thoughts of the fun she would have this evening lightened her mood.

She'd go to Frania's for an hour or so, then meet up with Kazia and Alina at the village park. On Friday nights it was the gathering place for all the village teens and a prime place for flirting with boys.

Veronika stared out the window as the late afternoon sunlight dappled through the trees. She yearned for the closeness she'd once had with Marek before it had been spoiled by Inna. That was more than a year ago, and Marek had changed. His voice had grown deeper and he had developed muscles. Sometimes he made his way over to her group and chatted with them. Did that mean he still liked her? She sent up a silent plea to God that it did, then felt remorse for troubling Him over such trivial matters.

She got up and went over to the dresser to fix her hair. She needed to get going if she was to have any time to practice reading Hebrew over at Frania's. She thought of how amazed both Frania's and her parents were that she could read and write in Hebrew.

"But do you understand what you read?" Tata had once asked her.

"Not a word," she had answered with a laugh.

Sometimes she would see Frania's father in the little room downstairs, wearing a fringed shawl across his shoulders and a round cap on his head. Holding an open book, he would sway back and forth, reciting his prayers in a singsong voice for hours.

"It seems so strange," Veronika said to her parents one evening after they had finished praying the rosary.

"Maybe strange to them that we pray with a string of wooden beads and say the same prayers over and over," Tata had said.

The other odd thing that Veronika could not understand was why Frania's family kept asking her to blow out the Shabbos candles while they stood around and watched her. When she was younger, she felt honoured, like it was a special privilege. Now that she was almost sixteen, it embarrassed her to have Frania or Izaak show up while she was at the park and ask her to come to their house to blow the candles out. Maybe Mama knew why they did that.

Walking into the kitchen, her hairbrush still in hand, she told her mother about it. "Why are they asking me, when they can do it so easily themselves?"

"It sounds like they're getting you to take part in some Jewish ritual."

"That's what I was thinking," Veronika said.

"Tonight, you tell Frania, politely, that you don't want to do that anymore."

— ✻ —

As usual, Frania and her family made Veronika welcome, this time by offering her a drink of water and a plate of knish buns filled with buckwheat, potatoes, and onions.

"Enjoy your time, girls," Frania's mother said. "Shall I let you know when it's time to leave?"

"Yes, please," Veronika said. "Then I won't be interfering with the start of your Shabbos."

When Veronika and Frania were upstairs in her bedroom, Veronika steeled herself to open the conversation about the blowing out of the candles.

"Frania, when I'm in the park, please don't come get me to blow out your candles. It's embarrassing."

Frania pressed her hand against her cheek. "I'm so sorry. It's just that you never seemed to mind."

"Why do you need me to blow out the candles? Just blow them out yourself."

Frania's mouth fell open. "You mean, all this time you've been blowing out the candles for us and didn't know why?"

Veronika shook her head.

"It's Jewish law! We aren't allowed to put out a lit candle on Shabbos, but Mama thinks it's dangerous to let it burn unattended, so we ask you to do it."

Throwing herself back on the bed, Veronika got the giggles. Every time she looked at Frania's puzzled face, a new round of giggles would start.

"Would you please tell me what's so funny," Frania asked.

At last, Veronika sat up and said, "It's funny to know the truth is so simple, when in my head, all kinds of thoughts were going around."

After leaving Frania's and thanking her mother for the knish, Veronika stood with Kazia and Alina in the park when Sonia joined them.

"Sit here with us," Alina called out when she arrived.

"Where's Julianna?"

"She's over by the swings with some of her own friends."

Moments later, they noticed some boys showing off their strength on the parallel and horizontal bars.

"Let's go yell some encouragement to them," Kazia said.

When they got closer, Veronika noticed Marek in the crowd, waiting for a turn on the bars. With ease he went hand over hand to the end then leapt off. Moments later, to Veronika's inner shrieks of joy, he stood beside them.

"You were great at that," Kazia said.

"Just one of my many manly strengths," he said with a smile.

"Listen to you brag," snickered Alina.

For the rest of the evening, Marek stayed mostly with them, trading funny stories of when they were children together, like when he had to walk Veronika to school.

"I could never keep her going. Always off in one direction or another. It was like trying to herd a goat."

When it was time to go home, Alina took Veronika and Sonia aside and said, "I wish the three of us could do something special, something to mark this summer of being sixteen, but I don't know what."

Sonia looked thoughtful. "We could all have a sleep-out in my barn tomorrow night," she suggested. "We could tell ghost stories and have a party."

"And I could sneak in some spiritus," Alina said, glee in her voice.

Veronika thought about it for a half-second and decided it would be the most exciting thing she had done all summer. "I'll come," she said, "if I'm allowed."

"Just say you're invited over to my place to sleep," Sonia said. "Your parents don't have to know it's in the barn."

"Let's do it, then," Veronika said. "But what about Julianna?"

"No, she wouldn't want to sleep in a barn. She's scared of bugs."

— ✳ —

The next day, Veronika told her parents, "Sonia invited Alina and me to sleep at her place tonight. Is that all right?"

"I suppose so," Mama said. "Janek?"

He nodded. "As long as you're home the next day by noon to help with chores."

That evening, when Veronika and Alina got to Sonia's, they spread blankets out on top of the hay and were quite comfortable, even before the bottle of spiritus came out. The first couple of drinks burned as they went down Veronika's throat. The third one got easier and the fourth one easier yet. Veronika felt a warm glow and a sense of relaxation while they talked about boys, a cure for pimples, how stuck their parents were in old ways, and then back to boys again; what boy they used to love and who they loved now or hoped soon to love. After a while, Veronika felt herself drifting off to sleep.

In the morning, she felt fine until she lifted her head and her stomach began to churn. She winced and lay back down again, trying to suppress her moans. An hour later she tried again with the same result. Finally, she had to get up and walk home, no matter that her head pounded and her stomach was queasy.

"What's the matter?" Mama asked when she got home.

"I don't know."

"Is it something you ate?"

"No, Mama. I just need to lie down."

Later she heard her mother telling Tata she was sick. "Alina isn't well either. I guess they're coming down with something."

By morning the next day, her parents were relieved to see that Veronika was over her illness.

> "*The Great Terror of 1937–38 ... During it, some 700,000 or so people were sentenced to be executed for political reasons ... as 'enemies of the people.'*"
> —Hiroaki Kuromiya, *The Voices of the Dead: Stalin's Great Terror in the 1930s*

62

VERONIKA

April 1938

When Veronika answered the knock on the door, she didn't recognize the middle-aged man who stood there, but seeing his peddler pack, and worn, rumpled clothing, asked, "You are selling something?"

"I am Ludka's son. I have news of Oryst."

Veronika stepped aside when Tata came to the door.

"Come in," Tata said, shaking his hand. "You must be Tadeusz. It's a pleasure to finally meet you. You have news of my brother?"

"If I could come in and rest a bit first."

"Of course. I apologize for my eagerness. Please, come. Sit down. Helena, a drink of spiritus for Ludka's son and something for him to eat."

As Veronika helped her mother put food on the table, she thought of the last time she had seen her Uncle Oryst and Aunt Ludka, a few months ago. It was New Year's when they had taken the train to Proskurov. She smiled to herself as she sliced bread, thinking of how Uncle Oryst still took his rabbits out for her to hold and, as always, had pressed money into her hand to buy treats as if she was still a little girl.

After setting food and drink in front of him, Veronika sat down, anxious to hear news of her Uncle Oryst.

Tata tipped a little spiritus into their guest's glass as well as into his own. Holding up the bottle, Tata asked, "You'll have some, Helena?"

"No, thank you," she said. "Not now."

Tadeusz quickly downed his drink. Tata silently refilled his glass. Taking another sip, Tadeusz shifted in his chair, but still did not speak.

Veronika glanced at her father. She could see he was becoming alarmed.

"You said you had news of my brother?" he prompted. "Is everything all right?"

"I'm sorry to be the bearer of such bad news," he said haltingly. "There is a great purge happening. Oryst has been arrested."

Veronika watched her father slump in his chair.

"Matko Boska. Not another purge," gasped Mama, reaching out for Tata's hand.

Veronika closed her eyes to the pain welling within her.

"But there is a good chance he can still be released."

"Released? How?" Tata asked. "The secret police don't release."

"Maybe his arrest didn't have anything to do with the purge. Mother was told that for enough gold, perhaps he could be released."

"Gold? How does anyone know about Ludka's gold?"

"Someone must have talked."

"What is Ludka going to do?"

"She's desperate. She said she'd do anything for her Oryst. She wants you to come, talk to the secret police. Help her negotiate."

Mama's lips trembled. "Janek, you can't."

Tata's jaw stiffened; his face drained of colour.

Mama clutched at his hand. "Don't even think of it. They would arrest you for being his brother, just like with Feliks and Vladzio."

"Mother has no one else to turn to," Tadeusz said, ignoring Mama's outburst. "The secret police could already be looking for me, to put more pressure on Mother, but they have no reason to arrest you, Jan. You're not related to my mother."

Tata went to the window and looked out. Mama followed him. "You can't leave us," she said, hysteria building in her voice.

Tata turned to her and said, "It was Ludka and Oryst who saved us when we were starving. I owe them." Putting his arm around her back, he led her to the table and sat beside her as she cried.

Veronika felt torn between hope and fear. She hoped Tata would go but feared that in trying, he would lose his own life.

She always thought her Uncle Oryst was safe, living in a big city like Proskurov. How many times had she heard him say that he would be safe as long as he kept his head down and his mouth shut? Who would accuse a lowly knife sharpener of anything?

"Veronika, get a glass for your mother," Tata said.

Returning with it, he poured in a little spiritus. "Here, drink this, Helena." Turning to Tadeusz he said, "You have to forgive my wife. Her nerves can't take much. Already she has seen many of her relatives arrested."

"And now another round of people is being executed," Tadeusz said.

"For what reason?" asked Tata.

"The excuse is disloyalty, but even the people most loyal to Stalin are being accused. The *Pravda* said in the past year, the secret police arrested 170,000 members of the Ukrainian Communist Party. Even the Ukrainian Prime Minister is dead."

"Dead?" asked Tata.

Tadeusz took another drink then said, "The newspaper said he committed suicide."

Tata snorted. "I wonder if he had two choices, his bullet or theirs?"

"Ordinary citizens in entire areas are being executed. Mass graves are being dug again. People are being lined up in front of pits and shot."

Veronika went to her room. She couldn't listen anymore. Long into the night she heard the murmur of her parent's voices.

In the morning, she could tell by her mother's sombre face as she packed food and clothes for Tata that nothing had changed. He was still going.

Veronika poured herself a cup of tea and sat down beside her father. She couldn't eat anything. She only wanted to be with him, to have the time to say goodbye.

"Where is Tadeusz?" Veronika asked, not seeing him or his pack by the door.

"He's gone," said Tata. "Until he hears word of Oryst's release, it's best that he remains in hiding."

Tata took her hand and looked into her face, scanning her eyes. "Don't be so worried about me. I think it will go well."

"Why?"

"I think it's just the gold they want. I don't think Oryst's arrest has anything to do with the purge the Soviets are having."

"Do you think you'll be back soon?"

"It's possible maybe even tomorrow. But for now, I want you to go to school. Don't wait for me to leave."

Veronika nodded, fighting back tears.

"You know I have to go. How could I live with myself if I don't try to save my brother?"

"I know, Tata. I understand."

Veronika drank her tea but couldn't eat. When it was time for her to go, Tata stood at the door and kissed her goodbye. She hugged him, squeezing every bit of love and protection she could into that hug, and then left before Tata could see that she was crying.

I trust no one, not even myself."
—Joseph Stalin

63

JANEK

Icy fingers clawed the inside of Janek's gut as he rode the train to Proskurov. So many disjointed images swirled through his head, but mostly he saw his brother's face as he imagined him waiting in his cell. Sometimes he thought of Helena and Veronika being told that he, too, had been arrested. Maybe it was a fool's quest he was on, going to the secret police. Yet what other choice was there? He closed his eyes and listened to the sound of the wheels clicking on the track.

When Janek knocked on Ludka's door, he caught a movement at the window. then waited while she went to the door and fumbled with the lock. When she finally opened the door, he was surprised at how much older and frailer she looked since the last time he had seen her a few months ago.

"You've come. Thank you, Janek," she said.

"What happened, Ludka?"

"Please come in and sit. I'll get us some tea."

Pulling out a chair, he said, "No tea. Just tell me everything you remember."

Using the table to steady herself, she sat beside him. "We were sitting here having lunch and there was a knock. It was the secret police. They searched the house. Everything they pull out and flip over.

"*What is it you are looking for?*" *I ask.*

"*Your gold.*"

"*Gold? I have no gold,*" *I say.*

They handcuff Oryst and say, "*Maybe if we take him, you'll find it.*"

Ludka looked up at him, her eyes filled with tears. "It was terrible not knowing if this was the last … the last time I would see him," she said, her voice breaking.

"Please, try to go on. It's important that I know everything."

After wiping her eyes and taking several deep breaths, she continued. "The officer came back by himself. I thought, now it is the end for me. He is coming to take me, too. But that's not what he wanted."

"What did he say?"

"He said his name was Mikhailov. He had heard that I had many gold coins, from my father. Who would tell him that, Janek? Who?"

"Who knows what people will say when they're seeking favours."

"He said to bring the coins in and ask for him. He would see if he could get the charges dropped."

Janek patted her hand. "Maybe he's hoping to keep the coins for himself. If that's so, then he must release Oryst."

"To stop us from reporting him?" asked Ludka.

"That's right. The Soviets shoot those who steal from them."

Smiling through her tears, she said, "You've given me hope. I'll get the coins."

"Wait," he said, reaching out for her arm. "How much should I give him?"

"I thought all of it," she said, blinking in surprise.

"Keep some back, Ludka. He doesn't know how much you have."

She hesitated.

"That's what Oryst would want."

"I'll see," she said.

After a few minutes she came back, a brown leather pouch in her hands.

"I'll do what I can. If I don't come back, you can let Helena know."

Blinking back tears, she said, "I'll be praying for you, Janek. God bless you for doing this."

Taking her hand in his and holding it for a moment, Janek hid the pouch inside his coat and left.

It took a while to find the prison. When he stopped to ask people along the way, their eyes widened and Janek could see the sympathy in their faces as they gave him directions.

Entering the building of the Soviet secret police, Janek felt lightheaded as he approached the soldier sitting at the front desk.

"Why are you here?" he asked.

"I have a private matter to discuss with an officer by the name of Mikhailov."

"What private matter might that be?"

"What I have to say can only be said to Comrade Mikhailov."

"What is it concerning?"

"A man by the name of Oryst Osiecki who's being held here."

"Wait."

"When he returned, he said, "He will see you. Come with me."

He led Janek through a dingy corridor to an inner office. The soldier opened the door and Janek walked in.

Mikhailov, a burly man with thick fingers, continued to work behind his polished desk, his double chin rubbing against on the top of his collar as he flipped though papers, writing on some but not on others. A minute passed and then another. Janek could feel sweat slowly dripping down his back, down the sides of his face. He looked to the left of Mikhailov's desk to the picture of Stalin on the wall and then to the right, to a row of pegs, where Mikhailov had hung his jacket and stiff-brimmed officer's hat. Finally pushing the last paper aside, Mikhailov looked up and said tersely, "Show me your identity papers."

With trembling hands, Janek undid his pack, pulled out his papers, and put them on the desk.

Mikhailov studied them. "I see you have the same last name. He is your brother?"

"Yes. I come on behalf of his wife. She couldn't come. Her legs are too weak. Please, I beg you, release my brother. He has done nothing wrong."

"You talk too much. What did you bring?"

"Here," Janek said, taking the pouch and placing in on his desk. "This is from his wife."

Mikhailov lifted the pouch, assessing its weight. He looked inside.

"Have you told anyone about this?"

"No one."

Mikhailov thrust the pouch into his desk. Rising to his feet, he said, "Wait outside. I'll see what I can do."

Janek stood outside the front doors of the prison, waiting. With each minute that passed, his hopes faded. When the door opened and Oryst finally came out, he swooped him up in a hug, as tears of relief flowed from both of them.

"Come on. Let's go," Janek said. "Ludka is waiting for you."

As they walked, Janek told of his meeting with Mikhailov and how Ludka wanted to give all of her gold, and of how worried Helena and Veronika were. Oryst didn't say very much. Janek could sense that something was wrong. After a while he said, "What's troubling you? You don't seem to be happy you're going home."

"There's someone I must see first."

"Is that all it is? Can't you go later? Ludka is very anxious to see you."

"Janek, I have something to tell you. I appreciate everything Ludka has done for me. But you know it was a marriage of convenience, a bargain that her son and I made. He would teach me a trade if I would marry his mother."

"Yes, yes. I know all this."

"But it was never possible to have children. She was too old already."

"Why are you telling me all this?"

"Janek, I'm in love with a younger woman. In fact, she's pregnant with my child."

Janek looked at him in disgust.

"Don't look at me that way, Janek. You have no right to judge me."

"How could you do this to Ludka?"

"Ludka is a friend, Janek, and she still is a very good friend, but she is not a wife. All these years I've been with her, it's like being married to an elderly aunt."

"How many years is it between you two?"

"I'm forty-nine. She's seventy-two. And I have never slept in her bed. She said she was done with that part of her life. But with Dorota it's different. Not only the sex, but we can relate to each other. We laugh, we talk. We both want children."

After a while Janek said, "Does Ludka know about her?"

"She does, in her own way, but we don't talk about it. Things have changed very little since I met Dorota. I still see Ludka every day. We sit at the table, have a visit, maybe a meal. I fix anything that needs fixing. I ask her what she needs from the market and then, after an hour or two, I leave."

"You'll continue to take care of Ludka?"

"Yes, of course. Anything she needs, she will have. That's the deal I made with Tadeusz."

"I'm going to go home to Helena and let you go to Dorota."

"You don't want to meet her?"

"Next time you come to our home, bring her. For now, I need time to adjust. Goodbye, brother. Don't keep Ludka waiting long. Tell her I wanted to catch the train and get home today."

When Janek got home, and after Helena's and Veronika's cries of joy and hugs, he told them about Dorota and that she was expecting Oryst's child.

Helena stared at him, open-mouthed, her hand held to her chest. "What? He's taken up with a younger woman?"

Janek nodded. "He met her by chance. They fell in love, a love he never had with Ludka."

"But him leaving her for a younger woman? It is outrageous. I never want to see him again."

"Mama. Please don't say that," Veronika said.

"It is only natural for Oryst to want to be with someone closer to his own age," Janek said softly. "And to have children."

Helena took a deep breath and after a moment or two said, "Maybe it's not for me to judge. It just will take some getting used to. For now, we celebrate and thank God for bringing you home and that Oryst is free."

64

VERONIKA

July 1938

A few months later, a letter arrived from Uncle Oryst saying that their baby had been born, and he and Dorota were hoping to come in September for a visit.

"I just don't feel good about that woman staying in my house. It's disloyal to Ludka," Helena said.

"Helena, please don't be like that," Tata replied.

Mama frowned. "And anyhow, where would they sleep?"

"They can have my room," Veronika offered. "I'll sleep at Aunt Agnes's."

Mama looked at her, defeat in her eyes.

"We can have some fun when they visit," Tata said. "Maybe I could bring Agnes over to help keep the conversation going, and it would give her a little outing."

"What do you think, Mama?" Veronika asked.

"I don't know. I suppose I could manage having Dorota here."

That night, lying in bed, Veronika hoped that when Dorota came,

Mama would be polite. It would be embarrassing if Mama snubbed her. Sometimes her mother could be so rigid about things—to her, marriage was a sacred and lifelong bond.

— ✴ —

The day they were to arrive, Tata borrowed a horse and wagon from the collective and brought Aunt Agnes over. Then he and Veronika took the horse and wagon to the train station in Gródek to pick up Uncle Oryst, Dorota, and the baby.

Uncle Oryst greeted them as warmly as he always did. Veronika looked curiously at Uncle Oryst's new wife, baby in her arms, as she waited to be introduced. She was a short, plain woman, not particularly attractive, but there was something about her, maybe it was her smile or the kindness of her eyes, that made Veronika like her.

"This is Dorota and our little girl. We named her Mela," Uncle Oryst said as Dorota leaned in to kiss Tata and then Veronika.

"Good to meet you," Tata said.

"And look at you, Veronika," Uncle Oryst continued. "A young woman already. Soon you will be getting married and leaving us."

Veronika laughed at his good-humoured teasing. "Not for a long time yet. I'm only starting the tenth grade in the fall."

Looking around, Uncle Oryst said, "Where is Helena?"

Tata cleared his throat. "She's at home."

"Oh," Uncle Oryst said. "I guess we'll just have to wait until we get to your house for Dorota to meet her." His cheerfulness sounded false to Veronika.

Veronika saw the blush on Dorota's face and knew the slight hadn't been missed.

When they got home and in the door, Veronika was relieved to see that Mama had the table set with sweet squares, her best teacups, and the samovar.

"I'll put the horse in the barn and be right back in," Tata said to his brother.

Veronika glanced nervously at her mother and was relieved to see her mother smiling as she introduced Aunt Agnes to Dorota.

Tata brought a bottle of spiritus to the table when he came in and poured a glass for Uncle Oryst and himself.

"So, how is everything in Kuzmin?" Uncle Oryst asked. "Hear anything about Feliks or Vladzio? Paulina?"

"No, nothing, from Feliks or Vladzio," Tata said.

"From Paulina we have heard nothing since that first letter," Mama said. "Her baby must be two years old now. Stasik would be sixteen and Julia seventeen."

Aunt Agnes looked at them, tears glistening in her eyes. "Every day I think maybe today is the day I will hear from Vladzio, but not knowing ... it's so hard," she said with a sob in her voice.

Veronika reached out and touched her hand.

"People have been saying they were taken to help build the railroad in Vladivostok, but we don't know," Mama said.

"Some days I think maybe it would be better if I went back to Germany," Aunt Agnes said. "What is left for me here?"

"Oh, no," Mama said. "Better you stay here. At least you have a home and something to eat."

"And people who love you," Veronika added.

"If only we could be rid of the Soviets, life would be better for all of us," Tata said, a bitter edge to his voice. "So eager are they to make arrests, they've got a truck now to put people in."

"It just makes me sick," Mama said, her voice rising. "Every time I hear a truck coming down the road, I think maybe the secret police are coming for Janek."

"They're taking whole neighbourhoods now, too," Tata said.

Uncle Oryst shook his head and took a sip of his spiritus, draining the glass.

"A little more?" asked Tata, reaching for the bottle.

Oryst nodded.

"During the day, they keep the truck parked outside the village's Soviet building," Tata said. "It looks like a delivery truck with double doors in the back."

"It sounds like the same truck the secret police use in our city," Dorota said. "The Black Raven is what some people call them."

Veronika looked around the table. Everyone seemed enveloped in gloom. Wanting to change the subject she said, "I have some good news, Uncle Oryst."

"Yes, enough of the Soviets. What good news do you have?" he said, smiling.

"This is my last year of school. In January I take my college entrance exams."

"Did you hear that, Dorota? Veronika wants to go to college. Na zdrowie, to your health," Uncle Oryst said, lifting his glass of spiritus.

"Na zdrowie," everyone said, lifting their glasses.

After dinner, Tata drove Veronika and Aunt Agnes to her home in the horse and wagon. Veronika looked forward to spending the night with her precious aunt, her confidante. Even though Mama had made a substantial evening meal, by nine o'clock Aunt Agnes had to put food on the table again at her house, just to make sure Veronika would have enough food in her stomach to tide her over until morning. Out came bread, butter, jam, and chamomile tea. They talked for hours, Aunt Agnes reminiscing about her childhood, and Veronika talking about her dreams of being a teacher and maybe one day marrying Marek.

"Marek? He's Kazia's cousin, is he not?"

Veronika nodded.

"If he's a good boy, works hard, and treats you with respect, then I say you should do what your heart tells you to."

Her aunt's words made her heart glow.

That night, as she was just falling asleep, she heard her aunt quietly walking over to where Veronika was lying on a pallet on the floor. She felt her quilt being gently pulled up until the top of her shoulders were covered. Slowly her aunt limped back to her own room and turned out the lantern. Veronika smiled to herself as she readjusted the quilt down to where it had been. Bless my aunt, she thought. She still thinks she has to tuck me in.

A few days later, when Uncle Oryst and Dorota were leaving, Uncle Oryst took Mama's hand and then seemed to think better of it, kissing her on the cheek instead.

Veronika heard him say under his breath, "Thank you for making Dorota feel welcome."

When Tata got back from taking them to Gródek, he asked, "How was it having Dorota stay with us?"

"Good," Mama said. "Dorota is a nice woman. I've been thinking. Maybe it's true that we shouldn't judge what Oryst did. I've never seen him so happy."

Tata held Mama and nodded. "See, that's what I was telling you all along."

65

VERONIKA

September 1938

Veronika sat across from her mother at the table. She knew from the unwavering steely look in her eyes, that Mama wasn't going to budge on her position. Veronika felt ready to explode into tears of anger and frustration, yet she knew, in the end, it would do her no good. It had already been decided by her mother and Kazia's mother that from now on, she and Kazia would spend every evening and night at Babcia's.

Veronika launched her most powerful appeal. "But Mama, how am I going to study?"

"Babcia will let you study."

"I'm sixteen. This is my last year of school. College exams are only a few months away. I won't be able to focus with her sitting across from the table looking at me. At least let me study at home in the evenings, and then go over to sleep."

"Look, Veronika," Mama snapped, "you and Kazia are just going to have to manage. Babcia is one hundred years old. She needs someone to be with her."

"Why can't Aunt Agnes sleep at Babcia's?"

"Because she won't."

That evening, with homework, books, and nightgowns in a sack, Kazia and Veronika walked to Babcia's, Kazia just as downcast as Veronika. Their evenings were going to be hell, indefinitely.

"At least we don't have to go over there alone," Kazia said.

"Yes, that's true, and we aren't scared of her like we used to be."

When they knocked on her door, Babcia seemed as pleased to see them as they were to see her.

"Where would you like us to sleep, Babcia?"

"You can sleep in Uncle Feliks and Aunt Paulina's bedroom, but don't touch anything."

The bedroom was just as their uncle and aunt had left it. Kazia and Veronika looked around, dismayed. The wardrobe was full of their clothes and the dresser cluttered with their hairbrushes and combs, shaving mug, and clips, and other little pieces of their lives. The girls wandered around the room and looked at everything. Veronika's heart ached. She sat down on the bed. "There's no room for us in here," she said.

"I know. It's bad enough living with Babcia but now this room. It's just so sad."

"I've got to get out of here. I'm going to Aunt Agnes's," Veronika said.

"I'll go with you."

When they told Aunt Agnes about the bedroom, she understood. "Just leave it to me. I'll see what I can do tomorrow."

The next evening when they came to Babcia's, she didn't answer their knock.

"Maybe she's at Aunt Agnes's," said Kazia.

"I don't think so, but maybe she knows where Babcia is."

When Aunt Agnes opened her door, she smiled, "Hello. Come in. Have you seen your room?"

"No, we haven't been inside Babcia's yet. She's not home," Kazia said.

"Oh, she's home all right. She doesn't answer her door when she's angry. Both of your mothers came over to see her today. I told them about your room. They cleaned it out and stored everything in Julia and Stasik's room. Babcia had quite a fit. I guess she's still not over it."

"Should we go home, then?" Veronika asked hopefully.

"Oh, no, just let yourself in and act normal. She'll get over it in time."

Timidly, they went back to Babcia's and opened the door. She was sitting by the kitchen table.

"Hello, Babcia," Kazia said.

She didn't answer.

"Let's put our books down in our room," Veronika said in a hushed voice. Walking into Aunt Paulina's and Uncle Feliks's room, Veronika looked around in astonishment. It had been transformed. New lace pillows were on the bed. The dresser had been cleared of its clutter. The wardrobe contained only their clothing.

As the days turned into weeks, Babcia returned to her old surly self and began to talk to them again.

"I wish she would show a bit of appreciation for what we're doing for her," Kazia said.

"I know. It's like she's the one being put out."

One thing that particularly annoyed Veronika was how low Babcia set the flame of the kerosene lamp.

"I can't see the words of my books, Mama," she complained when she got home the next day. "Then I end up with a headache."

"Just turn the flame up," Mama said.

That night, when Babcia had her back turned, Veronika turned up the lamp, just a little.

Kazia seemed amused. "Let's see how long that lasts," she whispered.

Babcia returned to the table, took one look at the lamp, and croaked, "Turn that lamp down. You'll get the ceiling all smoky."

Kazia gave Veronika an "I told you so" look.

At night in bed, Kazia and Veronika giggled about the things Babcia did, like pour a few drops of spiritus into her eye, then yelp and flap her bony arms, tears streaming down her face. When the pain subsided, she repeated the procedure in her other eye. Up she bolted again, leaping, gasping, and panting.

"Why do you do that, Babcia?"

Squinting at them through fiery red eyes, she said, "That's what keeps them strong and healthy. One hundred years old, and I still don't need glasses."

"Crazy old bat," Veronika whispered in bed. "Why does she always do such stupid things?"

Kazia tried to stifle a snicker.

"Be quiet! You're keeping me awake!" Babcia hollered from the kitchen where she slept.

Even that was strange, Veronika thought, as she rolled over and tried to sleep. Babcia had a bedroom, but never slept there, instead, she made up a little pallet on the floor, between the wall and the earthen oven.

"You don't sleep in your bedroom, Babcia?" Kazia had asked.

"It's warmer by the oven, and I don't hear the ghosts so much."

Kazia's mouth fell open. Veronika's, too. One more reason why Veronika hated being there. Ghosts.

— ✳ —

One night in October, after they'd been there for about four weeks, they were awakened by Babcia's yelling.

Veronika sat up, her heart caught in her throat. "What is it?"

"I don't know," Kazia gasped. "Maybe she's yelling at the secret police."

"Oh, God! Please, not that," Veronika said. "We have to go see."

Hand-in-hand with Kazia, she crept through the hallway toward the kitchen, her heart pounding as she strained to see through the blackness.

There was Babcia, standing in front of the open window, wraithlike in her white nightgown.

"Feliks, come! Vladzio, come!" she yelled into the stillness of the night. Then once again, "Feliks, come! Vladzio, come!"

Kazia and Veronika started to giggle.

"What is she doing?" Veronika asked.

"I don't know. Maybe she's gone crazy."

Finally, Babcia turned and went back to her pallet.

In the morning, Veronika awoke to Kazia shaking her shoulder. "Wake up, Veronika. Wake up."

"What is it?"

"Listen," Kazia replied.

"Listen to what? I don't hear anything."

"That's what I mean. It's too still. Babcia should be up making a fire by now."

Veronika bolted upright, her muscles tense. "Let's go see," she said, her breath coming in short gasps.

Once again, they crept through the cold hallway, holding each other's hand. Slowly they entered the kitchen, then stopped. Babcia lay motionless on her pallet.

"I don't hear her breathing. Do you?" Veronika asked.

Kazia shook her head.

They listened a bit more.

"Do you think she's dead?" Kazia asked.

"I don't know. I'll call her. Babcia, are you awake?"

No answer.

"Babcia, are you awake?" Veronika called a little louder. "Babcia, are you awake?" she called louder still, her voice rising in panic.

No answer.

Still holding hands, they crept up to Babcia and peered down at her. Her eyes were closed, her mouth open. Her skin looked white. Veronika gently touched Babcia's arm then pulled back. It felt like her arm was made of stone.

"She's dead! Babcia's dead!" Veronika yelled.

Out the door they ran, eyes popping, screaming all the way to Kazia's. "Babcia's dead! Babcia's dead!"

Kazia's mother froze when they burst into the kitchen, yelling and crying. At first, she didn't seem to understand what they were saying.

"Babcia's dead, Mama! She's dead. Veronika touched her."

"Her arm was cold and hard, Aunt Maria," Veronika said.

"Matko Boska! You two stay here. I'll get Helena and we'll go see."

— ※ —

Veronika knew it was true, that Babcia was truly dead, when the two sisters, her Mama and Aunt Maria, came back crying.

Babcia's body was brought to Veronika's home. She was glad to be at school while her mother and Aunt Maria washed and prepared the body for burial. When Veronika got home, Babcia's casket was in the living room, propped up on benches. Neighbours had already started coming over to pray and cry.

Mass was held for Babcia in Veronika's living room, with one of the men saying the words the priest would have said. Even though Babcia had been a big part of her life, Veronika couldn't find it within herself to cry. She wondered why and felt a sense of guilt.

"Why is it?" she asked Aunt Agnes the next day. "I should feel something but I don't."

"Did Babcia ever reach out to hug you or even talk to you?"

Veronika shook her head.

"There's your answer. You didn't have a relationship with her."

"I wanted to have a relationship with her," Veronika said, her voice coming out strained.

"Some tragedy in her earlier years, maybe," Aunt Agnes said, taking Veronika's hand in hers. "Or maybe she just didn't know what real love or compassion was."

Veronika stared down at her feet. "She loved Uncle Feliks and Uncle Vladzio."

"Yes, she loved her sons. That's why she was at the window, desperately trying to call the ghosts of her sons home."

Veronika searched her aunt's face. "You think they're dead, then?"

Aunt Agnes swallowed and glanced down at her hands. When she looked up, her lips were trembling, her eyes filled with tears. "Maybe so, Veronika. Maybe so."

66

VERONIKA

January 1939

Three months had passed since Babcia had died. During that time, Veronika went back to spending her evenings at home, preparing for the college entrance exams. If she passed, she would be eligible to take a ten-month course in childhood education and become a primary teacher.

"I don't know what I'm going to do, Kazia, if I don't pass. All my dreams will come crashing down."

"Don't worry, you'll pass."

"But what if I don't? Then what?"

"You could get married. You know Marek loves you."

Veronika pressed her lips together and said, "I'm only turning sixteen next month. I can't even think of marriage. At one time, I thought that's what I wanted, but now I need to go where I please and spend my money how I want."

"Have you talked to him about your feelings?"

"We talked, and I think he feels the way I do. He wants to learn the blacksmithing trade then maybe travel a bit."

"That's my feeling, too," Kazia said. "I'm longing to go to Paris and see the Eiffel Tower."

"For me, it's Germany. Aunt Agnes has told me so much about where she grew up in Heidelberg, with its castle on the hillside and medieval stone bridge."

— ✻ —

The day Veronika got the results of her exams, her fingers trembled as she broke the seal and opened the envelope. She scanned the paper, barely believing what she read. Not only did she pass, but she passed at the top of her class.

At the end of the school day, she could barely stop herself from running along the frozen, rutted road in her eagerness to get home. She could hardly believe that in a few months' time, she would go farther than she'd ever been before, to the city of Shepetovka, one hundred and fifty kilometres north of Kuzmin.

Bursting through the front door, she yelled, "I did it! I passed the exams! I'm going, Mama! I'm really going to Shepetovka!"

Mama and Tata smiled broadly, each taking her in their arms and giving her a big hug.

"We're very proud of you, the first person in our family to go to college," Tata said.

"Thank you, Tata. I didn't think of that," she said, basking in the love of her parents.

"Tonight, we're having a celebration dinner," Mama said. "I made your favourite—noodles and cream."

"So, you knew I would pass?"

"We never doubted it," Mama said with a smile.

— ✳ —

Before Veronika knew it, August had arrived. At the end the of the month, she'd be leaving.

Mama had sewn two new blouses and a skirt for Veronika, as well as knitting her a sweater. The only thing that troubled Veronika was her lack of winter boots. The ones she had were worn out and pinched her toes, but there was no help for it. She didn't even ask her parents for a new pair as she knew they didn't have the money, after paying her room and board for the year plus her train ticket. She hoped that the place where she boarded would be close to the college.

At dinner, a few days before she was about to leave, Veronika said, "I'm a little nervous about where I'll live."

"You'll like it. It's where Kazia's sister, Nellia, boarded a few years ago, with a very nice older couple," Mama said.

"Is it close to the college?"

"Very close," Tata answered. "Maybe a twenty-minute walk."

Veronika silently groaned. She'd have blistered feet all winter. Maybe Aunt Agnes had a pair of boots that would fit her.

67
JANEK

August 1939

"Veronika has gone off to say goodbye to some of her friends," Helena announced when Janek came in from morning chores.

Janek felt a wave of irritation as he dropped down in his chair.

"What is it, Janek?" Helena asked, her eyes troubled.

"Oh, I feel a little foolish saying this, but I was hoping Veronika would stay home with us these last couple of days. It'll be a whole year before we see her again."

"She'll only be gone for the morning," Helena said, smiling. "She wanted to say goodbye to Frania."

"Such a sad dream I had about her last night. I hope to God there's not a message in it."

"What was the dream?"

He could hear the alarm in her voice. He hesitated, wishing he hadn't said anything.

"Janek, you need to tell me. If there's a message in it, I need to know."

"In my dream, I saw Vladzio. He was playing his harmonica, and Veronika was standing in front of him. She was little, maybe two or three years old, listening to his music. Do you remember how she used to love his music?"

Helena nodded, her eyes misting over.

Janek felt a lump in his throat. He swallowed hard, not wanting to cry in front of Helena. He could see her looking at him, waiting for him to go on. After a moment he said, "In my dream, I became aware that the child standing in front of Vladzio was not Veronika, but her son. How happy I was. Her son. I wanted to see him, but no matter how hard I looked, I could not see his face. Then he was gone and there stood our Veronika, a grown woman now. I was aching to reach out and hold her, to touch the child, but I couldn't. It was like I was seeing them from a great distance. All I wanted was to be with her, but she was so far away, I couldn't reach her. Gradually she faded away. Vladzio spoke. He said that I would never see her again. I was filled with such great sadness that in my dream I started to cry."

"Your dream makes me so sad, Janek."

He nodded. "My poor little Veronika," he sighed. "I wonder what's going to become of her?"

"That scares me, Janek. We know what's going to become of her," she said, her voice brittle. "She's going to marry a good Polish boy right here in Kuzmin and give us many grandchildren."

"I pray to God that you're right."

She looked at him, tears glistening in her eyes and turned away.

68

VERONIKA

The bells hanging above the door of the general store jingled as Veronika walked in. Frania stood behind the counter, dusting shelves. She smiled. "Papa, Veronika's here. I'll be going now."

Her father came out from the back. "Veronika. How are you doing?" he asked, looking at her over his round glasses.

"I'm excited to leave but my parents are sad to see me go."

"It is a big change for them. They wonder if you will be safe on your own and make good decisions."

"I suppose that's it," Veronika said.

"Before you go off with Frania, I have a little something for you." He reached under the counter and held out a brown paper package. "For your trip."

Veronika felt herself flushing. "It's kind of you to think of me."

He smiled awkwardly. "It's not much, only a couple of scoops of candy. Enough to last you a month maybe."

"Her favourite candy? The one with the soft fruit filling?" Frania asked.

"But of course."

As usual, they went into Frania's room, sat on her bed and talked. Veronika opened her package of sweets and gave one to Frania.

"I'm going to miss you," Frania said. "In some ways I wish I were going with you."

"Why didn't you apply for college? Your grades were good enough."

Frania shrugged. "I wanted to, but my parents were against it. They think it best if I work in the store for a while and then get married."

"Oh, Frania. Do you want to get married?"

"Not if he chooses someone too old for me, but Papa says what matters is that he comes from a good family."

"What are you going to do?"

"Mama talked to me privately and said not to worry. She will let Papa think he is choosing but, in the end, she will have her say in it."

Veronika gave a snort of laughter. "That's the way it is with my parents, too."

After a while, there was a knock at the door and Izaak called out, "Mama wants to know if you and Veronika would like some cake."

"Cake?" Veronika asked.

"I think she made it because you're going away."

Sitting at the heavily polished dark wood table beside Izaak, Veronika noticed his freshly combed hair and how tall he was getting. "How old are you now, Izaak?"

"Eleven."

"Already he's studying for his bar mitzvah," Frania's mother said, setting a poppyseed cake on the table. "It won't feel the same without a rabbi present, but what can we do?"

Cutting the cake into generous slices, she said, "I heard that you'll be going away, Veronika. I thought I'd make a cake in celebration."

Veronika flushed with pleasure. "It is very kind of you to do this for me. My mother has been trying to keep it a secret, but I think she's also planning a celebration for me tomorrow. Going to have all my relatives over."

After Veronika finished her cake and was getting ready to go, she said to Izaak, "I hope you do well in studying for your bar mitzvah. I will miss you." Hugging Frania, she said, "I'll see you when I get back."

69
VERONIKA

August 1939

Veronika helped Tata carry their kitchen table and all their chairs and benches outside, setting them down under the leafy canopy of the walnut tree. Such a hot August day it was. The air inside the thick stone walls of her home made sitting inside only slightly cooler.

Resting from their exertion, she and Tata sat down beside the table. Tata took off his cap and, taking a handkerchief from his back pocket, mopped his head. Veronika looked across at the buckwheat field shimmering in the afternoon sun; she was enjoying the breeze that every now and then lifted her hair and cooled the nape of her neck. It hadn't been easy carrying out their heavy wooden table and all their chairs and benches. Mama had insisted. She wanted everything to be nice for Veronika's going away party. As Veronika sat beside Tata, she was acutely aware that this would be the last dinner she would have with her family until she returned home ten months from now. In the morning, Tata would walk her to the Gródek train station; from there she would take the train to Shepetovka, a ride of several hours.

Tata had just barely managed to save enough money from carving tombstones to pay for her room and board and to cover her train fare. There wouldn't even be enough money for her to come home at New Year's; she had not dared to mention new boots. She felt a stab of guilt for even thinking of new boots. She should be happy with what she had. So much work it had been for Mama to make her new clothes and a sweater for college. How often had she come home from school to see her mother, bent over at the river, beating flax stocks to loosen the fibre or sitting at her loom weaving fabric? Veronika would ask if she could help, but Mama always said, *"No, my Noosha. Better you spend your time studying."* How often had Veronika gone to sleep knowing that her mother was exhausted from working in the fields all day but determined to finish a hem or a sleeve, so that in the morning, almost magically, a new blouse or pair of underwear would be laid out by her bed, a silent surprise for Veronika. She consoled herself with the thought that there would probably be a lot of other impoverished students wearing worn out boots.

The idea of being on her own made Veronika feel excited and nervous at the same time. Once she stepped onto the train and it pulled out of the station, she imagined it would be like a dividing line in her life, a passing from childhood to adulthood and for that, she couldn't wait. Her whole life seemed to hinge around going to college and getting her teaching certificate; after that she could get a job and earn money, her own money. The whole world lay just beyond Kuzmin, waiting for her to explore and yet, how could she live without seeing her parents each day, hearing their words of encouragement, feeling their love? There was an ache in her heart already. Except for the occasional letters that Kazia would write for her parents, once she got on that train, she would be entirely on her own. What if the people

Tata had arranged for her to live with were horrible? What if she got too homesick and had to come home? What if she got sick like she had last month? Just like when she was a child, her mother had checked on her throughout the night, and in the morning had killed one of their precious chickens to make soup for her.

Tata picked up his cap and put it back on his head. "I should go get Agnes now. The others will be coming soon."

Veronika reached out and put her hand on top of his. "Thank you, Tata."

"Thank you? For what?"

"You know for what; for making this party for me, for helping to make my dreams come true."

"You don't have to thank me. It was always my plan to send you to college."

Searching his eyes, she finally said what had been weighing on her mind. "And you don't mind so much that I'm not going to be a doctor?"

Holding her hand between both of his and looking straight into her eyes, he said, "You know, becoming a doctor was my dream. Now that you're sixteen, you have to create your own dreams."

Veronika looked into his steady blue eyes and saw that he meant it; her soul lifted. "I love you," she said, "I'm going to miss you and Mama so much."

"We will miss you, too. More than you'll know."

Soon after Tata left, Kazia, Alina, and their mothers, brothers, and sisters arrived. Veronika noticed that Marek had not come and wondered if he would. In some ways, she hoped he wouldn't.

"Veronika, maybe you and Kazia can wash and peel the potatoes," Mama said, interrupting her thoughts.

"Of course," Kazia said, taking the bucket from her.

On their way to the well, Kazia said, "You must be excited to be going tomorrow."

"I am, and nervous, too."

"That's the problem with our life. Just because I'm a few months younger than you, we're always getting separated."

Although she said she wished Kazia was going, in some ways she was glad she wasn't. To be totally on her own felt so grown up, a challenge that would be lessened if someone else was with her.

"I wonder if Marek is coming over?" said Veronika, trying to sound nonchalant.

"Why wouldn't he come? Has something happened between you two?"

Veronika hesitated and then said, "He wanted us to become engaged."

"Engaged? And you didn't tell me? What did you say?"

"I turned him down."

"You turned him down? You've always been crazy about him."

"I told him I need time on my own before I can even think of becoming engaged."

"How did he take it?"

"Not so well. That's why I was wondering if he would come today."

"Did you say anything to your parents?"

Veronika shook her head. "I don't want anyone to know."

"Your secret is safe with me," said Kazia, giving her a little hug.

After a dinner of Mama's special white flour pierogi filled with sauerkraut and mushrooms, cabbage rolls, boiled potatoes, bread, and salads, and many toasts to Veronika, they played loteryjka all evening, with Aunt Agnes, as usual, the caller of numbers and the winning card checker. Although no one said anything, Veronika could tell that everyone felt the gap of the missing family members. So many had been taken, Veronika thought with a sigh. She couldn't help but look around and sense the missing presence of Kazia's father, Uncle Vladzio, Uncle Feliks, Aunt Paulina, Stasik, Julia, Alina and Marek's father, and Doctor Janczewski.

When Tata went to the barn to hitch the horse to the wagon to take Aunt Agnes home, she motioned for Veronika to come and sit beside her. "We haven't had a chance to talk all evening, just the two of us," said Aunt Agnes, holding out her arms.

As Veronika reached in to hug and kiss her, Aunt Agnes murmured, "My little girl."

"Not so little anymore," Veronika said laughingly, extracting herself from her aunt's plump and slightly sweaty embrace.

Aunt Agnes looked at her adoringly, her face open and childlike. "To me, you will always be my little girl. So, you're going away, and in one year you'll be a teacher."

Veronika nodded.

"In Germany, you have to go to college much longer to be a teacher."

"They're so short of teachers here, that's why. But the course is very intensive. It's six days a week with masses of homework."

"You'll do fine, such a smart girl."

"How will you do? I'm going to worry about you while I'm gone."

"I'll get by. I just don't like how quiet it is at home. Some days go by and I see nobody."

Veronika felt a wave of sadness go through her.

"Sometimes I think, oh, I'll go next door to tell Paulina something, then I remember she's gone."

As Aunt Agnes was leaving, she pressed a few rubles into Veronika's hand.

"I can't take this," Veronika gasped.

"You take it." she said firmly. "A woman always has to have money in her bag."

It was late by the time everyone went home. Veronika fell asleep right away and had no time to be sad or frightened about leaving. In the morning, her mother woke her up; it was time to eat breakfast and go.

When she went to kiss her mother goodbye, Veronika felt a lump form in her throat as tears welled in her eyes. Struggling not to cry, she avoided looking at her mother, but even so, caught a glimpse of her mother's forlorn eyes and the slight quiver of her mouth. As tears ran down Veronika's face, her mother kissed her again and again as she hugged her.

"I love you, Veronika. Do well in your studies."

Veronika nodded, and taking the handkerchief Tata silently proffered, she blew her nose. Suddenly she started laughing and crying at the same time.

"What is it?" her mother said, smiling at her in bewilderment.

"I could hardly wait to be going and now that I am, I cry because all I want to do is stay home and be with you."

Tata patted her shoulder and said, "It's time to go so we don't miss the train."

Giving her mother one last kiss and hug, Veronika said, "I'll think of you, Mama, every time I put on my new clothes."

Mama nodded, briskly wiping her own tears away with the back of her hand. "Write soon. Let us know how it is for you there with that family."

When they got to the Gródek station, they didn't have long to wait before the whistle blew. Veronika kissed her father on both sides of his bearded face and hugged him fiercely. When the train whistle blew a second time, Veronika picked up her suitcase and climbed the stairs.

Quickly finding her seat, she waved to Tata through the window as the train began to move. She craned her neck to see him for as long as possible, but after a moment, he was gone and she was totally on her own. For many miles, she discreetly wiped the tears that leaked from her eyes, and tried not to look at anybody until her breathing returned to normal and she became accustomed to her aloneness. When she finally looked up, an elderly woman sitting across from her smiled knowingly and nodded.

After eating the midday meal her mother had packed, she sat back on her hard wooden seat and thought of Frania. Here she was on her way to independence and adventure, and Frania was working in her father's store until a suitable husband could be found. She thought of how Frania had shrugged her shoulders and said, *"As long as he's young and handsome, and for my parents' sake, Jewish,"* but Veronika had seen the longing in her eyes.

Thinking of Frania, Veronika opened her satchel and pulled out the brown paper package of candy. She would miss seeing Frania's mother, always so warm and welcoming, yet in the background, not wanting to intrude on their visits. Even Izaak she would miss. She would even miss reading and writing in Hebrew, enjoying the challenge of Frania's mini lessons. She wondered if they would still be friends as the years went by or would they drift apart?

In the evening when it got chilly, she opened her suitcase, and to her astonishment found that a new pair of black boots had been slipped into her suitcase. A note in Kazia's familiar script said, *Your parents wanted you to have these boots. They say that they love you and will miss you.*

70
VERONIKA

August 30, 1939

As the train pulled into the station at Shepetovka, Veronika could barely contain her excitement. The station building was enormous, with ornate white trim around the windows. If the train station was this fancy, what would the rest of the town look like? And it would be hers for ten whole months.

Following the instructions given to her, she walked down the wide dirt road of the main street, with one-storey wooden shops interspersed with three- and even four-storey brick buildings. She wondered how it would feel to walk around on the top floor, knowing that there was layer after layer of people walking around below you.

When Veronika came to the home where she would lodge, she knocked on the door and a man, stooped with age, welcomed her in.

"I am Sergey, and this is my wife, Heike."

Right away, Heike showed Veronika to her room. Veronika could tell from the way Heike leaned in the doorway and smiled that she hoped Veronika would like it.

"This is a lovely room, perfect for my needs," Veronika said, taking in the small bed, wardrobe, wooden table and chair, and to her delight, her very own kerosene lantern.

"So you can study in your room and not be disturbed," Heike said. "I will leave you to unpack. Dinner is in an hour. Do you like pork and cabbage soup?"

Veronika hesitated before she spoke. Cabbage cooked with pork was something she had always found unpalatable.

"I'm sure it's delicious, but just a little bowl, please."

The following day, Veronika got directions to the college to orient herself to its location and to find out how long it would take to walk there. When her school came into sight, she couldn't quite believe that the grand four-storey brick building was where she would study.

In reception, the woman directed her to the second floor and the room that would be the focus of her dreams—a career working with children, financial independence, and a chance to see the world.

Her classroom was similar to the one in Kuzmin, except instead of desks, there were long tables that sat three students across, and charts on the wall that pertained to teaching.

After exploring the rest of the campus, which included a bookstore, a large empty room called a gymnasium, a cafeteria, and a common area outside with benches around plantings of trees, Veronika explored the main street of Shepetovka. After a little debate with herself, she stopped in a bakery and spent a few precious coins on a sweet roll.

Falling asleep that night was difficult; tomorrow was September 1st, the start of college. She woke up beyond excited. After a hurried breakfast of heavy dark rye bread, an egg, and tea, she took up her satchel and the lunch Heike had made for her and set off.

Her morning and afternoon were filled with absolute joy. As she walked across the main campus square at the end of her first day, she knew that this is what she was meant to be doing with her life.

Veronika's pace suddenly slowed and then stopped. Why were groups of students standing about, their faces frightened? She clutched her satchel and walked closer.

"What it is?" she asked a female student.

"Oh, my God. You haven't heard? Germany has invaded Poland."

Veronika's stomach churned. Kuzmin was close to the Polish border. Maybe the fighting would spill over the border?

Veronika approached a group and listened.

"It could lead to another world war," one student said, his voice raised. "Poland's allies will never tolerate this."

"Maybe the Soviet Union will be attacked next," another said.

Veronika hurried back to her boarding house, her stomach in a knot.

Sergey met Veronika at the door, his face tense. "Heike has taken to her bed. The invasion has brought back all her fears."

"Fears? Oh, my God. What happened to her?" she asked, dropping her satchel.

"She is from Belgium. During the Great War, German soldiers set fire to her city then went around shooting civilians. What happened to her mother,"—he hesitated—"and the other women was unspeakable."

Veronika sagged down into a chair, her mind numb. "What can I do to help?"

"Maybe help me make dinner. I'm not so good at cooking, then I'll take dinner to her on a tray."

Veronika helped wash, peel, and chop carrots, potatoes, and cabbage, putting together a simple meal of vegetable soup, bread, and cheese.

After Sergey brought Heike her tray, Veronika and Sergey sat down to eat their meal; the company of the old man was soothing.

"It must be hard to be away from your parents at a time like this," he said.

Under Sergey's kindly gaze, Veronika's anxiety came tumbling out. "I'm worried about my parents and family. The Polish border is so close, and this could mean the end of my dreams if the college closes down. There's not enough money to send me a second time."

"If the school closes, likely all the students will be given a refund. And as for your place here, we'll save your room for when things settle down."

Veronika felt weak with relief. "Thank you. You've eased my mind."

That night Veronika prayed for the safety of her parents, the people of Poland, and that college would continue.

The next day her teacher announced, "It has been decided that for now, classes will continue as usual. What has happened between Germany and Poland should not affect the functioning of this college, nor do we need worry about Germany attacking the Soviet Union. If they do try such a foolish move, they will be trounced upon."

Days later, Veronika heard that the United Kingdom and France had declared war on Germany, giving credence to those who felt another world war was coming, and raising her fears once again. To Veronika's relief, things settled down, but on September 17th, a shocking rumour went around campus. The Soviet Union had allied itself with Germany and invaded Poland from the east.

"What do you think is going to happen?" Veronika asked Sergey that evening.

He shook his head. "All we can do is wait and see."

Veronika went to her room, books to one side, and wondered what it would be like to be in a war. Tata had been in the Great War of 1914. He rarely talked about it. From others she had heard of the senseless deaths of young men ordered over a ridge, only to be slaughtered by a hail of bullets, followed by the second line. Those who froze in fear were shot from behind by their own officers.

The only time Tata seemed to enjoy talking about the war was when he told the story of how he had outsmarted his officers. When they ordered him to shoot, he aimed above the enemy's head so he would not have it on his conscience that he had killed someone.

That night, Veronika spent a long time in prayer instead of study.

By October 6th, Poland had fallen, and the country was carved up between Germany and the Soviet Union. Veronika took some comfort when Hitler announced that he would not be going to war with the United Kingdom and France.

After that, world events settled down for the next few months, and she once again focused on her studies, including the teaching of Soviet slogans, poems, and songs, with an emphasis on Soviet citizenship. She didn't like it, but what was she to do? She was training to be a Soviet school teacher, after all.

In May of 1940, Veronika sat in the college cafeteria as world events once more boiled over. Germany had invaded the Netherlands, Belgium, and Luxembourg, and two days later, Northern France. Veronika didn't know what to do next. Should she go back home?

When she got back to her lodging, Sergey was slouched in his chair. Heike had taken to fits of crying.

"Stay and get your certificate," Sergey advised her when Veronika talked to him about it. "You're too close now to quit."

He had a point. In only two weeks her course would end.

A few days later, Veronika received a letter that Kazia had written for Mama and Tata, expressing their concern. Was she safe there? Should she come home early?

She wrote back that she was safe and would continue with her studies.

The last few days of class were cancelled and the day of her graduation ceremony, a hurried affair, was not what she had hoped. After saying a heartfelt goodbye to Sergey and Heike, Veronika tucked her teaching certificate inside her suitcase and boarded a train, grateful to be going home. Whatever was to happen, she would face it with her parents.

71

VERONIKA

June 28, 1940

Veronika and her parents sat at the kitchen table staring at her teaching certificate. Glancing at her parents' beaming faces as they studied the document, her heart swelled with pride.

"Read it to us," her mother said, her finger gingerly touching the Soviet seal.

"It says: *Veronika Teresa Osiecka, this day 25 June 1940, completed at College of Shepetovka, Teacher's Certification program, Ministry of Soviet Education.*"

"You did well, Veronika. Today I'm a happy man. My daughter is home and now she's a teacher."

Mama gave Veronika a squeeze around her waist. "We are so, so proud of you, and to celebrate your homecoming, I made your favourite dinner."

"It can't be noodles in cream, can it?"

Mama nodded.

"How did you ever get the cream?" she exclaimed.

"I have a friend who works at the dairy. I told her that you were coming home and so she put a little bit of cream in a pail for me."

Eating Mama's meal of her tender potato and onion pierogi, the rich meaty broth of her borscht, and the noodles in cream, was even better than she had remembered. While she ate, she was bursting to tell them her other good news, but the moment had to be just right. Her application for a teaching position close to her home had been approved. If she took a shortcut through a path in the woods, it was only about six kilometres away. She would be able to come home on the weekends.

After Tata pushed his chair back and Mama had offered more food for the last time, Veronika said, "I have a surprise for the both of you."

"A surprise?" Tata asked.

"I've been given a teaching position for September."

"What? Mama asked sharply. "Where?"

"Don't worry, Mama. It's not far from here. It's in the village of Kalytintsy."

"Ah, that's good," Mama said, smiling. "You can come home every day."

"I don't know about every day," Tata said. "It's a bit of a walk."

"How far?"

"About six kilometres."

"Tata is right. After school, I'll need to stay and prepare lessons. Better if I board with a family during the week and come home on the weekend."

"Well, that's still wonderful news, Veronika," Mama said. "We get to keep you for another year."

"Kazia will be upset," Veronika said. "We'll be separated for another year, with her leaving for college in the fall to get her teaching certificate."

Tata nodded, a half-smile creasing the corners of his lips, as he tipped a little more spiritus into his glass.

"What, Tata?" Veronika said, noticing his smile. "It's sad that for the second year we're being separated."

"I was just thinking of the fuss you made when we first told you Kazia wasn't going to school with you. Thought I'd have to pack you over my shoulder and carry you to school each day."

"You're lucky to have a cousin like Kazia in your life," Mama said, leaning over and patting Veronika on the top of her hand. "You two are like sisters and probably always will be."

"Who knows," Tata said. "Maybe in your second year of teaching, Kazia can be assigned to the same school as you."

"Wouldn't that be wonderful? It can be our dream."

Hearing someone approach the house, Tata got up and looked out the window. "It's that Osip again," he said sounding upset.

Mama clucked her tongue. "Maybe he won't stay long."

"Him?" Tata said. "Probably wants to be here for the evening."

Veronika felt her heart sink. Osip was the one neighbour Veronika could not stand. She remembered how he used to beat his wife, Sofiya, and how she used to run to their house, holding her ripped dress together, spend the night, and go home in the morning when her husband was sober.

As Tata walked to the door, he said, "Say nothing to offend him."

"We know, Tata. You don't have to tell us," Veronika said, annoyed that this boorish neighbour was interrupting her first evening at home.

"Jan. You have time for a drink, don't you?" Osip asked, already entering the room and heading for the table. Taking off his cap, he nodded to Veronika and her mother. He was a burly man with ham-like hands. Veronika could smell liquor on his breath.

"So, you're back from college, are you? Going to be one of those nasty, mean-lipped schoolteachers?" he asked with a laugh, revealing a few missing upper teeth.

Veronika pasted a smile on her lips and shrugged.

"Helena, bring us some glasses," said Tata. "Please, sit down. We've just finished eating. Helena can make you up a plate."

"No, no I had my dinner." He looked at Veronika. "What do you think about Germany taking over almost all of Europe? Everyone must be talking about it in a big place like Shepetovka."

Veronika nodded. "I heard about it, but I've been too busy with my studies to think about it much."

"Thank you, Helena," Osip said, taking the glass from her. As Tata poured a splash of spiritus into his own glass, Mama managed a strained smile and said, "If you will excuse us, I think Veronika and I will go do some mending by the window where there is more light, and let you two men talk in peace." Glancing meaningfully at Veronika, she picked up a basket of mending and walked across the room. Veronika followed her, glad to be away from Osip.

Positioning her chair so that she could still see what was happening at the table, Veronika picked up a ball of yarn and a darning needle.

Osip drained his glass and held it out to Tata for a refill. "And I tell you, they're going to cross our borders next."

Tata looked at him incredulously. "No one will ever attack us. The Soviets are too strong, and anyhow, Stalin and Hitler are friends, like brothers."

"See the light of day, Jan. The German army is on the move. They've already invaded half a dozen other countries. We're next, I'm telling you, and when they do, it'll be a lot better government than this one."

Veronika looked at her father, wondering if he would say anything. All Osip had to do was go to the secret police in the morning and say he had heard Tata talking against the government and that would be it. He'd be gone. Maybe Osip was trying to set Tata up. She could see the muscles tighten in her father's jaw as he took a long, slow drink from his glass. He said, "The cow always wants what is outside the fence. I won't wish for what I don't know."

When Osip finally left an hour later, Mama said sadly, "This hasn't been the evening we had planned for you."

"It's all right, Mama. What could you do? But do you mind if I open the door for a while to air out the house? I can still smell him in here."

72

VERONIKA

The summer months passed quickly. Veronika's days were filled with helping her parents preserve enough food to see them over the winter. In the coolness of the morning, she weeded the garden and picked vegetables. In the afternoon, she helped her mother prepare fruit to dry as each type of tree in the orchard came into season.

In the afternoons, when there weren't any fruits or vegetables that needed to be tended to, they pulled out the washtub and scrub board and washed clothes, made candles or soap, or beat the stalks of flax to loosen the fibres for making thread. In their spare time, they spun the fibres into linen thread, then wove it into cloth so that Veronika would have new clothes for when she started teaching.

In the evenings, Veronika often went to dances at the homes of friends or cousins, but never at the dancehall the Soviets had made in what was once their church. She saw Marek from time to time. He was going out with another girl. She told herself, and everyone else, that it didn't bother her in the least.

In late August, Aunt Maria knocked on their door.

"Come in, Maria," Helena said. "What is it? Something good has happened?"

Veronika looked up from the sleeve she was sewing, her needle poised for another stitch, when she noticed the joy on her aunt's face.

"Agnes got a letter today," she said. "From Paulina."

"From Paulina? We'll be right over."

When they arrived at Aunt Agnes's, Veronika was asked to read the letter. Mama, Tata, Aunt Agnes, Kazia, her sister Nellia, and Aunt Maria watched as she unfolded the letter.

My dear family,
It has been a long time since I have been able to write, and I pray to God that this letter reaches you.

Through God's grace, the children and I are all still alive. Julia and Stasik send their love. They are nineteen and eighteen. My youngest is four. I named him Eugeniusz. Feliks would be proud to see how much the child resembles him.

We were moved from the family where we were living before to a large camp of women and children. When we first arrived, there were no barracks. We had to sleep in tents until the barracks could be built. It was spring. Very cold, sometimes snow on the ground when we woke up.

We are always hungry. Most meals are a thin vegetable soup, a few tablespoons of cooked oats, and bread.

The children and I work in the fields. Eugeniusz I have to leave in the nursery with the other children too young to work. Every day he cries when I leave him there. It breaks my heart.

Some of the women and children have been here for five years and are starting to be released. How we long for our time to be over. Perhaps in two years, we, too, will be released and will come home.

Have you had any word from Feliks or Vladzio? We are allowed mail now. Direct your letter to the name and number of this work camp.

Paulina and children

A silence filled the room.

"Poor, poor Paulina," Mama said at last. "How mangled her life has been."

"And if it hadn't been for my hip," said Aunt Agnes, pointing her finger for emphasis, "I would be in Kazakhstan right now with her."

"What did any of them do to deserve being deported?" asked Mama, her voice rising with emotion. "Nothing. Only that they are strong and healthy and can be used for slaves."

Blinking back tears, Aunt Agnes said, "I will never forget the day they took Paulina, the look in her eyes."

"Don't," Aunt Maria said. "You only torture yourself to think of it."

Lost in her own memories, Aunt Agnes went on. "She pleaded for them to come back after she had the baby. But they said she had to come now."

At that, Aunt Agnes broke down in tears. Veronika went over to her chair and put her arms around her. "But they are alive. Think of that. You heard what she wrote. Even the baby is fine."

"Thank God, at least that," Aunt Agnes said. "The baby lived."

"Maybe when he's five, we'll see him."

The room fell silent again. After a while Veronika's mother said, "I'll get some tea. I see Agnes has some already made."

"I'll help you, Aunty," said Nellia, pushing back her chair.

Aunt Agnes looked at Veronika, her eyes lingering sorrowfully, a half-smile on her face. "And now two more of our family leave us."

"But at least it's of our own choosing," Veronika said.

"When is it that you leave for your teaching job?"

"Friday. I want the weekend to settle in and get my classroom ready before school starts."

"And when do you leave for college, Kazia?"

"Wednesday," she said.

"You don't seem happy," Aunt Agnes said, reaching over and touching Kazia on the top of her hand.

Kazia shifted in her chair. "I just don't know if I should be leaving home at a time like this."

"The war between Germany and Britain is far from here," Aunt Maria said, crossing her arms. "Best you continue your education and get your teaching certificate."

"And if the war comes closer?" Kazia asked, chewing on her lip.

"You're only a three-hour train ride away."

Nellia and Mama came back into the room and set down trays of tea, honey, and mugs. As Kazia took her mug she said, "I can't help being nervous."

Tata nodded. "Things are very unsettled. Osip has been going around telling people that not only Germany has been invading countries, but the Soviet Union, too, now."

"What?" asked Aunt Agnes.

"That's what he said."

"Cholera jasna! What does that man know? He's always going around saying things," Aunt Maria said, her eyes flashing.

"He was very specific this time. He said the Soviet Union has invaded Lithuania, Latvia, and Estonia, and even parts of Romania."

"So, how does he know so much more than the rest of us, Janek?" she retorted sharply, passing around the honey and the spoons.

"That's the thing, he won't say," said Tata. "Who knows, maybe he has a crystal radio set hidden away somewhere."

"I don't think he would risk his life for owning a radio," said Mama. "He doesn't have that much courage. Just hot air and bluff he is."

"Good thing you never married him," said Aunt Maria, looking at her daughter Nellia and shaking her head."

"Mother, please. One date with him was enough for me. I just wish people would forget it. It makes me so annoyed. People keep saying, *Oh, it's a good thing you never married him.*"

"Well, it is," "Kazia said in a small voice.

Nellia lunged for her.

"Girls," Aunt Maria said, "that's enough. We'll finish our tea and then be going."

Walking Kazia home, Veronika linked arms with her, and they trailed a little behind the rest of the family. They talked of how much they missed Aunt Paulina and how Babcia used to be so mean to her. After a bit, their talk turned to when Kazia would be leaving.

"Don't worry, Kazia. You're not that far from home. If war breaks out, you could even walk home."

She could feel Kazia's arm tremble next to hers. "You think that comforts me? I can't even imagine how frightening it would be to have to make my way home all alone on foot, while a war was going on."

73
VERONIKA

August 29, 1940

The night before she left for her job, Veronika lay in the comfort of her feather bed, unable to sleep. She listened to the crickets and thought about how it would feel to leave home and start her new life as a Soviet primary teacher. In the morning, she and Tata would leave early for Kalytintsy, taking a short-cut through the bush. She told Tata that she could walk alone but he wouldn't hear of it.

It's too isolated that path, he had said. *Maybe someone might grab you. I'll go with you.*

Tata had found a woman in Kalytintsy willing to provide Veronika room and board during the weekdays. That way, she could stay at the school as late as she wanted, preparing lessons, and Tata wouldn't have to walk there and back each day to come and get her. Too much for him, she thought, especially after working all day and, in the winter, walking through the drifts of snow—in the dark. Impossible.

In the morning, Veronika could feel a bubble of nervous excitement building in her chest as she quickly dressed. She could hardly believe that today she would get to meet the principal for the first time. After that, she would have the rest of the day and tomorrow to get her classroom organized and lessons prepared for Monday.

Adjusting her new beige linen skirt and white blouse in the mirror, she turned to see if the skirt still flattered her hips and that the hemline hung evenly. Pleased that it fit the same as it had yesterday, she reached for her creamy wool sweater. Her mother had just finished knitting it last night. As she put it on, warmth filled her heart as she thought of how her mother had stayed up late every evening for the past month to have it and a matching knitted hat ready in time. It would certainly see her through the brisk fall mornings.

As she buttoned her sweater, she could hear the groan of the cast iron door of the woodstove as it swung on its rusty hinges. Her mother must be stoking the fire in preparation for breakfast.

Pinning her hair up into a bun, she hoped she looked older than her eighteen years. Again, a surge of nervousness fluttered through her stomach.

Standing back and looking at her reflection, she saw her timid, unsure eyes blinking back at her. Maybe her hat would make the difference. She picked up the hat sitting on her dresser and admired it. It was a lovely little hat, with a wool-covered leather brim. Mama had stiffened the wool into shape by soaking it in a solution of potato starch then re-shaping it as it dried. Veronika pinned it to her head at a jaunty angle. Standing back to take in her total look, she was satisfied, pleased, even. She definitely looked like a teacher, even if she didn't quite feel like one yet.

As she walked into the kitchen, she could see the pride in her mother's eyes.

"There you are. How beautiful you look. And that hat, it's perfect."

Just the reaction Veronika wanted. She hugged her and, stepping back, was surprised to see her mother struggling to regain her composure.

"You're not going to cry are you, Mama?" Seeing that her mother was indeed trying to hold back tears, she said, "Now, don't cry Mama. I'll be home in seven days. What are you crying for?"

"I know. I know you'll be home in a few days; it's not that. It's just that you look lovely in your clothes and your hair and all. And I'm so proud of you. My daughter, a teacher. And here I can't even read or write."

"Why didn't you stay in school longer?"

"Babcia said school wasn't necessary for a girl. And when I was your age, all I wanted to do was get married so I could get away from her."

"Oh, Mama, that's why I've always been so grateful to have you as a mother. Other girls sometimes used to say to me how they couldn't wait to leave home, or how they couldn't get along with their mother, but you, Mama, have always been like my best friend. No, stop, don't cry, Mama. It's true. Now look, you've got me crying."

Just then the door opened from outside, and Tata came stomping in from the barn. The smile faded from his face as he looked at them. "Something's wrong? What is it?"

"Nothing, Tata, nothing. We're just happy."

"Women," he muttered, smiling and shaking his head.

After they ate breakfast, Tata picked up her cardboard suitcase. Veronika hugged her mother goodbye, then walked out the door with a loaf of bread in a drawstring bag her mother had made for her new landlady.

As dawn began to break, Veronika and her father walked down the shortcut through the brush. They didn't talk much, but there was a feeling of companionable warmth between them. She felt special, cherished, that he would do this for her. For forty-five minutes they walked, meeting no one. Looking into the gloom of the brush that surrounded them, she was glad to have her father with her.

The village was smaller than Veronika had imagined, just a few houses, a general store, and the school.

"You won't hear any Polish here," Tata said. "The woman you're staying with, Ulyana, told me only Ukrainians live here."

"How old is Ulyana?"

"She'd be in her sixties, I guess. Nice lady. You'll like her."

Tata walked her to the door of Ulyana's home and knocked. When she opened the door, her kindly face crinkled with happiness. She was on the plump side with grey hair neatly pulled back into a bun; a large brown apron covered her print dress.

"You must be Veronika. I've been looking forward to you coming. Someone to keep me company. Come in. I'll make you both some tea."

"No, thank you," said Tata. "I have to be going."

"My father has to get to the collective," Veronika explained. Giving her a little hug, Tata gave them each a nod of his head, then headed back up the road at a fast pace. Watching him walk away, Veronika felt a sudden wave of loneliness. Turning and smiling at Ulyana, she chided herself. She would be going home every weekend. What was wrong with her that she was missing her father already?

Ulyana showed Veronika to her room. Although the home was plainly furnished, everything had the appearance of being clean and well-scrubbed. She admired the wooden plank floor that creaked beneath their feet as they walked through the living room and into the bedroom. Much warmer it would be in the winter than the hard-packed earthen floor of her home.

"This will be your room. Unpack while I make tea and I have some nice fruit-filled *varenyky*, pierogi. You like varenyky?"

"Yes, very much. Thank you."

Setting her suitcase down, Veronika took off her sweater and surveyed her room. A single bed pushed against the wall beckoned her to lie down on it, with its lofty feather quilt and pillows. A brightly coloured braided oval rug was at the side of her bed. On the opposite wall was a low dresser on which sat a large enamelled basin, a pitcher of water, and soap for washing. Beside the dresser were several hooks for hanging up her clothes and on the hook closest to the dresser, a towel and wash cloth. A small vase of daisies sitting on the windowsill cheered Veronika's heart and spoke of the woman's thoughtfulness. Veronika unpacked her few things, then slipped her empty suitcase under her bed.

In the kitchen, Veronika gave Ulyana the bread. "My mother wanted you to have this loaf, a little gift for having me stay with you."

Ulyana opened the drawstring bag and pulled out the bread. "Thank you," she said. "I'll make a sandwich for you to take to school."

"Thank you, Ulyana."

"And every day when you come home, I'll have a nice hot meal ready for you. We'll eat together, all right?"

Sitting at the table enjoying the tea and varenyky with Ulyana, Veronika's apprehension about living in someone else's home quickly disappeared. This was going to be a lovely place to stay, she thought as she took another bite of the sugar-coated plum-filled varenyky.

When she got to the school, the first thing she heard was the sound of a man berating someone loudly in Russian.

"Where are your manners? Are you being brought up by pigs? Are you? Answer me."

There was a sharp slap, followed by the sound of a child crying. Embarrassed and unsure of what to do, Veronika just stood there. Who could be hitting a child? She hoped it wasn't a teacher. It was forbidden to hit students.

Abruptly a door in the hallway opened and a woman walked out with two little girls, one about seven and the other about nine. The older one had a red mark across her cheek and was still crying. The woman was surprised to see Veronika standing there.

"I'm Veronika Osiecka, the new teacher."

"Viktor, come see. The new teacher is here."

A man of about forty, with short dark hair, beard, and full bushy moustache came out of the room and gazed at her sternly through small, round frameless eyeglasses perched on the bridge of his nose.

"Ah, there you are. The new teacher. I've been expecting you. Meet my wife, Stefania, and my daughters, Irina and this other, the naughty one, Nadya. Come with me. I'll show you your classroom." Walking down the hall, he said, "There are two other teachers here besides myself. You're the fourth, and the only woman. But perhaps you can be friends with my wife. She's been feeling quite lonely. Hasn't been able to make any friends with the village women; they're all intimidated by her. Think she's above them, with me being the principal and all. Of course," he said, lowering his voice, "you'll find out she isn't all that bright. Just a simple village woman herself. No education."

Shaken by his pompous attitude, Veronika's big moment of entering her own classroom for the first time was somewhat marred. She could hardly wait for him to show her around the room and then be gone.

After he left, she was still fuming as she organized her room and looked at the supplies. What a horrible man he seemed to be, to say such rude things to a stranger about his own wife. And slapping his daughter like that. She wondered what it was that the child could possibly have done to be treated so harshly.

At midday, she picked up her lunch pail and walked down the hall to where she heard the voices of the principal and the other teachers. She found them in a little room off to the side, eating their lunch. She entered the room and the other teachers introduced themselves, all smiles and nods, but she could tell that the presence of a lone female among three males made for awkward conversation. They soon finished their lunch and left.

The next day, she decided she would eat lunch at her own desk. No sooner had she unwrapped her sandwich, than the door to her room opened and the principal's wife, Stefania, popped her head in.

"I wondered where you were," she said in Ukrainian. "May I come in and visit with you while you eat?"

"Yes, certainly."

"It's good to have you here. Maybe we can become friends."

"How is Nadya doing?"

"Nadya?"

"She was crying yesterday."

"Oh, that," she said. "She's fine now. Poor thing. My husband is so good with the younger one. That one is his little darling. She resembles him, you know. But Nadya resembles me, and with her he has no patience."

Veronika was grievously sorry she had even mentioned Nadya. What if the principal should overhear such talk? He was her boss. She quickly tried to steer the conversation to a safer topic, but Stefania wouldn't have it.

"I should have listened to my parents and never married him. They were against the marriage, you know."

"I really don't feel comfortable talking about this," Veronika said.

"Oh, no, never mind. I'll keep my eye on the door. He'll never know. Anyhow, my parents were against the marriage because his parents didn't think I was good enough for their son. I gave him a little sample of what I would be like," she said, winking at Veronika, "if you know what I mean, so he was real eager to marry me."

Veronika felt her face flushing and she rose to put away her half-eaten sandwich.

"Have to go back to work now?" asked Stefania.

Veronika nodded.

"Well, I'll let you get back to it. I can sit with you while you have lunch every day. You probably won't want to be sitting with the men. Really nice meeting you, Veronika. I can call you, Veronika, can't I?"

"Yes, sure."

After she left, Veronika felt her head reeling. What had she just got herself in for? Maybe tomorrow she would have to eat lunch with the men.

74

VERONIKA

September 1940

On the first day of school, Veronika paused outside her classroom door to listen to the happy chatter of her third-grade students as they waited for her to enter. She was surprised at the flutter of nervousness that hit her. What if she couldn't control them? What if they didn't like her? Steeling herself, she opened the door and walked in. All talking stopped, as the children leapt to their feet and stood at attention.

Veronika looked at the rows of children standing before her, dressed in their finest clothing, some with eager smiles, others with curiosity, all trying to take her measure. On every child's desk lay a bouquet of garden flowers ready to present to her, as was Soviet tradition for the first day of school.

After introducing herself and explaining her rules and expectations, she invited the children to present their flowers to her, row by row. Thanking each child as they approached her desk, she thrilled to the look of their sweet, freshly scrubbed faces as they gave her their flowers. Most approached with a confidence that spoke of their eagerness to start a new year of learning. Others, such as Nadya, the principal's daughter, approached her desk shyly. Veronika determined that she would win her trust and build her confidence in any way she could. Maybe with her, Nadya could have a sanctuary where her dreams would soar.

After accepting her flowers, she led the children in songs and words of praise to Stalin and communism, as was required for the start of the school day. As the children sang, she glanced along the rows and noticed one boy looking uncomfortable and flinching away from the taller, leaner boy standing next to him. Veronika watched from the corner of her eye and saw how the taller boy kept his eyes on her with a steady calmness. When he thought she was looking away, he poked the smaller boy in the back. That one is going to be trouble, she thought.

When the songs and poems were done, she had the students take their seats then, looking at the tall boy, said in her sternest voice, "What is your name?"

"Jakiv."

"Come here, Jakiv."

The boy came forward, nervously glancing at the others. Veronika noted the shock of brown hair that hung to his eyes, the dirty neck, the shirt that was neither new nor clean. Standing in front of her, he flicked his head to the right to clear the hair from his eyes then looked up at her with a nervous smirk.

"You will not poke and disturb others while I am teacher of this class," Veronika said, with all the firmness in her voice that she could muster. "During recess, you will remain at your desk while the others go out to play."

She saw a slight flinch cross in his face and then, just as quickly, a look that said it didn't bother him in the least.

When recess came, Javik put his head down on his desk without being told. Veronika was surprised he didn't move or speak for the entire time. When the bell rang and the others came back in, Javik sat up and looked at her in a way that was unnerving. His eyes were like that of a beaten dog, sad and without hope.

At the midday break, she stayed at her desk, hoping that Stefania would drop by. She could use some inside information on this boy, Jakiv. Sure enough, moments after she unwrapped her lunch, there was Stefania.

"Did you notice that my Nadya is in your room?" Stefania asked.

"Yes. I recognized her right away."

"I'm so happy she has you for her teacher."

"She's a lovely little girl, with very nice manners."

Stefania nodded proudly.

"Stefania, what do you know about Jakiv?"

"That one? No one likes him. A real terror he is in the village. Ripping up people's flowers, slapping the other children."

"His parents don't stop him?"

"He doesn't have a mother. She left two years ago. Just walked out on her husband and left Jakiv and his sisters behind."

"That explains his anger."

"Having problems with Jakiv already?"

Veronika nodded. "I guess I'll have to go see his father."

"I wouldn't."

"Why not?"

"He thinks his children can do no wrong. When neighbours go to him, complaining about Jakiv stealing from them or bothering their children, he swears at them and won't do a thing."

"Oh," said Veronika. Her desire to meet with such a parent withered.

"Just send Jakiv to my husband. He can make any child quake just by yelling at them. I'll tell him you're having problems."

"No. Don't do that. This is only my first day. I don't want him thinking I can't handle my own class."

"All right," Stefania said. "Your secret is safe with me."

Veronika worked hard to get to know her students as well as make learning fun. She was careful to be very firm, yet gentle, with the children. Soon all of them, except for Jakiv, were doting on her, offering to help her with the after-school chores of sweeping the floor, cleaning out the woodstove, carrying in wood, and wiping the chalkboard. With Jakiv, she could see she was making some progress by praising what he did well, and by being consistent in her expectations.

Teaching school fell into a regular rhythm. She walked home on Friday afternoons, eager to be with her parents and to share all the news of the week. One evening after supper, as she was marking her students' artwork, she showed her parents Nadya's lifelike sketch of a horse.

"This was done by the principal's daughter, Nadya. Poor child, for any little thing, her father slaps her or calls her stupid. But he loves and treats his other daughter well, the one that looks like him."

Her mother shook her head. "That's another reason why I'm so happy I married your father. I've never had to deal with him acting that way. A woman doesn't have the right to interfere with how her husband decides to discipline the children."

"But it's not discipline, Mama. It's more like he's punishing the child for no reason."

"You have to stay out of it," Mama said, putting the kettle on the woodstove for tea, "Not only is he your boss, but he's also Russian. Maybe he has the ear of the secret police."

"Your mother is right," Tata said, looking up from the tombstone he was carving. "Maybe next year you should see if you can teach at another school."

"Maybe I should. Not only is he hard with his daughter, but with his wife as well."

"His wife?"

"She's really nice, but she tells me all kinds of private things I don't want to know."

"Like what?" asked Mama.

"Things like her husband is fooling around with other women."

"What?" said Mama, "A man of his standing?"

"She said her husband has a wandering eye, that most men do."

Mama snorted. "Not the men I know."

"He hasn't been bothering you, has he, Veronika?" Tata asked.

Veronika looked down and thought of how to word it, then looked into her father's eyes and said simply, "I make sure I'm never alone with him."

"Next year I want you to apply for a transfer," he said with an unaccustomed firmness to his voice.

75

VERONIKA

May 1941

One month before Veronika's primary school closed for summer break, there was a surge in rumours that they would soon be at war with Germany. It was said that the German Nazi government had massed troops and equipment at the border between Poland and the Soviet Union. An attack was imminent.

The principal of Veronika's school called an urgent meeting at lunchtime with the other two teachers.

"Things are just too unsettled with all the talk about the possibility of war. It's better for everyone to go home, and remain at home with their families where it will be safer. Tell your students that today will be the last day. We will resume school in the fall; what courses they have not completed, they should continue to work on at home."

Veronika said goodbye to her class. Some cried when she told them that today would be their last day.

Veronika saw them out the door and gave hugs to those who wanted one. When she turned around, she saw that Jakiv remained at his desk.

"Aren't you going to go, Jakiv? I thought you would be eager to be done with me."

He put his head down on his desk and cried.

"What is it?" she asked.

Wiping back the tears that coursed down his dirty face, he said, "You are kind of like my mother."

Veronika swept the hair out of his eyes with the side of her hand. "Would you like a special hug?"

Without answering, he flung himself into her arms and squeezed like he never wanted to let her go.

That evening as she packed her belongings, Ulyana knocked on her bedroom door.

"One of your students is here to give you something," she said with a smile.

Thinking it might be Jakiv, Veronika went to the door. It was Nadya, the principal's daughter.

"This for you," Nadya said, giving Veronika a drawing of two butterflies, one larger, the other smaller, flying toward a rainbow.

"Thank you, Nadya. It's a beautiful sketch, and look at all the detail you put into the wings. But why did you draw butterflies?"

"Because that's me and you."

"Oh, Nadya. Always remember that you are a good person. Someday you will show everyone how good and smart you are."

"Thank you," she said, wrapping her arms around Veronika. "I'll never forget you."

The next day when Veronika arrived back home, she showed the drawing to her mother, and then placed it on her dresser as a reminder of all the good things that had happened during her almost one-year teaching career.

76

JANEK

June 22, 1941

The drone of airplanes overhead caused Janek to look up from the row of onions he was hoeing. There were so many, all flying in formation toward the east.

"I wonder what's happening?" Helena asked, as she paused in her work to look up. "Do you think it could be the start of war?"

Janek crossed himself. "Pray that it's not."

"Why do you say that? We've been praying for an end to the Soviet government."

"It's not the rule of the German government I fear. Like Agnes says, they are a civilized people, not like these stupid-ass communists."

"What then?"

"I never told you what I saw in the war. Never told anyone. But I'll tell you this much, seeing the bodies of little children riddled with bullets is not something I want to see again."

"Matko Boska, Janek. Who would shoot children?" Her eyes widened in fear.

"Bullets fired in a village can't tell the difference between a child's body or a soldier's. Men, women, children, soldiers all get killed."

In the afternoon on July 7, while Janek again worked in his garden, Osip came over, spit flying from his mouth in his excitement.

"Did you hear? Kiev has been bombed. They are bombing all our cities. We are at war with Germany, just like I told you, Jan."

He left as quickly as he had come, eager to be the teller of news at the next house. His head spinning, Janek put down his hoe and walked to the well in his front yard.

War again.

He was glad Helena and Veronika weren't home. He needed time to think, to work thorough his rising panic.

Drinking from the enamel dipper that hung from a hook by the well, he noticed his hands trembling. He drank the dipper and then another, enjoying the trickle of cool water that flowed over the rim and down his neck into his shirt. He poured the third dipperful over his head and raked his fingers through his dripping hair, slicking it back. Slowly, he walked to the stone bench by his front door, where he eased himself down, his back and thigh muscles stiff from bending over all day.

What was he to do? What could he do to help Helena and Veronika survive? That was the thing. If only he could think of a way for them to survive until the shooting was over, they would be safe. If the Soviets won, things would go on as before. If the Germans won, things would be better. Nothing could be worse than living under the Soviets.

Hiding in the house would be no good. He thought of how villagers in the Great War thought they would be safe hiding in their homes. They didn't know that soldiers would fire into their doors and windows or set fire to their thatched roofs, not caring if there were innocent families hiding inside. Better that, the officers thought, than to risk their soldiers being shot at by an enemy hiding inside.

Where could they hide? He looked to the left, to the buckwheat field, still only knee high. Not tall enough yet. They could hide in the woods but for how long without food, water, or a place to keep dry? His eyes fell on the flat wooden cover of the root cellar, just beyond the well, a rectangle of weathered wood lying flat on the ground, and knew that he had found the answer. When Helena and Veronika came home, they would clear a space in the centre of the cellar by pushing the barrels of pickles and sauerkraut against the stone walls. After that, they would fill new barrels with well water. If the fighting came close, in the darkness deep under the earth they would go and hide.

77

VERONIKA

July 5, 1941

The early morning sun filtering through the leaves of the cherry tree felt good on Veronika's arms as she helped Tata pick cherries. Such a big crop they had this year. She hoped they would get a good price for them. When they were finished picking, she would leave with Mama for the farmer's market to sell them, and Tata would head to work on the collective.

Veronika's mind turned to the invasion. Except for the movement of Soviet troops and the drone of planes overhead, it seemed hard to believe that a war was going on. Already almost two weeks had gone by since they'd heard about the German attack. At first, Veronika had been terrified, especially when Tata said they had to prepare the root cellar to be an underground shelter for both their family and Aunt Maria's.

As the days went by and nothing happened, everyone began to hope their area might be spared. After all, there were no cities nearby, only rolling farmland and a scattering of small villages.

For Aunt Agnes, it was different. She seemed excited about the possibility of Kuzmin becoming a German village. It was like she had emerged from a cocoon of sorrow. She had a liveliness to her voice, a sparkle to her eyes. She started rising early and combing her hair.

A constant stream of people came to her door, seeking her out as an authority on what life would be like under German rule.

"*The Germans know how to run a country,*" she would tell people.

Veronika climbed down the ladder, her pail full of cherries, thinking about how Aunt Agnes had said that if the Germans took over their area, they would want Veronika to go back to teaching.

"*Germans think highly of education. They will need teachers.*"

Excitement pulsed within Veronika's chest at the thought of being back in the classroom again, doing something productive with her life.

Tata picked up the handles of the wheelbarrow. "I'll push as far as the turnoff to the collective. Let Mama know we're ready."

"All right," she said. She picked out yet another exceptionally large cherry from the wheelbarrow and popped it into her mouth, chiding herself as the skin ruptured beneath her teeth and the sweet fluid ran down her throat. This truly was the very last one she would eat. No more, for sure, no matter how firm or how plump they looked.

Tata looked at her and grinned. "It's a long walk to Kuzmin. I wouldn't be eating too many of those before you go."

"Tata. I'll be fine," she said to reassure him, but hoped he wasn't right. Cherries were her weakness, especially the ones that grew near the top of the tree. They were always outrageous in size and colour, a third larger than cherries from the lower branches, and so purple they were almost black.

Mama had on her new white headscarf and carried their lunch pails packed with dark bread, cucumber, and boiled eggs.

"Let's go," she said, closing the lids of their lunch pails. "I don't want to lose my spot at the market."

Veronika knew what she meant. If that woman Mama didn't like got there first, she would set up her produce stand in the space where Mama liked to set up.

"I thought you weren't coming," the woman would say and then refuse to move.

The wheelbarrow kept getting stuck in the ruts in the road and threatened to tip. Tata quickly worked up a sweat.

"Hot for July, isn't it?" Veronika said.

"You wouldn't be so hot if you'd wear a headscarf. Keeps you cooler," Mama said in a sharp tone.

Veronika snickered.

"What are you laughing about?"

Veronika tried to look serious.

"It's true. It keeps your head cooler in the summer and warmer in the winter."

Veronika shrugged and decided to try and change the subject. Sometimes her mother got emotional about such silly things.

After saying goodbye to Tata at the turnoff, Veronika and her mother continued walking to Kuzmin's village square, which was already vibrating with the bustle of vendors setting up their produce, and the friendly banter between people who had known each other for years.

Veronika had just lifted a basket of cherries when people began yelling, "Fire! Fire!"

Great billowing clouds of black smoke rose from the direction of the collective, followed by a series of explosions.

"Run! We're being attacked!" someone yelled.

All Veronika could think of was Tata. Her mother stared at the smoke now rapidly spreading and filling the entire eastern horizon.

"Janek," her mother whispered.

78

VERONIKA

Veronika stared at the commotion in the square. Some people were looking dazed, not knowing what to do. Others were scrambling to leave, hastily packing their wares and produce.

"Gather up the cherries, Mama. Let's go over there," she said, motioning to the trees at the edge of the square.

Pushing the wheelbarrow, Veronika and her mother hurried across the square to join a small group of vendors who were watching the growing spread of the smoke.

"I don't know that it would be the German army over there," said a man who sold soap and candles. "What would they want to be blowing up a collective for? I'm going to go see."

"I'm going to go with him, Mama."

Her mother looked at her, alarmed. "No, it's better to wait here. You could get killed."

"But what if Tata is hurt?"

"You have to stay away until we know what's happening."

Veronika looked down, trying to hold back her tears.

"It's what Tata would want," Mama said softly, taking Veronika's hand and squeezing it.

Under the shade of the tree, they anxiously waited and watched. A few minutes later, they heard someone yelling, "It's not the Germans. Soviet soldiers set the fire. The whole collective is burning."

Veronika looked at her mother, not knowing what to think. Out of the corner of her eye, she saw Osip.

"There's Osip. Maybe he's seen Tata."

Running and dodging around people, she called out, "Osip! Osip!" He turned.

"Have you seen my father?"

"Earlier, before the fires."

"Why? Why would they do such a thing?"

"They said Stalin ordered it. That's all I know."

Returning to her mother, Veronika told her what Osip had said. "Should we go to the collective and look for Tata?"

"No, better we go home. We could miss him if we go looking for him."

Walking home, they saw other workers coming from the collective. Mama approached each one and asked if they had seen her husband. None of them had. One worker suggested that he may have been hurt when the fuel tank blew up. Some of the soldiers as well as a few workers had been killed.

Veronika could see the anxiety growing in her mother's face. They quickened their pace. Turning the last curve before their home, they saw smoke coming out of the chimney. Veronika felt her knees become spongy as they both started laughing.

"He's home! He's home."

Abandoning the wheelbarrow, Veronika ran with her mother along their stone fence line and into the yard, and there, waiting for them in the doorway was Tata, his love for them radiating through his eyes, his smile. They threw themselves into his open arms.

"We were so worried about you, Janek. Thought I would never see you again," said Mama, sagging against him.

"Unbelievable what happened, Helena. Sit down," he said, gently guiding her to a chair. "Both of you, sit down. Rest. I made tea already," he said picking up the battered enamel teapot sitting on the table. Passing a steaming mug to Mama, he said, "The Komsomol were the ones who started the fires with gas-soaked rags. The soldiers just watched and made sure no one tried to stop them."

Veronika took the mug Tata held out to her and shuddered inwardly to think that at one time she had wanted to be a member of the Komsomol so she could go to Moscow. Just a nice club, she had thought, but as Tata had warned her, they also had to do Stalin's bidding.

Sitting down and taking his own mug, Tata said, "As soon as I got there, we were told to leave, that Stalin had ordered everything destroyed so that nothing of value would fall into German's hands."

"Did they burn the granaries, too?" asked Mama.

Tata nodded, a faraway look in his eyes. "Gone. All gone."

"No," Mama said, gasping.

"So much waste. All our work," Tata said, running a hand through his hair. "Only giving us a little bit of grain and now they go and burn it all.

"Don't they even care about us?" asked Veronika.

"We are nothing to them, never have been."

For a while no one said anything.

"Maybe once the Germans take over, things will get better," Tata said.

"Do you think they would bring in grain for us?" asked Mama.

"We can only hope."

— ✳ —

That evening, Mama and Tata went outside to sit on the bench for a bit. Veronika decided to prepare for bed. She had just started loosening her hair from its bun, when Tata called out to her, urgency in his voice. Dropping her hair clips, she ran outside.

"Look," Tata said, pointing to the glowing horizon and the smoke that billowed in the air.

"Oh, my God. What is it?" Veronika asked.

"The Soviets are burning Kuzmin," Tata said.

Veronika stared at the flickering red skyline in horror. "Frania," she whispered, as Frania's freckled face, her kindly father and mother, the sound of Izaak's laughter flitted through her mind.

Tata put his arm around Veronika. "Tomorrow we'll go see what is left of the village."

"Will they set fire to the farms next?" Mama asked.

"It's possible. I'll have to keep watch through the night."

Lying in bed, tears soaking her pillow, Veronika tried to stop worrying about Frania. She tried to think back to a good time, when all her family was around her, when Uncle Vladzio played the harmonica and Babcia danced, and they played loteryjka … a time before she learned to fear the secret police, and Stalin started taking everything that was theirs.

Not a single locomotive, not a single truck, not a kilo of wheat, not a litre of fuel must be left for the enemy ...

—Joseph Stalin, July 3, 1941

79

VERONIKA

Veronika got out of bed, anxious to hear if any farmhouses had been set ablaze.

"How was the night?" she asked.

"Didn't see anything burning, at least not out this way," Tata said. "I'll go have another look now."

Veronika and Mama followed Tata to their gate by the road and scanned the horizon but saw no sign of fire. All seemed quiet except for their neighbour, Jakiv, walking on the road. He carried an empty burlap sack and a shovel over his shoulder.

"Hello, Jakiv. Where are you off to?"

"The collective. Maybe there's grain to be salvaged."

"Won't you get shot?" Mama asked.

"The Soviets are gone," he said with a grin. "Moscow ordered them to evacuate. Even the secret police left in the night, their wives and children, too. One officer even took his feather pillows," he said over his shoulder, as he walked past them.

"Matko Boska," Mama said, tears springing to her eyes. "You're safe, Janek. How long have I prayed for this moment?"

"I never thought I would be spared," Tata said, with a disbelieving shake of his head, "when so many others had been taken."

As she watched her parents embrace, the sun peeked from between the trees, bathing them in sunlight. She put her arms around both her parents, laughing and crying in gasping sobs. "We're free," she kept saying. "We're free."

— ✳ —

After their breakfast, Veronika fell in step with her parents and another family going to see what was left of the village. Although they were only acquaintances, the magnitude of their joy and fears seemed to join them together like they were old friends as they talked of the fires, of famine, and the collapsing Soviet government.

Veronika knew it was true, what Jakiv had said, when they came to the Village Soviet building. The Soviets were gone. Everywhere, small groups of people stood around, laughing and talking in great excitement. Only charred sections of the building remained standing. A man picked up a rock, wound up, and pitched it at the building. Laughter again rang out.

They walked on, past the still smouldering shells of burned-out shops.

Mama groaned. "The waste of it all."

Everywhere people were bent over, poking through the charred rubble with sticks and shovels, seeing what they could salvage.

They stopped in front of the store Frania's father used to run. Like all the shops, it, too, had been burnt to the ground. Even though Veronika had mentally prepared for it, it was still shocking to see. She watched a man pick up a small blackened bell. Veronika wondered if it was one of the bells that had hung over the door.

"Would you like us to go with you to Frania's?" Mama asked.

"No, it's all right. I'll see you at home."

Walking the few blocks to Frania's, she knocked on their door. Frania's mother answered. She looked pale and nervous, not at all the person Veronika remembered from two years ago. Veronika could tell she'd been crying.

Veronika took her hand. "My parents and I saw the store. I'm so sorry."

She nodded. With a catch in her voice she said, "We are still shaken from last night, Veronika, but come in. I will get Frania."

At the sight of Frania's familiar face, her red hair and freckles, and the blue eyes that were always full of life and now so forlorn, the dam of tears that Veronika had been holding back loosened. They hugged, Frania's hair crushed against Veronika's cheek and the sweet, clean fragrance that was distinctly Frania's wafted over her. "Oh, Frania, it's good to see you. When I saw the fire, I was so afraid."

"Come, sit down at the table," said Frania's mother, putting her hand on Veronika's shoulder. "I will make tea."

While Veronika drank her tea, Frania told her of how they had watched the village go up in flames.

"What is your family going to do now?"

"I don't know. I'm trying to get Papa to see that there's no use staying here, that we should go to America," Frania said, "but he thinks it would not be safe to travel, and that the safest place for us is here."

80
VERONIKA

Two days later, as Veronika mindlessly drew up a bucket of water from the well, she became aware of a low beating sound, almost like threshing machines on the move. She glanced up to see clouds of dust rising from the road. Straining to see through the dust, she could make out a line of tanks coming closer, then turning sharply into the far end of the field behind their house.

She dropped her bucket, cold water splashing over her bare legs and feet. She turned and ran for the house. "Tata! Tata!"

"What is it?" her mother asked, clutching her stomach.

"Tanks are going into our field."

"Janek!" Mama screamed as she ran for the barn. "Janek!"

Veronika ran to the stone wall at the front of their yard. Hiking up her skirt, she shimmied up the wall. Horse-drawn wagons with massive guns were coming down the road, and Soviet soldiers were setting up machine guns along the riverbank.

Tata ran up to her, Mama at his side.

"What's happening?" he asked.

"Just more and more are coming."

Tata climbed the wall and stood beside her, watching the massive troop movement setting up along their road.

"What do you see?" asked Mama, her face ashen.

"It doesn't look good, Helena. The Soviet troops are setting up their defence lines."

"What should we do?"

"There's a truck coming this way. I'll see if they'll talk to me."

Veronika climbed down from the wall and stood with her father and mother at the edge of the road. A truck loaded with military equipment slowly lumbered closer, swerving to avoid the deep ruts and potholes. Veronika could see a tanned arm sticking out the window. Tata walked up to him.

"What's happening?"

The young soldier in the passenger seat leaned his head slightly out the open window and shouted above the noise of the truck, "You need to evacuate. The front is coming through. The German army is just over there behind that hill." He pointed to a low hill directly across the river from them. "Your house will be in the centre of the crossfire."

Veronika felt her breathing become rapid and shallow, her knees spongy.

Tata didn't think the fighting would be this close. He thought maybe along the major roads or in Kuzmin there might be some fighting, but more likely, only in the cities.

"Helena, go with Veronika and gather up blankets and coats. We're going down into the root cellar."

"Janek, you heard what he said," Mama protested, her voice shrill. "We need to run! Our house is in the middle of two fronts."

Tata's eyes hardened. "We stay right here."

"We should leave while we still can," gasped Mama.

"Yes, Tata, we should go."

"We are not leaving," he said, his voice harsh.

"Oh, Janek, please. We have to leave," Mama begged, crying.

Tata gripped both of her arms, his jaw a hard line. "Helena, you need to listen to me." "We are not going to run like mice in a field. Above ground is where the greater danger is. I have seen it before. People get shot. Women get raped. We will go below ground."

Mama stopped struggling. She looked at him, her eyes wide, then nodded.

Her body numb, Veronika went around with Mama, scooping up bread, coats, and blankets, her eyes going in and out of focus. All her life, this home, with its strong stone walls and thatched roof, was her place of refuge, but now it was a place of danger.

When they had finished gathering what they needed, Mama and Veronika watched Tata opening windows and blocking the doors open.

"Why are you doing that?" Mama asked.

"So when the Germans come, they don't have to worry that someone inside is going to shoot at them."

A high-pitched whistle and an explosion rocked the earth. Straw and dust rained down from the thatched ceiling.

"That's it, let's go," Tata said.

"No. My sister," said Mama. "We have to wait for her."

"They'll know where we are," he said, taking her sack and prodding her out the door to the cellar. Tata held the wooden hatch up while Mama made her way down the steps. Veronika followed, feeling with her bare feet for the cold edge of each stone step in the gloom. After spreading a quilt on the damp floor, Veronika sat beside her mother. Feeling her tremble, Veronika grabbed another quilt, gave one end to her mother and wrapped the other end around her own shoulders.

"Thank you," Mama whispered, taking Veronika's hand in hers.

"Are you ready?" Tata asked.

"Yes, Janek."

Tata closed the hatch and felt his way down the steps.

Veronika pressed closer to her mother as another whistle and then a thunderous roar deafened her. Dirt fell from the roof and sprinkled down on their hair and into their mouths. Veronika shrieked and clung to her mother.

"It's all right," Tata said, patting her back. "I built this strong. We'll be safe in here."

A few minutes later, something scuffled, then there was a knock on the hatch.

"They're here," Mama said with relief.

Squinting up into the glare of the light, Veronika could see the familiar outline of Aunt Maria. She was cowering at the entryway, her eyes wide with terror.

"Maria! Thank God you're here," Mama said.

"My neighbours are here with us," said Aunt Maria. "They had no place to go. Is it all right if they come in, too?"

"Come in, come in," Mama said. "We can make room."

Aunt Maria came down the steps, followed by a young couple with a baby in its mother's arms and two little ones in tow.

"Over here, Kazia," Veronika said, as Kazia came down the steps with her sister Nellia.

"The German soldiers are here already! Just across the river," Kazia said, her body quivering as she hurried down the steps, stepping over others, and squeezing in beside Veronika. "I thought at any moment we were all going to die."

Another explosion caused dirt to once again rain down on their heads and shoulders.

Veronika and Kazia sat shivering and holding one another as they listened to the sounds of gunfire and felt the earth shake with explosion after explosion. Together with their parents, they begged God to spare their lives.

As the hours passed, the younger children grew restless and began to cry. The air changed from chilly and damp to hot and humid, even though Tata had built a small air vent into the cellar. Gradually the children's wails turned to sobs and finally silence as, exhausted, one by one, they fell asleep.

About four hours later, they heard muffled German voices amid the shelling. Veronika squeezed Kazia's hand, knowing they were very close.

Please, God, let them not see the hatch.

Mama began reciting the rosary, and others joined in; the monotonous cadence of their voices had a calming effect.

Veronika sucked in her breath at the sound of scuffling, of something heavy being dragged across the hatch. Her thoughts spiralled downward. *Let my death be quick.*

Aunt Maria moaned, "He's sealing us in. We're all going to die."

"Quiet," Tata whispered. "If he hears something, he might toss in a grenade."

They sat petrified, waiting, listening.

Without warning, the cellar exploded with the rat-tat-tat noise of a machine gun.

Oh, my God! He's using our hatch as a platform for his tripod! Veronika thought.

She covered her ears and leaned into Kazia as the reverberating pounding went on and on.

During a lull in shooting, the young father frantically whispered, "Janek, slide something across the hatch so the soldier can't open it."

"No," Tata said.

"What's wrong with you? Lock it."

"It stays open."

"Janek, you've got to," Aunt Maria begged, her voice coming in short gasps. "When he's done shooting, he'll kill us all."

"We bolt nothing," Tata hissed under his breath, "or they will think there are partisans in here. If they open the hatch, just stand there and let them look at you. They will see who you are. That's the only protection we have—to comply and show that we're harmless farmers."

After an hour or two, the shooting became more and more sporadic, until finally it stopped.

Veronika's heart froze when she heard the abrasive sound of something heavy being dragged across the hatch.

"Quiet," Tata whispered.

This was the moment ... the moment of life or death for them. A white mist filled Veronika's mind, stretching and warping time. *Please, just go away. Don't look in here,* she prayed.

Someone pounded on the hatch. They gasped and moved closer to one another. Tata bolted up the steps and lifted the hatch. The brilliant light jolted Veronika's senses as she squinted and struggled to see. She caught a glimpse of a soldier's silhouette, the barrel of his rifle, and Tata cowering before him, his hands held high.

The grey-coated soldier shouted something in German, his words harsh and guttural. Everyone froze, not knowing what he was saying or what to do, as he stared into their frightened faces. He said the same thing again, this time motioning with his rifle that they should come out.

Everyone scrambled out of the cellar, hands held high, squinting in the daylight. Veronika visualized her family lying in a pool of blood and prayed that it would be quick.

After surveying them for a moment longer, the soldier seemed to lose interest in them and walked away to check out their house with the other soldiers.

Veronika looked at her family, astonished. She felt the wind blowing her sweat-dampened hair, the sun on her face, and felt like she was reborn.

After the soldiers had checked out the house and the barn, they were gone.

"Is it safe to go back in the house now?" Mama asked. "It looks like it survived the shelling."

Tata nodded. "The front has gone through. The Germans have the Soviets on the run. They'll be chasing after them."

Once they were inside, everyone began hugging and kissing each other. Tata brought out his spiritus and poured everyone a little glass.

"A drink to celebrate that we are yet alive," Tata said. "Na Zdrowie! Cheers!"

"Na Zdrowie," everyone said, holding up their glass.

"To the Germans for freeing Ukraine from the Soviets," said the young father.

"Na Zdrowie! To a free and independent Ukraine!" everyone cheered.

"And to the end of the collectives!" Tata said, his glass held up once more.

Maybe the worst is over, Veronika thought, holding up her glass. Once the new government is in place, life will be better.

The Soviet terror of the 1930's convinced many Ukrainians that there was nothing worse than Communist Russian slavery and nothing more welcome than the Army representing such a cultured nation as Germany.

—Andrew Gregorovich, World War II in Ukraine: June 22, 1941

81
JANEK

July 10, 1941

Janek stood shoulder-to-shoulder with hundreds of other people who lined the main street of Kuzmin. Dressed in their finest embroidered clothing, they cheered and threw flowers to their liberators. Smiling German soldiers sat in open-roofed cars wearing soft wedge caps, jauntily tipped to the side of their heads. Sometimes one or the other would stretch out their arm to try and catch a flower. A woman across the street held a large crucifix aloft, blessing the vehicles as they passed by. Other women made the sign of the cross as they passed. Janek glanced at Helena, Veronika, and Kazia standing in front of him and saw that they, too, were caught up in the enthusiasm, the waving and cheering.

Between the cars came motorcyclists, but these men looked serious in their steel helmets and did not smile or reach out to the people, only stared straight ahead. Behind the cars and motorcycles came endless trucks, loaded down with bulky equipment and boxes lashed and covered in tarps.

He wondered what it was about the convoy that he found unsettling, even threatening, then realized what it was. He had never seen a government that was not to be feared, not the Czar's, not the Soviets, and now not the German Nazi government.

Janek motioned to Helena that it was time to go to the square for the welcoming assembly.

"Did you see the black crosses on their trucks?" said Helena, her face alight with joy. "Think of it, Janek. A Christian government."

"Don't get too excited, Helena. We'll have to see."

Janek led the way to a roped-off area where the speakers were going to be. Hearing the mesmerizing sound of goose-stepping soldiers, their feet clip clopping in unison, Janek turned and looked. Grey-coated soldiers, arms swinging stiffly, entered the square. A black car with small red-and-white flags with that strange black cross that fluttered on each of the side mirrors followed the soldiers. Janek removed his hat and took hold of Helena's arm. He could see Veronika and Kazia craning their necks for a better view as the car came to a halt in front of the roped area.

Several officers emerged from the car, wearing hard-brimmed hats with what looked like an eagle with outstretched wings on the peak. From the heavy ornamentation on their jackets and the slight swagger as they walked, Janek knew they were very important people. When they got closer, he couldn't help staring at their boots and leather gloves. He had never seen leather gloves before, or boots so shiny. Such wealth and power these officers must have.

The officers walked to where a woman and two children wearing traditional Ukrainian clothing waited. The woman's hair was braided with a multitude of wide ribbons that flowed down her back, and she wore a crown of flowers, as did the little girls.

The woman held a board covered with a white embroidered ceremonial cloth. On top of the cloth were bread and salt, symbols of peace and long-lasting friendship. Janek heard the woman give the traditional greeting as she approached the officers with the tray. "With this bread and salt, we welcome you."

One of the officers, heavyset and seemingly neckless, smiled, swivelled his head, and took a bit of the bread, dipped it in salt and ate it, to the cheers of the crowd.

When the woman and children left, the officer who ate the bread turned to the assembled people. Everyone became quiet, ready to hear his first words.

"Heil Hitler."

Janek had never heard such a greeting before.

After a moment, the officer spoke to them in brief, clipped German phases, then paused as a man in civilian clothing translated what he had said into Russian.

"Everything is in the process of being put in order. You can be assured that everyone is now safe from the Soviets, and you have to worry about them no longer. You are now under the protection of the German government.

"It is the desire of this government that stores, schools, and churches be reopened as soon as possible."

The officer stopped speaking as a gasp rippled through the crowd and then an outpouring of cheering and clapping. Janek could see the disbelief on Helena's face. Dazed with happiness, he gave her a little squeeze, then smiled and nodded at Veronika as she turned and looked at him, a grin on her face. Everyone became quiet as the translator held up his hand and motioned for silence. The officer continued speaking.

"The Führer, Adolf Hitler, has ordered that the collectives will remain in place. Therefore, every collective worker will report to the collective at dawn and work until dusk so that the collectives can be restored as quickly as possible to full production.

"That is all for now. Once everyone is registered, then you will be able to go wherever you want, except for the Jews. They will wear yellow stars sewn onto the outside of their clothing so that everyone can know these dangerous parasites."

Janek felt his stomach clench as Veronika made her way over to them, her eyes downcast, her lips pressed together as she tried not to cry.

It's happening all over again, he thought. It's just like what the Soviets were doing to us, hunting kulaks. Now this new Nazi government is doing the same thing again, only it's the Jews they have it in for.

Within months of their arrival, the Nazis, and especially the SS execution squads (Einsatzgruppen), killed about 850,000 Jews.

—Orest Subtelny, *Ukraine: A History*

82

VERONIKA

July 15, 1941

Veronika tried to soothe the dull ache in her heart by mindlessly chopping weeds in the garden, trying not to think of what was happening in Kuzmin. The German troops she had smiled and waved at only a few days ago were gone, headed to the east to pursue the fleeing Soviet army. In their place came a new small group of German soldiers that people called the Einsatzgruppen. They were randomly beating and humiliating Jewish men and encouraging people to self-cleanse themselves of the Jews and Communists in their midst and do whatever they wanted to them.

When her parents came home exhausted from the collective that evening, she had a cold dinner of leftover potatoes, salads, and bread prepared. It was too hot to light the woodstove and cook anything. After dinner, Veronika sat outside with her parents, taking in the coolness of the evening. Like crooked horizontal fingers, bands of brilliant pink clouds alternated with bands of grey across the vast open sky above the fields. Looking across the field toward Kuzmin, she wished she could go see Frania and her family, and yet she was afraid of the Einsatzgruppen and of what she might see. What if she saw one of her Jewish classmates being beaten? Or what if it was Frania's father?

Hearing the voices of drunken men walking up the road, she looked at her father. He grimaced. "Maybe they'll just keep going."

"Not likely, if Osip is with them," said Mama.

Veronika's heart sank as Osip and a few of their Polish and Ukrainian neighbours walked into their yard, carrying stout sticks.

"Hey, Jan, want to come with us?" Osip asked.

"What's happening?

"The Germans say we can take anything we want from those blood-sucking Jews."

Tata shook his head. "I will not profit from what the Germans are doing."

"Why not? The Jews have been robbing us all these years with their high prices. And anyhow, if it's not us who take their things, it will be someone else."

"It's not right."

"Not right? Do you know how many secret police officers were Jews? Even in the highest government circles, the Soviets put Jews in charge. If we beat a few Jews tonight and take from them, it's only God's justice."

"I warn you," said Tata. "The Jews will know and remember who is taking from them."

"Come on, let's go," Osip said. "Better not be helping any Jews, Jan. I hear that in other villages, the Einsatzgruppen are hanging those caught helping Jews."

As they walked away, Tata, swore under his breath and said, "I thought I knew those men."

Veronika felt sickened, as waves of anguish swept through her. She could feel the bile rise in her throat, as all the terror returned from so many years ago, when she hid by the fencepost and watched helplessly as the secret police handcuffed the doctor she loved. How she had longed to run out to the doctor and save him, but she was helpless to do anything, just as she was now helpless to save Frania or her family. She ran to the bushes at the side of the house and vomited. She could feel Mama's hand on her back, steadying her.

"Here, take my handkerchief," Mama said. "Come in the house, Noosha. It's all right." She put her arm around Veronika. "Don't cry. You said they were thinking of going to America. Maybe they're there already."

At her mother's kind words, Veronika's heart seemed to crumble all the more. She knew that Frania's family hadn't gone away.

Veronika walked back onto the porch with her mother. "Do you think it's true, Tata, what he said about Jews being collaborators?"

"I don't know much about those things. All I know is that everyone is just trying to survive and take care of their family in the best way they know how. Look at how Yuri Rudenko collaborated with the Soviets. He was Ukrainian, but you can't say all Ukrainians are collaborators, or all Polish or all Jews. There are good and bad in all nationalities."

Veronika was silent for a moment, thinking of her father's words. "Tomorrow I'm going to see how Frania's family is doing."

"You cannot go. I forbid it," said Tata, his voice harsh.

Veronika felt her mother take her hand and squeeze it. She looked into her mother's troubled brown eyes as she said, "We know you're worried, but you can't be seen going into a Jewish home."

"You have to forget about Frania," said Tata. "You heard what Osip said."

"I can't forget her, Tata."

"Veronika," he continued. "It's just like with the Soviets all over again. Anyone who sympathized with the kulaks shared their fate. Don't you think I want to do something? But what can I do against the Germans? Go at them with my pitchfork?"

"Tata is right," said Mama. "All someone has to do is start a rumour, then they come and take all of us."

Veronika looked at her father and mother with tears in her eyes, knowing that they spoke the truth. If she went to see Frania, it was not just her life she was risking, but her parents' lives as well.

No one at that time could foresee accurately what was to come. Yet all of us had to make choices about which side we would take, what we needed to do in order to survive. As often as not the decisions we came to were poor ones. We were all afraid. None of us was truly free, none of us. That is too often forgotten now. It is easy today to say that you should have known better, that you should have been braver, or that you should have risked yourself and your family to save the lives of strangers. People who talk like that today have no idea of what living under a brutal occupation regime is like.

—Stefan Petelycky, *Into Auschwitz, For Ukraine*

83

VERONIKA

In the morning, the summer heat lay on the land, heavy and still, wilting daisies in the flowerbeds and making the hens jostle each other for shade as they settled their breasts into cool basins of dust they had made by the side of the hen house.

As Veronika continued her work weeding the garden, she could hear water splashing as her parents washed out barrels by the well in preparation for making sauerkraut. How she wished she could have some of that water splashed over her face and back. She decided to take a drink from the water bucket she had left under a tree at the edge of the garden. Straightening her back, she wiped the sweat from her forehead with the back of her hand and glanced toward where her parents were working. She was dismayed to see Marek talking to them. Why did he have to come now and catch her looking like this? She wondered if at least her face was clean. She waved. He waved back and came walking over as her parents continued working on the barrels.

"Veronika, I need to talk to you," he said as he approached. She noticed that he was tanned, leaner now. His blue eyes had an intense look.

She nodded. "We can go into the house."

"No, better out here where we can talk without being heard."

"Maybe by the tree, then," she said, looking at him curiously. When they were sitting under the tree, she asked, "Have you heard what is happening in Kuzmin? I'm so worried about Frania's father."

"Don't go to the village, Veronika. It's terrible."

"What's happening?"

"I went to Kuzmin to ask about Frania's father for you."

"How is he?"

"He was beaten, his wrist shattered, but at least he's alive."

Pressing her hand to her mouth, Veronika gasped.

"And her brother, too, they beat," Marek said.

"Izaak? He's just a boy. How is he?"

"I didn't hear. Only that they beat him."

"Oh, God, Marek. Everyone thought things would be better with the Germans here."

"Veronika, I want to tell you something. I'm going away. I can't take what's happening here anymore."

Veronika looked at him, surprised. "Going? Going where?"

"To fight with the partisans for an independent Ukraine."

"Oh, Marek. No. It's so dangerous."

"That's why before I go, I'd like you to promise that someday you'll marry me."

Veronika looked at him, his blond hair, the flicker of hope in his eyes, the softness of his mouth. "Marek, I can't promise. I think I love you, but I'm just not sure." She saw the hope fade from his eyes.

"Then I'll come back in a year," he said, "and ask you again."

She nodded.

Holding her by the shoulders, he looked into her eyes and said,

"Promise me you won't become engaged to anyone else while I'm gone."

"I promise," she said.

"I'm leaving in the morning. I'm just telling people that I am going away to find work. The Germans would kill my family if someone told them I had joined the partisans."

"I'll tell no one." Glancing toward her parents and seeing that they were not looking, she put her arms around him and kissed him.

When he stood up to go, he took her hand and said, "We should inform your parents that we're considering engagement."

A movement in the buckwheat field caught Veronika's eye. "Look."

They watched in astonishment as someone wearing a dress and a headscarf, taking long man-like strides, loped through the buckwheat field, crushing and breaking the waist-high stalks.

"Who could she be?" asked Marek.

"It's not a woman," said Veronika, starting to run toward her parents. "Tata. Mama. Look over there. I think a Jewish man is trying to hide."

As he approached them, Veronika's heart dropped at the sight of his desperation and the haunted look in his eyes.

"What is it?" Tata asked, "Why are you running?"

"I'm a Jew. German soldiers are going house to house shooting any Jewish man they can find. Please, hide me."

Tata looked at him and sadly shook his head. "I just can't do it. My heart is for you, but I just can't do it. They'll shoot us all."

The man looked away for a moment and then said, "I understand."

"Come, have a drink of water," said Tata. "Can we give you some food, dried fruit, maybe?"

He nodded.

Mama went into the house and came out with bread and dried apple rings.

He thanked her then ran back into the field.

"I feel sick about sending him away like that," Tata said.

"What could you do?" asked Marek. "Your house of stone rests directly on the earth. There are no hiding places in a home such as yours."

"We could have offered him the barn or the root cellar," Veronika said.

"The first place they would search," said Mama. "I know from when the Soviets were searching for wheat."

"Come, come inside," said Tata moaning to himself. "Such a life like this."

"It's just sick, sick, what they're doing. Oh, my God," said Mama.

Veronika sat in the house, stunned. "Marek was going to ask you something, but now I have no heart for it."

"What was it?" Tata asked.

Marek looked at Veronika uncertainly. She looked down at her hands and then nodded, knowing there would be no time later. "Go ahead, ask them."

"In a year we will consider becoming engaged. If we were to ask you then, would you give us your blessing?"

Tata looked at Mama and saw the approval in her eyes. "I would approve," Tata said solemnly.

Mama said, "We've always liked you."

Marek got up. "Thank you. On such a sad day, at least I have this to think of."

"Can you stay?" asked Mama.

"I would, but I'm leaving tomorrow to find work."

"Then you must go," said Mama.

Veronika walked him to the door. She took his hand and pressed it to her lips. "Be careful, Marek," she said under her breath.

"Come outside, just for a moment," he whispered.

She stepped outside, closing the door, and found herself in his arms.

"Remember your promise," he said.

Veronika nodded. "Take care of yourself."

They kissed and then he was gone.

Later that evening, as Veronika and her parents sat outside, Osip came to the door with his son, rifles slung over their shoulders.

"We're going Jew hunting. The Nazis have decided to kill all the Christ-murdering Jewish men."

"So we've heard," said Tata.

"Have you changed your mind about them yet?"

"I had enough of killing and seeing men die in the Great War."

"That's too bad, 'cause there are lots of them, hiding out in the fields and along the river around here."

"I just can't do it."

"If you change your mind, we're going out again in the morning."

Closing the door, Tata sat heavily in his chair and covered his face with his hands. "How can people be that way?"

"May God do to them as they deserve," Mama said, her voice shaking.

Veronika slumped down on the bench and wept.

84

VERONIKA

On a grey overcast morning two days later, their neighbour, Jakiv, hammered on the door of Veronika's home, his eyes wild with fear. "The Jews are crying out for revenge. This night they're coming to massacre us all. Already to the north, Jews are butchering Christians."

"Matko Boska," Mama moaned, her face ashen.

Standing in the doorway with her parents, Veronika felt a stinging numbness go through her chest and down her arms into her fingertips. Needing to steady herself, she put her arm on the doorframe.

"Why would they do this?" asked Tata.

"The men know they're going to die anyway, so they want to get revenge on those that were stealing from their homes," Jakiv said.

"What should we do?" Mama asked.

"We get everyone together to defend ourselves at the triplex."

"My sister's?" Mama asked.

Jakiv nodded. "It's the largest building, and it has a basement."

"Tell your family and the neighbours closest to you to meet there," Jakiv said, already loping down the path. Looking over his shoulder he said, "And bring weapons."

"Weapons?" Mama shrieked after him. "What weapons?"

"Pitchforks. Sticks. Anything!" he yelled.

"Veronika, take my axe," Tata said. "Helena, you take a kitchen knife."

Stunned, Veronika stood where she was, her head reeling in disbelief.

"Get going, both of you," Tata said, his voice sounding distorted, like it was coming from far way.

"But I can't use a knife, not like that." said Mama. "I can't even kill chickens."

"All right, take the grain flail then and go to Maria's. I'm going to Agnes's. If I help her walk, do you think she could make it over to Maria's?"

"I think so. It's not far. Should I pack food? Clothes?"

"No, take nothing, just the flail."

Veronika hurried into the barn to get the axe, but just holding it made her stomach contract in revulsion at the thought of using it on someone. Seeing the shovel leaning against the wall, she grabbed that instead. Smacking someone a good one with it—that she could visualize.

As Veronika moved quickly down the road with her mother, she thought of Osip. "I wish I could hit Osip over the head with this shovel."

Her mother nodded. "That vile creature and his type are the cause of all this."

— ✳ —

When they got to the triplex, close to one hundred people had gathered from all over the countryside. Men, women, and older children were taking positions around the perimeter of the triplex, armed with pitchforks, kitchen knives, sticks, and whatever farm tools they could get their hands on, while the young children and babies were being cared for by the elderly in the basement. Others were hastily barricading the doors. Veronika recognized Kazia's bed and dresser blocking one door and the heavy kitchen table and benches from Alina and Marek's home blocking another. How surreal it seemed that this home she had known and loved all her life was being turned upside down and made into a fortress.

She followed her mother into Aunt Maria's section of the triplex and found Kazia in her bedroom holding her weapon.

"I thought my weapon was poor, but yours looks even worse," said Veronika.

"Maybe, but it was all I could find," Kazia said.

When all was ready, dozens of men, women, and children waited, jumping at every sound, becoming more and more tense as each hour passed. In Kazia's bedroom, Veronika, Kazia, and Nellia, waited, armed and ready to fight to the death with a shovel, a rake, and Kazia's broken broom handle.

A dog barked in the distance. "Is it them?" people asked. "Are they coming?"

"There's a person crossing the river!" someone screamed.

"The Jews are already here!" yelled someone else. "They're crossing the river."

In an instant it was pandemonium as sheer panic overtook everyone. Weapons dropped, they ran screaming in all directions, the young children and the elderly in the basement abandoned to their own fate.

Aunt Maria, Nellia, and Kazia ran with Veronika and her parents. Wanting to stay together, both families plunged into a tall grain field.

Deeper and deeper into the field they ran, sometimes stumbling, sometimes falling, but always getting up and running some more. Finally, they could go no farther. Exhausted, they stood, trying to catch their breath as rain began to sprinkle down on them. Veronika looked up. Everywhere the sky was grey and overcast, except to the south where the sky was ominously darker.

"Who cares if we get wet," Kazia said. "At least we're safe."

Everyone seemed to agree. At least they were safe. Veronika stood close to her family as they huddled together for warmth; all was quiet except for the steady beating of the rain against the dry stalks. The wind picked up, driving the rain against everyone's face, arms, and legs. A few minutes later, the sky darkened as the black clouds passed overhead. Rain pelted down on them with a fury. Streams of water ran down Veronika's body. Her blouse and long skirt became sodden and heavy. Her legs and feet ached with cold and fatigue. She looked longingly at the ground, but everywhere puddles were forming. An hour went by and then another as they took turns leaning against one another.

"Is it ever going to stop?" asked Nellia. "I'm freezing, and I can't stand any longer. I have to sit."

"You can't sit down," said Aunt Maria. "Everywhere are puddles."

"I have to sit, too," Mama said.

"We're not going to get any wetter than we already are. Might as well sit," said Tata. "Pull up some stalks and lay them down in a pile so you can keep out of the puddles."

Everyone started yanking at the stalks of buckwheat and laying them down. When Veronika had a nice little pile, she eased herself down, thankful to be off her feet. Then she realized that Tata was wrong when he said they couldn't get any wetter, as the cold water squeezed up through the stalks and saturated her underwear.

All night they sat back-to-back against each other, legs bent, heads resting on their knees, sometimes dozing off, sometimes on high alert when a mouse or rat rustled through the stalks of grain or across their feet. Everyone shivered incessantly, grateful when the rain stopped and dispirited when it started again.

After what seemed an interminable length of time, the sky grew lighter by degrees. Veronika lifted her head from her knees and saw that some were still dozing, others awake. Her blouse and skirt felt cold and clammy as they clung to her body. How she wished she could go home, change into dry clothes and crawl into her feather bed.

When Veronika's father got to his feet and stretched, everyone else woke up, moaning and complaining as they stood, and stretched their stiff and sore limbs. Lack of sleep made Veronika feel slightly dizzy and nauseous as she stretched her arms above her head.

"I just want to go home," Kazia said.

"The rain has stopped," Aunt Maria said. "Let's hope the sun comes out to warm us up."

"I don't care if the sun comes out or not," said Tata, his eyes bloodshot with fatigue and the hair on one side of his head standing on end where he had run his fingers thorough it. "I've had enough. If I have to sit around and wait for an attack to happen, in my own home I sit."

Mama looked at him uncertainly. "But what if the Jews come?"

"The Jews know who was robbing them."

Mama and Aunt Maria glanced at each other. After a moment or two, Aunt Maria said, "Maybe he's right. I think the girls and I will go home and get warm."

"I just want to curl up in my feather bed and sleep until tomorrow," Nellia said.

"But first come to my house," said Mama. "Janek can make a fire and there will be a hot bowl of borscht for everyone."

Veronika and her family strode rapidly through the rows of grain and out onto the road. She could already feel herself towelling her hair and slipping on clean, dry clothes.

As they turned a corner on the road, a sudden shriek by Kazia startled her out of her daydream.

Like rain-sodden ghosts, a small group of people was coming out of the same field they had hidden in. Veronika and her family drew back.

"Jews," Aunt Maria whispered.

Veronika froze and stared, her heart thudding in her chest.

The Jewish group froze, too. Some raised their hands in surrender, others pulled their children close.

The tension left Veronika's body as she tried to make sense of what she was seeing. Was this sad looking group the enemies she had been so afraid of? The murderers? She scanned their faces and recognized the familiar face of Frania's mother. Lightheaded, Veronika took a few steps closer, tears sliding down her face, then let out a gasp.

"Frania! It's me!" Veronika shouted. "It's me!"

Frania's expression changed from bewilderment to joy, and suddenly they were running toward each other, arms outstretched. They clung to each other as they laughed and cried, and feelings of relief and sorrow swept through their broken hearts.

Soon everyone was laughing and crying and shaking hands as it was discovered that the Jews, too, had heard a rumour. Someone had told them that the Christians were rising up to massacre them all.

"We were so afraid that we hid in this field all night," said Frania.

"We were hiding in the field, too, just over there."

Veronika couldn't let Frania go. Frania, too, clung to Veronika, tears streaming down her face.

"It's all so ridiculous. Why did we believe these rumours?" Veronika said.

"I don't know," said Frania sniffing. "We just heard it and we ran."

Looking at the people around them and not seeing Frania's father or brother, Veronika asked, "Frania, your father ... Izaak, where are they?"

Sobbing and choking, Frania said, "They ... were shot."

"Oh, God, no, Frania, no."

Gradually, the two groups parted, the Jews to their homes in the village and the Christians to their homes in the country. Veronika and Frania were the last to let go of each other and walk their separate ways. Veronika turned often and, her heart aching, watched that frail downtrodden group walk away, alone and unprotected.

Our task is to suck from Ukraine all the goods we can get hold of, without consideration of the feelings or the property of the Ukrainians. Gentlemen, I am expecting from you the utmost severity towards Ukrainians
—Erich Koch, Nazi Reichskommissar (Governor) of Ukraine.

85

VERONIKA

Every day for almost a week, Veronika continued to see Jewish men running by the farm, stopping only long enough to plead with Tata to take them in. Some came from Kuzmin, others from villages farther away. Every time, Tata said no. In a few days the shooting was all over. The Einsatzgruppen shot all the Jewish men and teenage boys of Kuzmin. They shot them in their homes, in the street, and in groups outside the village.

As abruptly as the Einsatzgruppen soldiers had swept into Kuzmin, they were gone, replaced by an administrator and a small contingent of soldiers who wandered the village, seemingly more or less bored, other than when they were looking at the young girls as they walked by.

Every day Veronika battled waves of grief. Her mind kept going back to that grey misty morning, and the crowd of frightened people slowly rising up from the field ... the gradual awareness dawning on her that the Jewish people weren't out to massacre anyone; they were simply Jewish shopkeepers and craftsmen, people she had known her whole life.

What had happened to them? Some of the men must have escaped or been hidden away. How were Frania and her mother? She hadn't been able to go into the village when the Einsatzgruppen were there, but now they were gone. It was time to go in. She would seek out Tata and talk to him when he was alone. He'd be easier to convince than Mama that she needed to go into Kuzmin to see Frania. She bided her time until the breakfast dishes were done, then went out to the barn to see him.

"Tata, I need to go see Frania."

His face clouded over. "You cannot go."

"But there's no more shooting going on. You've heard that as well as I have."

"If you are seen with a Jew, you would be endangering us all."

"How would I? No one is bothering the Jewish women."

"Oh, no? You think not? They are being made to suffer, Veronika. Suffer for having been born a Jew."

Veronika felt her stomach clench. "What do you mean, suffer?"

"They're having to work hard. Dig ditches, that sort of thing. People can do what they want to them. Women are being raped."

"Oh, God, Tata, then we have to do something. Can we at least hide Frania and her mother?"

Tata's face crumpled as he slowly slumped down the wall to the floor. He covered his eyes and let out a grief-choked wail.

"What is it, Tata?" she asked, kneeling down beside him.

"I hate what I've become—a Judas. I want to help the Jews but I won't. I can't risk it, Veronika." He looked up at her with tear-filled eyes. "I know what would happen to you, to all of us."

He cried like she had never heard him cry before, deep from within.

"What, Tata?" she said, putting her arm on his shoulder. "There's something you're not telling me."

"I've been to Kuzmin, and I wish to God I had never gone. German soldiers were making an example of a family they caught hiding Jews. When I got there, a man and a woman were hanging in the market square, their feet still moving. A soldier was struggling to hang their baby, but he wouldn't die. He wouldn't die, Veronika. The soldier had to keep yanking on his little legs."

"Oh, Tata," Veronika said, her heart aching.

"Please, Veronika, I didn't want to tell you any of this, but please, wait for a month or two. After things settle down, then maybe you can go see her."

"All right, Tata. I'll wait."

— ✳ —

Two months later, in October, Veronika was shucking walnuts for drying when Tata and Mama came home from the collective with bad news.

"All the Jewish women and children in Kuzmin are gone."

"Gone?"

"Some German soldiers came and took all of them away. Loaded them up in trucks. Said they were taking them somewhere to work.

"To work? Where?"

"No one knows. Maybe Germany? But at least they'll be safer than staying in Kuzmin. It will likely be a more organized work camp or factory," Tata said.

"Why didn't I go see Frania while I had the chance?" Veronica cried.

Mama put her arms around her. "When the war is over, she'll come back, her mother, too. It's their home, after all."

Veronika went to her room, needing to be alone, to reassure herself that what her parents had said was true. She needed to believe she would see Frania's fluffy red hair again, sit on her bed and talk about boys, hear the peal of her laughter, and have tea and cake with her mother. It couldn't be that they would never meet again.

86

VERONIKA

Veronika was nervous. Today she and Kazia were going to the commandant's office to present a letter asking if Soviet teaching certificates would be valid when schools finally did reopen. First, though, they had to go to Aunt Agnes's to get her to write their request in German. Although both she and Kazia had taken two years of German in school, everyone thought it best to have Aunt Agnes write the letter. That way it would be worded politely and in the right form to address an official.

Veronika had just finished her breakfast when Kazia knocked on their door.

"I just need to wash up the breakfast dishes, Kazia," Veronika said.

"Do them later. We need to get to Aunt Agnes's early, otherwise we might have to wait in line."

"Wait in line? She'd make us wait in line?"

"That's what she does," Kazia said with a grin. "You know what a stickler she is for the rules. Everyone has to wait their turn, no exceptions."

When they arrived at Aunt Agnes's home, a man was already

sitting across from her, cap in hand, explaining the problem he was having coming up with the quota of eggs his family was expected to produce. Another man and his wife sat on a bench waiting their turn. Aunt Agnes looked up as Veronika and Kazia walked in, flashed them a brief smile, then motioned with her head to the bench where they should wait, third in line.

"See?" Kazia whispered. "No special treatment for us, and it takes forever for her to hear them out and then compose the letter."

Veronika nodded. It made sense. Aunt Agnes was the only one in the entire community who could communicate with the Germans. Everyone that had a problem or question for the administration was coming to ask if she could write a letter for them.

"I'm sorry you had to wait," Aunt Agnes said, when it was finally their turn. "Every day it seems that there are more and more people coming with this or that question."

"I don't mind," Veronika said. "It is good to see you busy again."

"And busier yet I will be. I had a visit from the assistant to the commandant. Said they were wondering who it was that was writing those letters in German for the people."

"What?"

"Yes. He wanted to know where I was born, and how long I was here, and what my name was before I married Vladzio, and things like that. In the end, he said I was a Volksdeutsche."

"What is that?" asked Kazia, leaning in.

"It means that I'm a person of German blood and heritage and as such, have extra privileges beyond what everyone else has."

A flutter of hope went through Veronika's body as Kazia grabbed her arm and squeezed it. With Aunt Agnes being favoured by the military, she could intercede on behalf of the family if it were ever needed.

"Then he said, as a Volksdeutsche, I'm ordered to continue translating for people, as well as translating their directives into Ukrainian and Polish."

Veronika's thoughts blurred. It was one thing for her aunt to be helping the community, but working for the military, translating their directives, was a different thing. "Aunt Agnes," she said, her words halting, "how can you work for them, after what they did to the Jews?"

"I don't know that it's so different. If the military can't communicate with someone in the community, and they go against an order, who'll be punished?"

Veronika could see her point.

"But there's more," Aunt Agnes said, her voice light. "When I told the assistant about Vladzio, he said that when Siberia gets liberated, they would make it a priority to have the husband of a Volksdeutsche released." Tears caught in the creases in the corners of her eyes.

"Oh, Aunt Agnes."

"Did you mention my father?" Kazia asked, her face hopeful.

Aunt Agnes's eyes softened. "I couldn't, not just now. It would be too much. But when they get to know me better, I will. I'll ask for help in getting everyone home. Paulina, the children, the doctor, everyone. You'll see. Soon everyone will be home."

Veronika and Kazia got up and wrapped their arms around Aunt Agnes.

When Veronika got home, her parents were anxiously waiting the evening meal for her. While they ate, Veronika recounted how busy Aunt Agnes was, and the hope that their family would be home soon due to Aunt Agnes being a Volksdeutsche.

Mama clutched her chest and looked at her, stunned. "My brothers coming home?"

Veronika nodded. "But she only mentioned Vladzio, not Feliks or anyone else. She thought she'd better wait for that."

Tears flowed down Mama's cheeks. "I never thought this day would come." In a broken voice, she continued. "Every day, I pray and I pray, God, bring our family home. Now, maybe, thanks to Agnes, the day is coming."

Tata nodded. "God bless our Agnes," he said, then he walked to the sideboard and poured a little spiritus into two glasses. Looking at Veronika, he asked, "Would you like some, too?"

"Yes, maybe a little, Tata."

"How did it go in the commandant's office?" he asked, pouring a third glass.

"We spoke with one of the office clerks. I was surprised at how polite he was and how much time he took with us, even got us chairs to sit on, but in the end, he said that until the war was over, nothing could be decided."

"Just as I expected," said Tata. "A waste of time."

"Not a total waste, Tata. He offered us jobs in Germany."

Tata's eyebrows shot up.

"What?" said Mama. "They offered you jobs? What kind of jobs?"

"He said there were plenty of factories and farms that needed workers and even in people's homes there were jobs as cooks and maids."

"What did you say?" her mother asked.

"I thanked him and said that we'd discuss it with our parents."

"Well, the answer is no," Tata said, raising his voice. "Don't even think of going to Germany. It will be just like with the Soviets—they will take you away, and we will never see you again."

"Don't worry, Tata. I just told him that to be polite. As soon as the schools re-open, I want to go back to teaching."

"I'm amazed at how polite he was to them," Mama said. "The Germans in Kuzmin have become more like the village managers than soldiers.

"It could be," Tata said. "Especially if we do all they ask of us.

"And did you hear, there's going to be an outdoor baptism?" Mama asked, her eyes bright. "Maria was telling me all about it."

"A baptism?" Veronika said. "Well, the Germans did say they would be opening the churches again."

"A Ukrainian Orthodox priest has come out of hiding. Several children are going to be baptized."

That night as Veronika lay in the comfort of her featherbed, her last thought before falling asleep was of Frania and the last time she had seen her in the field, how they had hugged and cried. Where was she now? Some said that the Jews had been put to work building hospitals and setting up soup kitchens. She prayed that it was so.

The Nazi vision of Lebensraum (Nazi concept of expansion into other countries) included the pastoralization of Ukraine and the elimination of major urban centers, whose population they otherwise had to feed, diverting resources from the Reich and its army. Thus, the policy was to starve the cities, whose inhabitants were driven by hunger into the countryside.
—Serhii Plokhy, *The Gates of Europe: A History of Ukraine*

87
VERONIKA

February 1942

A few days after Veronika's nineteenth birthday, sleep wouldn't come. Exasperated, she got up and pushed her bedroom window open and stared out at the silent stillness of the yard. By the faint light of the stars and partial moon, she could just make out the mounds that she knew were the shrubs lining the stone wall. Leaning her arms on the windowsill, she stuck her nose close to the open crack and breathed in and out deeply, enjoying how the crisp air calmed the agitation in her soul.

Almost a year had gone by since her teaching career had ended, and all she had done since then was help her parents on the farm. Once again, it was good that they lived on a farm. There were food shortages now and, in the cities, famine. Thousands of city dwellers were dying of starvation and even more had flooded into the countryside in hopes of finding food.

If only the schools had reopened. She could be doing something useful and earning a salary to buy food on the black market for her parents.

Even if the schools reopened, it seemed unlikely the Germans would accept her teaching qualifications. She could read some German but not really speak it. She knew everything about Soviet heroes and Soviet history, but what did she know of German history?

Without teaching, what would be her future? Marriage, perhaps to Marek, and then work on her own farm? Her back and legs suddenly chilly, she shut the window and climbed back into bed, glad of its warmth.

Closing her eyes and turning on her side, she thought of the posters that had sprung up all over the village. *Come to beautiful Germany,* they proclaimed, and *Germany needs you,* with pictures of smiling Ukrainian men and women. Another said, *100,000 Ukrainians are already working in Germany, why not you?*

In the posters were pictures of foods that were non-existent in Kuzmin now—eggs, milk, and bread. Maybe she should consider signing up for work in Germany. Get away from the miliary government and soldiers they had here, and the memories of how they had treated the Jews. Find some nice civilian family to work for, then come home with a whole new wardrobe, a few pairs of shoes, and money in her pocket. Maybe Kazia would go with her.

The next day, Veronika went over to Kazia's. She wasn't surprised to see Franek, Nellia's boyfriend, sitting in the kitchen, playing his accordion. They had been dating for over a year now, and there was talk of them becoming engaged.

She and Kazia went into Kazia's bedroom, where they could be alone, and she swore Kazia to secrecy before she told her anything.

"If my parents found out what I'm thinking, they would really be upset. No use to upset them needlessly until I decide what I'm going to do."

"I promise, not a word to anyone," Kazia said eagerly.

"I'm thinking of going to work in Germany."

Kazia's smile faded. "Germany?"

"Just for the duration of the war. And I'm hoping you will come with me. It would be an adventure."

"Oh, I don't know. It's so far away."

"It's not that far by train. And you don't even have to pack food beyond the first day. After that, they provide everything."

"How do you know so much?"

"There was a recruiter in the village. He said that with so many of their men at the front, Germany is desperately short of workers for the factories and even on the farms. Of course, we wouldn't work on a farm. We would work in a factory, and it would be fun, wouldn't it? Just think of all the clothes we could buy. And on our days off, we could go to the theatre, to dances. Please, please say you'll go with me," she begged.

"I don't know. Just thinking about it turns my stomach in knots."

"Well, at least say you'll think about it. I have to think about it, too. Anyhow, there's time. If I don't go on this train, there will be others, the recruiter said."

"All right. I'll think about it," said Kazia, somewhat reluctantly.

Veronika jumped up, threw her arms around her and hugged her. "I hope you say yes. We would have so much fun together."

88

VERONIKA

March 1942

The following day, Veronika's mother burst in from visiting Aunt Maria, her cheeks flushed, tears shimmering in her eyes.

"Mama, what happened?" Veronika asked, pressing her hand against her chest.

"Józef ... He's come home."

"Kazia's father?"

"Yes!" Mama said, her eyes wide. "He's been released from Siberia."

"How?" asked Veronika, clutching her mother's arms.

"All I know is that he's not well. That's why the Soviets released him."

"Not well?"

"He's dying."

"Oh, Mama, no," Veronika said, sinking into a chair.

"It's stomach cancer. But you know what, Veronika? We're not going to think of that. We're going to go over and celebrate that he's home."

"Yes, yes, of course," Veronika said, numbly. "We'll go over and celebrate."

When they got to Kazia's house, Veronika made her way past all the other well-wishers, to where Uncle Józef was seated in a chair in the corner of the room. Aunt Maria and Nellia sat on one side of him, with Kazia to his left. Kazia looked bewildered, as if she wasn't sure what to make of this feeble man with sunken eyes.

Memories flooded Veronika's mind of a strong young Uncle Józef being loaded into the cart and taken away, Kazia and her mother and sister clinging to him, screaming. After that, Alina and Marek's father and, finally, the doctor were loaded onto the cart. Tears streamed down Veronika's face as she looked at Uncle Józef stroking Kazia's hand.

"The doctor, did you hear anything about him?" someone asked.

Józef closed his eyes and looked down. "I never heard from him again."

"What about my father? Did you hear anything about him?" Alina asked. Veronika could see the apprehension on her face as she stood by her mother.

"After the first week, I was separated from both my brothers. I asked those who came in from other camps if they had heard of them. No one had."

"Oh, my Ludwik," Alina's mother wailed, collapsing to the floor. "Never will we see you again."

Alina and another neighbour helped her up, murmuring words of comfort. "Don't give up yet. Maybe he'll still come home."

Hollow words. They were likely dead. Maybe even in the first days of their arrest, just like in her dream.

After about an hour of talking, Uncle Józef's face began drooping with fatigue, his words coming out more slowly.

"You need to rest," Mama said. "We should leave."

Uncle Józef nodded. "I have to lie down."

The room quickly cleared, except for Veronika who lingered to speak to Kazia.

"With Tata home, I can't even think of going to Germany anymore," Kazia said.

"Of course, you can't leave him," Veronika said. "I understand."

89

VERONIKA

March 1942

The next day, Kazia asked Veronika to go with her to see Aunt Agnes.

"She's eager to know more of my Tata's return," Kazia said.

Veronika got on her warm coat and followed Kazia out the door. As she walked toward her aunt's duplex, Veronika thought of how much had changed since she and Kazia were children running across the bare windswept fields of spring.

"It still seems strange to me that Babcia doesn't live in the duplex anymore," she said.

Kazia nodded. "It must be lonely for Aunt Agnes to live there. Remember how we used to sleep at Babcia's? It was like the ghosts of Aunt Paulina and Uncle Feliks and Vladzio and our cousins haunted the place.

"And other days were so happy, playing knock-knock on Aunt Truda's door, the arm swings the doctor used to give us."

"All those people gone now," Kazia said, "and of all of them, only my father has come back."

"Come in," Aunt Agnes said when they knocked on her door. "Such wonderful news that your father has returned. Sit down and tell me all about it."

"Yesterday, when my mother opened the door, and my father was standing there, I didn't know who he was. Then when I saw the look on Mama's face and how she fell into his arms, I knew," Kazia said, her voice breaking.

Aunt Agnes reached for Kazia's hand and held it. "Such a day. A day we've all prayed for."

Tears streamed down Kazia's face. "It's not fair. Eleven years I waited and now he comes home only to die."

"It doesn't seem fair, does it?"

"There's so much I want to say to him but I can't. All the time he sleeps."

"Just hold his hand and he will feel your love."

"How can God be so cruel?"

"It's not God who's cruel. It's man."

"At least I'm not in Germany," Kazia said, "hearing all this by letter."

"Germany?"

"We weren't going to tell anyone," Veronika said, "but we thought of going to Germany to work, but it's out of the question for Kazia to even think of it now."

"Do you still think of going, Veronika?"

"I don't know. Maybe, and Kazia can join me later. I just feel so trapped, dependent on my mother and father again. I want to work and earn my own money."

"Do you remember how we used to sit on my bed and talk of Germany?" Aunt Agnes asked, a faint smile on her lips.

"Of course, I do. And I still dream of riding streetcars and seeing buildings as tall as castles."

"Maybe it's not a dream you should give up on, Veronika. But with the war, I would wait. At least to know what's happening. You have time, lots of time, to see Germany."

Veronika thought of Aunt Agnes's words as she walked home. Did she have a lot of time? Marek would be coming home in August. He'd want her answer. And what would she say? If she refused him again, it would likely be over between them, but if she said yes, then what? A life of living on a farm? Is that what she wanted? Maybe she shouldn't be here when he returned. In a few months the war would be over and then she could decide.

90

JANEK

May 1942

Janek knew something was wrong by the knock on the door. It wasn't the type of knock that friends or neighbours dropping by for a visit used. It was more like the pounding of someone's fist, jolting his memories of the Soviet secret police. He glanced at Helena and saw her gripping the table, her eyes wide. He opened the door and saw the grey uniform, the manicured hands, the polished boots, and a hollow numbness coursed through his body. He wondered what he had done.

"We're looking for Veronika Osiecka," the village official standing next to the soldier said.

"She's not here," Helena said, stuttering slightly "She's at her cousin's."

"So, she does live here?"

"Yes," Janek said.

"It is the order of the German government that all the youth between the ages of fifteen and thirty are to be shipped out for work in Germany. She has one week to get ready."

Janek felt as though he had been punched in the stomach.

"She will leave out of the Gródek train station. We will come get her May 8th. You will make sure she's here and ready to go."

Janek, struggling not to cry out, simply nodded.

"You understand that if she's not here, she will be held accountable."

Helena gasped.

"Yes," Janek said, in a voice barely above a whisper.

"She will need to bring a change of clothes, a warm coat, and food for the first day. Everything else will be provided."

When they left, Janek held Helena in his arms as pain squeezed his chest, like the pain he'd had when little Vladimir, his precious son, lay dying. Just as with his son, he was powerless to do anything to save Veronika.

"I'm so afraid, Janek," she cried. "What can we do?"

"We can do nothing. She has to go."

"Maybe we could hide her. Somewhere we could find a place," she said, clutching him.

"To resist only makes things worse. They would find her and make an example of her. It's the same as when the secret police were coming for me, that night they were parked across the road. I waited inside. It's why I couldn't help the Jews.

"We have to do something."

"Helena, listen to me. We have no money. No way to pay for a train ticket or for passage on a ship. A young woman alone, on foot, during a war? How long do you think she'd survive without some soldier raping her or killing her?"

"I don't know, Janek, I don't know," she said, collapsing into his arms and weeping.

Holding her close, he whispered softly into her neck, "The best way to survive is to follow their orders, just as we have always done."

Helena met his gaze and nodded. "I need to be with Veronika. Let's go to my sister's. Maybe they haven't heard yet." After a moment she said, "My poor sister. Losing her husband and now her two girls."

Janek wondered how Józef was taking it. Only home for a few weeks and now his daughters were being taken from him. Oh, God, this life, he thought with a sigh.

"You've heard, then?" Helena asked, when Maria opened the door, her face drawn.

"We heard. All over there are soldiers going from house to house."

"How are the girls?"

"Nellia and Kazia are taking it very hard. Veronika is with them. We haven't told Józef yet. Oh, Helena, I'm so afraid."

"Did you tell them your husband is dying?" asked Helena.

"I told them."

"And they won't give them a little more time to spend with their father?" Janek asked.

Maria shook her head. "He said there is a quota in place of how many people they need to send each month."

"Quota?" Helena said, her voice rising shrilly. "Matko Boska. Just like with the Soviets? Jezu Chryste, help us."

"Helena, stop," Janek said. "You're upsetting your sister even more."

Kazia and Nellia sat at the table, numb with grief. Beside Kazia sat Veronika. Helena rushed over to greet them.

"Mama. Tata. It's so sad. Nellia and Kazia are being forced to leave their father."

"I know, and you have to go, too," Helena said, her voice breaking.

"Please, Mama, don't be so worried about me. It might not be so bad. A few weeks ago, Kazia and I were even thinking of volunteering."

Janek looked at Veronika in surprise.

"Veronika, why would you even think of such a thing?" Helena asked.

"Because I can't get work here and they're offering good jobs to foreign workers."

"Good jobs?" Helena asked, her voice edged with sarcasm, "Once they get their hands on you, it will be just like with the Soviets. They will never let you go unless you're useless to them, and not even then. Only if you're lucky, they'll spit you out to crawl home."

"But the Germans are not like the Soviets."

"Look what they did to the Jews," Helena said.

"They had it in for the Jews, but not for us. Look at how polite they've been to us. They aren't beating anyone. They opened the churches and the stores. I think it might even be fun to work in Germany, a chance to see a new country."

Janek sat back in his chair, not believing the naivety of her words.

"What is it, Tata? Do you think it's wrong of me to want to go?"

"I think it's like Mama said. If you go, we may never see you again."

"Oh, Tata, no, no. Of course, you'll see me again. As soon as the war is over, all of us will be back, I promise."

Janek just looked at her, saying nothing. He could see her mind was made up. What was the use in scaring her? Since she had to go, maybe better this way, full of optimism.

"I will miss you both," she continued, "but I can hardly wait to look out the train window and see the places I've only dreamed of, like Ternopol. Remember how you always said that someday you would take me to Ternopol? And there's Berlin, Munich, maybe even the Black Forest."

Janek saw that Helena was about to say something. He caught her attention and shook his head ever so slightly to silence her protests.

There was an awkward, tense silence. Finally, Veronika asked in a lighthearted manner, "Did they say what we should bring?"

Janek paused, glanced nervously at Helena, afraid of the effect his words might have on her. Slowly, carefully, he said, "We were told you're not to bring much, that you would be given everything you need."

Helena burst out sobbing anew.

"What is it, Mama?"

"The Soviets ... that's what they said to Paulina, that Vladzio and Feliks wouldn't be needing anything."

91

VERONIKA

Veronika went around the house, gathering the few things she wanted to take when she left the next day. With only one small suitcase and a coat to pack, she couldn't take much. All the same, she found room for a few photographs, her high school diploma, and her teacher training certificate at the bottom of the case. Maybe she could get a job taking care of a wealthy family's children on an estate or a villa. She would tell Nellia and Kazia to take their teacher training certificates along as well.

"I've done as much as I can," she said to her parents. "I think I'll go to Aunt Agnes's now. She asked me to come see her this afternoon."

"Sit down for a minute before you go," Tata said. "There's something we have to tell you."

"Of course. What is it?"

"We want you to promise that no matter what happens, you three will try to stick together. Maria and Józef are telling Nellia and Kazia the same thing."

"Józef saw it in the camps," her mother went on anxiously. "Those that survived had friends."

"Yes, sure. I'll gladly stay with them. The thought of being all alone is the one thing that makes me nervous."

"Another thing is, listen to Nellia. She's older and knows more about the world."

"Yes, Mama."

"And there is Franek, too. Now that he's engaged to Nellia, he's a member of the family. He'll be watching out for you as well," continued her mother.

"Wherever you go, remember to pray," said her father. "God will always hear you."

"Yes Tata."

Veronika bent down and kissed them lightly on their cheeks. "You're both so worried. A lot of people have gone to Germany already. They seem to be doing fine. We will be, too. You'll see."

Walking down the road to her aunt's house, she tried to shake the feelings of guilt for being happy about going while her parents were feeling so much distress. Aunt Agnes would understand and be happy for her. Not like Mama and Tata, going around with sad faces, afraid she'd never come back.

The word *Germany* kept dancing in Veronika's mind, the land of her dreams, of castles and streetcars and, best of all, a job and money of her own to spend on whatever she liked.

Aunt Agnes opened the door to Veronika's knock. "Veronika, I heard you're leaving tomorrow."

"Yes, and I'm so excited." She looked around the room and, seeing no one else, said with a laugh, "Oh, today I see I'm special! I don't have to wait in line to see you!"

"Someone did want a letter written, but I said no, come back tomorrow." Sitting down at her old wooden table, Aunt Agnes held

Veronika's hands. "I wasn't much older than you when I left Germany to come here. I remember looking forward to having a new adventure and seeing something of the world."

"That's what I love about you. You've always understood me and supported me in what I wanted to do."

Aunt Agnes was silent for a few moments, a faraway look in her eyes. Finally, she looked at her and said, "But I'm worried, too, Veronika. I had always hoped you would see my Germany but not this way, not being forced to go."

Looking at her aunt's beloved face and the sadness in her eyes, Veronika was bewildered.

"War does strange things to people, Veronika, and with this new government they have now, the Nazis, it's not the same as when I left."

Stunned, Veronika didn't know what to say.

Reaching over and patting Veronika's hand, Aunt Agnes said, "Anyhow, I could be wrong, but that's what I've been thinking. How about if I get us some tea? It should be ready."

Slowly making her way back to the table with mugs of chamomile tea, Aunt Agnes said, "I hear that Nellia is engaged to Franek now."

Veronika nodded. "Her parents pressured her into getting engaged. I think part of the reason is that they want Nellia to have a man to look out for her and Kazia."

"It's a wonder they didn't try to get Kazia engaged."

"Kazia told me they were considering it."

"O mój Boże," Aunt Agnes said, rolling her eyes.

"They didn't pursue it because he's from another village and they weren't so sure about his family."

"Do you think your parents would have wanted you to become engaged if Marek were here?"

"Maybe," said Veronika. "They seem to really like him."

Aunt Agnes sighed. "How about Marek's sister? Have you ever heard from her?"

"Alina is working in a city north of here."

"She was your best friend for a while, wasn't she?"

"She was, but then I met Frania." Veronika felt a lump forming in her throat. "So often I think of the last time I saw Frania. Sometimes I dream that I could have done something to save her."

"Don't, Veronika. Drink your tea."

Veronika shook her head. "I should be going."

"Before you go, Veronika, I have something I've been saving for you. I think now is the right time. Maybe I won't be here anymore when you come back."

"Why not?"

"I'm getting older. Who knows how long I have."

"Oh, Aunt Agnes, you will be here! Don't talk like that."

Her aunt got up and walked into her bedroom. She came back with her large wooden jewellery box, the box that Veronika had always enjoyed going through as a child. Setting it on the table, Aunt Agnes opened the lid and took out the small piece of folded paper that Veronika knew contained the lock of Aunt Agnes's baby hair, some old postcards, pins and brooches, and a silver mesh coin purse from Germany. When she came to the silver necklace with the red garnets, she held it out.

"For you, Veronika. Something to remember me by."

Warmth filled Veronika's heart. It was the necklace she had always admired, the one Aunt Agnes had let her wear when she was a child. Veronika could feel herself tearing up as she hugged her aunt. She could see tears gathering in the corners of Aunt Agnes's eyes as well.

"Here, let me put it on you," she said. "You remember where I got it from?"

"Your mother."

Aunt Agnes smiled. "She said I was to give it to my daughter."

After a lingering hug and kisses for Aunt Agnes, Veronika left her house, shaken by Aunt Agnes's words. Once again tears sprang to her eyes. She wiped them away.

It's not true. I'm going for a few months and then I'll be back.

That evening, just as the sun was setting, Veronika sat on the stone bench outside her home. She loved this time of year, when spring was fully underway and the wisteria came into a profusion of purple bloom. Veronika knew this would be the way she would always remember her home. Although she longed to see another country, in her heart, this was her home; when her adventure was done, this was the place where she belonged. Veronika reached up to feel the necklace around her neck, enjoying the glow of love and comfort it gave her. Sighing deeply, she knew she would miss Aunt Agnes for the few months she would be away. She would miss all her family.

*Ukraine was, to the Germans, first and foremost a source of food;
secondly, of coal, iron and other minerals; and thirdly, of slave labor.*

—Alexander Werth, BBC World War II correspondent and writer

92

VERONIKA

In the morning, Veronika and her parents sat around the kitchen table, waiting for the solders to arrive to escort her to the train station. Her prettiest shawl, coat, and cloth shopping bag were sitting by the door. Her mother had packed bread and a few cookies for her to take along. She wanted to pack more but Veronika told her it was enough.

"I'm just so afraid," Mama said, "that you won't be treated right, that the Nazis will be just like the Soviets, and we won't see you again."

Exasperated, Veronika said, "What can I do now, Mama? The soldiers are already on their way."

Tata just sat there, looking at her, not saying anything, his face long and sad. She couldn't look into his eyes because each time she did, she felt his sorrow boring into her soul. At least he would be walking her to the train station, and they'd have a chance to talk and say their goodbyes along the way. It was a four-kilometre walk to Kuzmin and a further twelve kilometres beyond that to get to the train station in Gródek. Saying goodbye to Mama would be hard enough for now.

Why couldn't she make Mama and Tata understand? Why couldn't they just share in her happiness? They were so conservative, always thinking the worst. And suddenly she was flooded with a sense of guilt for being so annoyed with them. Remorseful, Veronika went over to her mother and put her arm around her shoulder.

"It's not going to be like you think, Mama," she said gently. "I'll make good wages. Maybe even enough to send home. And you'll see, I'll be back soon. Please, please, can't you just be happy for me?"

Veronika looked into her mother's face and could see she was struggling to hold back her tears. "Oh, Mama, it will be all right, really, it will." Veronika felt her own throat constrict as her mother held her hands over her face and wept.

"I'll make some mint tea," Tata said, getting up.

While they sipped their tea, Veronika felt compelled to look around the sunlit kitchen, to seal into her heart this home that her Tata had built, with its whitewashed stone walls and clay floor. The kitchen's multi-pane double windows were swung slightly outward, and the curtains fluttered now and then in the spring breeze. She looked at her mother, at the sorrow and age in her face. She saw that she was wearing her old sweater, pulled on top of two layers of clothing and on her feet were shapeless black work boots, ones that had been made many years before in their village. She saw her father's slightly stooped shoulders as he poured his tea into his saucer, and his gnarled arthritic hands that brought the saucer to his lips. And suddenly she saw clearly the fragility of her parents and felt a jab of fear. Her parents were getting old.

When I come home, I'll make it up to them, she promised herself. I'll buy new clothes for them, new boots. I'll marry Marek and be the daughter they want me to be, and with that thought, she felt comforted.

They were still drinking their tea when the knock finally came. They all jumped. Veronika looked over at Mama, who had the back of her fingers pressed to her mouth in an effort to keep from crying out. Suddenly the finality of the moment hit Veronika with a wrench in her gut. With a rush, she gathered her Mama in her arms and hugged her hard and kissed her, as tears streamed down both their faces.

Tata opened the door. Two local men and two German soldiers stood in the doorway; rifles slung over their backs.

"It's time to go," one of the local men said.

As they walked down the road, Veronika kept looking back at her Mama, standing there, waving and crying. She kept turning to wave until her mother got smaller and smaller. And then she was gone.

Tata and Veronika walked in silence. She wished she could talk to her father, to start saying her final goodbyes, but knew from the tightness in her throat that she would only cry. She wished she hadn't been so impatient with her mother this morning and could give her just one more hug and tell her how much she loved her.

She could tell that Tata was waiting until she felt calmer, by the way he kept checking her face and giving her hand a little squeeze. He, too, had things in his heart to tell her.

They stopped at the next farmhouse where there were other young people to be picked up. Veronika and her father watched while the soldiers knocked on the door and said, "It's time. You have to go to work."

Two brothers, about Veronika's age, protested that they didn't want to go. The younger one, wild-eyed, suddenly bolted. The soldiers took off after him. Veronika watched, her heart pounding as the soldiers caught up with him and brought him back, roughly pushing him ahead with the butt of their rifle as they walked. Veronika felt her stomach clench at the sudden change in the soldiers' demeanour.

They continued walking down the road, knocking on doors. Some, like Veronika, were more than willing to go and others fought against it. A cold numbness began to seep through Veronika's limbs as she watched Julianna and Sonia forced from their home. Stoic, kindly Sonia, now pale with fear, murmured encouragingly to Julianna, as they walked arm in arm.

At another home, the soldiers pulled Ania, a timid fifteen-year-old, from her mother's embrace. Her mother shrieked in anguish and clung to Ania. Visions swirled in Veronika's mind of the doctor and her uncles being handcuffed, her aunts crying, clutching at their hands as they were being taken away.

Tanya, a Ukrainian neighbour, also begged to keep her young daughter Larisa.

"Please, don't take her. She's all I have left."

Veronika knew the woman quite well. It was true what she said. Her husband and other children had died in the famine. Only this one daughter had survived.

"You don't want to be parted from your daughter?" said one of the local men with an indolent smile. "Then you can come, too."

Veronika was surprised. She was in her forties already.

"Tata, maybe you and Mama were right," Veronika said, her breath coming in short gasps. "Maybe they're no better than the Soviets."

Tata, his face pinched, didn't say anything. He just squeezed her hand and looked away. She could tell he was trying not to cry.

As they entered Kuzmin's market square, they stood with the gathering crowd, unsure why they were waiting and not already walking to the train station at Gródek.

"Look, there's Aunt Maria and the girls," said Tata waving to them.

As they made their way over, Veronika saw that Franek and his younger brothers, Jakub and Filip, were with them.

When a dozen or so German soldiers joined the soldiers that were already in the square, it became apparent why they were waiting. Immediately they began forcing the youth away from their parents and into the centre of the square and ordering the parents to move off to the side. Veronika thought she'd have another two hours to walk with her father, time yet to say goodbye. A German soldier briskly pushed them apart as she wept and clutched her father's hand. She felt as if her heart were being ripped open as her last chance to be with her father was taken from her.

"Tata," she called after him. "Tata."

"Stay with Nellia and Kazia!" he yelled. "Stay with your cousins!"

Hemmed in by a ring of German soldiers, they walked on, Veronika with Kazia, and Nellia with Franek and his brothers in the middle of a group of about two hundred other young people from their area. It was like there was a noose around them from which there was no escape. The Germans were in complete control. Outside the ring of soldiers walked all the distraught and weeping parents and relatives.

Veronika and Kazia kept turning and looking for their parents until they finally saw them keeping pace at the edge of the circle, a little behind where they were, but there were so many others around, they could only catch a glimpse of them every now and then for the two hours they walked to Gródek.

Long before they got there, a cacophony of wails could be heard coming from the train station, sending shivers through Veronika's body.

"There must be hundreds of people crying," said Kazia. "It sounds so eerie."

"I know," said Veronika through numb lips.

When they got to the train station and looked at the rail yard, Veronika stared in disbelief at the endless line of cattle cars.

"Where are the passenger cars," she gasped. "We can't ride in those, like pigs."

"It was lies they told you, Veronika," said Nellia. "Just like our parents said."

Trembling, Veronika stared out at the tracks. "How could I have been so blind?"

Veronika could see that some of the cattle cars were empty, their doors open, and others were bolted shut from the outside. It was alongside these bolted cars that small knots of family members were keeping vigil, some sitting, some standing, and some lying on the ground, weeping for those who were already locked inside. Crescendos of wails rose and fell as hundreds of family members wailed, *Oh, my child, my child. I love you so much. And now you are gone from me forever.*

"Nellia, I have to get away from here," Kazia said, her eyes wide with panic.

Franek grabbed her arm. "Look at all the soldiers," he said. "You'd be shot."

Suddenly their Kuzmin group was being forcefully swept forward toward the empty cattle cars. They were going. Linking arms with Kazia, Veronika desperately looked around, trying to see her father, but everywhere there were throngs of parents and she couldn't find him. The momentum of the crowd pushed them forward toward an empty cattle car as the German guards begin shoving and threatening those at the outer edges of their group.

"*Schnell! Schnell! Dreckschweine!*" they shouted, calling them filthy pigs, as they shoved those not quick enough getting in. Nellia and Franek hastily scrambled up into the cattle car followed by Veronika and Kazia, Jakub and Filip. All around Veronika there were cries of pain, as people were knocked against each other and crushed by the weight of those still coming in. Veronika and Kazia were forced by the weight of others toward the middle of the car. Still more and more people were packed in until the slam of the door blocked the light and they heard the sound of the iron bar sliding into place.

As their eyes adjusted to the darkness, they gradually became aware of the people they were crushed up against. Whispers of apologies were made as bodies were shifted to ease the strain and discomfort. There were about ninety of them crammed inside. Veronika knew everyone, some better than others. All were from Kuzmin.

Veronika stared at the walls that enclosed them, about five arm spans by two, enough room for about six, maybe eight cattle. In the upper corner of one wall was a small window covered in barbed wire, too high to see out of.

"Boost me up," Filip said to another boy.

At the window, he stood motionless for a long time, looking out.

"What's happening?" Franek asked.

Filip did not reply, but when he got down, they could see he was crying. Suddenly, everyone wanted a chance to look out. When it was Veronika's turn, her eyes were only looking for her Tata. She saw him, lying face down on the ground, beating his fists. He was wailing the funeral wail for her death. She fell to the floor, her grief so profound that she was unable to speak. She could only cry and say in her mind the words she wanted to say to him.

My Tata, my Tata ... you always liked to walk with me when you felt the road unsafe. Now, here you are, waiting outside my cattle car.

I had so much to say to you. I love you. Thank you for all your love. Thank you for taking such good care of me. I also want to say the things that you want to hear. Yes, I will be very careful and take good care of myself and yes, I promise, I will come back to you.

For two days they sat in that cattle car, waiting for the Germans to finish catching all the youth from the surrounding villages. They were given no food or water. The toilet was a bucket in the corner with an old blanket nailed up around it. The air was stifling by day, damp and chilly by night. All the time, they were only thinking about their families and crying. Together, Kazia and Veronika prayed, and then they cried, and then they held each other and cried some more.

From time to time, Veronika would ask for another turn to look out that window. Each time she looked, there was her Tata, keeping vigil beside her cattle car. He never saw her looking out that tiny window, but she saw him.

When the train finally pulled out of the Gródek station, the wails grew to a crescendo as frantic mothers and fathers ran alongside the slow-moving cattle cars, unwilling to let go of the train that held their children. Others ran and pounded the sides of the walls, calling out final messages of love and despair to the children. All Veronika could think of was her father, lying on the ground, as the cries of agony both in and outside the train intensified as the train slipped out of the grasp of their families' hands. Gradually the car became quiet. Kazia and Veronika put their arms around each other and cried. For the loss of their families, their homes, and their country. For their childhood.

The End

AFTERWORD

When Veronika said goodbye to her parents, she didn't know what would happen when she got on the train to work in Germany, other than it was a chance to travel and make some money before returning to Kuzmin.

Many years later, Veronika told her story to me, her daughter-in-law; her memories inspired this book.

Veronika's story will be continued in book two of the series, which picks up where *Black Sunflowers* leaves off, with Veronika, Kazia, and Nellia boarding the train for Germany.

Veronika Osiecka, Age 24
Germany, 1947

Kazia Janczewski, Age 24
Veronika's cousin and best friend
Germany, 1947

Janek and Helena, seated, with relatives, circa 1950

Veronika's parents and relatives at an Easter family celebration, circa 1950. Helena with baby, Janek seated next to her

Helena and Janek outside their home in Kuzmin. Helena standing, Janek with accordion, circa 1942

Janek with cane, Helena, and other friends and relatives outside Veronika's home, circa 1942

Ukrainian family, declared to be kulaks, being exiled, circa 1931

Child with signs of starvation on the streets of Kharkiv, Ukraine, circa 1933

Horses were poorly cared for because, with the introduction of tractors, the Communist Party considered horses obsolete

People died of hunger while Soviet government warehouses were filled beyond capacity with grain, Kharkiv, circa 1933.

Estonians being deported by cattle car to Siberia, Kazakhstan, and other remote areas for forced labour, 1949

Guarding the crop from starving workers on a collective farm in the Poltava region. Taking even five stalks of grain could mean the death penalty or exile.

Cynthia LeBrun

Joseph Stalin, leader of the Soviet Union from 1924 to 1953

Those living in the rural areas went to the cities in search of food. Instead, they found hunger, disease and lice, circa 1933

Not only Ukrainians were deported but Crimean Tatars as well, circa 1944

AUTHOR'S NOTE

The events, people, and places described in this novel are, for the most part, based on my mother-in-law Veronika's vivid memories of the times.

When I met Veronika in 2001, conversations often drifted back to her childhood in Soviet-occupied Ukraine, and the invasion of the German army when she was a teenager.

I began tape recording and asking deep, probing questions. At times it wasn't easy. Pent-up memories tumbled out as she thought of them, often skipping back and forth in time. As well, she used people's Polish names and their English names interchangeably. It took me a long time to realize that Stasik and Stanley were one person, and that Agnieszka also meant Agnes.

The interviews were both healing and painful for Veronika. She would be laughing as she recounted a happy memory, and suddenly a painful memory would be triggered and she would be sobbing. The memory that tormented her the most was when she looked out of the cattle car window and saw her father lying on the ground, wailing.

Veronika always enjoyed hearing passages read aloud from "her book." She smiled and nodded, hearing how her beloved friends and family members were brought to life.

One time she said, "You write so good! Some stories are boring but with yours, I want to hear what will happen next. I was never good with writing; for me in school it was math and science, but not chemistry so much, too many formulas."

A favourite memory I have of Veronika happened in 2009 when I went to Leduc, Alberta, for a family wedding. Veronika was living in Leduc with her daughter and son-in-law at the time. At eighty-six, Veronika still had a keen mind, walked an hour a day, and drove her pick-up truck around town.

After the wedding, I stayed an extra week to conduct interviews with Veronika in my hotel room. We had so much fun. I would read from the manuscript; she would correct parts that weren't quite right or nod with approval when I got it right. After two hours of reading, I would make a simple dinner for us in my kitchenette, then we would go to the Leduc Rapid Bingo Hall. Every night we would go, walking the two blocks from the hotel to the hall.

"I like going to Bingo. It reminds me of home," she said with a little sob, as a sad thought once again intruded on a happy one.

As we cut through a parking lot, she did a little skip and a hop and said, "Maybe I do the Hopak, just like Babcia!"

"You should act your age," I retorted, knowing that would please her.

What a chuckle we both had, me holding her arm to give her a little extra support as we walked.

The interviews seemed to give Veronika a deep sense of peace, knowing that her life and all that she suffered and overcame would be remembered by those far beyond her family circle. She marvelled when I told her that people she didn't even know were already interested in her life.

She died at peace in 2016, at the age of 93, not long after seeing a printed draft of her book, knowing that her family's and Frania's stories would be published.

After her passing, I felt an increased sense of urgency to finish the book. Each year more people of her era were passing away, and I was aging. I got an editor, pushed through, and finished the book. With that, I felt a profound sense of relief.

It is my hope that Veronika's family will be remembered as real people, with names, hopes, dreams, somehow representative of the millions who suffered and died, with their stories untold. At that point, I will truly have fulfilled my commitment to Veronika and to God.

The names of the Soviet officials in Kuzmin

Their actions and orders are as Veronika remembered them. I filled in the gaps of what she did not know by historical research for the years this book takes place. Every effort has been made to provide an accurate historical account of what Veronika and her community went through under both Soviet and German occupation.

Kuzmin was not typical of most villages in Ukraine

Veronika lived in Kuzmin until the age of nineteen and so was able to give me an in-depth description of the village and surrounding rural areas. She said it was a mixed community of people who identified themselves as either Polish, Ukrainian, or Jewish. Her father often said that their village was unusual in that, for the most part, the Ukrainians, Polish, and Jewish people lived peacefully together, and it wasn't like that in other villages.

Names of villages and towns

It can be confusing to find where Veronika and her family lived because towns and villages in Ukraine have different names depending on the language and year of the map. For example, Gródek, can be spelled as Gorodok or Horodok. Another point of confusion is that there may be more than one town or city in the *oblast* (province) with the same name. In Ukraine there are at least five towns with the name Horodok and two towns with the name Kuzmin. Veronika's village is on the Smotrych River in the Khmelnytskyi province.

Polish and Ukrainian Names

Some of the names in the book have been modified from the correct Polish or Ukrainian spelling in order to provide clarity to the English-speaking reader.

I have chosen to follow the Polish tradition of ending a man's name with an "i" and a woman's name with an "a." For example, in Veronika's family, the following was correct: Jan Osiecki and Helena Osiecka.

Why was a Polish family living in Ukraine?

For centuries, the border between Poland and Ukraine was very fluid. From the 14th to the 18th centuries, Ukraine was at times under Polish, Lithuanian, or Russian rule. After the Russian Revolution in 1917, most of Ukraine became a part of the Soviet Union. Many Polish people decided to remain in Ukraine because the land they were on was their home and had perhaps been in their family for decades.

Babcia

Babcia is entirely real and was as ornery and feisty as Veronika described her, including having her finger bitten off by a rabid dog and pouring straight vodka in her eyes to "clean them out." Veronika and her family always believed that she lived to be 105 but that might have been an exaggeration on Babcia's part. In the book, she died at 100, but I'm more inclined to believe Veronika.

Did Feliks and Vladzio survive?

When Paulina got a letter from the government saying, *"After ten years then you can hear from him,"* everyone in the family believed what it said, that they would hear in ten years, and so Agnes, Paulina, and the whole family waited.

Not long into my research, I was deeply distressed to come across a similar terminology, *"sentenced to ten years without the right to correspond";* for those in the know—i.e., Soviet officials—it was the euphemism for executed.

I did not tell Veronika that her uncles were likely executed not long after they were arrested.

Frania's fate

Veronika never knew what happened to Frania and the other Jewish women and children of Kuzmin. It was only very recently that I came across an account of the murder of Jews at Gródek, where Kuzmin was mentioned. The account sickened me with grief. After years of meditating about Frania, I felt that she was someone I knew and loved, and I needed to spend time grieving her loss. What follows is the true story of what happened to Jewish women and children in German-occupied Ukraine.

In the fall of 1941, approximately 300 Jewish women and children from Kuzmin were taken to a ghetto in Gródek and forced into hard labour. No food was provided, but children managed to sneak out from time to time and barter with the villagers for food.

In the early morning hours of October 1942, the ghetto was surrounded by a German unit and Ukrainian auxiliary police. They ordered the occupants through a megaphone to come out and bring all their valuables with them. They were taken under guard to Gródek's town square and told they were being sent to Palestine. From there they boarded a train to Yarmolintsy, approximately twenty kilometres away.

All the Jewish women and children from the surrounding villages were taken to Yarmolintsy, along with some Jewish men who had escaped the initial shootings. They were told if they handed over their valuables, they would remain alive.

Under guard, they were walked to a derelict three-storey barracks four kilometres from the railway station. It was fenced-in with barbed wire and guarded. For three days they were given no food or water. Some committed suicide.

After three days, the German soldiers started taking people out to the nearby pits. Many refused and put up a resistance, killing some Germans and policemen.

The resistance ended when the Germans set a fire in the barracks and smashed their way in. People were taken in groups of fifty and ordered to strip naked and lie face down in the pit. They were shot by the Germans standing on a plank over the pit. The shooting lasted for days. In total 6,400 Jews were killed.

AUTHOR BIO

Cynthia LeBrun grew up in Kelowna, British Columbia, and studied to be a teacher at Simon Fraser University. She taught in a northern one-room schoolhouse west of Fort St. John, as well as the isolated logging camp of Phillips Arm, and finally in Campbell River. *Black Sunflowers* is inspired by the vivid memories of her mother-in-law, who grew up in Soviet Occupied Ukraine. Cynthia now lives and writes in the beautiful Comox Valley on Vancouver Island, where she enjoys time in her garden and being with her grandsons. *Black Sunflowers* is her first novel.

ACKNOWLEDGMENTS

My deepest appreciation goes to **Marsha Skrypuch** who, over the years, has moulded and sharpened my writing skills, and who was there to uplift and support me at every point when I needed guidance or advice. I could not have asked for a better mentor and friend.

My husband, **Edward (Ed) Tomaszewski**, has always been there for me, with unfailing love and support during the never-ending reads, rereads, and edits. His understanding and encouragement have allowed me to succeed, and I thank him with all my heart.

Many thanks to my daughter, **Jessica Akehurst**, for believing in me and inspiring me to go on. She kept nudging me to push through and get it published. I couldn't ask for a more loving daughter.

Thank you to the late **Sharon Fitzhenry** and to **Holly Doll**, at Fitzhenry & Whiteside, for having faith in my book.

An immense thank you goes to **Sarah Harvey**, my editor and coach. I am grateful for her unparalleled knowledge and insightful expertise in editing. Without her help, the book would not be what it is today.

I would like to express my heartfelt appreciation to my son-in-law, **William Akehurst**, for the countless hours he spent designing a professional website for me as well as for his general help and sense of humour that has kept me laughing.

The synergy of the group mind at **KidCRIT** helped me polish and refine my manuscript. I would like to thank the group leader and moderator, Marsha Skrypuch, as well as group members Evangelene, Stephen, Corinne, Mar, Ian, Christine, Adrian, Shirley, and Don for all the hours and hours they helped me develop *Black Sunflowers*.

I'd like to thank my mother, **H.B. (Sue) LeBrun**, who always said that someday I would be a writer.

My deep appreciation also goes to my sister, **Diane Preston**, for constantly asking me to dig deeper and find out more about Veronika's life when the manuscript was still in its infancy. Diane spent hours on the phone with me while I read each chapter to her. Her exemplary listening skills and brilliant suggestions helped shape the book into what it is today.

Thank you to my sister, **Nance-Ann LeBrun**, who kept reassuring me that this book would someday get published and would be a success. Thank you for believing in me. You've always been there in my hour of need and my brightest day.

Thank you to my sister, **Phyllis Bowman**, for persevering in teaching me the alphabet. At the age of six, I was very reluctant to learn the meaning of those abstract markings on the page. Where would I be today without her help?

Many thanks to my cousin, **William (Bill) Deacon-Rogers**, for listening to each chapter with such overwhelming enthusiasm. As I read, I'd watch his face to see if the point I was trying to make with the readers would be a hit or a miss. His face told it all!

Thank you to **Janet Murphy** for her enthusiasm and absolute faith that this story needed to be told. I also thank her for her suggestions, proofreading, and feedback, as she read each chapter not once but multiple times.

I would like to express my deepest appreciation to **Valentina Kuryliw**, Director of Education, Holodomor Research and Education, (University of Alberta) for recognizing my manuscript as historically accurate. I also appreciate her assessment, as Department Head of History and Social Sciences for the Toronto District School Board, that *Black Sunflowers* is relevant to a wide range of readers.

A very special thank you to **Dr. Mateusz Świetlicki**, Professor at the University of Wroclaw, Poland, specializing in Ukrainian and Polish studies, for checking the manuscript for errors and omissions in writing about the culture and history of Soviet Occupied Ukraine. I cannot thank him enough.

I am extremely grateful for the assistance of **Dr. Yohanan Petrovsky-Shtern**, (Northwestern University of Evanston, Illinois) for checking the manuscript for errors and omissions in writing about the culture and history of Jewish people of western Ukraine in the 1930s–40s.

I would like to thank the **Peterson Literary Fund** for recognizing my manuscript as a distinguished written work whose Ukrainian subject matter is relevant to a global readership. Receiving that award was a tremendous boost of confidence. For the first time, I felt that my years of research and writing were not in vain.

Bibliography

Applebaum, Anne. *Red Famine: Stalin's War on Ukraine*, Toronto: Signal, 2017.

Belov, Fedor. *The History of a Soviet Collective Farm*, London: Routledge, 1998.

Conquest, Robert. *The Harvest of Sorrow: Soviet Collectivization and the Terror Famine*, Oxford: Oxford University Press, 1986.

Gregorovich, Andrew. *Written for InfoUkes history of World War Two* (www.infoukes.com/history/ww2/page-04.html)

HREC Education. *Information from: Holodomor: The Aftermath*
Website: education.holodomor.ca

Kostiuk, Hryhory. *Stalinist Rule in the Ukraine: A Study of the Decade of Mass Terror (1929–39)*. New York: Frederick A. Praeger, Inc., Publishers, University Place, New York 3, New York, 1960.

Magocsi, Paul Robert. *A History of Ukraine*, Toronto: University of Toronto Press, 1996.

Petelycky, Stefan. *Into Auschwitz, For Ukraine*, Kingston, Ontario: The Kashtan Press, 1999.

Plokhy, Serhii. *The Gates of Europe: A History of Ukraine*, New York: Basic Books, 2021.

Radzinsky, Edvard. *Stalin: The First In-Depth Biography Based on Explosive New Documents from Russia's Secret Archives*, New York: Doubleday, 1996.

Revutsky, Valentyna. Video recording of song sung by children of the Holodomor in the city of Khmelnitsky, interview recorded by VIMEO, called "Valentyna's Story": vimeo.com

Service, Robert. *Stalin: A Biography*, Cambridge: Harvard University Press, 2006.

Snyder, Timothy. *Bloodlands: Europe Between Hitler and Stalin*, New York: Basic Books, 2012.

Subtelny, Orest. *Ukraine: A History*, Toronto: University of Toronto Press, 2000.

US Congress Report Summary of Public Hearings. *Investigation of the Ukrainian Famine 1932–1933*, Commission of the Ukrainian Famine, April 19, 1988.

Viola, Lynne. *Peasant Rebels Under Stalin: Collectivization and the Culture of Peasant Resistance*, Oxford: Oxford University Press, 1996.

Viola, Lynne, V. P. Danilov, N. A. Ivnitskii, Denis Kozlov. *The War Against the Peasantry 1927–1930: The Tragedy of the Soviet Countryside*, New Haven: Yale University Press, 2005.

Viola, Lynne. *The Best Sons of the Fatherland: Workers in the Vanguard of Soviet Collectivization*, Oxford: Oxford University Press, 1987.

Wodoslawsky, Andrew. *The Red Harvest: faminegenocide.com/2003-competition/04-wodoslawsky-red_harvest.html*